THE
MANGROVE LEGACY

THE
MANGROVE
LEGACY

Kit Marlowe

www.foxspirit.co.uk

The Mangrove Legacy copyright © 2020 Kit Marlowe

Cover Art by S.L. Johnson Images

Typesetting and ebook conversion by HandeBooks.co.uk

ISBN: 978-1-910462-32-4

Previous edition published by
Tease Publishing

This edition published by
Fox Spirit Books
www.foxspirit.co.uk
adele@foxspirit.co.uk

For the women who've longed in vain for pockets

Chapter One

From behind the door, Caroline Alice Mangrove could hear the unaccustomed sounds of disagreement between her parents; which is to say, she heard her father's throat clear and her mother's gentle weeping. Lord and Lady Mangrove had been arguing in near silence for many days on end. Alice (as she had been called since childhood when her nurse trembled before the three syllables of her initial name and, struck dumb, failed to speak again until the child was weaned) feared that the topic of their disagreement was likely to be her impending marriage. To whom she had been given was not yet clear. Her parents had come to some sort of impasse and the meaningful glances they exchanged that morning at breakfast could only signal that things had worsened to nigh on a fever pitch. When she heard her father rustle his newspaper, Alice's eyes brimmed with tears and she fled the chaos to take refuge in the solarium.

The gentle green fronds of the ferns and orchids soon soothed her troubled nerves. Life was a harrowing prospect when you were eighteen, unmarried and wealthy. It was a very dangerous age—almost too old for an advantageous marriage but still in the realm of possible. Her parents had been too protective, she thought for the hundredth time. As if to chastise her for this disloyalty, the bland face of Mr. Radley, the gardener, appeared before her.

'Evening, Miss,' he said, pulling at his cap, oblivious to the fact that it was only mid-afternoon. 'Mind the orchids, they're a bit stroppy today. Forgot to water them yesterday.'

'Yes, Mr. Radley, I won't be a moment,' Alice said hastily, gathering up the pages she had spread before her, blushing with embarrassment that he might see what she had. Why do dresses seldom have pockets? she thought crossly, folding the papers roughly.

'The philodendrons are all right,' Mr. Radley called, but Alice had already scurried for the library, hoping to encounter a sanctuary at last. But as she opened the door, whom should she find but her cousin Elizabeth Jane, whom everyone called Lizzie. Well, not the servants, obviously—they in fact called her Miss Elizabeth Jane. As if to demonstrate the fact, Mrs. Perkins stepped in behind her and said 'Miss Elizabeth Jane, a letter has come for you.'

Alice was unprepared for the sudden change in her cousin, whose handsome face had blanched white. While Lizzie remained unmarried still at the age of twenty, there were those in the family who held out hope for the lively woman. To be fair, there were probably more who held that her very spirited nature was completely antithetical to the notion of marital union. Alice's own father had set his seal upon her cousin's fate at the St. Stephen's banquet not three years past, when he had taken in his niece's most recent witty retort and said, 'Good god, woman, no decent man will marry you.' For some in the family, that was that.

Alice emerged suddenly from her reverie as her cousin gasped. Lizzie clutched the letter to her breast. 'It's from the king!'

'Our king?' Alice demanded breathlessly as Lizzie coloured significantly.

'No, you—you misunderstand me,' her cousin stammered. 'King, King — I only meant...Mr. King. In Harlow. The collector of...spindly-legged insects. You know my interest in insects of all kinds, Alice.' Lizzie seemed to have quite recovered herself, but for the slight pink flush at her neck. However, Alice did notice that she had also tucked the letter in question into the recesses of her sleeve. Hmmm, thought Alice, she had never considered the uses of sleeves. It would render pockets obsolete, although it would require one to wear unfashionably billowing sleeves.

'Insects,' Alice repeated, with some suspicion still lurking in the shadows of her vocal tones.

'Insects!' Lizzie repeated with some of her former venom. 'That will be all, Mrs. Perkins.' Lizzie waved off the hearty domestic. 'My cousin and I have much to do.' The house-keeper looked distinctly disappointed as she curtseyed perfunctorily and slipped silently away, closing the library door with some evident reluctance. 'I hope she's not going to go gossiping,' Lizzie muttered once the door had whispered shut.

'I doubt Mrs. Perkins has much time for gossiping. There's the laundry to manage, dishes to wash, dinner to direct — she has rather a lot to do,' Alice said, suddenly realising what a trying life poor Mrs. Perkins must have. I shall not complain about the lumpy darns in my stockings ever again, she thought with a surge of pity that would be forgotten within a fortnight.

'I can only hope so,' Lizzie continued, oblivious to Alice's ruminations. 'Now if you'll excuse me, I have to read the king's letter.'

'You mean Mr. King's letter,' Alice corrected.

'Alice,' Lizzie said softly, stealing a glance at the door, 'I have a secret to share with you.'

'Oh, I love secrets!' Alice crowed. 'Tell me! Is it about that handsome young man we spotted talking to Mr. Bennett at the Assembly Ball last month?'

Lizzie regarded her cousin with obvious puzzlement. 'Why on earth should it be about him? No, no, it is about this letter.'

'Oh.' Alice had entertained many pleasing thoughts about that still nameless young man in the idle weeks since. 'Oh, it's not from Arthur Boylett,' she continued with dismay. She knew her father had leaned in his direction as far as her suitors went and was very cross to imagine that she may indeed have to marry that dull young man.

'Alice,' her cousin said, rousing her from a growing despondency, 'not everything is about you. This letter is actually from —' and she paused again to ascertain that they were still alone in the library, then whispered, 'the King of Naples!'

Alice paused thoughtfully. 'Africa?'

'We paid Miss Travers far too well,' Lizzie said, frowning as Alice's father was also apt to do when speaking of the recently sacked tutor. 'No, Alice. Naples is in Italy.'

'Ah.'

'The King. Of Naples.' Lizzie cocked an eyebrow at her younger cousin.

'Why is a king writing to you?' Alice asked at last.

Lizzie smiled. Alice had long ago noticed that when that happened, Lizzie looked very cunning indeed. It was most unbecoming in a lady. 'We have worked out a plan to—'

Just then the door of the library flew open and a very flustered Mrs. Perkins shot into the room again. 'Oh, Miss Alice!' she sobbed. 'Come quick, your mother needs you!'

'What is it, Mrs. Perkins?' Lizzie asked, looking somewhat cross at having her own revelation upstaged.

Mrs. Perkins was wringing her hands as she blurted, 'It's your father, Miss Alice—he—he's dead!'

'Dead?' Alice said with wonder.

'Dead!' Mrs. Perkins was adamant.

'Are you sure?' Lizzie asked. After all, Lord Mangrove had been a man of legendary silences, and Lizzie was to be forgiven the doubts that prompted such an otherwise impertinent question. There was a time not five years past when Lord Mangrove had gone without more than a harrumph for over six months. At that time Lord and Lady Mangrove had come to some rather ineffective disagreements about a parlour maid. It was perhaps the worst of their silent struggles, but it was far from the only one.

Mrs. Perkins, however, was not to be dissuaded. 'Oh, child, I hate to give you the news in such a terrible manner,' she said, flustered, offering a perfunctory half-curtsey.

'It's all right,' Alice soothed. 'I hardly know what to feel. I do feel extremely odd and a bit queerly dizzy.'

'You must sit at once,' Mrs. Perkins and Lizzie said in tandem, both fearing that perhaps that she was about to faint. Alice followed their advice, collapsing into a sensible pine library chair. Dead! Her father was dead! Perhaps, Alice thought excitedly, she would not have to marry Mister Boylett, after all.

'And how is Lady Mangrove?' Lizzie asked the faithful servant.

'She… she is rather shocked, as you might imagine, miss,' Mrs. Perkins said.

'What happened, Mrs. Perkins?' Lizzie demanded, artfully pulling out a second chair for the weary servant. 'Tell us from beginning to end.'

10

Mrs. Perkins sank into the proffered chair and rubbed her troubled brow. 'It was a most peculiar thing,' she said. 'Not that people go on dying every day, child. Oh, and my greatest and most humble sorrow for your loss, Miss Alice.' She seemed on the verge of rising once more if only to curtsey, but Lizzie restrained her with a gentle gesture that belied her growing impatience with the strange mystery.

'Go on, Mrs. Perkins,' Lizzie encouraged her. 'How did it begin? Start there and then go to the end. Then stop.'

Mrs. Perkins drew in a breath. 'I was just about to set to the kitchen, a million and one things to do as well you might guess — not that such work should be any worry of fine young ladies like yourselves,' she added, patting Alice's soft white hand. 'All of the sudden I heard a horrible sound, like a wild bird's squawk or something.'

'African? Or European?' Lizzie asked, but Alice shushed her with a wave of her hand and bade Mrs. Perkins go on.

'I rushed to the door of the morning room and there such a sight awaited me! Your father, Miss Alice, was lying on the floor in a most peculiar disarray, arms clutching at the air and legs in a most ungainly crouching position, but him flat on his back like a puppy.'

Alice thought of the image and could not quite hide a smile. 'It must have looked most… curious,' she finally said, coughing a little to cover up her involuntary merriment. Her cousin, she noticed, did not grin but looked ever more intently at Mrs. Perkins.

The housekeeper did not notice Alice's inappropriate mirth, but continued with her tragic tale. 'Your mother looked up from her needlepoint with a most shocked appearance, her hands frozen in the air as if unable to move. Until I finally gasped and your mother at last said, and I shall always remember these terrible words: 'Mrs. Perkins, I believe something has happened to my husband.' Truer words were never spoken,' she added with a shudder.

'And are you sure — that is, have you truly ascertained, that he is… dead?' Lizzie said gently.

'I have sent young Master Spiggot for the doctor. We shall know soon enough now,' Mrs. Perkins intoned sagely, her composure returned.

Suddenly, there was a loud crash and a scream in the hall.

'Heavens!' cried Lizzie, forgetting all propriety in the shock of the moment. 'What can that be?'

Alice stared at her, thunderstruck. She had never heard the word out loud with such a charged tone. Yet, the sound had been startling. The three of them were just turning toward the door when it flew open once again to reveal Janet the scullery maid, breathless and red-faced.

'It's your mother,' she squeaked.

While her addressee was uncertain, Alice had no doubt she herself had been meant. Lizzie's mother was seven years dead, and Mrs. Perkins—well, honestly she had no idea whether Mrs. Perkins had a mother living or dead. Oh certainly, a mother she must have had! Alice corrected her wandering thoughts. But she realised that she had never once inquired about Mrs. Perkins' mother, alive or dead, and was conscious once more—fleetingly—of how cavalierly she treated the trustworthy woman who had ordered her life since before birth. I shall do better, Alice swore to herself—a promise quickly forgotten in the ensuing hours yet one we really ought to honour her for, nonetheless. She rightly considered whether her disordered thoughts were the result of all the shocks. After all, she could only assume the worst. Her mother, too, was dead, perhaps. And while to lose one parent might be considered a distinct misfortune, Alice was quite certain that to lose both would leave her out of all sympathy as someone who ought to have taken better care of her predecessors.

Janet, however, clarified her initial remark to the relief of all three women who evidently had been thinking along similar lines. 'She discharged your father's pistol!' All three of her addressees breathed a sigh of relief.

Lizzie was the first to recover. 'Why on earth did she do such a thing?' she demanded of the trembling maid. 'Surely, not—' and the horrible conclusion that presented itself to the wise young woman fortunately escaped Alice for the moment.

Janet was quick to restore equilibrium. 'Oh no, miss,' the maid assured them, 'it was only on account of the young man. She meant no harm.'

'Young man,' said Alice with a great deal of curiosity. 'What young man?'

'Why Mr. Boylett, of course,' Janet finished, turning to her young mistress with a hint of a smile. Mr. Boylett was a great favourite among the house staff for he generally dropped large amounts of coinage from his pockets as he made his awkward way through the house.

He was less than a favourite of Alice's, however, as may already be plain. 'But my mother is all right?' Alice asked somewhat peevishly. It *would* have to be tiresome old Arthur who caused such a fuss just when she was thinking she would be free of him.

'Your mother is a bit bewildered and a trifle deaf,' Janet continued. 'The doctor is already on his way, so he will be able to determine the extent of her hearing loss. Begging your pardon, miss,' Janet said with a hasty curtsey, 'we're so sorry to hear of your loss.'

'Thank you, Janet,' Alice replied with great gravity. The shock of her father's death had not yet reached her heart although it had begun to sink into the relatively calm, still and shallow waters of her mind. 'How did my father pass anyway? We are sorely pressed for details!'

Lizzie nodded agreement. 'We should like to know more about what happened. This is all so sudden!'

Janet nodded sadly in agreement. 'I had just brought him his daily tincture of arsenic when he simply keeled over all of the sudden. It was like a bolt from the blue!'

Lizzie was about to bring forth her pet theory that arsenic, far from being the tonic her uncle assumed, was in fact extremely dangerous, when a figure pale as a spectre peered from the half-open door of the library and whispered weedily, 'Alice, Alice…'

The women turned and gasped.

'Oh for heaven's sake,' Alice said crossly. 'What is it, Arthur?'

Alice's lack of compassion for the young man was understandable, perhaps, given her strong likelihood of being married to him in the very near future. But surely the sight of his pale visage peering round the door would have stirred the sympathies of any heart not already obdurate to his welfare. Of course, a conversation of even five minutes would easily have remedied that initial stirring, for Arthur Boylett was an inveterate bore.

There was no subject on which he could not wax mind-numbingly, tediously dull. And most subjects of his choosing inclined sharply in the direction of boring—land management schemes, tax redundancies and the obscure minutia of the lives of the long dead kings. Alice could scarcely conceal her tendency to yawn when Arthur got going on the effects of adding furrows to increase drainage or spoke at length on Edward the Confessor's collection of holy relics and spoons.

However, this time Arthur managed to be brief. 'Is the doctor on his way?' he exhaled wearily.

Janet was the first to answer, which was handy as she was the only one with first-hand knowledge of the issue. 'Yes, sir,' she said with another little curtsey. 'He should be here directly. Oughtn't you be sitting down, Mister Boylett?'

Rather than respond, Arthur simply sank to the floor. As he fell, his arm flew out, revealing the rather large stain of blood that had soaked through his shirt. Alice gasped and Lizzie once again blurted, 'Heavens!'

Mrs. Perkins, however, was quick to act and dragged the unfortunate young man toward a chair. 'Help me, dear,' she said to Janet, who stepped forward eagerly enough but gingerly tried to avoid touching the blood-soaked shirt.

'You don't mean to say my mother shot Arthur, do you?' Alice was impressed. She had certainly never thought of doing that.

Janet tried to curtsey as they lifted Arthur to the chair, causing Mrs. Perkins to grumble. 'Yes, miss, she did, but I don't think she did it on purpose.'

Alice wisely kept her thoughts to herself. She knew all too well that her mother did not share her father's keenness on Arthur as a suitor. 'Poor mother—she must be terribly upset.'

Lizzie nodded. 'We must go to her at once. Two shocks like this will be quite dangerous, even for a woman of her

14

robust health.'

She grabbed Alice's hand and the two walked swiftly to the morning room where they found Lady Mangrove bent over her needlepoint before a large mass covered by a tablecloth. Alice was just thinking she had never noticed that there before, when it occurred to her that this was no doubt the body of her father, now frozen in the curious posture Mrs. Perkins had described. She thought perhaps it wouldn't be quite the right thing to remove the covering to see her father in an attitude he would never have chosen to take in life, but her hand inched toward the tablecloth as if on its own.

Before she got to it, Lizzie interrupted her morbid fascination by shrieking, 'How are you, Lady Mangrove?' at very nearly the top of her vocal capacity. Why is she shouting? Alice wondered, derailing her mind from the curiosity about her father.

Lady Mangrove failed to react, however, sewing away deftly with her needle and thread. It was only when Lizzie touched her shoulder that Lady Mangrove looked up, smiled and announced, 'I can't hear a thing. That damn pistol is much too loud for indoors.' She cast a glance at the instrument itself, lying innocently on the small oak table. 'Is Boylett dead?' she asked Lizzie.

Lizzie answered no, and made sure to shake her head as well.

'Pity,' Lady Mangrove said, echoing Alice's desire. 'Though I didn't mean to shoot him. I thought he was someone else when he walked in.'

'Who?' Alice asked, suddenly realising that she did not really know her mother all that well. But her mother had not heard her. She was about to attempt a louder shout when the door flew open and Doctor Ponsonby entered, exclaiming, 'No one must touch that body! The constable is on his way to investigate this murder!'

'What did he say?' Lady Mangrove said with some consternation. 'Why is everybody whispering?'

'He's here to investigate,' Lizzie stated as loudly as could still be considered genteel in front of the doctor.

'Instigate? Instigate what?'

15

'I am here, Lady Mangrove,' the doctor clarified, his own tone pitched loud enough to rattle some of the cutlery in the next room, 'to investigate the murder!'

'Murder,' snorted Lady Mangrove, in what Alice could not help but notice was an unsuitably ungenteel fashion, 'what murder?'

Doctor Ponsonby snatched a small blue bottle from the table. It was marked with what appeared to be two triangles, one inverted, the other missing a little bit in the bottom line. He thrust it before Lady Mangrove's perfect nose. 'I put it to you that this is arsenic, my lady!'

'Of course it's arsenic,' Lady Mangrove continued, her tone now matching the shouting of the others. 'That's my husband's arsenic concoction. Vinegar, I believe,' she added, touching a finger thoughtfully to her lips. 'I believe he mixes it with vinegar. My sister always added chalk, but my dear husband would have none of that. Always preferred the ruddy complexion. Suits a man, he always said, did he not, Alice?'

'Yes, he did, Mama,' Alice said, remembering to modulate her voice appropriately. The tension in the room was becoming unbearable, but she hoped that it might endure just a bit longer. It was the most excitement there had ever been in the nearly always-silent house. Unused as her ears were to the thunderous tones of this day, it was certainly a pleasant change. Not that she had forgotten the death of her father, mind you, but she should surely be forgiven for being caught up in the excitement that surrounded the unexpected events that day.

'So, you poisoned your husband!' Doctor Ponsonby shrieked at last, brandishing the bottle with its horrid alchemical symbol before the stoic face of Alice's mother.

'Stuff and nonsense,' replied the unperturbed woman.

By Lizzie's expression, Alice gathered her cousin felt an unaccustomed sense of admiration for Lady Mangrove, whose accomplishments heretofore had seldom crept outside the arena of needlepoint and disapproving of whist. Alice herself was quite done in with astonishment. Was this the same woman who meekly responded, 'yes, dear' to nearly every didactic pronouncement of her father? While she was temporarily distracted by wondering whether she had used the word 'didactic' properly in her thoughts, Alice soon returned to astonishment at her mother's daring.

'Lord Mangrove was in the habit of taking his arsenic daily. He believed it to be a powerful tonic—'

'Powerful tonic!' the doctor shouted with a great deal of bluster. But his bluster failed him at that moment, and he merely repeated, 'Powerful tonic?'

'There's no need to shout,' Lady Mangrove continued. 'I believe my hearing has at last returned. As I say, he took the mixture of arsenic and vinegar — with a little basil in the summer times — on a daily basis for his health. I'm certain the amount of arsenic cannot have been sufficient to have killed him.'

'Well,' the doctor relented, 'perhaps not. I shall have to perform an —'

'Doctor, do you mind?' Lady Mangrove deliberately set aside her needlepoint and stood up. At her height, one might not initially consider it to be an impressive move, but she had a way of making her not quite-five-feet of height matter more than people twice her size. 'My child is traumatized and fatherless. Please do not injure her further with your talk of horrid and mundane tasks!'

The doctor bowed his head, crestfallen. 'I only thought... well, for once I might have to... yes, Lady Mangrove, I apologise most heartily.'

'Never mind! Lizzie, take Alice's other arm. We must escort her to her room, she has to recover from this terrible blow. And we have a funeral to plan — call Mrs. Perkins once we've deposited poor Alice in her bed.'

Alice had a curiosity worthy of her cousin that made her wish to stay there and see what the doctor might do next, but the two women each grabbed an arm and whisked her from the room before she could think of protesting. At the door, her mother seemed to recall something to mind and she paused, turning.

'I nearly forgot, Doctor Ponsonby! Do check on Arthur. I'm afraid I shot him. Perhaps you will have a murder to investigate, after all.' And she turned back to bustle her daughter to her room with Lizzie's help, there to administer a helpful dose of laudanum which caused Alice to slip into a dream almost at once.

Chapter Two

Alice awoke and stretched languorously. It was some minutes later, after admiring the fair weather and the pleasing warmth of the sun, that she finally recalled the shocking events of the day before. Giving a little gasp, she threw back the covers and dashed across the room for her wrapper. Where on earth was MaryAnn? She needed to dress at once! Smoothing her unruly locks back with her hand, Alice rang for the maid and tapped her foot impatiently while she waited. For the umpteenth time she wondered why her robe had no handy pockets for her unoccupied hands. Sighing, she went to the window to stare prettily, if vacantly, at the immaculate garden. To her surprise, voices floated up from below, so Alice unlatched the window and leaned tentatively out.

'Oh, it's only Arthur,' she said to herself with a sigh and leaned back, the better to close the window. All at once she remembered the excitement of the day before and quickly leaned forward once more to see how the young man was faring, although it must be said as well that she took the precaution of shielding her face with the lace curtain. No need to attract Arthur's attention just because she was mildly concerned with his health. After all, she hardly wanted to encourage his attentions now that she might be free of them.

With the window swinging open she could now hear the conversation in progress.

'...rather than the original head of King Edmund, which of course, if you have been following my story, you could not possibly believe. After all, if the body of the saint has lain incorruptible these many years, with only the thinnest red line to indicate the site of the martyrdom—by site, naturally I mean to indicate the location on his body rather than the location where the martyrdom occurred, but certainly, despite the vendor's attempts to render accurate arrow marks and even the tooth marks of the wolf in question, surely even the novice collector would be able to—'

'Oh, do stop droning on, Arthur! I am beginning to regret

having spared your life,' Alice's mother interrupted suddenly, relieving her eavesdropping daughter as well as herself of the seemingly endless murmur of Arthur's toneless ramble.

'Lady Mangrove!' Arthur said with evident surprise. 'You claimed the shooting to have been an accident and I took you at your word. You don't mean to say—'

'Good heavens, Arthur, must you take everything so personally?'

Alice was just giving in to a most ungenerous giggle when the ever-inappropriate MaryAnn tapped at the door and entered. Rather than be seen spying on her mother and former fiancé, Alice hastily pretended to be regarding the fine blue sky, and then turned slowly to greet the flustered maid. This behaviour should make clear to the unbiased viewer that Alice was a young woman accustomed to being something less than entirely truthful. While one might not call MaryAnn 'unbiased' in the most truthful sense of the word (one which your author is at pains to follow implicitly), she was certainly not fooled by Alice's attempt to cover up her recent eavesdropping.

'So what does your mother have to say to young Mister Arthur now?' MaryAnn asked impertinently, all too aware of the gentleman's presumed aspirations with regard to her young mistress.

Alice pretended to be deeply insulted by this show of familiarity. Although she usually confided the most personal information in the various maids in the household (a most undignified practice for a young woman of her station, she ought to know), Alice disliked it immensely when one of the maids believed this confidence to be a two-way path. (While this was not entirely fair, it is often the sad duty of authors to have to point out that world is seldom fair and if it were, writers would be better paid; however, it would be unseemly to dwell upon such a point and bring attention to the author that ought really be lavished upon the characters, so my lips are henceforth sealed on the matter.)

'I really don't know,' Alice replied stiffly, stepping away from the window.

MaryAnn ignored her and slipped over to the window and

twitched the curtain aside. Alice admired her swift, silent movements without ever wondering what other uses they might be put to in the course of a normal day. 'I'm surprised he's back again, after yesterday I mean. He must really love you, miss,' MaryAnn said, not without a note of amusement as Alice was quick to realise.

'I hardly think that is your concern,' Alice said with all the smug superiority she could muster. 'Will you please dress me now?' She turned her back on MaryAnn with a swirl of curls that she imagined had a dramatic finality. In so doing, she missed MaryAnn's frank look of contempt and further amusement. One might suspect that the young girl might harbour literary pretensions.

If only she had been literate.

MaryAnn began stuffing Alice into her various layers and flounces with a good deal more roughness than was her wont, but her mistress steadfastly refused to be moved by her evident displeasure and kept her complaints to herself in stubborn silence. MaryAnn was just slipping the soft silk gloves onto Alice's admirably petite hands when Lizzie burst through the door with her face aglow with a strange excitement, as if she had just discovered a new type of moth.

'Alice!' she crowed, then looked abashed at the maid's unexpected presence and the three at once retreated into an uneasy silence as MaryAnn put the finishing touches on Alice's apparel.

Alice saw Lizzie could barely contain herself until MaryAnn curtsied and ever so slowly wandered out of the room. It was like the maid was lingering for some specific purpose. MaryAnn had no more than turned the handle and closed the door before Alice's cousin could no longer contain her excitement.

'Alice, can you imagine?'

Alice could easily imagine many things. Ask her to imagine the finest feast the cook could devise and she would be quickly immersed in delectable mental pictures that varied from cream buns to the very tastiest lemon tarts. Or ask her to imagine the very finest clothes and she could picture herself awash in crisp crinolines and silks from the East. Or ask her to imagine the very cutest of small animals and she could at once see herself surrounded by the most adorable of puppies and the most precious little kittens, with lovely little colts and fillies prancing around the gathering and even an utterly adorable baby wombat beside her (she had once seen a drawing of an adult creature and could only guess that an infant would be too charming for words). Yes, she could imagine.

However, her cousin was in fact asking a rhetorical question and well aware of her younger relative's easy ability to drift off into daydreams. In fact, what she had in mind was revealing a secret heretofore locked in her own private breast without the knowledge even of her guardians. I'll give you a hint that it has much to do with the King of Naples, but unfortunately at the moment Lizzie was about to divulge this momentous mystery, a most peculiar thing happened.

Far below them in the garden came a singular sound of alarm. Alice and Lizzie's eyes met and like one woman (though they were in fact still two) they ran to the window. They unlatched the window and thrust themselves out, leaning precariously over the sash to take in the scene below.

Alice's mother stood transfixed, a pair of gardening shears in her hand, the other hand shading her view from the morning sun. Arthur stood stock still, his mouth agape (a look which did little to credit him to either young woman, although perhaps Alice more particularly, for she saw in him the progenitor of a bevy of slack-jawed children that she dreaded to be the mother of in any consequential way). A small number of rather sweet honeybees droned on without alarm, nestling in the fading flowers of the honeysuckle, tasting perhaps the last dregs of what had been until lately a rather fine late spring.

Alice and Lizzie, however, gasped in horror as the ghost of Alice's father sternly beckoned from the rhododendron (or should that perhaps be rhododendra? Alice could not help wondering, confusing her Latin and horticulture). As in life, he was nigh on wordless, but grim and formidable. Clearly, he had a mission today, important enough to drag him away from the parlour where his lifeless body lay awaiting the funeral photos and cortege of reluctant mourners.

'Millicent!' Lord Mangrove intoned with a sonorous boom.

Alice could be forgiven for wondering for a moment who on earth he might be addressing. However, it did not take her very long to recall that her mother's given name was in fact Millicent, a fact the latter often neglected to recall herself.

'Millicent,' Lord Mangrove's ghost continued, 'you must obey my dying wish!'

Lizzie heard Alice's involuntary intake of breath. What could it be? The mystery hung before them like a small rain cloud waiting for the words of Lord Mangrove to dispel it.

'Do you mean about the azaleas?' Lady Mangrove asked hopefully.

Lord Mangrove's ghost was quick to respond. 'Not the azaleas! Alice!'

Alice's attention perked up considerably at that remark, as you can easily imagine. She was always more interested in conversations about herself.

'Oh dear,' Lady Mangrove grumbled, 'you don't mean to say —'

'Indeed I do!' Lord Mangrove's ghost countered rather irritably. 'Alice must marry Mr. Boylett!'

Lady Mangrove and Arthur both looked surprised as well. Alice could not help noticing that her vantage point above the young man did nothing to improve his appeal. Having escaped the undesirable attachment once, she was displeased to find herself thrust once more into the arrangement. Why did young women such as she have less control over their lives than they did over their clothing? This reminded her once again of her scheme to add more pockets to her day dresses, but the thought once raised had little time to perch on the outstretched limb of her mind and soon flew off for more welcoming vistas.

Her father's ghost did likewise, fading into insubstantiality before disappearing altogether with a mild cough.

'Oh mother, must I?' Alice could not help noticing that while Lady Mangrove grimaced, Arthur's face took on a look she could only describe in her mind as something approximating the appearance of the Mrs. Perkins' visage when someone disparaged her blueberry scones. While Alice's kindly heart could not help regretting having made her distaste for a lifetime union with Mr. Boylett plain, she felt a strange sense of defiance, too, for she really could not imagine that union without a particular sense of dismay that magnified the unpleasantly dull conversations of the years past.

For her part, Lady Mangrove regained her aplomb with customary swiftness, and gathered her gardening tools and parasol. Then she straightened, beckoned to Mr. Boylett and announced in her clear bell-like voice to all present, 'The viewing of the body will begin precisely at eleven. I suggest we all get ready to meet the mourners.' With that, she tucked her basket under her arm, turned on her heel and headed toward the solarium.

And that was that. Arthur hesitated, then followed her retreating steps, his head hung dejectedly low.

Above them, Alice and Lizzie exchanged glances and quickly smothered fits of giggles. A disinterested observer might fault the young women for their mirth so near the deceased remains of a loved one, but the peculiar determination of Alice's mother coupled with the clear displeasure of Arthur combined to produce a giddy effect on the two that they were helpless to resist.

'Oh my,' Lizzie said, recovering herself first as befit her more mature years. 'I fear Mr. Boylett is displeased.'

Alice still muffled a lingering giggle. 'I don't care—I'm sure mother will not make me marry him! She was decidedly evasive when father spoke with her just then.'

'Alice, did you not think it odd that your father's ghost appeared just now in broad daylight?'

'Actually, it was rather overcast.'

'Alice, that's not the point. Have you ever seen a ghost before?'

'No, I don't believe I have.' Alice thought a moment. 'What about Aunt Susan?'

Lizzie narrowed her eyes. 'Aunt Susan is indeed rather pale. She is not, however, dead, the primary requirement for a ghost.'

'Ah,' Alice responded with some considerable embarrassment. Her cousin had such a nimble mind that she often felt at a disadvantage in moments like this. 'I suppose this is my first ghost, then.' The thought immediately cheered her, however — novelty had its own charm. 'Do you suppose Father will be returning regularly?'

Lizzie looked thoughtful. 'I believe that to be possible as long as he has a reason to do so. In most novels the ghost appears for a particular reason. Once it is accomplished, there is no more ghost.'

'That would be a pity,' Alice said. 'After all he died so suddenly, I have hardly had time to get accustomed to the idea. Having his ghost around would make the change less drastic. Particularly if we needn't listen to anything he says.'

'Alice, you should always listen to your father,' Lizzie scolded. 'Alive or dead.'

Alice thought it was all very well for Lizzie to say so, having no parents to listen to at present, but she kept that thought to herself. I need someone to share all these thoughts with which I must keep to myself, Alice thought further, wondering indeed with whom she might share such scandalous thoughts.

Alice was about to voice another daring thought when Mrs. Perkins rapped sharply on the door and stuck her head around the edge to announce, 'The guests — I'm so sorry — mourners have begun to arrive! Alice, your mother wishes you to appear downstairs at once. Good heavens, why aren't you in black?'

Within a short time, Alice was completely enveloped in proper funeral attire by the roughly competent hands of Mrs. Perkins. Feeling slightly dizzy from the process, Alice wavered at the door, uncertain whether she was indeed ready to meet the prying faces of the public. Her cousin, she noted, had already dressed appropriately. Well, such speedy changes left one in a muddle, she thought crossly. I could hardly be expected to remember everything about the day to come.

'Come now, child,' Mrs. Perkins said with a somewhat gentler tone than she had used while dressing Alice. 'We need to help your mother on this difficult day, and a quiet—' Alice could not help noticing that the housekeeper paused and laid some considerably emphasis on that word, '—and obedient child will be a great assistance on such a troubling day.'

Alice resolved to be just such a child and dutifully trooped out the door behind Mrs. Perkins and Lizzie. They made their way to the sitting room, which was already draped in black crepe. At the centre of the room on a catafalque, lay the coffin holding Lord Mangrove. In and around the open coffin lay a profusion of blooms that threatened to quite overwhelm the perpetually silent lord of the house.

'Mr. Radley has outdone himself,' Lady Mangrove commented upon walking into the room. 'I hope there are still some flowers left for the tea table.'

'My heartiest condolences for your sudden loss,' Mrs. Perkins said sadly with a subtle yet effective curtsey that managed to avoid the usual explosions of knee popping that so often accompanied her curtseys. She was nothing if not thoughtful about the ambience of the moment.

'You needn't repeat that sentiment every time you see me, Mrs. Perkins,' Alice's mother responded a tad testily. 'Once will do. Can you allow the trampling hordes of mourners in now? I believe we are ready to receive them at last.'

Mother is surely suffering from the sudden loss or she would not be so needlessly curt, Alice thought, ignoring her own lack of feeling with regard to the loss. Surely the arrival of the others would cheer her mother once again. Mother loved parties, Alice comforted herself.

In the few moments before the guests were to arrive, Lizzie managed to whisper a few hints to Alice about how she ought to behave. 'Do not giggle, and do not employ your usual mode of conversation. Keep to brief acknowledgments of other people's condolences. Remember to curtsey for older people and shake the hands of your peers.'

'What about Arthur?'

'Arthur should be greeted with a curtsey and handshake to indicate his special relationship with you.'

Alice bridled at this suggestion. 'Perhaps with Father dead, I won't have to marry him after all.'

Lizzie looked scandalized. 'Perhaps not, but if your father's ghost has made one appearance, it is possible he will make another. It often happens that way in novels. It would be best if we were to avoid such types of public displays at this time, my dear cousin. Think what people would say.'

Alice was tired of hearing this oft-repeated refrain, but for the moment she thought it best to not to mention her fatigue at this juncture. 'I suppose I should be crying, but somehow I think I feel very little desire to do so.'

'That is often the case at such events,' her wise cousin advised, 'but there are ways to adapt. You should find in your right hand dress pocket a suitable black crepe handkerchief, which can be as useful for drying your tears as it is for hiding your lack of them.'

Alice was delighted to find just such an item in her pocket. Now why cannot my usual dresses have such convenient pockets? she thought, but at once employed the kerchief in the manner Lizzie indicated, dabbing at non-existent tears and fancying herself in the role of the mourner even as her mother idly looked through an old copy of *Punch* while awaiting the arrival of the cadre of sympathetic lamenters.

Just then, the door of the sitting room flew open and a shrill scream entered the room.

The scream was closely followed by Aunt Susan, who swept toward Lady Mangrove with outstretched arms, clasped her in a warm embrace, sobbing, 'I cannot believe he is gone! You must be so bereft, my dear Millicent! Whatever will you do?'

Lady Mangrove did her best to withstand the smothering while nevertheless maintaining her sense of dignified poise, but eventually sought to extricate herself from the octopusian arms of her sister-in-law. 'Dear Susan, how lovely to see you. Perhaps you should comfort poor Alice,' she suggested a little icily. For the thousandth time, she marvelled again that this fluttering creature was actually a sibling to her taciturn husband. Late husband, she amended, though no one had heard her thoughts.

Susan took the hint and wrapped her considerable arm-lengths around a startled Alice who had not even begun to practice using her new black lace-trimmed handkerchief. 'Poor, fatherless child! What will become of you? I cannot believe he is really gone.'

Lady Mangrove nodded approvingly and looked around for Mrs. Perkins. As usual, she was there at once, as if summoned by her mistress' desire to employ her in an essential task. She curtseyed in her practiced way, but remembering her earlier chastisement, refrained from expressing her sorrow at Lord Mangrove's sudden departure, although surely it was still uppermost in her mind. Anything that shifted the routine and balanced relationships of the house was sure to cause disturbing ripples in the normally calm waters of the manor. The frightening spectre of the late Dowager Mangrove, mother to the recently departed, was ever in the back of her mind (not unlike the very visible spectre of her son lingered in the garden earlier). When her husband had likewise departed the mortal coil unexpectedly one summer day, Mrs. Perkins, then her lady's maid, had been scandalised to find her mistress take to playing cards in the afternoon shortly thereafter. She shuddered at the very memory. Consequently, she was already on the watch for such radical changes in behaviour in the current lady of the house.

She needn't have worried — Lady Mangrove despised the playing of cards, as Mrs. Perkins well knew, and the shock of her husband's untimely death did nothing to change the status of that frivolous activity.

'Mrs. Perkins, has the hearse arrived already?'

'Indeed it has, Lady Mangrove.'

'I thought I detected the scent of gin,' Lady Mangrove said disapprovingly. Like many of her class, she loathed that particular elixir, the scourge of the working classes. But doubtless Mr. Bird, the seldom-seen butler, was lubricating the waiting coachmen to ease the burden of standing around while the mourners gave genteel vent to their grief. Indeed, the expected gaggle of mourners had arrived more or less en masse, none desiring to be the first (although of course Aunt Susan had had no qualms about that). However, their mass arrival proved to be a problem as the murmuring throng had bottlenecked at the parlour door, none able to enter without proper deference to the others in an unending roundabout of politeness that threatened to continue until the turn of the next century.

A raised eyebrow from Lady Mangrove was all that was necessary to send Mrs. Perkins forth and with effortless efficiency, she popped the cork, so to speak, and the mourners streamed in full of appropriately cheerful expressions of profound grief and regret, so that they were quite unable to resist bursting into leaky tears which were at once dabbed away by a variety of stylish mourning handkerchiefs.

Alice was impressed.

She was also immediately enveloped in the arms of many long-lost kin who weepily conveyed their sorrow for her loss and their own, then headed quickly for the buffet table, which was smartly decorated with an abundance of flowers rivalling the coffin where Lord Mangrove reposed. Through their tears they marvelled at the sweetness of the scones, the tartness of the black currant tarts, and the delectability of the funeral meats. Mrs. Perkins had outdone herself as usual, rearranging cook's treasures to their best appearance, and soon the table was enclosed by a murmuring throng that only minutes before had stoppered the door.

This arrangement left Alice free to suffer the attentions of her former tutor, the former Miss Travers, while Lizzie merited the copious tears of consideration from Aunt Susan, who wailed on with remarkable perseverance. Lady Mangrove had taken refuge behind the catafalque to distance herself from that performance.

'Alice, dear child, how good it is to see you!' the former Miss Travers crowed, quite unaccountably cheerful. 'It has been weeks, has it not?'

Alice nodded with what she hoped was a measured dose of grief-ridden poise, or so she hoped. She may only have appeared to have had a stiff neck. To feel more confident, she pulled her lovely handkerchief out and dabbed delicately at one eye and then the other as she had seen many of the more experienced mourners do. It seemed to have the desired effect of reminding Miss Travers (or, she quickly corrected herself, Mrs. Martin) of the gravity of the occasion.

Indeed, Mrs. Martin pulled out a similar handkerchief and patted likewise at her blue orbs which had so far remained stubbornly tear-free disregarding the depth of feeling she was sure she felt for Lord Mangrove, despite the fact that most of her memories of him were probably of his rumbling shout of annoyance when he tripped over one of her various fascinating art projects for her young charge that usually involved copious amounts of plaster of Paris and string, or suffusing the house with the less than enchanting scent of drying gypsum. Poor Miss Travers (as she was then) lived in mortal terror of Lord Mangrove then, often shaking so much at the tea table that she would drop her spoon into the marmalade or treacle and bring upon herself further impassioned bellows of annoyance that made her cringe upon her seat and attempt to hide behind the tea cosy.

'Oh, my poor, poor Alice!' she cried with renewed vigour as her husband stood silently by with an unaccountably pleasant look on his face.

Just as if he were gazing out on the fields like one of his cows, Alice thought rather uncharitably. Mr. Martin's cows were a bit of sticking point with Alice, who had entertained rather grand thoughts of marrying off her sweetly vague tutor to someone of rank and privilege, and though this was a bit to expect from the young woman who once dwelt upon the bonny shores of Lyme Regis, Alice had had hopes of raising Miss Travers (now Mrs. Martin) to a stature somewhat beyond that which birth had chosen to allot her. She could hardly bear to imagine that Miss Travers had become the wife of this farmer with not only resignation but also a considerable amount of pleasure. It was disappointing, to say the least.

Oblivious to Alice's chagrin, Mr. Martin dutifully nodded to his wife's former charge and commented, 'The flowers look quite nice, Miss Alice, not to say abundant as well. Look at the head on that one! Why, I wonder what ol' Radley's using for mulching these days?'

Alice felt her sight dimming, but Mrs. Martin swiftly grabbed her elbow and began fanning her with a lovely black mourning fan that Alice could not recall having seen before and at once wished to have. Mrs. Martin, guessing the reason for Alice's delicacy, turned back to her husband to admonish him, but charmed once more by his plain and affable face, merely twittered, 'Perhaps you should step into the solarium and inquire. I'm certain he would love to share some of his secrets with you, my dear.'

With a nod to Alice, Mr. Martin did just that. He turned on his heel, ambled over to the funeral buffet to grab a scone, and walked down the hall toward the solarium with a confident tread. As if he had lived here all his life, Alice thought crossly. It was the chief aspect of Mr. Martin that riled her: his refusal to acknowledge his social inferiority. Alice would not have minded the farmer quite as much had he been more willing to bow and scrape to his betters, but she could have been no more happy to have Miss Travers pass up any number of more suitable attachments (regardless of their apparent lack of interest in the scatter-brained tutor) to marry this man who seemed to find joy in all he did, even patiently milking his cows every morning. The mere thought of this abominably physical activity threatened to make Alice swoon again. Mrs. Martin recognised the signs and steered her toward one of the parlour chairs heavily draped with black crepe. Alice sank gratefully into it.

'Oh, Miss Travers — I beg your pardon, my dear, Mrs. Martin — whatever shall I do? How bereft I feel without the comforting presence of my own papa!'

Mrs. Martin patted one of Alice's pale hands comfortingly. 'Ah, but he's right here, Alice — at least for a little while.' She smiled uncertainly, somehow realising that this was perhaps not the right thing to say. The former tutor had a heart of gold and a head of a rather comparatively dense metal of some kind. Struggling for a better comment, she ventured to say, 'And he will always be in our hearts.' Mrs. Martin felt a shock of surprise at having come up with an admittedly thoughtful comment and lapsed into a grateful silence.

'I suppose,' Alice at last answered with some reluctance. While her father had never taken up residence there previously, there was always a chance that it might occur now that he was at least somewhat beyond the mortal coil, although his appearance in the garden rather cast that thought into doubt. What on earth could it mean, this insistence on her marrying Arthur? Of course, he had wished that prior to his death, but surely one could not feel strongly enough about a subject like that (or someone like Arthur) to actually journey back from the land of reward to insist upon the point.

However, Alice's musings were cut short when her mother, reacting to the sudden and silent appearance of Mr. Bird, drew the attention of the buffet gathering with her announcement, 'It is time to ride to the cemetery! Do please gather your things.'

The awkward exit from the parlour did not match the peculiar antics of the crowd's entry into the room, but it seemed to have an untoward air of haste that Alice thought most unbecoming to the scene as she folded Mrs. Martin's lovely fan negligently in her hand. Lizzie took the opportunity to disengage herself from Aunt Susan's mournful wails, and slipped her hand around Alice's elbow, hastening their exit from the house.

'By all rights,' Lizzie muttered somewhat peevishly, 'we ought to have been allowed a little more time for expressing our grief, rather than being hustled off so expeditiously.'

Alice reflected. 'Perhaps it is to move us more quickly to recovery.'

'Grief does not disappear in a day,' Lizzie said simply, but Alice blushed to recall that Lizzie had lost both parents unexpectedly at the same time and had never ceased to miss them. She could hardly imagine the same feelings arising in her own breast for the strange and capricious man who had been her father, but she endeavoured to reflect the more gracious expression her cousin exhibited. Thus she might earn some sympathy, if not in fact the trappings of true grief, beyond of course the lovely new fan she had liberated from her former tutor.

The profusion of carriages that met them set the two young women into momentary confusion. They did not remain in that state long, for the nigh on invisible Mr. Bird appeared, ushered them to the second carriage, then just as silently and swiftly disappeared. Lizzie and Alice looked out the window to see the remainder of the party sort themselves between the various carriages according to rank, need and propriety. Alice's mother, encumbered by a weeping Aunt Susan, stood clear-eyed, waiting for the coffin to be placed in the hearse, whose gin-infused driver swayed like a poplar at the heads of his horses. The creatures seemed to wonder at the curious smell their master exuded, although certainly as a hearse driver, it could not have been all that unusual. Yet even the horses turned their heads curiously to observe the arrival of the coffin.

'Oh dear,' Lizzie thought helplessly as she caught her first glimpse of the procession of Lord Mangrove's final earthly remains. It was indeed an unfortunate sight, one that would have infuriated his lordship, had he still had the means to become irate — and certainly recent events suggested that such temper was still possible. Perhaps this is one of the matters keeping his spirit from equanimity and rest, Lizzie thought, as she watched the mismatched crew of pallbearers stagger along.

It was not simply that the various heights of the men in question veered greatly from the moderate stature of Doctor Ponsonby to the demi-stature of Rector Chancel, then upward to the imposing figure of Lord Dagenham, although this did cause the coffin to rest at an unbecomingly rakish angle and undoubtedly, Lizzie mused, squashed the fragile remnants of Lord Mangrove into one end of the coffin. There was, however, the additional factor of the pristine sarcophagus itself, covered with any number of admirably detailed designs, ornate accoutrements reflecting the wealth and distinction of its interior dweller, ringed with gold and, popular this year the funeral director had insisted, a nautical design that included a fantastical ring-prow that would elicit looks of envy as the hearse drove through the village, assuring that the fine sense of privilege of the Mangrove clan would remain intact.

However, the additional weight of these items cast considerable taxing duty upon the pall bearers who, try as they might, found it difficult to maintain an elegant pace on their walk toward the hearse, instead listing and lurching first to the left, then to the right, depending entirely upon whether the rector managed to keep up with the gait of his taller compatriots, or whether he did in fact stumble in his attempts to do so. Fortunately it was only a short number of steps to the hearse from the front entrance, although one serious stumble did make Lady Mangrove reach out involuntarily toward the remains, the casket's forward momentum was halted by the surprisingly quick hand of Lord Dagenham whose elegant glove proved both swift and sure. In another moment the coffin was slipped into the glass enclosure of the hearse and the gentlemen could be forgiven for using their mourning handkerchiefs to mop their brows like common workmen.

Alice could not help feeling strong admiration for Lord Dagenham, despite her never having noticed him before other than as a place setting card on the dinner table. Her unremitting admiration was dampened, however, when she saw him take a nip of gin from the flask offered by the driver in a congratulatory way, for she had inherited from her mother very strong feelings about spirits.

But there was no time to wrestle with her conflicting thoughts. Lady Mangrove used the proffered hand of that man to alight to the phaeton, which she had insisted upon using despite the brisk air. No doubt she felt it important to show herself and her grim grief to the lowly folk of the village and provide an example of their betters. Alice felt a fleeting sense of admiration even as she bundled up, feeling colder by contrast, before she felt the lurch of the carriage taking off. With Lizzie brooding beside her, Alice stared out the window as they headed toward the cemetery.

Alice could hear the crisp sound of the wheels of the phaeton ahead of her, mingling with the rougher tread of the hearse. She waved to Mrs. Perkins as they pulled away, then glanced worriedly over at Lizzie to see if that was in fact proper behaviour, but Lizzie remained disconsolate, so Alice sank back into the seat and wondered how long the trip to the cemetery would take at this slow pace.

She was in danger of becoming bored.

As they turned the corner from the manor onto the road, she saw a number of the local farmers gathered into a respectful clump as the hearse passed by. Alice was amazed at the stoic faces set in grim masks of no doubt great feeling as they wheeled past. She found herself surprised that her father might awaken such emotion in the hearts of others when such sensations were hard put to find purchase in her own heart. Alice thought perhaps she was quite wicked and the thrill of horror this supposition gave her proved to be very warming, which probably restored a little of the usual rosiness to her cheeks.

Yet she could not wholly dismiss the persistent concern that she had missed something important in her father's personality all these long years. 'Lizzie,' she said, forgetting her cousin's distraction, 'was my father much beloved by the farmers? Did he have a special bond with them that they mourn him so?'

Lizzie drew her penetrating gaze away from the soft mists of memory and brought it to bear upon her cousin, an act that never failed to make young Alice quail. All too often that look hinted at scorn and judgment, two attitudes that were no favourites of the young woman.

'Why on earth would you say such a thing?'

Alice felt her blush deepen, which doubtless added to her rosiness of cheek, perhaps going a bit too far from rosy to red and diminishing her loveliness ever so slightly. 'The farmers gathered at the gate to pay Father their respects. They looked quite sad, I think.'

'Of course they looked sad, my dear,' her patient cousin counselled. 'They all owe their livings to the family lands. They are uncertain how Lady Mangrove will handle things in the wake of Lord Mangrove's death. There are many stories over the years of bereaved women turning unstable and causing all manner of fuss. They will not look happy until there has been some assurance that all will continue as it has been for many years, without rents being raised or land redeveloped in some modern way.'

Alice thought about these words. One can only imagine it to be due to the shock of her circumstances, the gravity of death, and perhaps the boredom of the carriage ride, that she did so, but Alice did ponder the issue, albeit briefly and with only the slightest of concerns.

'I cannot imagine Mother doing much to change the arrangements. She doesn't particularly like to have anything at all to do with the lands. In fact, she is quite happy dealing with her garden which, now that Father is away—' Alice waved her hand to demonstrate that she was well aware that this euphemism was precisely that, but also that she found it admirably suitable to the alternative; namely, that he was quite nearby but lying in the rather fanciful coffin not twenty yards away, '—she may replant as she has desired without interference.'

'That is exactly how it starts,' Lizzie said gravely. 'A woman suddenly loosed from the heavy bonds of matrimony may become quite giddy with the heady perfume of freedom. Countries have fallen for less cause.'

Alice frowned. 'You hardly sound interested in the idea of marriage. While I do not wish to be pledged to Mr. Boylett, I certainly have every faith that marriage will be an awfully big adventure.'

Lizzie positively glowed. 'While I may seem averse to the idea, I am not. In fact, if I reveal to you this letter's contents,' she remarked as she drew the much-glimpsed missive from her sleeve, 'you will see that I have much excitement to reveal—'

'Lizzie,' Alice exclaimed, her cousin's entreaty unheard, 'there he is again!'

'There is who?' Lizzie said with some understandable annoyance, for she was beginning to think she would never be able to unburden her secrets to anyone, not even to her cousin who was far less the kind of confidant she would have preferred, but there were few in the small number of folk around her who could provide suitable ears.

'The handsome young man from the Assembly Ball!' Alice shrieked, as oblivious to her cousin's mood then as she had been for most of her life. And certainly, there was the young man she had admired from across the room just before Lady Mangrove had notified her somewhat peremptorily that they were leaving the Ball. Once again it was due to her father's rather peculiar notions of propriety, in this particular instance, his dislike of comments that ran counter to his own singularly fixed opinions.

Alice remained ignorant of the nature of the disagreement her father had had with Lord Darlington that evening (as indeed she remained ignorant of a great many things such as the ultimate depths of the ocean, the distance between England and France [soon to be remedied by experience if not actual learning], the number of houses in Parliament at present, and the airborne speed of the average magpie); however she and mother both patiently bore his grumbling on the carriage ride home which consisted of unedifying snippets of angry muttering that seemed to form little in the way of a coherent pattern, ranging as they did from 'Newts!' said with great vehemence, a more measured utterance of 'impossible!' and finally the seemingly unrelated, 'miners!' (or perhaps 'minors!' — it is always difficult to be sure with homonyms).

Lord Mangrove did not choose to share the nature of the problem with either of the women, so they were left to their own thoughts, which for Lady Mangrove meant peaceful ruminations on spring planting and the dreamy prospects of a Sunday afternoon with her husband grumbling to himself in the library, while for Alice it meant the growing suspicion that the love of her life had appeared just when her father had whisked them away. Over the ensuing weeks, this imaginary affront had grown into a sizable if petty temper for the young woman, who felt a pout coming on at any recall of the subject. Although, to be entirely fair, such recollections came at greater and greater intervals as time went by.

However, the sight of the young man at the Darlington's very gate aroused Alice's remembrance of this terrible tragedy and she thrilled anew at the sight of the handsome young potential beau. 'There, see!' she crowed at her cousin, pointing out the window with a great absence of breeding.

Lizzie sighed, then turned her own gaze outward once more. 'Of course, that's Kit Barrington,' she explained to Alice just as the young man chose to make a polite bow in the direction of their carriage — or perhaps it was directed toward Lady Mangrove in her speedy phaeton, which now drew some rather more significant distance from their slower carriage (which may have had something to do with the amount of gin young Dick Spiggot had swilled prior to being pressed into service this day upon realisation of the shortage of drivers).

Alice, however, claimed the act as deference due to her as the doubly aggrieved party, having missed the chance to assess his charms at closer range during the Assembly Ball, as well as of course being part of the funeral cortège occasioned by the untimely death of her father. All of which made her tremble considerably, suddenly recognising just how romantic her state had become. She cast a furtive eye toward the group bunched at the Darlington gate, but had little time to assess whether they had made the same realisation, although she did note that young Mister Barrington had bright blue eyes, rich wavy dark hair and an admirably pale complexion.

'I do hope he is not Irish!' Alice thought, once more exposing the shortcomings of her class and its prejudices even as she did hope that he noticed her delicate blush and soft skin even from this distance. Perhaps the Darlingtons would speak of her pale and tragic beauty at greater length before they all arrived for the funerary tea or some other condolence event, Alice hoped.

Lizzie, however, apparently had had no such romantic thoughts clouding her mind. In fact, Alice noticed her cousin's head was cocked at a funny angle, as if she were hearing something strange. Good heavens, Alice thought, the shock of the day overcoming her natural distaste for such vulgar language, perhaps it is my father's ghost again. She quailed in her seat with a little bleat of distress, her new romance nearly forgotten.

Lizzie turned her penetrating vision back to Alice, who noticed a peculiar shine to her cousin's eyes that did not bode well for her comfort. 'I think something is about to happen!' Lizzie cried with alarm. Alice had no time to respond, for at that moment the carriage made an unexpected lurch, then picked up distressing speed.

Chapter Three

'Lizzie!' Alice cried at last, overcoming her annoyance at having the delightful view of Kit Barrington wrested from her gaze only to feel a growing sense of panic as the carriage declined to slow at all. 'What's happening?

Lizzie, for her part, seemed to be wondering much the same thing, but forbore to reply acidly to the obviousness of Alice's question and reached instead toward the intent.

'Why on earth is the carriage moving at such a fast speed? It might be that the horses startled at something, but surely the driver would be able to rein them in fairly soon. No, there is only one logical answer: We are being kidnapped,' Lizzie announced with some horror and not a little worry, but sounded unable to conceal completely the exciting nature of the proposition. Had Alice been able to divine her cousin's thoughts, she would have known that this was the best thing to happen to her in quite some time. While it did not make up for being orphaned from parents she genuinely loved, it was an improvement even on her secret romance, which, while quite thrilling to contemplate, remained a secret unshared, and thus, less than fully exhilarating. Alas, she had no idea of Lizzie's complex ruminations.

However, Alice, for once, was speechless.

She had waited all her life for some grand adventure. From the nursery to the parlour, her life had been an endless string of more or less what had been expected for a young girl of her stature and wealth. Even the death of her father (which was rather swiftly fading into the back of her somewhat over-taxed brain) failed to meet the expectations of excitement (although the possibility of there being something suspicious about the death raised the stakes considerably for a brief time). But here, Alice and her cousin were on the brink of a very big adventure indeed. So many words expressing her supreme joy raced one another to jump to the front of her mind and expel themselves from her lips, that they met in a great jumble, blocking further thoughts and clogging her throat to such an extent that unfamiliar feelings rose to her breast in the agitation of the moment and unexpectedly, rushed into her heart.

Alice burst into tears. She was quite surprised. Lizzie, too, looked shocked. Assuming these unaccustomed droplets indicated fear, she grasped Alice's hand consolingly and attempted to reassure her. 'I am certain we will come to no harm, my dear cousin. Undoubtedly some evildoer has seized the opportunity of the funeral to realise some terrible plan, probably to procure money, knowing the wealth of your family.'

Alice was too overcome by her unexpected tears to answer immediately. She wanted to say many things, which unfortunately only made it more impossible to get them out. As unaccustomed feelings battled for dominance in Alice's heart and mind, a muddle of words struggled to pour from her throat, which only brought forth a tremendous moan and yet further tears.

Lizzie still seemed nonplussed by her behaviour, but acted as if perhaps a new tack would jolly Alice out of her unexpected emotional display. 'Come now, Alice. If you keep crying like this, the coach will soon be full of tears and we will both drown.'

Rather than the laughter she hoped for, Lizzie's words only provoked a wail as Alice wiped teardrops from her cheeks. Lizzie was just about to dab at her cousin's eyes with her handkerchief when Alice cried out with elation, and she reached into her own sleeve. At last, she thought, I get to use my mourning handkerchief!

Alice dabbed her eyes then carefully tucked her mourning handkerchief into the special pocket in her dress. How had she forgotten to put it there before? Old habit, she scolded herself, and old habits must be broken. With a sudden rush of giddiness, Alice realised that henceforth she should demand to have all her dresses made with pockets. Why not? Who is to stop me? she thought wildly. With her father gone and mother unconcerned with such niceties, there was little to impede this new era of profligate pocketing. She very nearly swooned.

'Lizzie,' she cried, nearly breathless (if she had in fact been breathless, doubtless she would not have been able to say anything at all, so she must well have had some breath left, at least enough to make some sound). 'Do you know what I have realised?'

Lizzie, staring grimly out the window, seemed oblivious to her great joy. 'Indeed! The kidnappers will be leaving terrible demands for your mother, which she will not see until her return to the house after the funeral itself. It may be an hour or more before anyone begins to wonder where we have been taken.'

This was not at all what Alice had been thinking, but as soon as her cousin spoke, her previous thoughts evaporated like the last spoonful of tea in her cup, leaving not even so much behind as a few leaves, although the word 'pockets' continued to echo gently in the back of her mind like a small silver bell. However, because Alice spent so little time there, she was unlikely to hear it any time soon.

'Will no one miss us sooner?' she asked Lizzie somewhat peevishly. It was bad enough to suffer the indignity of a kidnapping (although if pressed, Alice would be unable to articulate how she might be suffering at all at present), but not even to be missed — that was simply intolerable. 'I should think everyone will be asking, 'Where's Alice?' as soon as they get to the graveside. I am Lord Mangrove's daughter, after all.'

Lizzie, however, paid no attention to her misfortune, engaged as she was with employing logic and observation to some useful end. 'We are heading south at present, and appear to be nearly out of the village altogether.'

'Perhaps we are heading for Africa,' Alice interjected hopefully. While she did not in general have a very good sense of the positions of various continents and countries around the globe, she had a very strong sense that Africa lay to the south of England and was sufficiently confident to voice her assumption out loud to her often censorious cousin. Surely this time she would win a gratified smile from her close relation, of the sort that dear Miss Travers used to award to her often less than entirely correct answers in the school room at home.

This was not, in fact, one of those times.

Lizzie refrained from looking very pained at her wild assertion and merely stated, 'We shall likely be heading somewhere in England first, although I suppose we cannot rule out Africa as a final destination, but we will be able to guess that as a more likely location after several months of sea travel have indicated such.'

While Alice bowed her head in chastised chagrin, Lizzie mused to herself that there was really no way to know what their final destination might be, and likewise, they had little idea by whom they had been abducted. While her own thoughts were better company than her cousin, Lizzie had begun to feel more than a little worry about their situation, and this she voiced at last aloud.

'I wonder who has kidnapped us?'

'Perhaps it is Kit Barrington,' Alice said. 'He has fallen madly in love with me and must have me, although my father has forbidden the union!' She looked near to swooning again at the prospect of such a plot.

Lizzie brought her cousin back down to earth in the most unfortunate way, as was her habit. 'Was it not he you were looking at through the window as we were spirited away?'

She saw Alice's cute little snub nose was quite out of temper now and trembled most unbecomingly. 'Yes, I suppose you are right,' she responded glumly.

Lizzie, feeling some modicum of pity, threw her a small bone of hope. 'I suppose it is not out of the question that he might have arranged for some bravoes to carry out the task for him…'

'Do you think so?' Alice said with a quick rushing return of her initial excitement.

'No, not really,' Lizzie answered honestly.

Alice sank back on the seat and reached for her handkerchief once more. 'Logic is a great enemy to romance.'

For a time nothing at all happened, which was infinitely disagreeable to Alice. Lizzie was not much happier. While she had entertained her nimble mind for a time with calculating their possible trajectories southward (Southampton seemed the most likely candidate, she declared to herself with some satisfaction), there was little to do afterward but admire the countryside, which was lovely indeed, but such an unremitting sameness of even pleasant charms quickly paled for the young women.

Boredom arrived amidst the creaks of the carriage and the monotonous drumming of the horses' hooves as they kept to their comfortable but persistent pace.

Alice, already peevish from the lack of fawning attention, looked as if she felt an illness coming on. This was not unusual for young ladies of Alice's stature (that's her civil stature not her physical stature — though neither disinclined her for such opportunities). In fact, Lizzie knew one young girl who spent an entire year suffering from brain fever after an unfortunate faux pas at high tea one September afternoon. Many women were known little beyond their maladies, for their sufferings always provided a safe topic of conversation sure to wring voluble commentary from both interlocutor and respondent equally and tended to discourage all other discussion.

Lizzie heaved a gentle sigh at having left behind the very interesting novel she had been reading (*The Echo on the Moors*, a cracking good yarn of intrigue, ghosts and family secrets written by an author who modestly chose to remain anonymous), for she had expected only the brief journey to the churchyard, not this prolonged incarceration. She lamented having never realised the vital importance of earnestly carrying reading material wherever one went. Life is uncertain, she told herself firmly, always carry a book.

Alice, however, had clearly convinced herself that she felt rather ill and was growing more distressed by the minute. 'Lizzie,' she croaked, as if her life were already hanging by a thread and in the throes of some fashionably delicate condition.

'Yes,' Lizzie answered, although her mind was now helplessly cataloguing all the novels she had yet to read.

'I fear I have come down with something!' Alice wheezed, her breath growing short and agitated.

Lizzie turned to her cousin and was mildly alarmed at the

43

sudden blotches of red on Alice's cheeks. In the time-honoured tradition of women since Erishkigal's time, she put her palm to her cousin's forehead and concentrated. What was she supposed to feel anyway? She recalled reading Galen's commentary on the writings of Crispinus, but only that the latter had been discredited by the former, who labelled him *lupus in fibula*. After a moment, she removed her hand and gazed penetratingly at Alice, although well aware how this intimidated her cousin.

'How do you feel? Give me details.'

Alice considered for a moment. 'I have an enormous feeling of lassitude,' she began carefully, quailing a bit under Lizzie's scrutiny, but bravely continuing, 'and I feel somewhat dizzy and I have a headache and there's a tingling… in my… left hand!' Alice raised the injured appendage as if its state could be ascertained visually.

'Do you feel at all confused or disturbed or restless?'

'Indeed!' It was quite accurate. To be fair, it was often true for the young woman, who found much of life confusing and disturbing and who could be counted on to feel restless at any event that required much sitting still.

Lizzie pondered the symptoms. 'It could be neurasthenia,' she said at last, although her furrowed brow seemed immediately to discount the likelihood of that judgment.

Alice nearly swooned. 'How exciting! I have never heard of the malady, but I love the name immediately.'

'However,' Lizzie continued without a thought for her happiness, 'I think you're simply bored.'

Alice gasped. Surely there was something more seriously wrong with her than mere commonplace boredom. 'But — but, what about my fever?' Surely that would count for something!

Lizzie sighed. She was beginning to feel as if her life were an endless repetition of what it was like now, to be trapped in this increasingly close carriage with her rich and dim cousin, on an endless journey to who knew where. While Alice assumed herself to be the captive of some delicate condition, Lizzie knew her own tribulations to be far more painful largely because she was so acutely aware of them. She fancied with some horror that she could imagine some overly fastidious Frenchman one day writing at length of the horrors of just such an existence, where the endless prattling of others would become a condition not even Milton's grand hero could endure forever. It seemed a perfect picture of purgatorial despondency.

But, for now, there was her responsibility to Alice who, if she was not entirely cognizant of the fact or appreciate of the effort, should be forgiven for her fewer years, her lesser learning (oh, the horrible neglect of Miss Travers), and her all too often pampered beauty. How sad, thought Lizzie privately (as so many of her thoughts had to be), that those who are given loveliness of face are seldom given any other qualities to complement it. However, her cousin should surely be able to marry someone on the strength of that beauty, who would not find himself deceived on that account until many years had passed. Other disappointments might come more quickly.

Alice was still pouting, which did little to restore her aforementioned looks, as her lips were drawn much too tightly together to give her pout any piquancy. As if by magic (or long habit), the realisation of how unappealing she must look finally brought Alice around with a sigh. I suppose I haven't any interesting disease, she admitted to herself at last, but then, left without a way to amuse herself, turned as always to her cousin. 'Did you bring a deck of cards, by chance, Lizzie?'

One can imagine somehow that the ever alert Mrs. Perkins undoubtedly dropped whatever was in her hands at that moment, for even far away she must have been conscious of this dangerous precedent slipping from the lips of one of the Mangrove family women. Unaware of this distant accident, Alice felt hope renew with the thought of entertainment.

Lizzie shook her head, however, dashing Alice's hopes. 'If only I had thought to put something aside for entertainment. A nice game of Authors would be pleasant even if we were not on a green river bank,' she said with unaccustomed wistfulness. 'If I had had the good sense to carry a book, I could have read aloud to entertain us both.'

'We should have had to be careful of bumps,' Alice said

somewhat distractedly, for there had been a number of good ruts in the road, which had lately brought the girls' attention back to their method of conveyance.

'One can always pause,' Lizzie reminded her, kindly but firmly. 'That's the beauty of a book. You can pick it up anytime, anywhere and be entertained. It is sublime simplicity itself!'

'Not in the dark,' pointed out Alice, who felt unusually thoughtful that moment.

'No, not as a rule,' Lizzie agreed. 'But one usually has a candle to hand and then reading can recommence.'

'Or one can call for a servant, who would surely have a candle. And matches,' Alice said, still thoughtful, although Lizzie was beginning to see that future Frenchman a little more clearly, as well as feeling a sense of understanding grow as to why most murders happened within the home.

All at once, though, Lizzie became alert. 'Listen,' she cried. 'Do you hear that?'

There was no mistake about it: the carriage was slowing its relentless pace.

The two women hugged one another with excitement. 'Perhaps we will be freed!' Alice said excitedly. The swift return of hope was enough to fill her cheeks with the flush of happiness again. 'Perhaps it was all a mistake and we're back home again!'

Lizzie, however, was slower to leap to frivolous conclusions. 'Alice, I believe we would have seen more recognisable landmarks by now if we had returned,' she said, returning to a lecturing mode. 'And note how the sun continues on the same side of the carriage. If we had changed directions, we should have noted a change in the direction of the sun as well.'

Logic was a dry subject, which even Alice knew, but she meekly replied, 'As you say, Lizzie. But surely we have arrived somewhere.'

Indeed, the horses were slowing to a walk, no doubt fatigued by their hasty journey. Lizzie furtively peeked out the window of the carriage but found it difficult to make out where they were. 'I see a sort of house, or perhaps it's a public house. There is a sign hanging outside it, so I suspect it may be the latter.'

'It could be a baker's,' Alice ventured shyly.

'Perhaps,' Lizzie admitted, 'But I suppose it more likely to be a kind of place for refreshment. See! We are heading around the building. Perhaps the horses will be stabled and we will have something cool to drink.'

'Look, there is a pot of flowers!' Alice meant to be help-ful, but even she could not see anything of gain in that observation.

'We have stopped!' Lizzie had unconsciously lowered her voice to a whisper. At last, their abductor might make himself known. The excitement was nigh on intolerable. The two felt the carriage lurch as their driver leapt down from the box. Voices drew near, undoubtedly addressing their abductor. The horses were being led away, undoubtedly to be well fed and watered. Alice gasped as footsteps approached the side of the carriage; Lizzie grabbed her hand and they both stared toward the door.

When it suddenly opened, however, they were immedi-ately blinded by the bright sunlight streaming through and ruining their first glance at the daring highwayman. Well, Lizzie had fancied some dashing robber perpetrating the crime, while Alice had still hoped for Kit Barrington's visage. They were both soon disappointed by the squat, masked man in the black hat who stepped into view. He was not the strik-ing figure they had hoped for; further, he did not regard them with a cool, appraising stare nor did he smile devilishly at their beauty and vulnerability.

No, he simply pointed a pistol at the pair of them and demanded (in something less than dulcet tones) that they alight from the carriage to refresh themselves. 'And look sharp about it, too, or my master will hear about it!'

This pronouncement had the immediate effect of motivat-ing the two young women to scurry out of the carriage, but it also inspired them with a sense of relief that this unprepos-sessing figure was not in fact their nemesis, but only his servant.

'It could still be Kit,' Alice whispered furtively to

Lizzie, blushing before she corrected herself, 'I mean, Mr. Barrington.' They both blinked to be out of the carriage's shadowed interior and were scuttled into the public house without much of a look outside. Lizzie did manage to glance at the sign hanging from the front of the house and mentally recorded its name.

Never had the words 'Pig and Whistle' provoked such an ominous gloom!

The squat, masked man in dark clothing hurried the two young women forward with his pistol and his muttered demands. 'Get along, get along, would you, haven't got all day, hurry along.'

It was most provoking when one was doing one's best to 'get along' and yet still be told to 'get along,' Alice thought with some peevishness. She turned to Lizzie to repeat her sentiments aloud, but for her effort only received a very peremptory poke in the small of her back from the brigand's pistol.

'The nerve of the man!' Alice thought. 'We have never even been introduced.' No, she affirmed to no one but herself, this cannot be the work of Kit Barrington. Surely he would have taken the effort to hire experienced and kindly henchmen to carry out his surreptitious deeds. Alice contemplated for some time her knowing (and recalling, it must be added) a word like 'surreptitious' with a good deal of unbecoming smugness.

Lizzie meanwhile was trying to gain as much information from her surroundings as their hurried march would allow. They went into the building without much more detail being visible apart from that sign. 'The Pig and Whistle' presumably meant this was a public house (how common, Lizzie thought with a shiver) but it appeared to be empty, which was not the usual practice of such locations as she understood it. Lizzie had an abhorrence of alcohol quite out of all reason (something the King of Naples had been trying to get her to overcome in their rather considerable correspondence over the many months, for his land was rich in the grape with many a fruity reserve delectable and sweet with a variety of local dishes) and attached, perhaps not unreasonably, the taint of alcohol to her Platonic ideal of the public house.

Much to her surprise, the interior of the place, while dark, smelled pleasant and seemed remarkably clean. While the two captives were hustled along a side corridor toward the back of the house where the lodgings appeared to be, Lizzie had scant seconds in which to glimpse solemn oak panelling and comfortable benches for the public, presumably, to cosy up to one another. It was with a bit of a shock that she realised it all looked very comfortable indeed.

One can almost see a smile crossing the face of the King of Naples in his distant land at that moment.

However, it was far away and of no immediate concern to the events involving the kidnapped young women, who were whisked into a chamber by the squat man. He slammed the door behind them, trapping them once again, although in a new location which at least had novelty to recommend it, Lizzie thought with a small brightening of hope in her breast.

Left quite alone for the moment, the two women sighed with relief, hugged briefly, then turned to examine their new confines. It was a dismal room with two wooden chairs, a table, a tiny and very dirty window which showed only the courtyard where their carriage yet awaited (although without its original pair of horses), a small painting of King Henry the Eighth (rendered very poorly it must be added, for they could recognise him only from the general outlines, his face giving little clue to his identity and in fact appearing almost to have melted perhaps in the sun of some zealous anti-Catholic endeavour) and a second door.

'Dare we try the door?' Alice asked with some trepidation.

Lizzie took a breath and, deciding fortune favours the bold, strode across the room to take firm hold of the handle, turning it down, with all her courage she flung it open.

It was a small room with a water closet.

Both young women blushed. Raised with a proper sense of modesty and decorum, they were supremely embarrassed by this needful invention, and quite unable to admit, despite the thunderous need on both their parts, of the desire to use said apparatus.

They might well have stood there for a very long time, silent and bursting, had not the other door sprang open to

49

admit a most curious figure that made the two women shudder and leap to each other's comfort.

Through the door came a woman with a bright red turban swathed around her hair, wearing a loose dress of bright blue and startling white, with skin the colour of luxurious chocolate. She was the last thing they expected to see come through that door, so the two cousins remained clasped together, mouths open in surprise.

'What're you standing there for, m'dears?' The woman at last addressed them after her own look of surprise. 'You do not have much time they tell me, so let us move along swiftly and get things done.' Her voice had a lilt that sounded so unlike the measured tones heard in Mangrove Hall. Alice could easily imagine her father cocking one eyebrow at the face of one who spoke with such unnecessary music in her tone.

Seizing on Alice as the clearly junior partner in the association, the woman bustled Alice across the room and into the convenience before she could rightly blush or show her unwillingness to enter such a room.

There Alice found in addition to the water closet (that modern prurience bids we mention) there was a lovely basin with fresh clear water. While Alice was greatly relieved by her use of the unmentionable invention, she was much refreshed by the water after the close air of the carriage. While she made her ablutions, the woman spoke almost constantly, twitching at Alice's dusty mourning clothes and tutting over the state of her hair.

'What have you been doing, child? Looks like you have been on a wild ride. If you were my daughter, I wouldn't allow you to walk abroad like this. If the good Lord had meant for women to go traveling such long distances, he would have created a better conveyance than the carriage. My goodness, your hair is just a disaster — here, let me brush it a little or you'll have to hack it all off at the end of your journey, it will be so full of rat's nests.'

Alice could not utter a word until her hair had been brushed to a new sheen of restored beauty, her clothes had received a good slapping to release dust and her face scrubbed to a pink liveliness which covered well her embarrassment at the whole proceedings. Whisked once more into the outer chamber, Alice whirled dizzily as their interrogator darted to repeat the same procedure with Lizzie, who just as quickly demurred and swiftly latched the door to the convenience behind her to take care of matters herself.

Feeling the floorboards firmly under her feet, Alice turned at last to regard this stranger with her yet blinking eyes. 'Who are you, miss?' she asked of the whirlwind with some trepidation. In her young life, Alice had little experience with such forceful people, apart from Mrs. Perkins, who was no match for sheer exuberance, although she could be far more peremptory.

She was greeted with a broad and friendly smile. 'I am Emma Saint John.'

'Ah,' Alice said, at a loss for further questions when faced with such a succinct response.

'You probably want to know where you are, don't you? You are at the Pig and Whistle, that much I can tell you, but I am forbidden to tell you more on pain of being beaten severely by my master.'

'How awful!' Alice said with genuine feeling. The world's wild ways were beginning to seem quite hideous to this heretofore-sheltered girl. Novels, she must admit, did not lie. If even England could be filled with such reprehensible people, how much more dangerous the barbarian lands beyond its borders?

'Indeed,' Emma continued, 'you will not be here much longer, for you are to be taken to Southampton and across the waves. I can say no more —' She paused and turned her head toward the door as if she had heard a sound, but after a moment, turned back to Alice. 'You are in great danger!'

Alice felt a thrill such as she had never before known. It was as if she had become an exciting novel's heroine. Surely that meant they would be rescued before anything too untoward were to happen to them! She was about to ask Miss Saint John more about the danger, but just then Lizzie returned, bursting open the door as if she, too, had heard that they were in danger.

'What can you tell us, Miss Saint John?' Lizzie demanded.

'I can tell you no more,' Emma said with grave sorrow. 'Your captor will return any moment and you will be on your way. Bless you, girls — there is nothing to be done for you now but hope for the best.'

Lizzie impulsively took Emma's hands in her own and implored her, 'Do you have some paper and writing implements? I must write a letter!'

Emma reached into the folds of her dress and drew out a small bundle. 'I carry my master's writing kit with me always.' She snapped open the leather case to reveal some small scraps of parchment, a pen and ink in a small cylindrical bottle, and thrust it at Lizzie, who took it without hesitation and immediately set to scratching out a letter.

'We have been kidnapped,' Alice said, feeling that she had been ignored far too long, stung slightly by the thought she had no one to whom to write. Perhaps Mother, she thought, but was sure little good would come of her writing except a longer than usual lecture on her penmanship.

'Yes, child, I know. It must be horrible,' Emma agreed, patting her hand.

'Do you have anything to read?' Alice asked with sudden inspiration. 'We have no amusement of any kind in the carriage.'

Into another pocket Emma's hand went to retrieve a small volume and place it into Alice's eager palms.

'Oh, thank you so much, Miss Saint John! This will go a long way to relieve our boredom. It has been so desperately dull and boring, I can't tell you how tedious and drab our whole day has been. I have been so fed up, uninterested...' Alice floundered, thinking of other words to reflect her boredom.

It seemed, however, that Emma grasped the situation well. 'I can well imagine, miss.'

Just then, Lizzie snapped the writing case closed and thrust it and the letter back into Emma's hands. 'Please, if you can, see that this letter reaches its destination. I would be ever so grateful for your help!'

Just then they heard a shout in the hall. Their captor

was returning! Emma nodded quickly, thrust the letter and the case into her pocket and turned to face the door. Alice glanced down at the book in her hands.

Oh dear, she thought, it looks like an improving book.

The door was flung open by the surly and squat man. In the light of the room, Alice could see that he was remarkably ugly and that suited her sense of justice long nourished by exciting novels. Bad characters were inevitably homely and heroes handsome, although sometimes dangerous, too. She would be sure to recognise the hero when he arrived.

'C'mon,' the rumpled man ordered them. 'Back in the carriage with you two.'

Lizzie and Alice exchanged a look of distaste, but were uneasy to think how this low character might injure them, so they swiftly gathered themselves and headed for the door with a last imploring look at Emma.

'She can't help you none,' the kidnapper chortled with evident disdain, causing the two young women to cower helplessly. 'And you,' he continued, turning toward Emma. 'Make sure to tell your master that I expect my payment in full when we arrive in Southampton.'

'I will do so,' Emma said with palpable revulsion, even as she threw one last kindly glance toward the departing women.

Down the stairs they went, back through the public house and once more into the hated carriage with its new team of horses. I shall walk everywhere from now on, Alice promised herself, fully intending to maintain that rule, although the likelihood of a lazy girl like herself doing so seemed tolerably slim. Her intention was, if not pure, then honourably motivated, so perhaps we should not criticize her too harshly.

Lizzie appeared thoughtful as they took off once more. 'We have learned some things today, Alice,' she said eventually, drawing her words out slowly. 'Our kidnapper is not the man on the box, but someone at a remove. He has perhaps been to the West Indies, for he employs a woman of that region.'

'How do we know that?' Alice asked, perplexed.

Lizzie looked at her. 'Emma, Alice.'

Alice wrinkled her nose, working out the connection. 'Emma?' she echoed unhelpfully. It really was most provoking to always rely on hints and puzzles.

Lizzie sighed. 'Emma is from the West Indies. She spoke of her master, who sounds like a most cruel and objectionable person, as did the man who drives this carriage.'

'How do you know she's from the West Indies?' Alice asked with wonder.

Lizzie stared at her. 'Did you not notice the manner in which she spoke?'

Alice squirmed, feeling her cheeks grow warm. 'I thought perhaps she was Welsh,' she ventured to say with something less than confidence. 'Who did you write to?' she asked, desperately seeking to change the subject.

Lizzie frowned. 'To *whom* did I write?' She emphasized the interrogative pronoun for Alice's benefit, which escaped its intended target entirely. 'I wrote to the King of Naples. He will surely want to deal with this unfortunate occurrence himself.'

Surely she would have been tempted to let more of the mysterious story drop at this point, had not Alice suddenly recalled what she had in her hand. 'We have a book to read! Oh, do let us read it now. I am so desperately bored.'

'What is the volume?'

Alice brought the book up to her gaze. 'It is *The Governess* by Sarah Fielding. Perhaps it is a gothic,' she said with some hope in her tone, but thought to herself, oh yes, an improving book, no doubt.

'Here,' said Lizzie, stretching out her hand. 'Shall I begin?'

Alice was delighted. She was afraid she would have to start. It is always better to be read to than to read. Although it must be said that even her mother could not bear to have Alice read aloud for long, as she would inevitably lose her place, mispronounce words and skip over lines.

Lizzie cleared her voice and then began, 'There lived in the northern parts of England, a gentlewoman who undertook the education of young ladies; and this trust she endeavoured faithfully to discharge, by instructing those committed to her care in reading, writing, working, and in all proper forms of behaviour. And though her principal aim was to improve their minds in all useful knowledge; to render them obedient to their superiors, and gentle, kind, and affectionate to each other; yet did she not omit teaching them an exact neatness in their persons and dress, and a perfect gentility in their whole carriage...'

Oh dear, thought Alice, it *is* an improving book.

Chapter Four

Alice suddenly found herself drowning.

She paddled like mad, gasping for breath, striking out in vain to reach some solid ground, something upon which she might grasp hold, save herself from the swirling, endless waters. Another mouthful swallowed and she feared that all too soon she might just give in. The water had a terrible salty taste as if she were drowning in tears of sorrow. Then a giant sucking sound began and Alice shrieked because she knew that the plug had been pulled and there was no way to avoid being sucked down to the bottom of the ocean to drown and never see Mangrove Hall again or her mother, or Lizzie, or Mrs. Perkins, or her father — well, at least her father's ghost — and even Arthur, she might miss Arthur at this point, although when it came right down to it —

'Alice, wake up! You're dreaming again.' Lizzie looked up from the book with the air of irritation she always demonstrated when Alice was being particularly obtuse. At the sight of the horrid book, Alice recalled what had made her drift off in the first place.

'I shall continue,' Lizzie said, much to Alice's dread, then commenced to do the same. 'Miss Jenny, with her heart overflowing with joy at this happy change, said, 'Now, my dear companions, that you may be convinced what I have said and done was not occasioned by any desire of proving myself wiser than you, as Miss Sukey hinted while she was yet in her anger, I will, if you please, relate to you the history of my past life; by which you will see in what manner I came by this way of thinking; and as you will perceive it was chiefly owing to the instructions of a kind mamma, you may all likewise reap the same advantage under good Mrs. Teachum, if you will obey her commands, and attend to her precepts. And after I have given you the particulars of my life —"

'How dark it has grown,' Alice interjected with sudden inspiration. 'Lizzie, you must not strain your eyes with reading this late. It's not as if we have a lamp.'

Lizzie looked thoughtful. For a moment, Alice feared that she might implore the driver for a light, but at last she resolutely closed the small volume and leaned back on the seat with a sigh. Alice did what she could to hide her own sigh of relief. Go hang Miss Fielding and her improving book, she thought deliciously to herself. If Lizzie only knew!

Alice had no way of knowing how phenomenally bored Lizzie was at that very moment. Her only solace in the book had been that the useless chatter of its words had kept her worried thoughts at bay. While reading aloud to her cousin, Lizzie could keep herself from all her anxieties about what the next day would bring. As they continued to bounce along the road, unchallenged, unpursued as far as she could tell, Lizzie could only wonder endlessly what would become of them. With no new information, however, she knew her worries to be pointless, endlessly circling like water down a drain with no end.

It was ironic how similar their thoughts had tracked, like horses in traces together.

Neither remarked upon the coincidence as neither became aware of it. Instead they sighed separately, yet together, apart and alone.

'Perhaps we should try to sleep,' Lizzie suggested at last, taking in the woebegone countenance of her cousin, so ill-used by circumstance, so unaccustomed to the life of drab drudgery.

'It has been quite a day,' Alice said, her eyes getting heavy in spite of herself.

'Tomorrow is another day,' Lizzie remarked brightly even as she thought to herself, what an odd thing to say, and how unlike me. Well, fiddle-dee-dee, she scolded herself, everyone runs out of pithy sayings at one time or another.

'I only hope I shall not dream of water,' Alice said, quite unable to finish her thought before yawning gapingly and barely bothering to cover her mouth.

We shall become quite the barbarians if this keeps up, Lizzie thought, but rather than chastise her sleepy cousin, she, too, leaned back and settled herself as well as possible given the hard seat, the lurching motion of the carriage and the uncertainty of their destination.

The two were startled awake with the shouted words. 'Southampton, ladies!'

This cheery greeting seemed to come from a long way away, although it was perhaps the reflected light of the seaport that shimmered across the open door of the carriage and lent a not quite ethereal air to the short, squat man who had conducted them so far from home.

Lizzie sat up abruptly toward the beckoning hand and instantly felt the pain in her neck from sleeping none too comfortably in the upright position for the night. As her hand went up to massage her painful nape, she heard Alice stir and in her usual way say, 'Oh just let me lie in a little longer, MaryAnn. I feel unaccountably tired today!' Alice stretched herself with admirable ease, clearly forgetting where they were.

'Let's not take all day, speed of the essence, etcetera, etcetera,' their too cheerful conductor called forth, waving his hand further to encourage them to disembark.

Alice looked with alarm at Lizzie. 'I had quite forgotten where we were.'

'I only wish I had,' Lizzie said, stepping forward to alight from the carriage, but pausing for a moment on the top step to look back into its depths at Alice. Suddenly she feared leaving its darkness for the flat light of dawn, but Alice could not be bothered to allow such sentiments to settle in. She was cramped and cranky, and consequently could not wait to bound out of the carriage into the sun, weak though it was.

'Are we to be free now?' she said hopefully to the driver.

He merely laughed. 'You're going on a journey, my ladies. Your ship is just along here.'

Lizzie looked at him coolly, taking in his small stature and common countenance. 'And if we scream, a constable will surely come to our aid.'

The driver laughed even harder than the first time. 'You don't know Southampton! And anyway, miss, you forget about this little treasure of mine.' He pulled the pistol from the side pocket of his coat. 'Say hello to my little friend.'

Lizzie swallowed uncomfortably, but Alice managed to say,

'Hello, little friend.'

'Now, ladies, if you'll follow me—'

There was little choice in the matter, so follow they did. Truth to tell, the streets along the docks did not appear to house the very finest of houses nor, must it be admitted, of people, as it seemed everyone they passed looked to be engaged in activities every bit as unscrupulous as they. Indeed, those who were abroad in the early light (if sensible, for admittedly, many they met seemed to be the worse for drink, which made both young ladies reach for their stylish mourning handkerchiefs rather than call for assistance) regarded them furtively and with great suspicion.

'There it is, your next conveyance,' the pistol-waving man announced as they turned a last corner. 'You'll be on board and away from England before the tide lets out today.'

Lizzie felt a sudden chill looking upon its timbers, though she could not have said what sort of boat it was or why she found it so ominous. Perhaps it was only the combination of the eerie dawn light, the strangeness of their companion, and of course, the fact that they had been spirited away from the funeral of Alice's father's sudden, and admittedly, slightly mysterious death.

'The *Demeter*,' Alice read off the side of the boat. She looked to Lizzie for approval. 'Italian?'

'Greek,' Lizzie corrected, barely noticing her cousin's crestfallen look.

'Aye,' said their kidnapper. 'But she is set to sail as far as the Caspian, I hear, to the land beyond the forest.'

Lizzie gazed with sorrow at the ship whose sails picked up a portentous billow from the wind. Where were they bound now?

Alice looked up at the ship, voicing much the same thoughts as Lizzie. 'Where are we bound? Who had wished us conveyed hence — and when would they be serving breakfast?'

Lizzie had not been thinking the last, her appetite dampened by the unpleasant chain of events they had undergone, but surely soon she would be thinking of food, too,.

'Particularly once her stomach started to rumble; then no

one would be able to think of anything else except perhaps growling dogs,' Alice muttered. 'I must be quite hungry, I am beginning to make very little sense.'

Their kidnapper ignored this, continuing to speak. 'We shall meet here the captain of this ship who will be responsible for taking you further. Indeed! Here he comes now —'

Lizzie had a moment of hope, thinking of the glorious men of the sea who had been celebrated in story and song, from Captain Cook to Sir Francis Drake, fearless men who lived proudly and sailed courageously across the globe, heroes and honourable men. She shaded her eyes from the dawning sun's rays and looked up the gangway to where the short, squat man pointed. Alice, too, found her eye irresistibly drawn in that direction, holding her breath as she hoped that this ship's captain would prove to be reputable, strong and, of course, be in possession of a well-stocked larder.

'Captain Bellamy! I have some cargo for you here.' The short, squat man chortled with good humour at his own witticism. May he trip and stub his toe, Alice thought without a modicum of charity for his feelings. It was probably due to hunger, but it is quite likely that she was developing bad habits far from the comforts of home, a good hair-brushing and clean clothes. I shall never wear mourning clothes again, Alice promised herself rather rashly.

Lizzie, however, had kept her eyes trained upward and her attention fixed on the gangway as their new tyrant made his way down to the dockside where they stood. She must make a study of him for he would be their only avenue of escape, the squat man proving to be amenable to no appeals of any kind. They must not be allowed to leave England and safety for some foreign shore!

In the soft morning light, Captain Bellamy strode down the gangway like a man who knew his worth down to the penny. His fulsome brow arched beneath a captain's hat of such elaborate styling from its crisp black lines to its stately plumage that it seemed to announce to the world a man of such repute that none could dare venture a word against his courage. Lizzie was pleased to see manly shoulders thrust below the epaulettes of his jacket, where its nine buttons gleamed jauntily in the dawning sun. His buff vest looked neat and trim and his boots, she saw as he stood majestically before them, were shined so well that she could see her face reflected in the smooth leather as she looked down. Here, surely, was a man who would take pity on two young women, ripped from the bosom of their family and thrust into the untoward company of brigands and ne'er-do-wells of a distinctly lower class.

Captain Bellamy cleared his throat, looked at the two young women, and then in a high-pitched voice burbled, 'Wheh is my money, you heawtless bwigand?'

The short, squat man laughed with his head thrown back. 'Always business with you, eh, Bellamy?'

'You would be the vewy same if you wewe in my position,' Bellamy glowered, his menace somewhat undercut by the screechy tone of his voice. 'Wapscallions like you awe always a twial.'

'Well, here's your merchandise,' the kidnapper shouted, shoving Alice and Lizzie toward the imposing-looking figure of the captain. 'And here's your payment, you sea dog,' he said, thrusting a leather purse into the captain's hands. 'Bon voyage,' he said lifting his cloth cap in mock polite regard to the two young women. Then he turned on his heel and strode away, whistling as if he hadn't a care in the world.

'I shall hate him forever,' Alice whispered fiercely, although it is doubtful that she should keep such an all-encompassing effort foremost in her mind. There had been many occasions on which Alice had planned similarly long-lasting and comprehensive vendettas, such as the time she declared she would never eat anything but lettuce, or the day on which she vowed to always coordinate her hair ribbons and gloves. However, it did seem entirely likely that Alice would indeed loathe if not in fact hate that short, squat man for a very long time, as she been terribly inconvenienced by him, and things looked likely to deteriorate further before they improved.

'Come with me, giwls,' the captain wheezed, patting the purse full of money fondly. 'You awe my wesponsibility now!' As if to emphasize the point, he drew a revolver from his belt and waved it at the two of them, who meekly trotted up the gangplank to the ship's deck.

'Welcome aboawd the *Demetew*!' the captain said with surprisingly sincere zeal. 'We sail with the tide fow the land beyond the fowest.'

'Are we really going all the way to Transylvania?' Lizzie asked with admirable coolness. She had come to the conclusion there was little to lose now (although she still held out hope for the letter Emma Saint John had promised to post on her behalf), so she might as well be bold with the captain. Perhaps it was that he had rank, she feared less his anger — with the short, squat man of indeterminate class, they had no way to anticipate his conduct. Surely a captain would uphold some of the general laws of behaviour and show good form.

She was somewhat nonplussed to see the weather-creased face break into a smile as prelude to a cackling laugh. Very bad form, Lizzie thought, and shared her disapproval with Alice by means of an archly lifted eyebrow. Alice appeared to be uncertain what Lizzie intended with this gesture as she had been mesmerized by the captain's strange laugh.

'Twansylvania? Oh no, my child, you will not be going to Twansylvania. We have othew plans fow you. At pwesent, howevew, you shall be going below decks to youw cabin whewe you will be spending much of youw time.' He cackled again and Lizzie felt her heart sink.

As they turned in the direction the stern captain indicated, a thought unbidden rose to Alice's mind. 'Oh,' she said, turning suddenly to Lizzie. 'We have forgotten our book!'

Lizzie groaned inwardly — another long journey and nothing to read, but Alice could not help thinking that she was glad not to know what immeasurably valuable lessons Betty Ford would be learning from Mrs. Teachum.

It seemed but a few minutes and the two women were safely stowed away in their cabin after running the gauntlet of stares provided by the men on deck. Alice seemed particularly perturbed. 'How dare they stare! And anyway, it was not our fault if our clothes had begun to look a little worse for the wear. How I would adore a bath! Perhaps with so much water around, I shall have a bath.'

Lizzie did not bother to explain that Alice was, of course,

ignorant of the preciousness of fresh water at sea. One need not whisper that in her ear just yet and she could live in happy ignorance of that fact as she did of the price of wheat and the chemical nature of alum powder.

Lizzie, however, despaired.

'Leawn to love this life, my little fwiends,' Captain Bellamy advised the two in his peculiar high-pitched voice. 'The men might get a little westless if they think too much about such pwetty ladies hiding on boawd.' The menace in his words was clear if somewhat mitigated by the sound of them. While before they were in the hands of a single ruffian, now they were faced with the horrors of a ship full of nefarious men of undoubtedly low birth and worse morals. The bos'n, in particular, with his single eye and black swan tattoo, seemed to be particularly ghoulish despite his rather jaunty top hat. He had a tendency to mutter mysteriously as he swabbed past their cabin. If only this were a book, thought Lizzie, I could peek ahead at the next chapter and see if the heroine survived her perilous journey.

With a sudden lurch, the ship was afloat. Alice grabbed Lizzie's hand and the two of them watched sadly as Southampton receded from their view, slowly getting smaller and smaller as the vessel crested the waves. The gentle rocking of the ship broadened as they headed out further into the channel. This is life at sea, Lizzie thought, as the wind whistled through their rather small window, the cries of the gulls punctuated the calls of the men on deck, and the sea air filled her with a strange sense of familiarity. It was as if her fear receded somewhat and she could imagine coming to enjoy such a life. There was a freedom in the ship's movement, a camaraderie among the men that spoke of secret knowledge, of mysteries. Lizzie could begin to understand how men were drawn to its open expanses, the drift of the waves and the salty tang of the air.

Alice, however, felt a curious sensation that she quickly realised was going to bring the contents of her very light meal much closer to her lips. With a look of mute appeal to Lizzie, she pressed her mourning handkerchief to her lips, sobbed once, then ran to the window and violently vomited out it.

The smartly hatted bos'n grinned up at her like a leering skull and merely mopped her leavings away off the side of the boat and winked (or blinked, it is rather hard to tell with only one eye to go by) at her.

Perhaps I am dead and this is hell, Alice thought, though she could not bring herself to believe she had done anything to deserve such a fate. The next few days would make her wish dearly that she had gone to hell instead of Southampton.

The waters swelled and rolled. The horizon appeared then plummeted. Alice's stomach grew apart from her in coldness, stubbornly keeping to a schedule of events unwelcome to her vanity, but she found herself unable to reason with its demagogic turn and resigned herself to misery, weakness and parboiled tea.

Lizzie, on the other hand, found herself exhilarated. The sea air in her nose made her senses sing. The salt wind in her hair convinced her to bundle the offending locks out of the way and, scandalously unbonneted, she strode the deck under the watchful eye of Captain Bellamy but with the grudging admiration of the top-hatted bos'n, who at first — perhaps somewhat doubtful of this gentlewoman's mettle — had sneered quite openly behind his hand at her attempts to negotiate the deck. In no time at all, however, Lizzie had mastered the firm but flexible pace of the sea-going veteran, and fought her way against the winds to walk the ship from stem to stern and take in all manner of sights and portents. Lizzie learned to listen to the different calls of the gulls, to glimpse the fish that leaped from the waves, indeed, even the different slopes of the waves across the sides of the vessel that relayed the minute changes in the weather. Lizzie thrilled to the cry of the albatross and came to welcome the cold drops of rain from the sky that broke the sun-drenched deck's heat.

In any case, it was better than watching Alice vomit.

Infinitely worse, perhaps, was that one must also hear and smell her distress. The bos'n was kept busy much of the time, but still he managed to wander abroad and catch Lizzie just in time to point out something intriguing about the scent of the wind or the particular cry of the gull. Although Lizzie feared that they were already heading south of France, she could not let go her fascination with the sea and her thrill at the wonderful freedom of the life on deck.

Even Captain Bellamy seemed to notice, although he spent much of his day alternately brooding in his cabin or lashing at the crew with his black bullwhip. He was never less than polite with Lizzie, but his tone often betrayed a sense of risibility that made Lizzie wonder if he did not mock her new excitement.

'How is ouw little sailow this aftewnoon?' the captain would quiz her as she reached the forecastle. 'Have you gained youw sea legs?' If the wind was right, they might be able to hear the sounds of Alice violently discarding any attempt at lunch. Otherwise, Lizzie had only her contempt to distract her from the captain's scathing insinuations.

'Are we making good progress?' Lizzie would inquire, inevitably turning the captain's thoughts ahead to the time when he might get rid of the two women and, consequently, receive good payment to do so. It tended to work.

At this latest moment, however, the captain seemed distracted. He was about to finally answer her when the bos'n appeared and whispered — far too loudly for Lizzie not to hear — that a black sail had been sighted on the horizon.

Lizzie was relieved to close the shutter on their window (although she had a brief wonder about whether it was still called a shutter on board the ship — everything else had a different name) and no longer see the rictus grin of the top-hatted bos'n who reminded her more and more of some evil portent despite his smile (or perhaps because of it). Alice had lain down in her bunk and was whimpering softly in her sleep. At least she was not vomiting at the moment.

It was a strange thing to be at sea — literally in this case, although Lizzie could not help remembering that they were very much at sea metaphorically, too. It was with this sense of melancholy that she slipped unobtrusively into the world of dreams without even sensing the change of location.

She may have been tipped off by the strange aroma of roses but it did not seem odd to her just then, nor was it at all unexpected to find herself in the Regent's Park (why only two days a week? Lizzie groused to herself, it should be open

to the public at all times and filled with roses all the year).
Indeed at that moment, it was and she wandered her way
among them, smelling the intoxicating blooms and letting
her fingers trail over their velvet blossoms.

All at once she heard a voice; his soft accents betrayed an
Italian influence and Lizzie knew it was the King of Naples.
She turned swiftly but could not see him, so she ran. As she
did, the rosebushes — which had seemed so lovely and soft
moments before grew large thorns and pluck at her dress as
she sought to follow the dulcet tones ahead of her. This is
ridiculous, Lizzie thought, redoubling her determination but
the roses began to climb and the thickets impeded her way.
Before she knew it, she was trapped and the sweet smell of
the roses had turned to a fetid swampy air. Lizzie gasped for
breath and felt a sense of being trapped. How would she get
out? Panic rose in her breast and she cried out.

'Oh dear,' Alice said suddenly. 'I do beg your pardon, but I
believe I have purged myself again.'

Alice woke to feel her head pounding and her heart beating weakly. She looked out the window to see in the dim light
of the dawn that appalling rictus grin of the bos'n, his jaunty
top hat failing to make her the least bit jolly. His skull-like
countenance for once was nearly welcome.

If you are Death, Alice thought, I do hope you have come
to claim me. She had expelled every bit of food that had been
in her stomach, and some bits of food that she particularly
did not like to believe had ever passed her lips at any time,
having been of such unappealing form and substance as to
have questioned the reasonableness of anyone allowing such
morsels to grace her mouth. Just let me die, she whispered,
not even aloud.

The hideous spectral figure drew closer and Alice very
nearly thought that at last her pain was at an end. No more
adventures, no more kidnapping, but sadly, no return home
and hero's welcome. She would very much have liked to be
welcomed home with a great deal of pomp and circumstance
(not to mention tea, cakes and very nice crispy bacon) but
she feared now such was not to be. For death's head loomed
before her about to cut short her promising beauty and

loveliness (or so she liked to think even in this moment of unremitting pathetic suffering).

The bos'n, however, far from being a representative of Death on this earthly plane, merely took her soft white hand with surprising gentleness, turned it over and tapped repeatedly just below her wrist.

Alice was too shocked and sickly to muster an objection. Surely if Lizzie were there, she would have done so, but Alice merely stared with wonder as this episode took place, then just as uncomprehendingly watched as he dropped the same hand and, smiling, walked away across the deck. She stared at his retreating back, her misery not so much lifted as displaced, when suddenly she felt the oddest sensation.

'I could quite go for a plate of kippers,' Alice said aloud wonderingly, a phrase she had never used prior to that day. Suddenly, the world looked brighter, and it was not simply because the sun was up.

Lizzie regarded Alice's returned appetite with some misgivings. It was not so much the ravenous vigour she exhibited — although that was rather common and more than a little off-putting —- no, it was rather the unladylike choice of her food. 'Vulgar' kept popping into her head for some reason and for the first time her own stomach made rather unexpected turns as she watched Alice consume yet further quantities of the small silvery fish that seemed far less than entirely prepared for such consumption.

'Aren't these marvellous!' her cousin crowed from her seat, a small dollop of oil shining from the corner of her upturned mouth. It was at least good to see Alice's humour returned, Lizzie reminded herself, even if the results were less than appetizing. She would stick to the hard biscuits the sailors shared amongst themselves and the somewhat tepid water that came in her cracked cup when she requested it. No need for extravagances like the slippery little creatures Alice continued to consume with all the zeal of a cormorant.

It was not like her to make unflattering bird comparisons to members of her family, but Lizzie was feeling uncharacteristically peevish at the moment. She hated to admit that Alice's illness had left her to her own devices in a welcome respite from her dear, beloved cousin's inquisitive — if easily bored — nature and sometimes ceaseless chatter. It was unkind to think it, Lizzie scolded herself, and one should certainly not admit that one's dearest relations might be less than wholly good company on a long sea journey, although it may be slightly more truthful to confess that she had been more than a little relieved at the thought of Alice quietly spending the perilous journey in her bunk.

I am not a good person, Lizzie sighed to herself. Poor Alice was suffering and I was walking the deck without a care on my mind. 'You are feeling much better, my dear.'

'Indeed!' Alice agreed, munching and swallowing yet another little fish, its tail slipping between her moistened lips. 'I feel quite recovered and I am not at all certain why. I could not raise my head for illness just an hour ago, yet now I cannot imagine ever having felt so poorly. I am quite restored!'

'How wonderful,' Lizzie agreed with, it must be admitted, something less than the full force of her enthusiasm.

The captain chose that moment to look in on the two prisoners, taking in Alice's renewed appetite with some surprise and then a hearty laugh. 'I see the bos'n has worked his magic on the weluctant young lady.'

Lizzie looked at him quizzically. 'The bos'n?' Whatever did he mean?

She did not get a chance to inquire further, however, for just then the first mate ran up breathless and agitated.

'What is it, Wandall?' the captain asked somewhat disagreeably. 'Out with it, man.'

'Black sails,' the mate hissed darkly. The captain sucked in a breath and then the two turned and walked swiftly toward the deck.

Black sails, thought Lizzie. That could only mean one thing — pirates!

Chapter Five

There was no doubt about it. A shiver seemed to run through the whole of the crew and Lizzie herself saw the black sails now. The sight of the Jolly Roger whipping madly atop the mast made her draw her breath with a mixture of alarm and excitement. Only Alice seemed unfazed by the excitement, licking the last of the cod liver oil from her fingers as she sat on the sunny deck's bench.

'I would advise you to wetweat to youw cabin, miss,' the captain said with a snarl. 'If you think you are in dangew now, wait until the likes of piwates get hold of pwetty young giwls like you. Thewe is nothing they will not stoop to doing!'

Lizzie was chagrined at having to miss the excitement, but she knew that she and Alice needed protection. At least their cabin was on the starboard side. They would be able to peek out the window. 'Come, Alice!' Lizzie cried and took her cousin's arm.

Alice was meekly compliant, her stomach full of various kinds of fish, which made her feel rather sleepy. I know I shall have a wonderful dream tonight, she thought, confused about the time of day from her topsy-turvy adventures. For, although the moon could be seen in the sky, it was the middle of the day. Alice did not even wonder about that fact, she simply accepted that things were different at sea. She was so grateful not to be feeling poorly that all other facts could be faced with sanguine complacency.

Lizzie latched the door behind her and ran to the porthole. No doubt about it, the ship with the black sails was getting closer. If only I had a spyglass, Lizzie fretted, envying the mate's clearer view as he gazed across the waves with his.

'No doubt about it, captain,' Randall shouted to Bellamy, 'it is she!'

They must recognise the ship, Lizzie told herself confidently, for she knew ships were always referred to as if they were female. But which ship? She was bursting to know.

'I'm going to sleep now,' Alice announced dreamily, and

then proceeded to lie down on her bed. In a twinkling she was breathing deeply, completely unaware of the excitement on board.

The sailors were running to and fro, stowing gear and preparing weapons. They would be ready for a fight. Lizzie could not decide whether it was horror or a thrill of excitement that made her heart beat so. Clearly the captain wanted to avoid a fight if he could, for the men were busily swinging the sails around in an attempt to pick up more speed.

Far on the horizon—though not as far as before—Lizzie could see the dark vessel gaining on them, sails bulging with wind and the trim rigging taut with their speed. She could see that the flag flown from its highest mast was no ordinary skull and crossbones, but one that featured a bright five-pointed star as well. That image rang a faint bell in Lizzie's memory. She tried to cast her mind back to consider it. Where had she seen that flag before? Brighton came to mind. Her mother's uncle had lived in that seaside town, selling newspapers to the sailors, merchants and holidaymakers. She had often visited as a small child, and she remembered well her uncle's ruddy complexion and rough, but kindly hands. It was there she first knew the delight of adventure stories, for he knew them all, from the lament of Dorigen to the triumph of Palamon, and told them to her eager ears as she sucked on sweets. All at once, a name welled up in her memory.

'Black Ethel!' It was the pirate queen herself out there—and she was gaining on them.

The sailors ran nimbly across the decks. Every one of them seemed stretched as taut as the wind-belled sails about them, but their frantic movement could not hide the fact that as the black vessel was steadily closing the distance between them they threw concerned looks behind them. Lizzie sensed the fear growing among the crew even as Captain Bellamy continued to bellow orders preparing for the seemingly inevitable encounter.

It was all so exciting!

Lizzie wished she could be some useful part of the crew. She threw a glance over at the blissfully sleeping Alice and wondered how she could sleep at a time like this. Here was the stuff of adventure—here the thrills of the novel's pages in real life.

If I were any sort of heroine, Lizzie thought peevishly, I would be out there helping prepare for the battle. She watched a handful of sailors head below decks and soon heard the rumble of the cannon being rolled into position below her. 'I could load gunpowder,' she murmured under her breath. 'Or perhaps I could light the cannon!' But the more she thought about it, the less she was confident that she could do anything of the kind. While she had always been known for her cool head and sensible thinking, but truth-fully—she blushed to admit it—there was little to actually test her abilities in the past. Until the sudden string of events that had led them to being kidnapped and on board Captain Bellamy's ship—why, it was beginning to seem months ago that Lord Mangrove's mysterious death had occurred, the strange haunting and their precipitous removal from the funeral train.

And she had thought life in Surrey dull.

But look! The black sails drew ever closer. Lizzie swore she could hear the wind whipping that giant black flag. That speck on the deck—surely it must be Black Ethel herself with a splendid hat. That was one of the things she could recall from Uncle Frank's exciting stories. Her raven hair and her splendid hat. There was a lot of folderol about the many men she had murdered, but Lizzie was certain that she would have the gentle heart of a woman underneath.

Although now that she thought about it, Lizzie felt a shiver of fear as she remembered another tale that told of death himself employed as her bos'n, his skeleton fingers itching for the taste of flesh. In fact, there was a poem, was there not?

Lizzie paced the tiny cabin, while Alice slumbered on. (No doubt the steps would echo in her head and enter her dreams, but Alice's dreams will have to wait for a while). If she could just remember the first line, no doubt the rest would come to her in time. Surely, Lizzie scolded herself, it started with her name. She paced a few more steps—the words were proving elusive—until the image of the albatross came to mind. That was it!

Black Ethel, the pirate queen, sailed the seas,
Her bos'n was Death and he gathered his fees
From all those who would dare to challenge her sword;
They fell with a curse or a grovelling word.

Way-hey, Black Ethel is here!
Way-hey, let's give her a cheer.

The albatross must be in the second verse, she thought uncertainly. Although why one would cheer a pirate who is about to kill one dead, escaped Lizzie. Perhaps it was all part of the romanticism of adventure, which she was beginning to understand, paled beside the real thing. Lizzie gathered her courage and stepped out of the cabin. The salt air stung her cheeks and the loud cries on deck were thrilling, to be sure, but as the black ship drew within firing distance, Lizzie could feel her mouth go dry.

Suddenly there was an explosion of fire and a boom from the other ship. The first cannon had been launched!

The first ball fell short and the crew heaved a collective sigh. Another crack! And a second cannonball flew across the waves, and this one did not fall into the salty sea, but took a bit of the stern with her. The shouts of the crew redoubled and Captain Bellamy's orders flew ever faster.

The black pirate ship was hastening down the wind, drawing ever closer and putting them all in greater danger. Lizzie hung out the window as far as she could, unable to bear the idea of closing the shutters and finding safety within, but with no chance to follow the developing battle. The sailors all had their cutlasses drawn, the captain himself had a pistol in each hand. Even the ship's mascot, a salty old parrot with only one leg (and a penchant for language that was not fit for a lady's ears) wrestled a bit of stick in his mouth as if he, too, would fight for the decks of the *Demeter* and its precious cargo.

Lizzie could only hope that she and her cousin would be considered part of that estimable cargo and not ballast that might be jettisoned to quicken the pace of the journey. She glanced over at Alice to see her oddly still dreaming away, oblivious to the chaos crying all around her. How could she sleep through such a time! Lizzie returned her gaze to the decks just in time to see another cannonball fly through the air and land in a shower of splinters on the deck. It crashed through to the lower deck and, judging by the sound, hit some of the rum below. The anguished cries of the crew seemed to suggest that it hit its mark squarely.

Another projectile flew over the cabin from which Lizzie looked out on the fray. She could see now the decks of the pirate ship before her, and like magic, the second verse of the song came back to her memory:

> *The albatross sits on the skeleton bow,*
> *And calls to the sailors who suffer below—*
> *The captain, she wields a bright scimitar now*
> *And the men fall before it like corn in a row.*
>
> *Way-hey, Black Ethel is here!*
> *Way-hey, let's give her a cheer.*

Lizzie could see that the black pirate ship bore the name that chilled many across the wine dark sea: it was the *Bonny Read*! No doubt about it now, it was Black Ethel herself and there was little hope to be had that any of them would live to tell the tale of this battle.

As if to underscore that realisation, Lizzie saw the pirate queen herself standing proudly on the fo'csle of the ship, her scimitar in the air as she shouted orders to her crew. The air was so full of smoke that Lizzie could hardly see what was ship and what was sea, but Black Ethel's men seemed to be gathering together for a singular purpose. As one they turned to face the *Demeter*, and Lizzie could not help ducking down behind the wall to avoid being seen. When she finally worked up the courage to look again, her eyes nearly popped out of her head with horror and alarm.

The pirates were climbing up ropes, ready to swing over. They were going to board the ship!

Lizzie drew back in horror—the pirate ship was within yards of the *Demeter*. She could see the terrifying crew, a band of cutthroat rebels, not one fit for a gentleman's home. None

73

of them acquainted with the finer things in life, helpless to deal with a standard array of forks, let alone the intricacies of the oyster fork's manoeuvring. No, they were brigands through and through, Lizzie thought, untamed, unmanageable and uncompromising. She very nearly swooned, and as we all know, Lizzie is not a swooning sort of woman.

At the front of the deck on the pirate ship there strode a woman dressed all in black, save for a plume of deep purple in her hat. It could only be she, Black Ethel, the scourge of the Atlantic. Through the mists of the evening and the smoke of cannon-fire, Lizzie squinted her eyes to get a better look at the legend. If only I had a spyglass, Lizzie cursed. Suddenly she remembered that they were in fact in the captain's cabin. If there was an advantage to being kidnapped, surely this was it. She rummaged through the drawers she had neglected while moping over their fate or exploring the open decks. There was a treasure trove here!

In one drawer she found a wonderful adventure book ('I must read this to Alice when things get back to normal!' she thought), several gold doubloons in rather sad neglect, something that looked suspiciously like a monkey's paw, a kind of gold bug, some pale greenish liqueur, several rolled up scrolls of parchment that might have been maps or directions of some kind (indeed, one looked like it could have been a piece of skin—Lizzie abruptly dropped that item as soon as she made that realisation) and in the last drawer, alas, only a thimble.

But there was still the cabinet to explore, and in the second compartment (after jiggling the lock free—well, desperate times called for desperate measures) Lizzie found what she needed, the captain's spyglass. Employing it at once, she ran to the porthole and peered out. The sudden closeness of the pirates gave her a shock, but she quickly recovered once the glass was withdrawn to show the pirates still a good distance away.

Lizzie drew the glass once more to her eye and set a curious eye upon the captain. A woman, indeed, she was, but a woman like none Lizzie had seen. While Lady Montague was certainly a woman to be reckoned with on any playing field

of fine society, here was a woman who could be her match—
no doubt on any field of play. From the tip of her tricorne
hat to the heels of her black leather boots, Ethel was a scal-
awag of the worst sort, that much was clear. But there was
even more to it. She had a fiery eye that Lizzie could not help
but admire, a gaze that many a man would quail before. She
pitied the men who had to face that pirate queen, but not
very much—for only the weak would not match her steely
eyes and they would be better off dead.

Heavens, thought Lizzie, I am condoning a pirate!

'Fire away, boys!' Black Ethel shouted, her voice ringing
out clearly amidst the din of the battle. At once the report of
cannon fire belched forth from the ship's sides, hurtling the
little black missives toward the *Demeter*'s groaning sides. How
much more could they take?

Captain Bellamy yelled orders in his inimitable style,
clouting the slower members of the crew about the head in an
attempt to get them to scramble faster. Everyone seemed to
be going in the wrong direction at once, cannon balls sometimes missing their trunks by mere inches, and all too often,
not missing at all, but carrying the unlucky few over the side
of the boat and into the great wide ocean. It was beginning to
look an awful lot like chaos.

Through the smoke and noise, Lizzie could hear three distinct sounds: the throaty laughter of Black Ethel, the rasping
snoring of Alice, and what she could only imagine to be the
cry of the albatross perched high above the deck of the *Bonny
Read*. Watching the fight from the window of the captain's
cabin, Lizzie feared that things were not going well.

For one thing, she could see that Captain Bellamy's visage
was becoming beet red, a sure sign of indignation, as was the
tendency of his voice to rise ever higher and skate over more
and more consonants. For another, she could see more than a
few holes in the deck of the *Demeter*, which signalled a slight
tendency to take on water.

I must wake Alice, Lizzie thought. Surely it was only to
have her cousin prepared for any eventuality, and not simply
because her snoring was becoming unbearably loud and
coarse. In any case, she shook her cousin's shoulder gently yet

firmly and called her name. 'Alice, Alice! You must wake up! We are under attack—by pirates!'

'What?' Alice asked, rubbing her eyes and smiling vacantly as was her habit upon waking. 'Parrots?'

'No, no, pirates,' Lizzie hastily corrected her. 'They are at present firing cannonballs at the *Demeter* and will no doubt board her soon.' Well, perhaps an exaggeration, Lizzie scolded herself, but she needed to find a way to get Alice moving. She was so lethargic!

'Is there anything to eat?' Alice asked as she stretched luxuriously, raising herself slowly to a sitting position. 'Where is Mrs. Perkins?'

Lizzie groaned. 'We are not at home, Alice! We are on board the ship, remember, dear? Captain Bellamy is our latest kidnapper and we are sailing for who knows where!'

Alice burst into tears. 'I had thought that was all a bad dream! Oh, Lizzie, please tell me, can it be so?'

Lizzie patted her cousin's shoulder. 'I am so sorry, my dear, but it is true. We have been kidnapped, we are under attack from pirates and all looks quite dismal at present.'

'No, no,' Alice said, shaking her head sorrowfully. 'But is it true I ate eels?'

'And many other kinds of fish, much of it raw, Alice.' Lizzie could not quite help the scolding tone of her voice even as she tried to comfort her cousin. 'But that is not the most important thing just now,' she continued as she moved the bucket once more to the bedside.

'What could be worse?' Alice asked in a strangled voice, turning a pale and not too becoming shade of light green.

With a sudden blast of splinters and shattering glass, a cannon ball crashed through the window of the cabin and made a hasty exit out a new hole on the opposite side.

'That, my dear, could be much worse!' While Alice cowered on the bed, regretting having woken up, Lizzie peeked carefully out the smashed window. The *Bonny Read* was a mere two yards away and the pirates were swinging ropes between them. They meant to board the ship!

In the burst of noise that suddenly and cacophonously surrounded them, Alice wished with all her heart that she had not awakened from her dream. In it, she was surrounded by a bevy of admirers, chief of which was the elusive Kit Barrington, whose fine head of hair and gentle manner charmed her exceedingly. There was such a crowd that Arthur Boylett was quite lost at the back, jumping up occasionally to get a glimpse of her beauty but otherwise quite unable to approach.

This was just as Alice wished.

Although the parlour seemed to have become surprisingly drafty, Alice chose to ignore this fact. She also ignored the increasing din from what appeared to be Mr. Radley dropping large rocks into a very large bucket and Mrs. Perkins pummelling the walls with a very large and somewhat sinister rattan carpet beater. Desperately she clung to the dream even as Lizzie in both dream and reality shook her shoulder gently, yet insistently.

How horrible to awake to the chaos of the pirate attack! How infinitely worse to know that no such throng of admirers surrounded her at present. When she heard herself begging Lizzie to say it was all a dream, that she might return to the fantasy of her slumber, Alice felt a small measure of shame as well as a much larger one of disappointment.

What a burden I have been! she thought, and vowed once more to be a better person and to help her dear cousin to bear the trials to which they had been subjected. This was a solemn vow that might last minutes altogether.

With horror, the two young women stared out the newly fashioned porthole to see the grappling hooks settle into any nook where they might find purchase. Several went high in the rigging and only a few were cut by the flashing swords of the crew. Within a short time, pirates of all sorts swung over to the deck of the *Demeter*.

Look! There! Three black-clad devils hopped onto the deck, spinning left and right to parry the blows of the sailors. Each carried a short dagger as well as his blade. One had a pistol tucked in his belt, another had a club hanging from his.

There! On the prow, another pair of marauders grappled with the *Demeter*'s stalwart crew. Blades flashed and alarming sprays of blood filled the air as the rugged pirates battered back Captain Bellamy's sailors. The clink and clack of the weapons rang out through the air and the two cousins cowered in their cabin. What was to become of them?

As if to seal their fate like a barrel of Caribbean rum, they heard a shrill whistle and a hearty laugh. It was Black Ethel! She leaped across the short distance between the ships and landed on the deck, both swords drawn and a broad smile on her face. A gold tooth glittered in the lantern light as she roared with laughter. 'Where are you, Captain Sam? We have a little matter to settle here on deck!'

'Bellamy!'

Black Ethel strode across the deck, searching for the captain. Lizzie cowered behind the window of the cabin as the pirate queen passed, her purple plume bouncing and her two swords gleaming.

'Cuwse you, Ethel!' Bellamy roared as he ran from the prow toward her. 'You will not have my ship!'

Black Ethel planted her boots firmly and laughed good and loud. 'I take what I want, Bellamy. And I want your cargo and maybe a few of your men.'

'You will nevew escape my cwew!' Bellamy shouted, waving aloft his own heavy sword. A few of his men, who weren't busy battling the other pirates, did likewise. Shouts of great audacity arose and Alice, who had joined Lizzie at the window, felt her heart strengthen with the sight of so many courageous men. Surely, they would be saved from the pirates' predations.

'I have no need to escape. Not before I have purloined your ship from stem to stern. Bring them on, Bellamy. My lads will dispatch with your scalawags. But you,' she smiled an evil smile, 'you are mine!'

And with that the two crews fell to in earnest once more, swords clanging and the occasional pistol ringing out. Bellamy and Black Ethel came together amidships, well within view of the cabin's window. Black Ethel struck with both swords at once, scissoring Bellamy between their blades. He parried one then the other with his own sword, rapidly batting it between her two. One of his more quick-witted

78

crew shouted a word of encouragement and tossed his own sword to the captain. For his pains he was at once attacked by a pair of pirates, one with a large club, the other with a razor-sharp rapier. In vain he sought to halt the downward thrust of the club with his small knife. The rapier's blade bit into his arm and scarlet bloomed from the gaping wound.

'Hardly sporting,' Lizzie muttered under her breath.

Alice was speechless with indignation. Had pirates no morals at all?

Their attention flew back to Bellamy and the pirate queen, just as the captain declared, 'Wevenge, deaw lady, wevenge shall be mine tonight!' He darted forward with the second blade, thrusting toward the vulnerable side of the pirate. She was too quick, however, blocking his single sword with her two, throwing his blade up and making Bellamy regroup for another attack.

'You're going to have to be faster than that,' she shouted, a grin still widening her too- red mouth. Lizzie could see a fine white scar crossing the woman's cheek and disappearing into her raven hair. She did not draw Alice's attention to that detail, for fear that she might swoon right away. Imagine the rough life the pirate queen must lead, to be in such danger, to suffer such injuries. Lizzie did not wish to admit that the idea was simply soppy with thrills. To be completely independent! To never again be thrust into uncomfortable clothes and uncomfortable situations, to never again smile politely at the endless line of tedious people that were most of her relations, to no longer be the poor orphan with no marriage prospects—but suddenly she remembered, blushed at her lapse and touched the letter still secreted away in her sleeve. There was much to live for. They must triumph against the pirate queen!

Bellamy thrust again and Black Ethel neatly dodged his blow, spinning around lightly and parrying back with her left hand, holding the right in reserve, waiting for her opportunity. 'Don't tell me you're running out of steam already, Bellamy! The fight has only just begun.'

True enough, Bellamy was looking a bit overwhelmed, but her taunting reinvigorated his flagging spirits. 'Nevew! I shall defend the Demetew with all my heawt and skill. Take that!' and he launched a renewed attack of such vigour that he fought the pirate queen back to the railings.

Suddenly a bright light seemed to burst all around the fighting pair. Lizzie ducked and clunked heads with Alice. Smoke seemed to be everywhere until the night breeze wafted through the clanking night.

'Look,' cried Lizzie, grabbing Alice's arm. 'Over there!'

A fiery missive had exploded right in the middle of the cabin's wall, blasting a blackened hole into the wood and allowing the ocean winds to whistle through as Lizzie and Alice cowered back from its splintery force. Small flames cluing to the charred wood, but they were no match for the wild night winds and were soon extinguished.

'We were nearly killed by cannon fire!' Alice said indignantly.

'I think it was some other kind of missive,' Lizzie said examining the hole and the complete lack of cannonball.

Some shattered glass around the opening gave her a clue. She peeked out at the deck of the *Bonny Read* to see a doughty tar preparing another flaming bomb. He stuck a bit of cloth into the neck of a bottle and lit it the strip, hefting it in his blackened hand while he looked at the *Demeter* for a likely target. Lizzie held her breath, her tender heart concerned lest the pirate inadvertently set himself on fire. At last he seemed to see something suitable as a target and hurled the bottle across the decks toward the stern. Another explosion rocked the ship and it gave a groan as if it were in pain.

Or perhaps it was just the moans of the crew, many of whom were feeling the worst of the battle. The pirates fought ruthlessly and without scruples. Bellamy's men were no gentlemen, but Lizzie could not help but side with the men who were not rapscallions of the sea and in thrall to the daunting pirate queen.

'Where have they gone?' Alice asked, looking over at Lizzie who was still lost in her thoughts. Startled, she wondered for a moment who it was that her cousin meant, but recovered herself quickly. Where were Bellamy and Black Ethel?

As if in response to their queries, the clash of swords

returned to their ears as the fearsome pair fought their way back across the deck toward the cabin where the young women waited. The air around them almost seemed to swirl with the force of their battle. Perhaps it was the smoke from the cannon-fire and flaming torches that gave the wind an almost visible presence, or perhaps it was the swift slashing of the blades of the two combatants. It was hard to be sure, but Lizzie and Alice watched in awe as the fight wore on and the steel clashed over and over again.

'Chin up, Bellamy!' Black Ethel laughed with glee, a little hoarse from the fight, but still grinning widely. 'You can always become one of us. Haven't you always wanted to be on the pirate side? You got more than a little buccaneer in you, Bellamy.'

'Nevew!' Bellamy cried once more. 'You awe a cheat and a cwiminal.'

The dreaded pirate queen then looked at Alice and Lizzie, who were peeking out from the blasted hole in the wall, and laughed even louder. 'At least I don't kidnap young women for nefarious purposes. I never took you for a white slaver, Bellamy.'

Lizzie and Alice both glared at Bellamy. Was this the fate that awaited them? Oh, the horror of it! Bad enough to be spirited away from her father's funeral, but to find at the end of the journey a fate worse than death—it was too much.

'No!' Bellamy shouted as he parried another of her seemingly endless thrusts. 'Theiw fate is something faw diffewent, you see—'

But before he could finish his sentence, Black Ethel struck once more, the shaft of her sword striking Bellamy's ribcage.

'Cuwse you, Black Ethel!' Bellamy cried, grasping his side in pain. She merely guffawed louder and fought ever harder. Bellamy was hampered by his injury, but still he fought on with a good deal of spirit.

Lizzie and Alice hardly knew for whom to root. If Bellamy won, it seemed that they might be destined for the nefarious white slave trade—about which they knew rather little other than the horror with which those words were met by any heroine of their favourite gothic tomes and by the beloved

Mrs. Perkins, who had been the one to obtain said volumes by mysterious means and possessed a surprisingly thorough knowledge of their authors and adventures.

This heinous fate was among the things she could never bring herself to explain to the eager young readers. She had relented on various methods of torture once young Alice had passed her thirteenth birthday—explaining with relish the intricacies of the Iron Maiden, the rack and the Spanish Tickler while the two girls shrieked with barely suppressed horror.

Many a quiet afternoon had been passed in rapt terror while the patient and kindly housekeeper detailed the implements of the Inquisition. 'The Renaissance,' Mrs. Perkins was fond of saying, 'meant a whole new attention to the machineries of torture. The medieval era was crudely kind in comparison. The artistry of the sixteenth century—why when Father Gerard was in the Tower!' She would detail his sufferings in a hushed whisper, reading long passages from the book he had penned after his escape from Queen Elizabeth's henchmen.

But never would she explain the nature of the horror that was white slavery. Lizzie suspected much and Alice wondered often, but neither could have their worst fears confirmed nor denied.

It was most provoking.

The ignorance in which they were held on this account made its fiendishness that much more. The suspense of knowing that they might be headed for that fate was positively-swoon inducing. Alice searched her pockets for her handkerchief, feeling a strong desire to dab at her cheek with some delicacy, but the tiny lace friend was nowhere to be found, which left her in a puzzled state. What could have become of it?

Lizzie, on the other hand, busied herself wondering what might become of them if Black Ethel were to command them. Would they become piratical maids-of-all-work? Think how their delicate fingers would be roughened! Think how they would be drained of all vivacity! I shall be aged beyond recognition in mere months, Lizzie thought with a gasp.

White slave or pirate maid? Which was worst—yet, she recalled that Bellamy had sworn that he was not planning their descent into white slavery. Should she trust that? Lizzie looked at the captain as he continued to fight doggedly against the gleeful pirate's blows. He was an Englishman, and that still counted for something, she decided. Black Ethel was French after all!

'Fight on, Captain,' she called boldly, drawing a disapproving look from her cousin. 'We do not wish to fall into the clutches of wild pirates!'

The pirate queen laughed heartily, making another stab for Bellamy's ribs. 'How do you know life wouldn't be better with the corsairs, eh?'

'We are Englishwomen,' Lizzie said primly. 'We shall not go over to the enemy.'

'Enemy?' Black Ethel repeated, ducking away from Bellamy's *contre sixte*. 'I would merely set you free, unlike your gentleman.' She accentuated the latter word with a withering tone.

'Free?' said Alice, forgetting her handkerchief for a moment.

'Free!' said Lizzie, grabbing her cousin's hand.

'Two hundwed pounds!' gasped Bellamy as he was unable to sidestep Black Ethel's double, falling precipitously to the deck with a groan.

'Two hundred pounds!' Lizzie said with great venom. 'You mountebank! You captain queernabs! You were going to sell us into white slavery!'

Bellamy groaned, grasping his side. 'It's not like that, miss. I pwomise you!'

Alice became indignant as well, spurred by the passion of her cousin's harsh words. 'You horror, you...you...dangler!' She very nearly swooned quite away at the daring she felt using such rough language on such a pointed occasion. What would father say, Alice thought, her breast heaving with the exertion of uttering such a word. All at once she remembered that her father was quite dead and he would never again rail at his incorrigible daughter.

Perhaps it was the excitement of the moment, perhaps it

was the recognition that that audience would never again be able to express its disapproval in no uncertain terms, but all at once Alice felt a strange sensation in her heart.

'This must be grief,' she said, more to herself than anyone else—not that anyone else would have heard her low utterance. Alas, she was again wrong, for it was not the unaccustomed feeling of grief that she was experiencing but a heretofore-unexpected bout of nausea. This time it was unrelated to seasickness, for Alice had at last found her sea legs (albeit somewhat late and in a rather unlikely moment). It is possible that it was the sight of blood, for blood was pouring copiously from Captain Bellamy, which, after their initial expressions of scorn and derision, had a softening effect on the two soft-hearted cousins.

Black Ethel, however, was unmoved by the all too common sight of a foe's blood. Indeed she laughed loudly and exclaimed, '*Mon dieu!* Who knew there was red blood left in you, eh, Bellamy? I thought it had all turned to black like your heart!'

'Black Ethel, you wascally villain! You have slain me, no doubt. Kill me now and save me the suffewing death by thiwst when you abandon me on this ship.' Bellamy sank even lower upon the deck, the sounds of the other fights gradually sinking into the background as their attention focused upon him.

'You will live to fight another day, *mon cher!*' Black Ethel crowed. 'I care nothing for your life. I wish only to take your wealth.' With that she put her fingers to her lips and blew three loud whistles. All at once the fighting on the deck ceased and all the men turned their eyes to the dreaded pirate queen.

'Your captain is defeated! If you continue to fight, I will throw him to *le requin, le ange de mer* and burn this ship under your feet. If you wish, however, to save the life of your master, lay down your weapons and help my men haul away your goods. What do you say, *messieurs?*'

The men looked back and forth between themselves. Lizzie looked in vain for the strange bos'n, figuring the men might look to him for advice, but the skull-like visage was not to be seen. Alice had a strange pang at the thought that he might be among those killed in the battle. Despite his frightening appearance and strangely quiet ways, he had been so kind to her at the start of this difficult sea voyage.

As if agreeing, the captain's men dropped their weapons and shuffled forward to the hold. Two of the crew grabbed Bellamy's moaning body and carried him to what was left of his cabin.

'And now, *mademoiselles*, you must come with me!'

Alice and Lizzie exchanged a fearful look. What was to become of them on the pirate queen's ship?

Chapter Six

With some difficulty, the two young women were helped over the small gap between the ships and onto the *Bonny Read*. Some of the pirates were busy putting out the fires, which the fierce battle had sparked in the rigging and on the deck. The crew seemed to pay no attention to their latest acquisitions, being far too engaged with control of the damage.

Black Ethel shouted encouragement in the way of dark curses. 'What're you thinking, you lazy miscreant! Get that rigging restrung, *tout de suite*! You—*bricon*! Get some planks down over that hole. Load that cargo faster. Put your backs into it, *merdaille*!'

Alice exchanged a frightened glance with her cousin. If she was this harsh with her own men, imagine what the pirate queen would be like with poor captives like themselves. Alice considered fainting dead away, but found she was far too excited about the change of ships to give in to such a wistful impulse.

Lizzie, for her part, was bearing up well, as always, braced by the excitement of a new challenge and unknown horizons. While she observed the rough speech of the corsair queen, she also noted how the men shrugged off her hard words for the most part, doubling their efforts to be sure, but not cowering in fear as she might have expected.

Captain Bellamy's men, on the other hand, quaked quite visibly before the dashing black figure of Ethel, afraid no doubt that she would be putting them to the plank or setting fire to their ship and abandoning them to the horror of choosing between death by fire or water. They trundled their goods onto the deck and scurried back over the side to their own familiar decks. Black Ethel strode back and forth, her curt commands punctuated with a gleeful laugh. No doubt she was proud of the loot they were taking and the humiliating beating she had given Bellamy.

'I do hope the good captain will recover from his wounds,' Lizzie said confidentially to Alice as the latter gawked in a very unladylike manner at the proceedings whirling around them.

'Fie on the good captain,' said Alice with what Lizzie saw as a want of charity. 'If he had been such a good captain, he would have taken better care of his charges.'

'Now Alice,' Lizzie scolded, 'he was our warden, so to speak. How was he to know on what charges we were brought there? Perhaps he thought we were ungrateful little women who never did our lessons or deferred to our parents' wishes.'

We must assume Lizzie was in high spirits to tease poor Alice so, but her cousin—in her usual artless way—was taking her at her word. As she was more than a little prone to being ungrateful on the whole, avoiding her lessons at all costs and seldom taking into account her parents' wishes at all, Alice was a might peeved to think her cousin meant these jests seriously.

She was just about to let fly words in a squeaky and most unbecoming pitch when Black Ethel returned to their side and motioned for the two to follow her to her cabin. One could presume it was her cabin because it had the grammatically incorrect yet emphatically feminine '*La Capitaine*' painted on the door.

'*Entrez, ma petites.* You have a new sort of adventure ahead of you!'

Lizzie and Alice trembled but obeyed and entered the dimly lit cabin. The first sight to meet them was a mop and bucket and the horrible truth sank into their hearts.

They were to be maids after all. *Horreurs!*

Black Ethel saw the looks of dismay on the two young faces and laughed out loud. 'Set your minds at ease, little ones. I am not setting you to work as maids. Madeleine! Perhaps you could move your accoutrements out of my cabin for a time.'

As if from the shadows, a small dark figure with a pale face swept silently across the room and vanished at once with the mop and bucket and a whispered, '*excusez-moi!*' It was impossible to tell from the brief glimpse they had whether Madeleine was a small child, a tiny woman or simply a hunched over figure of normal size. She whisked away so

87

quickly that they were left only with the impression of trailing black clothes and a pallid visage that would make Aunt Susan swoon with envy.

Black Ethel threw her tricorne hat upon the broad oak desk and lounged on the stout chair behind it. '*Assez-vous!* Please be comfortable, take your ease. You are not prisoners here, you may do as you wish.' She laughed, however, and gazed shrewdly at the two young women. 'However, you may find it safer to stay close to my cabin. I cannot keep my men in check too much, they are not prisoners either. Many of them are not well-accustomed to...' She paused and looked them up and down. 'Let us say, women of your upbringing. You have lived sheltered lives of little dangerous experience, no?'

Alice and Lizzie both blushed to show this was indeed true. Merely imagining the rough attentions of the pirate queen's uncouth crew brought them to the edge of swooning. Alice tried hard to imagine what sort of conversation she might have with the one-armed rapscallion who had gurgled a sort of greeting as they walked to the captain's cabin. Lizzie, meanwhile, tried to picture herself dancing a scotch reel with the swarthy brute who at present berated the other pirates on the deck who were repairing the rigging as best they could while he stomped back and forth on his peg leg.

It dawned on them both in their separate musings that a pirate's life was one fraught with much danger of bodily harm.

'Would you care for something to eat?' Black Ethel asked them, the kind meaning of her words somewhat tempered by her brash tone of voice. Clearly she was more accustomed to ordering around her gang of buccaneers than conversing over a tea tray.

'That would be most kind,' Lizzie said with renewed spirit. Food would return the rosy glow to Alice's cheeks and restore her own sense of confidence, Lizzie was certain.

'Bos'n!' Black Ethel shouted, causing the two genteel women to jump with alarm. 'Bring something tasty from the larder!' In a minute or so, the door opened to admit a very familiar figure. It was the nattily-hatted bos'n of the deathly pallor and the kindly manner. Lizzie and Alice could not have been more surprised to see Captain Bellamy himself.

The mysterious bos'n laid a simple repast upon the desk, which nonetheless looked far more appetising than anything they had seen upon the *Demeter*. There were many cheeses and dry crackers, but there was also fresh fruit—a veritable miracle it would seem. Alice could feel her mouth beginning to water, but looked quickly over at Lizzie to see if she would allow any compromise of manners. Finding her cousin firm in her regard of propriety, Alice instead caught a glance from the bos'n who gave her a conspiratorial wink and a roguish (if somewhat toothy) smile. He still looked cadaverous to an alarming degree, but seemed far more cheerful to be on board the *Bonny Read*.

After a proper incantation of begging grace, Lizzie and her cousin tucked into the plain supper with a very keen appetite. Lizzie was the first to recover her sense of conversational requirements. 'We owe you much for your rescue of us, *Mademoiselle Capitaine*.'

'Think nothing of it. I shall enjoy the conversation as we sail to France.'

Lizzie wanted to ask about the possibility of being returned to England instead, but decided it would not be prudent to press upon such short acquaintance. Instead she tried a different tack for conversation. 'If it is not too personal a question,' Lizzie began with some hesitation, uncertain what were acceptable topics to a pirate, 'I would be very interested to know how it was you became a renowned pirate.'

'Me too,' Alice chimed in with a mouthful of cheese, which earned her a reproving glance from Lizzie that she chose to ignore.

'Well,' Black Ethel said as she inhaled the aroma of a Cuban cigar, 'it is a very exciting tale which I shall be glad to relate.

'*Alors!* Where to begin?' Black Ethel lit her cigar and puffed on it thoughtfully.

'Perhaps at the beginning,' Lizzie offered encouragingly. 'Where were you born?'

'I was so small at the time, I can hardly recall.' The pirate queen smiled to show that this was indeed intended to be humorous. 'But what was made clear to me at an early age was that my parents had not been there for much of that time. In fact, they had died and left me to my own devices, or rather, those of some distant relatives.

'I was raised in the town of Angoulême. Do you know it?'

'A medieval town, is it not?' asked clever Lizzie, impressing her cousin again with a passing thought that she must stuff cotton in her ears to keep all those facts retained. Alice herself had never been troubled with such an overabundance in that department.

'Indeed! Surrounded by the Remparts, which are ancient, and then the cathedral, which I knew so well. I was raised in the shadow of the Cathédrale Saint-Pierre d'Angoulême—at least in the afternoons, that is. Early in the day, we often had sun.'

'We?' Alice inquired curiously as she stuffed another piece of fruit between her lips. 'Who took care of you once your parents were gone? I have lost my father. That is to say, I have not mislaid him, but he is dead also. Like your parents. Mother is still alive, or so she was the last we saw her.'

Black Ethel looked at Alice with a penetrating gaze that soon made the latter drop her gaze and continue to gnaw on fruit rinds. 'When I say 'we', I refer to my relatives, whom I believe to have been distantly in my mother's family. The Perkineiss family was obliged to take me in after the unfortunate event of my parents' demise.'

'How did they die?' Alice could not help asking despite the fear of another severe look from either the pirate queen or her cousin. Death being such a new subject for her, its fascination was strong.

Rather than pierce her with another steely look, however, Black Ethel looked thoughtful. 'It was a rather unexpected cheese-related accident,' she said at last. 'The making of hard cheese involving a press has always proved to be a dangerous undertaking. My father, being of a rather mechanical bent, had invented what he hoped would be stunning new machinery for the pressing of cheese and revolutionize the industry for this modern age. Unfortunately, due to a small flaw in the bolting apparatus, the pressing aperture went wild, completely crushing my father and mortally injuring my mother who had been assisting him in the venture. Her last words to me were 'Always treasure the curds of life."

'Wise words,' Lizzie murmured with some faltering of confidence that they were in fact the appropriate words to offer in such a peculiar instance.

'C'est vrai! My only other remembrance of my beloved parents was a small plaque from the cheese press that my father had placed on the side in a moment of whimsy. We hung it over the fireplace in my room when I went to stay with the Perkineisses. Lady Dowdy—that was the mother of the family—she thought it would do me good and teach me my good Christian duty.'

'What did the sign say?' Lizzie asked, her interest piqued.

Black Ethel smiled and in that moment the two young women could see the lonely little girl she had been. 'It said, 'Blessed are the cheese makers.' I will always believe that with all my heart.'

'What was your life like with the Perkineiss family?' Lizzie inquired, helping herself to a piece of cheese with rather renewed vigour for the dangerous labour involved.

Black Ethel blew an enigmatic smoke ring into the air, twirling her cigar to dissipate it just after, as if she were loath to let anything last too long. 'It was a dour time of much palaver about duty and a great deal about being grateful. Mostly about my being grateful for the kindliness of the Perkineisses.'

'What a trial to be dependent upon other people,' Lizzie said with a subdued voice but great feeling, casting a surreptitious eye toward Alice, who was completely rapt with attention for their rescuer's story and completely unaware that the remark may have had anything to do with her.

'Indeed,' said Black Ethel, who had not missed the glance toward Alice and understood more than she acknowledged. 'While Lady Dowdy Perkineiss continually pressed me to maintain my good Christian duty, Lord Surfeit Perkineiss spoke to me only gruffly and at indifferent intervals when he chanced to notice that there was yet another mouth to feed in the shadow of the cathedral spire.'

'I shouldn't like to live in the shadow of anything,' Alice said with a mouthful of orange. 'It would be most vexing and hardly show one in the best light.'

'Quite,' said Black Ethel while regarding the oblivious child stuff yet more fruit in her mouth. 'It is indeed vexing as you say to be in the shadows. I saw little chance in being out of it for some time, however. The Perkineiss family was family, my only claimed relatives, my mama being related to Lady Dowdy indirectly. That she had married a cheese maker (however blessed) was regarded with a good deal of hand-wringing and distasteful alarm.'

'Even those years later?' Lizzie asked, considering her own secretive plans. Although she was hardly considering the hand of a cheese maker!

'I was looked upon as a pitiable thing, which made no inroads into their Christian charity and pity as far as I could tell,' Black Ethel said with a dry laugh, stubbing out the last of her cigar and swilling her glass of rum so the brown liquid coated the sides of the glass. 'The very worst of it was the daughter whose age fell closest to my own and who, it was assumed, was bound to become my *ma meilleure_amie*. Instead, she became my *bête noire!*

Alice looked up with a puzzled expression. 'Black dog?'

Lizzie was rather surprised to find her cousin on so very nearly the right cricket pitch. 'Quite close, my dear. While it means literally a 'black beast' it has come to mean someone, or I suppose, something that has become the bane of your existence. This is what you meant, is it not?'

She turned to regard the pirate queen, who nodded sagely. '*C'est vrai!* And by the age of five, I had a most egregious *bête noire*.

'Her name was Miss Surfeis Perkineiss!'

The two cousins exchanged a look of puzzlement.

'Miss Surfeis Perkineiss was the trial of my youth,' Black Ethel continued, pouring herself another measure of rum and settling back into her captain's chair once more. 'While she had a certain charm for people she enjoyed, she could be unutterably cruel to those she did not.'

'Perfectly loathsome!' Alice pronounced before cramming another orange slice into her gaping mouth.

'Indeed,' the pirate queen assented while raising an eyebrow at Alice's unusually robust consumption. 'Any number of faradiddles by Miss Surfeis succeeded in putting me in a very awkward state. She was never quite caught out, but I was always being punished on some whim of hers to blame me for one farrago or another.'

'Did not her parents chastise her for her lack of truthfulness?' Lizzie asked, knowing all too well the blindness of parents to their beloved children's naughtiness. 'I am shocked, shocked to hear such things!'

Black Ethel gave a wry grin. 'You are perhaps less surprised than you say, eh *mademoiselle*? You are correct to guess that her parents indulged to no end her relaxed attitude toward the truth of matters. Lord Surfeit Perkineiss himself was known on many an occasion to sweeten the account of events to his own advantage, so I am little surprised to see such things encouraged.

'One of the most reprehensible of these childhood traumas came when we were both about eight years old. It was a small thing but seemed much larger at the time, as such occurrences do to young children of an impressionable age.

'We were with a small group of children at our favourite gathering place, an old linden tree with many well-loved low branches from which we would swing and have great adventures.'

'We have an old oak like that in our garden,' Alice broke in eagerly, but at a gesture from Lizzie, subsided with a reluctant sigh. 'Do go on, ma'am.'

Black Ethel sipped her rum and then, with a meaningful look at Alice—who found herself suddenly feeling very meek indeed—continued with her tale. 'This day we had been playing revolution as we so often did. I was taking the role of Robespierre as I often did, and Surfeis was as usual Marie Antoinette. I enjoyed being on the opposite side from her. Our games were the only place where I could occasionally get my own back, as you English say, on my tormentor.'

Alice and Lizzie made murmuring sounds of sympathy

and approval as the situation no doubt required.

'That day, I had captured Marie and confined her to the Bastille—our favourite tree, *naturellement!* I was just in the midst of giving a stirring speech to the peasantry, rallying them to the cause, when Marie decided to make a break for it.

'Unfortunately, she made her escape by clouting another unfortunate child on the *tête* and shoving her to the ground. Poor Madeleine! She came away with a large bump of purple, which the naughty *Mademoiselle* Perkineiss blamed on me.

'Lord Perkineiss corrected me with a sound thrashing that made me forever his enemy. But worse than that was the sniggering face of Surfeis who watched my beating with laughter and glee. I swore from that moment I would have my revenge!' Black Ethel stared into the distance, lost in thought.

'Do go on with your tale,' Lizzie said, caught up in the exciting adventure of Black Ethel's childhood. 'I hope something terrible—er, something morally instructive happened to Miss Surfeis Perkineiss.'

Black Ethel smiled and blew some smoke from her cigar. She swirled the rum in her glass and said, 'We LeBeaus—for that is my family's illustrious name—we do not take kindly to insults. I swore upon the cheese-scented grave of my parents that I would have revenge upon Miss Surfeis. Her mother Lady Dowdy, to give her some credit, was kindly to me after Lord Surfeit whipped me for his daughter's naughtiness, but she too drew the line at suspecting their petite angel capable of the deed herself.

'I plotted and planned and at last saw my opportunity. There was a soft little fribble of the name of Algernon — a true *demimonde*, always in *le dernier cri*, his parents owned the most successful flower shop in Angoulême, so successful that they did not soil their hands with any kind of soil but had servants and shop girls to do it for them. This Algernon earnestly pursued the life of the fashionable young man even at our childish years. Although he was more hair than wit, Miss Surfeis had a ceaseless desire to flatter him and win his friendship, treating him as if he were a *nabob* of the first order. I fancy it was only because she had her family's stoat-like hunger for money.'

'The little cormorant!' Alice said with explosive vehemence, startling both Lizzie and the pirate queen. 'How unutterably common!'

'Indeed,' said Black Ethel as Lizzie tried to smother her laughter and Alice looked mildly confused. 'I knew that on a certain day the two would be riding forth in his little pony cart to go pick strawberries at the meadow's edge, beyond the walls of the city. Algernon fancied himself quite the horseman even at the age of eight. Miss Surfeis—with her family's unerring compass for the ways of the ton—would always join him in his little cart as he whipped his little pony to charge down the cobblestones with all manner of speed.'

Alice could not abide such cruelty even in the past. 'The poor little pony! I cannot bear the thought of his being so callous. I should never whip my pony, dear, dear little Bosky.' Indeed, Alice's frequent playmate was so idle as to have exceeded his ideal weight by at least two stone, so that very often he wheezed as he trotted, unable to work up the effort to accomplish even a mild canter. It is doubtful that whipping would have done much to increase his pace even if he were able to feel the sting of the crop upon his well-padded hindquarters. But let us think well of Alice for her kindness, regardless of the dubiousness of the object of her affections. It would not be the first time those near to her would need to turn a blind eye to her ideas.

'Knowing her plans, I gathered my few friends together for a dastardly plan. My playmates were mostly from the less fortunate side of town, rough young boys whose ideas of games were often quite dangerous and careless of the rules of society. We found our position for the attack at the base of the hill, where the rains of the last few days had gathered in a considerable pool of murky waters across the road. My confederates armed themselves with large scoopings of mud and some small rocks. We ran a purloined laundry line across the road.

'And then we waited.'

Black Ethel took a sip of rum before she continued with her riveting tale. Lizzie thought to herself how exciting the story would be when she revised it for her secret pen pal with the proper flourishes that the pirate queen seemed to find unnecessary. A good Gothic should have more atmosphere, Lizzie mused, listening to the rain falling outside the cabin window, aware once more of the occasional shouts of the pirate men as they went about their myriad duties required to keep the ship running. No doubt about it, Lizzie assured herself, this tale could be embellished grandly.

'It was late afternoon,' Ethel began again, 'and we knew that Algernon and Miss Surfeis Perkineiss would be returning any time in their fine frocks and with their basket of fresh strawberries. They were part of my bribe to the other children. I assured them we would plunder the basket and enjoy the spoils of our attack.'

'Did you look forward to the strawberries with cream?' Alice could not keep herself from wondering aloud even as she wistfully sighed for the lack of such delicacies on board the *Bonny Read*. 'Or even with a little bit of sponge cake...'

'What did I care for strawberries?' Black Ethel waved away such details, intent upon her tale. 'My only hunger was for revenge against mine enemy, my *bête noire*! Miss Surfeis was going to pay for her many unkindnesses and if her little toad-eating friend had to share the cost, so much the better!'

'Oh, horrors!' Alice said with considerable alarm, seeking in vain for her mourning handkerchief to cover her swiftly watering mouth. 'I can hardly abide toads at all, let alone consider eating them! It is too much to contemplate.'

'Where you come by this ridiculous toad prejudice, I can hardly understand,' Lizzie said with a cross tone that suggested this to be yet the latest round in an ongoing battle of wills. 'Toads are essential for the smooth-running garden, they provide a simple solution to common pests and insects and are clean and friendly—'

'I was merely using the phrase 'toad-eating' to indicate that M. Algernon was a sycophantic flatterer,' Black Ethel broke in, looking somewhat dismayed at the suddenly fractious turn of the conversation and eager to return to the traumatic events of her childhood. 'We despised him for it. And when I say we, I mean my little friends of the town who were immune to the charms of Miss Surfeis because they could not get past her evil words and her snooty attitude, and thus had come to hate her nearly as much as I.

'We were watching the road closely. A few carts had come by and the mail from Paris, but all of a sudden we saw the bright little pony cart that held those two and we prepared ourselves for the assault. I knew that however much I ended up in the basket, as you English say, it would be worth it to see that superior smirk wiped from the face of my mortal enemy.

'Faster and faster, the little pony trotted along. I looked to my comrades and they each had a look of grim satisfaction as the shiny white cart drew nearer with its large basket of strawberries and its two well-dressed passengers. With a quick whistle, I signalled to my men, two of whom pulled taut the laundry line across the track, stopping the gentle pony in his traces, and causing young Algernon to drawl idly, 'What can be the meaning of this, you mangy dogs?"

"I will show you the meaning, *mon petit losengeor*' I said to him, hoping he would catch the irony in my insult, and ordered my men to begin firing…'

'Oh my,' Alice said with horror, forgetting for a moment that the people in peril were Black Ethel's mortal enemies. 'The poor pony!'

'Never fear,' the pirate queen said, waving away the young woman's fears with her still-smouldering cigar. 'The pony himself was unhurt. My enemies, however, did not fare so well.'

Her face seemed filled with a grim satisfaction as she recalled the events. 'My compatriots let fly with the best of their weapons and soon the glistening white cart had become spattered with the foulest mud, its gilt edgings dimmed. The snooty pair who had dismissed us so peremptorily now gasped with shock as they were met with volley after volley of the viscous glop gleaned from the depths of the muddied waters.

'My nemesis, Miss Surfeis Perkineiss, cried aloud in alarm as the handfuls of mud splashed against her white frock, every pleat pressed laboriously by me the night before—yet another punishment for my imagined wrongs. I hated her, I hated that dress and I hated the way she was coddled and cosseted, assured of a cushy life without the least bit of effort—all from an accident of birth. My parents were the kindest people on earth and I had been robbed of their comforts.'

Alice suddenly began to cry, so overwrought by the story as to imagine herself much wronged by the death of Lord Mangrove, although the spirit departed had not (at last encounter) yet managed to depart completely and that she had already some difficulty in recalling any event of kindness or thoughtfulness demonstrated by her late father and so, lapsed into a puzzled silence as she tried to imagine him doing anything other than muttering behind an endless succession of newspapers or fuming red-faced at her mother or the servants.

Lizzie was, on the other hand, deriving a great deal of vicarious satisfaction from the narrative, events she could never have brought herself to take part in (to be entirely truthful) but which she was delighted someone of Black Ethel's mettle had had no scruples about. 'Go on,' she encouraged the buccaneer, who had paused to raise an eyebrow at Alice's tender-hearted weeping (which had since dwindled into sniffles and a furrowed brow). 'Was Algernon greatly displeased?'

The pirate queen laughed gleefully. 'He was quite beside himself! I could not tell if the indignity or the mud was worst for him, but his face was red as a pomegranate and he let loose with most ungentlemanly words of the blackest vituperation. My comrades and I only laughed in delight, some of the rougher fellows sought to pull him from the bench and toss the young dandy headlong into the floodwaters.

'They were still struggling with the recalcitrant lad, while Miss Surfeis was weeping bitter tears, when the authorities at last arrived. My compatriots, hardened criminals all, made rude gestures, called even ruder names, and quickly eluded the gendarmes, but I was too overcome with triumph to bother.

'I was dragged to the home of my keepers and true to form, the Perkineisses turned me out without a kind word after a tearful accusation from Surfeis. I no longer cared. I

was glad to be sent to *Les Orphelines de Brad*, once I had rescued the last remnant of my parents from the wall of my tiny
room. I looked with scorn at my ungrateful relatives and spat
on the ground at their feet. A door was closing behind me,
but I was sure things could be no worse than at that hated
home.

'Oh, la la! What a child I was!'

Lizzie and Alice both nodded in eager agreement.

'My thoughts were less confident when I was ushered
brutally to the doorsteps of the grim orphanage,' Black Ethel
continued. 'While I had been eager to leave my unkind relatives and their uneasy scorn, I was somewhat abashed when
the tall black doors loomed before me.'

'I have never seen an orphanage,' Alice said, her voice
betraying a curiosity she was little able to hide. 'It sounds perfectly monstrous, though.'

'I shudder to consider your fate,' Lizzie added, thanking
her lucky stars once more for the sometimes tiresome but
always cushy home of her aunt and uncle.

'It is to be shuddered at,' Black Ethel agreed, stretching her
battered boots before her and tousling her long black hair.
Lizzie noted that the pirate queen looked much less intim-
idating with her hair down and her face relaxed from the
scowl she often wore on deck. Nevertheless, Lizzie suspected
that it would not be wise to remember the ruthlessness of
which she could be capable.

'I was admitted to the grey walls of the institution and
immediately sized up the situation. Most of the children
appeared to have been beaten into a sullen submission by
the head of the orphanage, *Madame* de Pautonnier. While
the orphanage may have been founded by the holy man who
had been a friend to children everywhere and an artiste of *bon
repute*, this leader seemed to have come from the opposing
camp.

'Only infernal realms could have been responsible for this
dictator in a redingote. I can see her dull grey eyes before me
in my worst dreams and hear that piercingly high-pitched
voice. Her cruelty was legendary, her conscience non-existent. Pautonnier's only concern was making the most of the

stipend the city offered her for caring for the cast off children without a *sou* or a relative. Thus she clothed us as meagrely as possible and fed us little more than gruel and vegetable soup. A lump of meat was a rarity that might turn up in the bowl of an unfortunate only at odd intervals, and often resulting in an impromptu battle.'

'How awful,' Alice said, appearing to be genuinely shaken by this picture of the rough life. Cosseted in her stately home, she had had no idea of the lives of others beyond her class. Although a very ignorant girl, her heart responded with lively empathy and she vowed, 'I shall make sure we have no such horrors in our village! When I return,' she added somewhat more sombrely, dabbing at her eyes with a mixture of sympathy and self-pity.

'That would be a good thing,' Black Ethel agreed. 'We were poorly fed, beaten and used as cheap labour. Hour after hour we girls were forced to tat.'

'To what?' asked Lizzie. Alice looked on with alarm, fearful what the answer might be.

Black Ethel looked at the two of them with surprise. 'Tatting? *Frivolité*? The horrible lace with which one makes collars and doilies.'

Lizzie could feel a sense of indignation building. 'Children labouring to make lace? It's an outrage!'

'And we have so many lace collars,' Alice said wonderingly, before blushing and begging the pirate queen to continue. 'Why were children particularly used for this?'

The buccaneer raised her rough but petite hands for their inspection. 'Our fingers were tiny and nimble. We could move the shuttles to and fro with alacrity. The hooks would not catch on our short-sleeved garments and our young eyes could see in the faint light allowed by the grimy windows of the workroom.

'But one day, I decided I had had enough!'

The cousins cheered.

'One day,' Black Ethel continued as Lizzie and Alice drew closer with the excitement of her tale, 'when we were all in the main hall where we received our paltry meals and did our endless tatting, I made a decision. No more would I tat for this horrible woman who leeched the vital souls of innocent children, no more would I work for anyone but me as the beneficiary.'

'How brave you must have been!' Lizzie said with undisguised admiration. The pirate queen was like a novel's heroine come to life. How pale the stories of Miss Radcliffe seemed in comparison, whereas once she devoured them by candlelight when the sun had long since gone to sleep. Perhaps when she has finished relating her adventures, Lizzie mused, I can trust my great secret to her bosom. Surely she can be a stalwart confidant! She turned to the tale once more with an even greater excitement.

'I could do nothing alone. That was the lynchpin, as we say. I needed a few confederates to join me. This would be difficult,' the pirate queen said confidentially to the pair raptly listening. 'I was not known as a kindly sort, I must admit. I was quick to temper, eager to use my fists and the envy of all because of my beautiful long hair the colour of a raven's wing.' Black Ethel swept her long locks over one shoulder, combing her fingers through the ringlets to emphasize her point.

Lizzie and Alice both cooed appreciatively, although the latter might be excused for thinking her own golden locks were more attractive. She associated this shade of hair with the chimera of Kit Barrington, now sadly fading from memory with only the light anchor of black hair and blue eyes to tie him to her memory and the vague thought that he had been so charming, though truth to tell, Alice was unable to recall a single witty remark or clever observation. She would have to quiz Lizzie later and see if her memory were better (it generally was).

'However, as I spread the word about my desire for rebellion, I found there were many who desired an opportunity to rise up against the despot, Mme. de Pautonnier, and to break free of that horrid place. They only lacked a leader. I decided to embrace the necessity and draw them together for the attack. Our plans were laid in the dark of the night. Whispers floated from bed to bed and room to room. At last on a night with the full moon's light, we struck.

'Our attack began in the kitchen. Without the sour-faced staff who usually tortured us, the place was cavernous and foul smelling. We filled our shirts or kerchiefs with what food we could find, slinging it over our backs for the night. Tripping past the sleeping Francis, *Madame*'s lazy cousin with his short sight and his cruel stick, we filed into the great hall and gathered our tatting work into a pile, throwing onto it all the shuttles, a few wooden buckets and some small kindling from the woodstove. I drizzled some olive oil over the combustibles and then I drew out the box of matches I had liberated from the kitchen, right under the nose of the chef.'

'Oh, no!' Lizzie could not help but gasp.

'Oh yes,' Black Ethel said with a wicked smile. 'I set fire to the pile there and then, and laughed aloud as the flames shot into the air.'

'Goodness,' said Alice, gobsmacked with pure admiration for the destructive young girl.

'Goodness had very little to do with it,' the pirate queen said with a wave of her hand. 'I admit my motives were good, but what happened next turned the night into a *mêlée*.'

'Oh dear!'

'Yes, the other children equally enraptured with the flames, grabbed their uncomfortable stools and chairs where they had spent hour after miserable hour tatting, and thrust them onto the pyre as well. Within moments the fire was blazing out of the control. *Madame* de Pautonnier and her staff were roused from their own comfortable beds and desperately tried to extinguish the flames but it was far, far too late.

'In the helter skelter of the noise and panic, as the fire brigade arrived tardily and tried to contain the fire, most of us children escaped from our overlords, nipping out into the streets and running into dark corners to await the morning light and the freedom it brought us. I breathed in the night air, and though it was choked with burning tat, it smelled like freedom. I was fifteen and the world lay before me like a lazy opponent whom I had every expectation of besting at the first match.'

Chapter Seven

'Fifteen—and on your own!' Lizzie could not help uttering those words with a tone of disapproval, although whether she truly disparaged Black Ethel's wayward independence or simply envied her boldness, it was hard to tell. She was beginning to form a distinct sense of awe before the fearlessness of this raven-haired buccaneer.

'Indeed!' chuckled the pirate queen as she lit another cigar and turned down the wick of the lamp. Late as the hour was neither of the two young women seemed the least bit tired as Black Ethel related her exciting adventures. 'Although I was of course rather tall for my age. It is all in the bones,' she said, turning to Alice. 'Cheese is good for the bones!'

Alice winced although she tried not to show it. She had always been somewhat delicate around the subject of cheese. Her parents had tried all the types to find a flavour she would enjoy, but she had tasted them all and continued to demur. It was always the same: Wensleydale, cheddar, Stilton, Derbyshire, brie, gouda, Dachsteiner, Herve, Havarti, Lappi, Beaufort, Camembert, Desmond, Kilcummin, Shropshire Blue or Double Gloucester, Alice had nibbled a bit from one side or the other and yet had seen no perceptible change in her feelings. It is quite possible that she would always remain recalcitrant when it came to fermented curd.

The pirate queen returned to her narrative with no knowledge of the curtly curdly tumult in Alice's brain. 'I knew that I would never find my dreams in the town of my birth, so I began the long trek to Paris, sure that something there would lead to the wonderful life I knew awaited me.'

'How could you be so certain?' Lizzie asked, thinking pensively of her own doubts and fears.

Black Ethel laughed. 'Paris was the City of Lights! I had heard about it since childhood. I was not foolish enough to think the streets were paved with gold, though I had hopes nearly as unrealistic. For the first month I was there, I swept the floors in a café so dirty that the very rats would not eat off the floor. In the second month, I kneaded dough in a *boulangerie* where cockroaches routinely substituted for sultanas.'

'Oh my,' Alice said, turning a rather pale shade of green.

'Oh, that was not the worst!' Black Ethel gave a sinister laugh. 'In the third month, I was hired to beat linens in a laundry that supplied the local *infirmière*, although they were less than scrupulous about the care they gave the linens. How many times the cruel *madame* barked at me not to waste the bleach that might have saved one more of the soldiers from horrible infection, I cannot have kept count.'

'How horrid!' Lizzie said, aghast in her gentle heart.

'Indeed,' the buccaneer agreed. 'I knew that it was not to be my life's work. But one day I saw a glimmer of hope. A man walked into the *infirmière* while I was delivering linens. He was grim-faced and bearded with huge guns at his side and all the hallways filled with whispers of his name.

'It was...the pirate Lafitte!'

'Lafitte!' Lizzie said with alarm and disbelief. 'The horrible pirate? Oh, I beg your pardon.' How awkward it was to suddenly find themselves rescued by a pirate from what had appeared to be perfectly respectable men. As fixed as her ideas had been about pirates and highwaymen, Lizzie could not keep herself from regarding Black Ethel with a mixture of puzzlement and admiration. She would be loath to admit it even to her dear cousin, but Lizzie was quite fascinated and intrigued by the free life the pirate queen lived, not only freed from the bonds of tutelary but also from the restrictions of family and town. She wore what she liked, spoke as she wished and was entirely careless of housekeeping details.

It was quite dizzying to consider.

Black Ethel continued to suck on her cigar thoughtfully. 'He was certainly notorious, *c'est vrai*. All those who faced him in the corridor that day eagerly gave way after one glare from his glittering eyes.'

Alice quailed visibly. 'Were you not frightened?' she asked with awe.

Black Ethel waved her hand dismissively. 'He was the one person who could take me away from the all that drudgery into a life of freedom and adventure. I knew that the fusty luggslugs who ran the *infirmière* had long been his paramour, so I decided to make the most of his brief visit to Paris.'

'Paramour?' said Alice, her brow furrowing.

'Paramour!' said Lizzie, her cheeks blushing pink.

'Indeed,' said Ethel, oblivious to the reactions of the two young women as she warmed to the telling of her story. 'By listening to the gossip of the staff, I knew that it was the habit of M. Lafitte to visit the kitchen first and obtain a little sustenance from the gallimaufry that served as the primary meal of the *infirmière*—except of course for those too ill or injured to eat.'

'Was there a war on?' Alice asked hesitantly, afraid that she might be asked to name the particular war and aware that she could only remember the battles that had interesting names like Marathon and Waterloo but had no memory to recall the other wars categorical.

'There is always a war on,' Lizzie said with some bitterness, all too aware how the current situation in the Mediterranean affected her own romantic interests.

Black Ethel nodded sagely. '*Quel dommage*, eh? It was fortunate for Lafitte, as it was far easier to recruit men to the piratical life once they had seen action in the armed forces. They knew how to use pistols and they were accustomed to the sight of blood. Quite often, too, they were somewhat less idealistic and more eager for results.

'I left my linens behind and sneaked into the kitchen. The usual Gorgon who ran that sweaty room had departed for fear of Lafitte, who sat on a chair shovelling some food into a bowl with a mug of ale at his side. He was everything the tales had told: surely six feet tall or more, with an ugly scar down the left side of his face, blocked only by a jet black patch where his eye ought to have been. I quailed at the thought of his roughness, but I was determined to join the pirate life and lay waste to all that my blackguard relatives held dear.

'I gathered my courage and at last said, 'M. Lafitte, I wish to join your crew!' He looked at me through his single eye, set down the bowl of gallimaufry and then burst into loud guffaws of laughter.

'This only made me more determined. Quick as a fox, I

snatched a knife from the cutting board and held it to his throat. 'M. Lafitte,' I said triumphantly, 'I suggest you consider my offer!"

Alice drew back in horror. 'Did he quail before your daring?' She thrilled to think of the bravery of the pirate queen, holding a knife to the throat of the renowned buccaneer. Lafitte himself—such daring! Alice longed to be such a heroine herself, but she was hampered by the prime defect of being quite cowardly. It was so inconvenient.

Black Ethel meanwhile had allowed a lazy grin to move across her features as she contemplated this episode from her youth. The young orphan had indeed possessed daring. She shook her head in response to Alice's question. 'Indeed he did not, he never moved or showed the least bit of worry.'

Lizzie smiled. Although he was admittedly a pirate, she could not help a thrill of admiration for the unflappable rapscallion. 'What a man of considerable mettle he must have been to remain so complaisant in the face of a wild young thing.'

'C'est vrai!' Black Ethel continued, taking another puff on her latest cigar. The thrilling narrative had kept them all rapt with fervour to let the yarn unfurl and they waited impatiently for her to continue. 'He simply reached for his spoon and began to eat once more, keeping a weather eye on my hand to see if it would tremble. I suppose now that he was more concerned with my fear leading to his injury rather than my wrath.

'After a time, when I had demonstrated that I was no less stubborn than he, Lafitte pushed the empty bowl away from him, grabbed the mug of ale and took a deep draft, my knife still at his throat. When he set down the empty glass, he looked once more into my blazing eyes and grunted.

"What is your name, cherie?' he asked me. I gave him the name my dear parents had bequeathed me, but he shook his head. 'That is no name for a pirate.' My heart leaped of course to know that he would accept me into his crew.

"Merci, mon Capitan! I shall do all that you ask, I shall work hard, I shall be ruthless...' I was effusive in my delight, but the old reprobate merely grunted again and asked for more food. I sprang to work finding him sustenance, rooting through the cabinets with alacrity. He said nothing more until he had devoured some Bretagne ham and half a loaf of pumpernickel. And all he said then was that I must disguise myself as a boy.

'I laughed, because I had already anticipated that possibility. In my bindle I had stuffed such clothes as would fit the life of the cabin boy for some time to come. It took only a few minutes to run and fetch the rucksack, but I feared the whole time that the bloody pirate would abandon me to the ravages of the Gorgon once more, but he was still filling his pockets with smoked meats when I returned breathless. He looked at my bindle and wordlessly handed me a string of sausages. I took it upon myself to liberate the few good wedges of cheese to be found in that sorry excuse for a kitchen, and turned to follow at Lafitte's heel as he strode once more out of the *infirmière*.

'As we walked down the filthy streets of Paris, I turned once more to look at the workplace that had oppressed me for a time and spat on the ground with contempt. Lafitte saw me do so and laughed out loud as we walked toward the banks of the Seine.'

'Did he have his ship waiting there in Paris?' Alice asked the pirate queen as she recalled the day she met her mentor, the legendary pirate Lafitte.

Lizzie coughed to cover her inadvertent chuckle at Alice's seemingly bottomless ignorance. Poor Miss Travers must not have worked her way through much in the way of geography with her young pupil. Black Ethel narrowed her eyes at the guileless Miss Mangrove, but perceiving only ignorance in the question, at last deigned to answer.

'No, *ma petite*. He had only a barge there and a handful of his crew. The crew was picking up various supplies while Lafitte himself had been delivering a rather special item.'

'Special item?' Lizzie said, trying in vain to smother an inadvertent yawn. Surely that was not the first rosy light of dawn brightening the ink dark sky? Could they have talked all night?

'I did not learn this until much later, of course,' Black

Ethel said, as she opened a drawer in her massive desk. 'But Lafitte had met with no less a person than the king himself.' She smiled expectantly at the two listeners.

'Our king?' Alice asked breathlessly, daring to hope.

The pirate queen frowned. 'No, *mademoiselle*! *Our* king.'

'Oh.' Alice immediately perceived the frown lengthening, so she added, 'How lovely!'

'Quite gratifying, I'm sure,' Lizzie added quickly, her ability to size up awkward social situations benefiting her as always. 'What a surprise, too, to know that the king was intimate with the man who terrorized the seas across the world! Such a brave man.'

The buccaneer leaned back and nodded appreciatively. 'He had rescued a rather important item for his majesty and was being appropriately rewarded. I don't suppose that either of you have been in such a situation, but it is quite a thing to be in the presence of a king.' She leaned forward to fish through the open drawer, obviously seeking something special.

'Well, as a matter of fact,' Lizzie started cautiously, as the late hour and the thrilling conversation had made her somewhat indecorously reckless regarding her secret understanding with the King of Naples. She had been just bursting to tell about the many months of letters back and forth, the detailed information exchanged about the habits of certain spindly-legged insects, and the growing feeling of esteem so beautifully shared over the lengthy and rather well-spelled (for a foreign national) letters. 'I must confess, that I—'

'Ah, *voilà!* With a flourish, Black Ethel withdrew the item she had been in search of. 'See here, given from the king's own hand.' She repeated the gesture, passing the object to Alice because she was the closer of the two.

Alice gazed at the small metal disk with something approaching concentration. 'How very lovely and that's the king's image, is it not?' She bit her lips hoping she had guessed correctly. Black Ethel nodded curtly. It was not the time to wish that she had paid more attention in her interminable French lessons. The language always sounded better when Miss Travers spoke it with her elegant Stratford accent. When Alice tried to repeat the words they failed to sound as trippingly from her tongue, instead bumping into one another in a rush as the servants did back home when Mrs. Perkins was in a foul mood.

Lizzie took the disk from Alice's outstretched hand while the pirate queen awaited a more suitably effusive response. Lizzie was ready to oblige despite smarting under the abruptness with which the subject had once more wheeled away from her secret correspondence. But she was no rag-mannered chit and had had many of her years devoted to the concealing of disappointment.

'Medal of honour,' Lizzie read off the top of the disk, which despite its rather unkempt look, she saw was made of solid gold. 'From the king himself—look Alice, there's his name.'

Alice nodded with what she hoped looked like confidence.

'For extraordinary valour, to M. Jean Lafitte,' Lizzie continued reading from the back of the disk. Despite its missing a ceremonial ribbon of some kind, this was indeed a precious object. The buccaneer captain herself smiled with reflected glory at this acknowledgment of respect. 'Whatever had he done?' she could not help asking.

'He delivered a most important article to the king. It was…a woman!'

The orange tendrils of dawn were lifting across the sky as Black Ethel stretched and then stubbed out the last of her cigar. 'Oh la la, we have talked a long time.'

Tired as she was, Lizzie could not conceal her curiosity about the adventure that had brought king and pirate together. 'Is it a very long story?'

'Oh, *oui, Mademoiselle* Lizzie,' the pirate queen assured, 'It is rather complicated and quite intriguing tale, but it is late—or rather, very early.' She chuckled quietly and pointed to Alice. 'Besides, your young cousin has already fallen asleep.'

True enough, Alice had finally succumbed to fatigue despite the exiting tale spun in the captain's room that night. She would be sorely vexed to be awakened now, but Lizzie was quite practiced at manoeuvring Alice in that condition, which took an application of firmness and gentle cajoling in equal parts. While Black Ethel made one last round of her ship, growling at the occasional laggard and clapping a few stalwart lads on the back, Lizzie coaxed Alice out of her much wrinkled day clothes and into one of the night gowns they had received from the kindly pirate queen.

'I know I shall have the most peculiar dreams,' Alice yawned as she collapsed into nearly instantaneous sleep. Lizzie looked down at her young cousin and sighed slightly before pulling the covers up to her shoulders. Alice seemed to pay it no mind, but said groggily, 'Mother, please, I don't want any treacle,' before turning over and beginning to snore softly.

Lizzie smiled and turned to prepare herself for bed as well. Out the window she could see the clear signs of dawn, but she did not care two pins for propriety. If they could be spirited away from her uncle's funeral, kidnapped twice and caught in the midst of pirates, Lizzie could reconcile sleeping late on a weekday. She thought it was perhaps a weekday, anyway. It was increasingly difficult to be certain.

Lizzie got into bed, glancing over at her cousin and making certain she was safely in Slumberland before she reached once more for the much-read letter secreted as always in her sleeve. But as she ran her eyes over the neatly formed words, they failed to give her the usual thrill she would feel on most occasions.

For the first time Lizzie experienced a twinge of doubt. It wasn't the king himself, of course. He was sublime. She still found his words stirring, especially when she dared to read between the lines. But for the first time she doubted it would all work out somehow. How could the king find her in the middle of the wild seas? The pirate queen was kindly enough—far more so than they had any right to expect—but what were they to do? No one knew where they were; no one might even be looking for them anymore, supposing perhaps they had perished, if not when sold into the white slave trade as had been planned, then certainly once they had boarded a pirate vessel.

Lizzie sat up anxiously, the thoughts preying on her consciousness. What is to become of me? What is to become of us? Will the king forget me before he has had a chance to even make my direct acquaintance? He had letters, a lock of hair—was it enough to bind her love to him when all hope seemed lost?

Unable to bear the weight of her thoughts, Lizzie sank back to the supine position, tears dampening her pale cheeks. As the sun rose, her hopes fell and she slipped into a fitful slumber.

It was late morning when Alice heard the distinctive sound of horses' hooves on a well-trod road. She turned on the sunny bench where she had slumbered in the afternoon light and shaded her eyes to see who was coming up the lane. Two young gentlemen on fine steppers, cutting very fine figures indeed, were trotting toward the garden bower. Alice squinted even though she knew it was not to her best advantage to be seen that way, as she was not able to discern who was coming her way looking so corky.

'It's those two young gentlemen,' her father said unhelpfully as he continued to poke at the roots of the forsythia. 'Those two dangling after you, not quite right, either of them. Ought to set them down.' He made as if to get up from his semi-recumbent position, but Alice shushed him with her fan and rose herself to greet the two gentlemen.

'Don't make a cake of yourself,' Lady Mangrove said sharply from behind the fairy fountain, her head hidden by a satyr's trumpet. 'No mawkish trifles, now.'

Alice was stung both by the unkindness of her mother's words and by her undignified use of cant. What is the world coming to, Alice thought peevishly, if one's parents try to use the latest slang? It was entirely wrong, she could not help thinking, and it was as bad as imagining her parents suddenly playing croquet with herons for mallets. Once she had put the image in her head, it refused to leave for some interminable moments.

She only succeeded in throwing it aside when she suddenly realised that the one young man was no other than the mysteriously handsome Kit Barrington, who was once more restored to vivid glory before her eyes. It is hard to believe that his brief absence had seemed so long, Alice thought in an agony of regret. How could she have forgotten those handsome black curls, those piercingly blue eyes and the jaw that promised firm decisiveness? Alice could see now that he rode magnificently upon his steed with a certain attitude that showed he had pluck to the backbone. How wonderful that he was calling on her.

It was another moment before she noticed that Arthur Boylett rode beside him on a horse of far less striking beauty and without that set of the shoulders that presaged decisive boldness. If Mr. Barrington were the pinkest of the pink, then surely Arthur was the grey. Alice felt her smile withdraw into a frown of disappointment, until she recognised that it must be making her a shade less attractive. Her smile sprang back like a fresh young sapling in the wind. Mr. Barrington must find her to be admirably agreeable.

'The ants are returning,' Mr. Radley said by the wisteria, a trowel in one hand and a bottle of gin in the other. Alice was momentarily distracted. If Mr. Radley were taking to the gin, that would be the end of their famed garden. Perhaps he was only using it to tease the ants. She had to think—did ants drink gin? Would it lure them within range of the trowel?

'Alice!' It was Kit Barrington. Alice turned back, but he seemed farther away now. He and Arthur were riding at the same pace, but they seemed to be retreating from her nonetheless. Alice furrowed her brow, heedless of its unattractive pull at her features. She decided to walk toward the gentlemen as if she happened to be going that way, trying not to let her panic show.

Yet each step seemed to slow her further. The wisteria was spreading far too quickly, flopping across her path and impeding her progress with gentle insistence. 'The seed pods are poisonous,' Mr. Radley was saying somewhere in the distance but Alice was unable to hear his additional pronouncements on the progress of the ants. The elusive Mr. Barrington was nearly out of sight, yet his voice was becoming clearer all the time, calling 'Alice, Alice!'

It was with great sadness and frustration that Alice opened her eyes to behold her cousin offering a plate of comestibles for a late breakfast. Alice sulked as she chewed on some jerky and did not notice the dark circles rounding Lizzie's gentle eyes.

The day, which had begun so promisingly, soon darkened precipitously. Black Ethel stood in anxious conferral with the mysterious bos'n and her pilot as the rising winds whipped about them. Lizzie looked up from her sewing and glanced at the small huddle with some trepidation. She was loath to imagine even a fine ship like the *Bonny Read* tossed about by a tempest on the wild seas. No Prospero had she to command the winds and no Ariel flew to their behest on the bat's back.

An anxious glance toward Alice revealed her cousin to be in unaccustomed deep thought, her mending forgotten. Perhaps it was for the best, Lizzie reflected, as usual sheltering her younger cousin from harsh realities of life. Let her preserve the time remaining in pleasant ignorance, free from concern about the dangers of the ocean. Truth to tell, however, it did seem that Alice had some thoughts that pressed upon her heart with rather more pressure than usual.

Lizzie considered simply turning back to her stitching without distracting her cousin's musings. They had volunteered to do some mending for the sailors and were quite overwhelmed by the volume of shirts and inexpressibles that had been heaped upon them. Nonetheless, Lizzie had set to work with her usual efficient sense of duty and they had begun making headway despite Alice's tendency to sew poorly and very slowly, necessitating the removal of many of her mended patches. Lizzie was no brilliant seamstress herself, but long-term need had supplied her with sure skills if no great love for the tedious work.

Indeed, Lizzie had once more bent her head to her work—a rather well-worn elbow of the third mate's attire—when Alice herself broke from her reverie and turned to her cousin. 'Lizzie, dear, do you suppose that dreams can mean anything of import?'

'You've dropped your mending,' Lizzie said first, pointing to the inexpressibles that had fallen to the deck while Alice had meant to be repairing one leg that was frayed at the bottom. As Alice retrieved the fallen garment, Lizzie cast her mind back to her own reading and quickly recalled a suitable analogue.

'In *The Odyssey*,' Lizzie said with a pleasant sense of authority, something long missing from the tumultuous ordeals of late, 'Homer has Penelope talk about the two kinds of dreams.'

'Are there only two?' Alice said, sounding somewhat disappointed.

'Two types, but far more many individual dreams,' Lizzie answered, snipping a length of thread from a spool. 'But Penelope says— '

'Was she very clever? Was she a professor? I only ask,' Alice said shyly, 'because I hope to know the truth.'

Lizzie smiled. 'Penelope is not a professor, but I will certainly argue that she is indeed clever. And if you recall Professor Slough, you will also recall that the title need not confer wit.' Alice nodded, abashed. Her pupil now contrite, Lizzie continued. 'Penelope spoke of the two types of dreams as those which came through the gateway of ivory and those which came through the gateway of horn.'

'Where did the gate lead from?' Alice could not resist from asking.

'From Elysium, which I'm sure you'll remember from your lessons.'

Alice though it best to pretend that she did.

'The gate of ivory,' Lizzie continued, pleased with her avoidance of another digression, 'brought dreams of foolish fancy that had no more substantial weight than a will o'the wisp. But through the gates of smoothened horn come dreams that offer truth to the dreamer.'

Alice seemed almost awed into silence. 'How can you know which gate the dreams have passed through?' she said at last.

'It is very difficult to tell,' Lizzie said with a rotund echo of wisdom in her tone, for she could not immediately recall what, if anything, Penelope had had to say on the subject, although she had a vague notion that Chaucer might have been helpful at that moment. 'Only time can make you certain.'

'What if the dream was a warning?' Alice asked with some anxiousness betrayed in her tone.

'What was your dream about, Alice?' Lizzie asked with a small knell of foreboding. But before her cousin could answer the ship took a sudden pitch in to the air before falling with a sickening abruptness into a trough. A sudden din arose as enormous drops of rain pelted the deck.

'Quick, get below!' the third mate barked at the two women as they grabbed their pile of mending and rushed for safety.

Ensconced once more in the safety of the captain's cabin, Lizzie looked with some alarm out the thick windows. The sky had become a precipitous black and the rain pelted against the windows as if it sought entry to their haven. Periodically the darkness was lit by wild slashes of lightning. The pitch of the ship grew until it seemed like some wild steed freed from its traces to plunge and charge at will. Its motion made her own strong stomach flip over on its own. It looked to be an ominous night.

Their mending now forgotten, the two young women crouched at the window and tried to see out into the black air. It was fruitless, though. There was simply nothing to be seen in the inky sky.

'Oh Lizzie,' cried Alice, 'we're going to die, aren't we?'

'Hush, Alice! There's no need to be ridiculous. This ship has sailed across oceans, back and forth and been part of many a sea battle I would wager. The *Bonny Read* will keep us safe.' But in her heart Lizzie feared the same thing. Such a night! And the captain herself had seemed rather concerned… but she could not let that trouble her nor frighten Alice. How to keep their minds off such horrors when the ship pitched so wildly? Her eye lighted upon a book lying on the captain's desk and inspiration struck.

Lizzie lurched across the room to the desk and picked up the small volume. She was somewhat aghast to find that it was yet another copy of Miss Sarah Fielding's inexplicably popular tome, *The Governess*. It would, nonetheless, suffice to keep their attention off the growing tempest or so she hoped. Lizzie beckoned to Alice and they sat side by side in the flick-ering light of the captain's lamp. It would be a struggle to keep the pages still enough to read, but Lizzie thought it best to distract themselves.

'We were up to, ah—the story of the giants, I think.' Alice's eyes were wild, paying no attention yet but darting toward the opaque windows. Lizzie cleared her voice and began in a rather loud voice to compensate for the wild dash of the waves and the soaring cry of the wind.

'The story of the cruel giant Barbarico, the good giant Benefico and the little pretty dwarf Mignon,' Lizzie said with great expression. 'A great many hundred years ago, the mountains of Wales were inhabited by two giants; one of whom was the terror of all his neighbours and the plague of the whole country. He greatly exceeded the size of any giant recorded in history; and his eyes looked so fierce and terrible, that they frightened all who were so unhappy as to behold them.' A sudden crash of lightening made her start and Alice jump, then erupt with hiccoughs as the ship pitched up once more.

'The name of this enormous wretch was Barbarico. A name, which filled all who heard it with fear and astonishment. The whole delight of this monster's life was in acts of inhumanity and mischief; and he was the most miserable as well as the most wicked creature that ever yet was born. He had no sooner committed one outrage—'

At the peak of another wave, the ship gave such a groan as a very evil giant might indeed give and both women cried out in horror and latched onto one another. 'Oh, Lizzie,' Alice shrieked. 'We're going to die!'

'Hush, Alice,' Lizzie said, but her calm words belied a much more turbulent state of mind. It was impossible to go on reading in this hurly-burly. She slipped the book absently into her apron pocket and considered what they ought to do. Her first thought was about the importance of buoyancy, should the worst happen, but there were other practical concerns to consider. Lizzie rose and stuffed a good amount of the mending into workbags along with a few spools of thread and a packet of needles. She tied one around the wrist of her uncomprehending cousin and the other around her own.

'What's that for?' Alice said, quailing before another peal of thunder as it ripped the chaos of the night.

Lizzie ignored her question and cast about the room for useful items. What was left of the cheese she also stuffed into the mending bags It would be something, anyway. What else, Lizzie thought, a finger tapping her lips. She held a loop of rope in her hands, knowing it would be handy, but the problem of buoyancy remained uppermost in her mind.

'Barrels,' Alice said dully and Lizzie turned to regard her with some surprise. Not only had Alice seemed to have grasped the dire situation—which was astounding enough—but she also had come up with an excellent suggestion.

Except that the barrels were all on deck, Lizzie thought. A glance at the door revealed nothing but darkness outside, perhaps though, it would not be so bad to step outside and secure a small powder keg or two. Better to be safe, *ne c'est pas?*

Alice and Lizzie crept to the door and pulled it open. At once they were hit with the massive force of the gale, a wind that slapped them rudely as some ill-mannered hooligan and then rushed past them to the interior. But there, beside the cannon, a couple of small barrels slid precipitously back and forth in the wild storm. As the rain crashed down upon them, the two staggered toward the cannon, protected only by their light shawls and dragging the mending bags. Bending swiftly, Lizzie knotted a rope around the first one then tied another secure knot about the waist of her cousin. One good thing about living with sailors, she thought absently, one did learn quickly how good knots were tied. In another moment, Lizzie had secured herself in a similar fashion.

Their safety assured, the two young women turned to regain their sanctuary. The midnight hue of the sky belied the mid-afternoon hour and the gale roared like a furious giant. There was no one to be seen on deck and Lizzie paused in wonder as the ship reared up once more on the back of an enormous wave. As they staggered toward the beckoning door, the ship pitched back down into the sea as if it were a muskrat heading for the river bottom. Lizzie had no voice with which to shriek when she saw the wall of water coming across the deck. Alice, mercifully, was looking the other way and so saw nothing before the swell lifted them both aloft, barrels chopping the surface. In a moment they were over the side of the *Bonny Read* as it leapt up once more into the black night. Lizzie swallowed a quantity of salt water before bobbing once more to the surface with a gasp and a shriek, for she saw Alice borne upon another wave some yards away from her, her hands grasping the rope around the barrel, her mouth open in a silent scream.

The last thing Lizzie saw before the waters closed over her head once more was the pale white face of the friendly bos'n, quizzically staring in her direction before lifting his hat in an unmistakable gesture of farewell.

Chapter Eight

Lizzie supposed that she had added significantly to the ocean's salty waves with her tears by the time she lost sight of both the *Bonny Read* and her dear cousin Alice, whose gentle face she now beheld in her thoughts touched with the warm white light of loss and regret. The violent stabs of lightning continued to rend the night sky, but the thunder seemed to be growing somewhat less tumultuous and the sound of the waves soon became that which filled her weary ears. She bobbed along the sea surface, although many a wave still o'er reached her head, dumping miserably cold water upon her wearied skull.

As she wiped her lips dry for the umpteenth time, Lizzie considered what important preparation they had not made: the securing of drinkable water. If she had known any oath stronger than 'to the fiend with it!' (a phrase her late father had been much enamoured of using in moments of extreme agitation), she would have used it then, for Lizzie knew all too well that without water to drink she and Alice would be parched in very little time and dead in not much longer, particularly if one gave in to the temptation to drink sea water. It was a death warrant, as well she knew, but would Alice remember?

It was hard to imagine Alice coping on her own, paddling her way through the water alone. Lizzie sent up a desperate prayer that her young and often foolish cousin should not perish due to either her own neglect or Alice's often-inefficient thought. It was too much to be borne! Lizzie could reconcile herself to the thought of death, full of regret as she might be to never see the King of Naples with her own eyes (for well she knew that fantasies were most often far more rewarding than realities ever proved to be), but she could not quite bring herself to picture poor dear Alice perishing in the cold waves, alone, confused and without adequate recognition and preparation for death.

If we are not near land, we shall perish, Lizzie thought

119

with harsh simplicity. She looked in vain through the inky night but could discern no sign of stars or other signs but the occasional flash of lightning far in the distance. Did storms go out to sea or toward land? she wondered. If toward land, she might be floating in the right direction, for she was more or less moving in the same path as the storm was retreating. She hugged the barrel tightly, trying not to think of the lack of water, nor of the hungry fish that might be floating below her. She did not believe in sea monsters of any kind. Or so she told herself; when on dry land Lizzie had found the idea patently absurd and filed such notions away with the fancies of *Gulliver's Travels*.

Now the idea of some ancient and tentacled monster rising to the surface, disturbed by her passage on the waves, not only seemed possible but entirely imminent. Lizzie anxiously tried to berate herself for her lack of logic, but found it impossible not to violently kick her feet whenever she imagined something brushing against her leg. It might be only a fish, she admonished her suddenly wakeful imagination, but her increasingly frantic mind whispered back, it might not be a fish at that.

In such a way, Lizzie floated like a cork upon the wide ocean with not another soul in sight or within sound of her occasional pitiful cries. Done to a cow's thumb, exhausted by her fears and her struggle to survive, the brave young woman fell into a fitful slumber just as the first bright fingers of dawn lightened the darkness upon a much calmer sea.

When Lizzie awoke, the sun was high in the sky and the crush of her thirst an unbearable manacle that clung to her body with unutterable misery. She tried not to lick her lips and increase the misery, but the salt water inadvertently swallowed in the night had raised a salty hunger that burned to be assuaged. Lizzie, with some considerable difficulty, wrestled a small morsel of cheese from the workbag knotted to her wrist. She spoke a small prayer to the winds and waters for safe delivery, thinking Poseidon and Amphitrite might be more nearly within earshot than a contemporary deity, then nibbled on the small wedge of cheese in hopes of making it last as long as possible.

Although Lizzie commanded herself to careful and delicate consumption, the tiny portion quickly disappeared, leaving her still hungry and perhaps doubly thirsty. She drew her eyes to the horizon and searched in vain for some sign of land or humanity. The water gave a curious brightness to the sky and almost seemed to shimmer in the distance. Lizzie considered kicking her feet to aid in her progress, but the horror of removing herself even further from safety froze her to inaction. Best to let the sea carry her forth, she told herself grimly, if there was to be any hope.

She had no sense of time or its passing. Although the passage of the sun across the sky could be tracked over time, Lizzie faded in and out of consciousness as the merciless orb beat down upon her. She did not dream, but her mind filled with random snatches of memory, from the long lost visages of her parents, to the distant and restrained images of Alice's family, and of course, the inescapable oddness of their contemporary adventures since the funeral. As the day wore on and the glint of beams upon the waves taxed her already overwhelmed brain, Lizzie experienced feverish dreams of the King of Naples that she knew she would recall later only with supreme embarrassment, but which at the time proved somewhat soothing to her delirious spirit.

In this way, beleaguered by fancy, salty waves and savage thirst, the day passed, although Lizzie could not believe it was but one. She could hardly dare to believe that she could survive another like it, but put the thought away as soon as it rose to the surface of her consciousness. Sounds and voices echoed in her ears but Lizzie could never tell with certainty whether they came from without or within and feared that the merciless sun might deprive her altogether of her wits. After a time it was all she could do to cling to the barrel and try not to cry.

It was with a start that she awoke some indeterminate time later, to find the sun down and the black night once more holding sway. 'Where are you now, Alice?' she whispered aloud, but there was no response in return save the waves lapping against the sides of the barrel. At least the cooler night air restored some sense of hope against the derangement of the bright day. Lizzie rallied and considered whether to give in to the urge for another bite of cheese, or to steel herself for another cold night without sustenance.

She was quite unprepared for the strange sensation she felt next as something brushed against her foot. The offended limb recoiled with sudden horror and Lizzie looked vainly into the ink-black water, where she was unable to see anything at all. Raising her head once more, Lizzie was startled to see something white in the distance. Could it be a mirage? As she squinted into the dark, Lizzie relaxed her legs once more and behold! They were touching the sandy surface of the ocean floor. The long white shape must surely be the strand along the shore! She was safe, safe at last. She had never been more grateful in her young life as she strode awkwardly through the water toward the approaching prize of land, sweet land.

For a time, Lizzie could do nothing more than lie on the soft white sand and cry tears she did not realise had been waiting for release. Chary of thirst, she had held them in as she floated upon the black waters, but upon the shore once more, they came with relief, happiness and not a little grief. Alice, sweet Alice, where might she be? It was too much to hope that her dear cousin, too, had survived the pitching waves, but Lizzie would not give in to despair.

But where was she?

Once the tears subsided and the night wind chafed her cold wet clothing, Lizzie shivered and looked about. To find someone! That must be her next quest, but Lizzie stopped the shout that had risen to her lips. Many a thrilling gothic adventure rose from her memory—bereft gentlewomen, far from the care of family, so often became the terrified prey of an unscrupulous (yet often handsome and dashing) young man. Such a thing ought not happen to her.

Lizzie was cold, miserable and lost without a friend, but she knew she had a clever wit, a good sense of propriety and a reasonable knowledge of human nature. She pulled at the ropes knotted around herself and the barrel as her mind thought rather feverishly of the options. There must be warmth, or else she would soon catch her death. There must be water or she would faint from dehydration all too soon.

After that, food would be the most needful thing, but fresh clothes—how were they to be obtained? She had no money of any kind and little in the way of bargaining.

With great effort she finally released herself from the barrel's company, chafing at her wrist and scouting about her on the strand. Now that her eyes had become accustomed to the dark of the night and the brightness of the strand, Lizzie could see that there were some cottages nearby. Probably the fishermen, she mused. I hope they don't have dogs, Lizzie thought, as she headed in that direction, telling herself that no doubt they had cats (somehow cats and fish seemed to connect naturally in her mind). While she was eager to be near people once more, Lizzie felt certain that a damp and friendless young woman like herself would be in far too vulnerable a spot to ask for assistance from people to whom she had never been introduced.

As she approached the nearest cottage, Lizzie could hear the gentle sounds of snoring and took some comfort in it. At least she was no longer alone. Approaching the corner of the little house, she peeked nervously around and drew in her breath sharply, thinking she had been seen. When no sound materialized, Lizzie drew up her courage and looked round the edge of the wall. It was not a person, but only the laundry hanging in the night breeze. With relief, Lizzie let out the breath she had not been aware of holding.

An idea struck her. While loathe to purloin from these poor folk, Lizzie knew she would be in grave danger should she not get out of her wet clothes soon. As she examined the laundry in the moonlight, she was somewhat taken aback to see nothing but boy's clothes.

'Any port in a storm,' she muttered and grabbed a pair of breeches and a shirt that appeared to be about the right size. Looking carefully around, Lizzie saw no one watching and scooted away toward the next cottage to slip between it and into the darkness once more. When she was some distance away in a small tangle of shrub, she deemed it safe to disrobe and try on her new apparel. What a surprise to find that the unmentionable garment was far warmer than her frilly dress and the shirt quite a bit more comfortable than the fussy sleeves of her usual attire. Lizzie looked back at the cottages after she had knotted her wet clothes into a bundle and stuffed them inside the still damp mending bag.

She could not have known that the feeling she had was much like that of any successful thief, for if she had Lizzie might have been ashamed. Instead she felt only satisfaction that far from home and on her own, she had succeeded in the first step of her own rescue.

Vestis virum reddit, Lizzie thought, as she wiped the water from her chin after gulping a healthy amount of water from the well. Although its dark shape had alarmed her initially, she was grateful for its cool, restorative waters. She was nervous of lingering long by the group of cottages, but Lizzie was reluctant to leave the well behind immediately. It had been too long since she had drunk so deeply of fresh water.

Where would she go anyway, Lizzie reminded herself. She peered in the midnight dark toward the lane that led right up to the well. Many a cart had travelled this way; no doubt the fishermen had carried their catch to market daily. They would head out long before dawn, surely.

Strangely, she had no desire to be noticed. While at first Lizzie had longed to knock on a cottage door and be welcomed into the friendly warmth of a nearby hearth. Caution had checked her wish then, but what about now? Surely she could risk meeting others in her guise as a young man, hair carefully pulled back, pants attesting to her stature as a man.

But Lizzie found herself desiring instead to strike out on this unknown lane and see what she might encounter along its curves. She had already begun to consider what her name might be in this masquerade. George, surely, seemed the most suitable name for some reason that she could not quite recall. Lizzie had considered Cesario, but discarded it as far too romantic a notion. After all, there would be no likelihood of meeting a Duke Orsino, as she already had a nobleman's heart (although she felt a stab of pain remembering the state of the King of Naples' letter and hoping that once dry it would still be legible). She would keep the Bennett surname, as it might prove useful.

With one further deep drink from the well, 'George' set

out on the lane heading away from the sea. If only I had some boots, Lizzie tutted, but if wishes were horses—well, there she was. In time, no doubt, her feet would become accustomed to the rough life of the traveller. No doubt there would be much to get used to in this new life, Lizzie thought as she jumped at a strange sound, only to realise it was an owl hooting on her late night hunt.

I am alone, thought Lizzie. This thought had terrified her on the wide ocean's waves, but now she regarded it with a strange sense of wonder. Had she ever been truly alone in her life until this singular voyage? She had certainly felt bereft when her parents had died, suddenly plunged into the position of poor relation and lonely orphan. Lizzie had been at an awkward age: not quite old enough to be on her own, yet not young enough to be the fawning child who might make new parents love her as their own. Admittedly, Alice's parents were hardly the warm home of tender novels. The peculiar and nearly silent Lord Mangrove frightened her at first, as did Lady Mangrove with her sudden passions and constant wrangling with Lord Mangrove. Alice was sweet enough—if only she could manage to interest her in books without pictures!

Ah, Alice, Lizzie thought with a sudden stab of longing—where are you now?

As she trudged along the road, Lizzie—or rather George, as she must now consider herself—considered the likelihood of carrying out her masquerade. How did men behave in general, she quizzed herself, how were they likely to speak?

Lizzie put away the poetic lines of the King of Naples and tried to ponder more ordinary gentlemen. She kept herself to that class, as Lizzie feared being unable to reproduce the noise and behaviour of the lower classes with any accuracy. Besides, she pondered, there was little information for her to go on with regard to that behaviour. She called to mind the very strange Mr. Radley, who seemed to always be out in the garden planting carrots or deadly nightshade (the latter, he always said, had a grave purpose to safeguard the family, but Lizzie had never known of him actually employing the flowers in any kind of scheme; perhaps that was all for the best). There was also Mr. Bird, the butler, but he seemed to slip in and out of rooms without leaving behind so much as a shadow and thus offered little in the way of useful instruction.

The less said about Master Dick Spiggot the stable hand, the better.

So she was left with the examples of various affable young gentlemen like the persistent Arthur Boylett, whose conversation never failed to drive Lizzie to find someone more charming to talk to or a dance to join. She sighed as she walked along, remembering the pressure Alice had been facing to marry that very tedious young man. When he got going on the kings of England, a very dull night was promised for all. To hear him extrapolate on the true nature of Æthelred the ill-advised was to know the true meaning of infinitude and envy the unlettered people of hinterlands who might be spared the droning experience that Arthur's stories offered.

The constantly changing swirl of young men who appeared at various house parties and assembly rooms offered little more help. They were dressed in like manner, they spoke in the same lazy tones and, unlike Arthur, mostly spoke about horses, complimenting this or that 'beautiful stepper' or threatening to draw someone's cork if their favourite hunter were not sufficiently praised.

What we need, Lizzie thought with a certain peevishness that might be forgiven in light of the early hour and her strenuous journey, is a better class of men.

I shall simply act as myself, she vowed. I will recall to keep my voice low, to speak as little as possible and not offer any opinions. I may be thought a stupid young man, Lizzie scolded herself, but I will not be discovered as a woman. With that resolution, she picked up her pace, seeing the first outlying buildings of a small town coming into view with the dawning light.

It was early yet, but there were those here and there who stirred. Here and there, a carter hitched up his horses and a landlady opened her shutters as her meat pies baked. The smell so bewitched Lizzie's nose that she thought for a moment she might simply swoon away with the delicious aroma of that simple meal. As she slipped along the quiet streets, Lizzie pondered the relative requirements of morality and hunger. While she was not one to pay close attention to the vicar's advice on most Sundays, Lizzie had the same moral compass as most girls her age had.

Trained by novels sentimental and gothic, Lizzie knew that rules were rules, but also that rules could bend when circumstances called for it and the heroine were sufficiently in need. If she found herself in a strange country, far from home and without succour, it was perfectly understandable that a heroine might find herself taking part in activities or going places where a young woman might not be expected to wander alone.

Without comprehending it, Lizzie had turned her steps toward the public house from which rose the enchanting scent of baked meats. A more seasoned observer might have guessed that Lizzie already planned to partake of the food one way or another, seeing her singular focus and the way she licked her lips as she slipped along between the sparse buildings in the dawn light. Our heroine herself, however, still sought to find thoughts reconciling her to thievery in the pages of the many novels she had read. It was unfortunate that the tome, which rose to the top of her consciousness happened to be Miss Fielding's instructive volume of school-girls and their governess. Miss Fielding's heroine would not allow such a thing as she was contemplating; no, her self-denying good girls would sooner starve than steal.

The kitchen window was in sight now. Lizzie could feel the marvellous scent assaulting her like an unseen mist. Now she knew how the dogs outside the butcher's shop on the high street felt. It would have been quite undignified to have her tongue hanging out, but Lizzie had never felt quite as hungry as she did then. It was with a start that she recalled her last meal aboard the *Bonny Read*. It gave her a disconcerting moment of confusion. None of it seemed real.

Alice, sweet Alice! Where could she be? Alone! Lost! Worse than that, she could not allow herself to go. Her head seemed to fill with a grey fog and she froze halfway across the alley, uncertain. Just then the rising sun hit her with a shaft of light and Lizzie swallowed as best she could with her dry mouth.

I shall think about this later, Lizzie told herself as resolutely as any of Miss Radcliffe's heroines. She drew in a deep
breath and plunged across the road, intent upon the pies just
beyond the window. She flattened herself against the wall of
the public house and listened for a moment. All seemed quiet
enough and she was about to dart a hand in when a loud
voice startled her.

'Boy! Come here!'

Lizzie—or rather, George, she hastily reminded herself—
turned to see the person who had hallooed her. A striking
young man had just alighted from a tall chestnut hunter, its
flanks wet from exertion. 'I say there, boy! Come take my
horse.'

Lizzie froze. She willed herself to step forward, but for
once her body was not responding to her mind's prompting.
This was precisely the moment she had anticipated, but she
found herself terrified at the idea of impersonating a young
male. Surely frozen terror was worse than the poorest disguise, she scolded herself and made her numb legs take a step
toward the young man who was looking impatiently at her.

'Oh heavens, I forget myself,' the young man continued
smacking himself on the forehead. '*S'il vous plaît, garçon. Mon
cheval*—oh, hang it. Horse? You understand, right? The fiend,
seize it! I can't keep this slippery language in my head for five
minutes at a time.'

It seemed so long since Lizzie had heard one of her countrymen speak that she grinned at once, cheered to feel a little
bit of home so far from it. 'Not to worry, sir,' Lizzie said,
remembering to lower her voice as much as possible, 'I'm an
English lad.'

'Are you then? 'Pon rep, that's fortunate. Give me German
any day, these Romance languages just don't suit my mouth,
I swear. There now, be good to my Darcey here—he's a prime
bit of blood.' The young man patted his horse affection-
ately and Lizzie made sure to praise its fine lines and good
musculature.

'There then, lad, see my horse well-groomed and put away
and there's good coin in it for you—sink me! You're not
a stable lad, are you? Look at those hands. You're not some

rough.' Lizzie became acutely aware of the probing intelligence behind those hazel eyes, belied as it might be by his lazy tone and slipshod canting vocabulary.

'N-n-n-no, sir!' Lizzie stammered, thinking swiftly. 'But I may have to make my living soon enough in that manner. I don't have a feather to fly with, you see—destitute!'

'Heavens!' the young man looked surprised and not a little intrigued. 'Well, lad, take this horse around to the barn, see that the groomsman takes him in hand, then join me inside for a hearty breakfast. I'm fair gut founded and you look like you could do with a bite as well. Then you can tell me what a young gentleman like you is doing without a sixpence to scratch with so far from home.'

'Yes, sir!' Lizzie said and led the chestnut off to the stables behind the inn. A sleepy groom met her there, scratching himself elaborately and yawning as he took the reins from her hand. Lizzie could only imagine that she might have been spared the sight had she been there in a fine frock and her usual accoutrements, but the revelation of the male world was already proving interesting.

Speaking of interesting, Lizzie was deeply curious about her unexpected benefactor. His lively eyes and cultured voice intrigued her. Of course, she reminded herself, her heart belonged entirely to the King of Naples, but the dangerous situations she found herself in of late required her to adapt to the unusual circumstances in all sorts of ways. A short time alone with young gentleman could not possibly prove of any scandalous difficulty, Lizzie assured herself. She was merely curious, that was all, what it was like to speak with a man as a man. A scrape it was, but a most interesting one. Lizzie had every confidence that she would prove to be its master.

Stepping into the cool darkness of the public house, Lizzie was struck once more with the strangeness of being treated like a man. No one rushed forward to lead her to a table, no one greeted her with more than a grunt. It was a bit disconcerting, but less so than the fact that she was about to sit down to eat with a man to whom she was a stranger.

'Here, lad,' that same easy voice called over to Lizzie as she peered into the gloom of the inn. The young gentleman lounged easily at one of the small wooden tables near the far window. The morning sun was just beginning to work its way round to the angle, so when he sat up Lizzie was able to take a second glance at her young patron.

No doubt he'd be considered a swell of the first stare, Lizzie thought as she too cautiously lowered herself into the chair opposite. Tall and a bit thin, but with the swift movements of a man of action. Wiry rather than muscled, but with a strong sense of confidence that belied his lazy drawling manner of speech. It told her something that he was conscious of his effect on people and sought to affect it against him. It bespoke intelligence, Lizzie was certain.

'Name's Tilney, Sidney Tilney. The Manor House, Woolton, Hertfordshire. Pleased to meet you, eh—?' Tilney used this speech to clasp Lizzie's hand in his and shake it vigorously.

Lizzie swallowed and finally stammered out the answer, 'George Bennett, pleased to meet you.' There was an unexpected squeak in her voice as she spoke which she tried to cover up with a cough. 'No family, no home at present, although I hope to make my way back home eventually.'

Tilney's eyes seemed to dance with amusement. 'Must be a bit of a tearaway, Bennett. Penniless and far from home. Too ripe and ready by half, I must say.'

Lizzie smiled, feeling a little puzzled by the high flung cant, but she determined to press on enthusiastically. 'And you, sir? Are you adventuring at present?'

'Now, that's enough of this 'sir' business, Bennett. We're going to be good pals, eh? Now can we get this devil of a landlord to spring us some eggs and decent bread, d'you think?'

Lizzie called over to the landlord in her accurate if somewhat timid French and the man waved his assent and waddled toward the kitchen.

'Damn clever of you to know this French tongue so well,' Tilney said with evident relief. 'I spend half my day trying to remember the right word. Half the time it comes out all German anyway.'

'My gov—er, tutor always insisted on reading Voltaire in

130

the original language. My father thought Voltaire essential to the well-educated young… man,' Lizzie finished lamely.

'Sound like your papa was a task master,' Tilney said, not unkindly.

'He was a very good man,' Lizzie thought with a stab of loss, that melancholy pain of great sorrow that lingers softened only by the joy of one so beloved. She was glad the landlord bustled up just then to lay two trenchers of eggs and sausage before them. To the devil with a genteel appetite, Lizzie thought wildly as her mouth watered, and tucked into the breakfast with breakneck speed.

'Gad, you were hungry!' Tilney said with a chortle before lifting his own fork to eagerly join in the meal. They passed the next few minutes without any kind of talk at all, each enjoying his meal fully.

'Well, Bennett,' Tilney said languorously as he set his fork down at last, 'where were you bound anyhoo?'

Lizzie tried to cover her momentary panic with a bit of a cough, necessary anyway as the sudden constriction of her throat had caused a bit of her egg to go down the wrong way. 'Bound—er, well, nowhere in particular, I suppose,' she said, remembering to keep her voice low and gruff as she might.

'Anyway the wind blows, eh?' Tilney laughed and the hearty sounds rang through the mostly empty inn. The landlord polishing glasses, looked up at the sound, but returned to his own thoughts when there seemed to be no immediate order behind their sounds. 'So is that the adventurous spirit that got you into hot water in the first place?'

Lizzie tried not to betray the confusion she felt, until she remembered that she had suggested calamitous happenings were in her past and responsible for her destitute present. 'Ah, yes…' She swallowed and took a big mouthful of coffee to hide her confusion. Why, oh why, did I think it was going to be easier to pretend to be a man? Lizzie scolded herself firmly. She had chosen her path and now it must be followed until another opportunity came her way. Lizzie tried to maintain her composure. Mr. Tilney must not glean from her appearance just how much she was attempting to hide.

Sure enough, there seemed to be a twinkle of amusement

in his eyes that Lizzie was determined should not undermine her confidence in the charade. However, she was not well prepared for his next conversational sally. Tilney picked up his own cup and used it to gesture lazily at Lizzie. 'Let me guess: was it a press gang? Somehow I can imagine something of the sort, a wild type of lad like you, frequenting taverns on the coast—we all know the typical hellholes.' He winked at Lizzie. 'Too much ale and the poor sort of acquaintances who don't watch out for your best interests, I'll wager.'

A flush of indignation rose from Lizzie's breast, but she checked herself from a hot retort. Why not a press gang? She had read of them in her uncle's newspapers, so she was familiar with the basic narrative. From a press gang she could easily work her way around to the pirates with a convincing ring of familiarity. With the pirates she could stick more closely to her experience and away from the need to tell expansive lies (which were, she admitted, much harder to keep in memory).

'From Southampton, I'm afraid. I was at the Three... ah, Three Crowns when I was pressed. Service on the seas for some days, I couldn't tell you how long. I was rather seasick at first.' Lizzie was loathe to portray herself as prone to seasickness, particularly because she had perhaps some immoderate pride on behalf of her good stomach, but expediency in narrative must overlook such small matters as truth.

Tilney seemed quite enraptured by the tale. 'Heavens, lad. What a confounded havey-cavey business! They were free-traders I suppose, that was a bit of a hobble.'

Lizzie was a bit flummoxed by his outrageous cant, but she forged on as fearlessly as possible. It was with a full knowledge of the effect of her words that she said carelessly, 'Oh, that was nothing compared to the pirates.'

'Pirates! Lawks! You don't mean to say...?'

'Captured.' Lizzie smiled to herself as she bent her head down to the last few bites of bacon. It was a delight to be listened to with such rapt attention. I should not get used to this, she scolded herself, yet she found the pause before resuming her tale even more delicious than the crispy bacon she popped into her mouth.

'Well, blow me down!' Tilney exclaimed with surprised

delight. 'I shan't take another bite until I hear everything. Were they cruel? Were they heartless? Out with it, Bennett! I must hear everything.'

'Aye, aye,' Lizzie answered, savouring the last salty bite of her bacon. 'Don't come a Nastyface with me,' she said, savouring, too, the chance to pelt him with some nautical cant of her own. All that time on board the two ships had trained her ears to a whole new rhythm of speech. 'I don't mind finishing the story, just hold onto your hymnal.' Tilney seemed suitably cowed into expectant silence, nibbling on his oatcakes and sipping tea.

'We had been sailing along that day, not knowing where we were bound—at least I didn't know where we were bound,' Lizzie added with a careless shrug. 'Over the horizon a great black ship appeared, the ominous colours on its mast —'

'You don't mean —'

'Indeed! It was the *Bonny Read* and at the wheel —'

'Not, not—she, herself?'

'Black Ethel Le Beau! She was fearless, ruthless and exceedingly handsome,' Lizzie said, turning her head away as if abashed.

'Oh lad, you didn't fall for her,' Tilney asked with some amazement, as if such a wild woman were no more than a tiger or panther.

'She was extraordinary, quite a force of nature.' Lizzie warmed to the narrative now, caught by the force of her imagination and the rare gift of a rapt listener. 'She commands her men with an iron fist and they cower before her like dogs, though they are the wildest pirates on the seven seas. In moments they had leapt aboard our ship and captured all hands who had not fallen or jumped overboard from sheer terror.'

'But did she not kill all the men?' Tilney's brow wrinkled perplexedly. 'I'm sure I have heard that she cruelly murders the men of the ships she destroys. I must have read it in the *Examiner*.'

Lizzie, to her credit, hesitated not in the slightest. 'She was on the verge of doing so when I pleaded for us —'

'Pleaded?' Tilney said, one eyebrow raised.

'Yes, pleaded,' Lizzie continued like a terrier after a rat, 'pleaded to become a member of her crew, to know the dangers of the wild seas, to live a vagabond life in the sun and to seek out the four corners of the globe. She accepted after we swore our loyalty in a suitably bloody oath.' She was elated to see that Tilney appeared inestimably impressed. 'What a time we had, plundering the seas, capturing, er, wenches and drinking rum all night.'

'I'm envious, lad. You are a nonesuch and no doubt about it. But how came you to this dreary place?'

'A storm at sea,' Lizzie said sadly, feeling the loss of the *Bonny Read* and her dear cousin anew. 'Washed up here and, fearing that the town people might take me for the pirate I had been, I was making my way secretly through the streets when I chanced upon you.'

'A damn fine thing you did,' Tilney said, clapping Lizzie on the arm with a little too much force for that delicate limb. 'We shall be great friends. Would you like to accompany me on my journey to Marseilles? It will not be quite the adventure you have had, Bennett, but I daresay the two of us can get into some scrapes together.'

Lizzie grinned. 'I should be delighted. Particularly if we can rustle up some trouble,' she added, fearing she had not been sufficiently rakish in her response.

'I see great things ahead,' Tilney said, clapping her tender mitt into his larger hands and rubbing it violently.

Chapter Nine

Alice began to think that she had always been in the water, that the life she had once imagined had been only a dream and that she was to spend the rest of her days in a purgatory of tears cried by some heartless giant. The salt waves lapped at her incessantly and she had no energy to rescue the cheese that they had so carefully secreted away for sustenance. Die today, die tomorrow, it made no real difference. It must sometime come, and sooner rather than later.

She longed for a friendly face, particularly when the sun rose to its heights and made her sleepy and desirous of a drink of water. The constant lap of the waves worked like a soothing voice lulling her into a twilight state that was not quite awake and was not quite asleep. Alice thought she heard Lizzie's gentle voice and turned to see only the sunlight rippling off the waves and not even an albatross to be seen. Alice was not entirely certain that she could identify an albatross at sight, but she felt certain that somehow she would know when she had met one.

How to greet an albatross properly, Alice mused. 'Good afternoon, Sir?' or would a more general 'How do you do, Miss?' be a better choice. 'How do you find the seas today?' would undoubtedly be welcome to a weary traveller like herself. Would an albatross have a title? Doctor Albatross seemed unlikely—Lord or Lady Albatross? Duke or Duchess seemed even less likely, Alice had to admit after some thought, as she licked her dry lips and tried very hard to remember why Lizzie had been so adamant about not drinking the water.

It had all been such a hurly-burly. The pirates shouting, the waves slapping the sides of the boat and the thunder making such a pullulating noise that one had very little room for thought in one's head. Lizzie's hurried instructions amid all the confusion had stuck at first with the ironclad weight of a divine hand. Don't drink the seawater, Alice. She had been quite firm.

But she was so thirsty! Surely it could not be wrong to

have a little sip. Alice could not quite work up the interest in eating a piece of cheese and anyway, she feared it might make her thirstier rather than less. It was hard to imagine being thirstier than she was, however. Each lap of the wave seemed to want to jump into her mouth as if to say, 'Drink me! Drink me!' Would it be so wrong to give in?

'It would certainly be most unfortunate,' a calm voice at her elbow said suddenly. Alice turned her head to see a large white bird floating beside her. 'It is really most ungrateful of you to ignore the advice of one much more experienced than you, who only has your best intentions at heart.'

'Dear Albatross,' Alice responded, suddenly feeling so woebegone that she did not hesitate to address the bird so familiarly. 'I know it is wrong, but I feel such a strong compulsion to drink the water, I hardly know how to avoid doing so.'

'You must think of home and your loved ones. What about that handsome Kit Barrington? Does he not delight and distract you?' The Albatross leaned toward Alice expectantly.

Alice let her mind drift back to that wonderful night of dancing. Surely that young man had left a strong impression. 'Did he not have the most beautiful blue eyes? And his hair was glossy and black, curled like a halo around his head. His voice,' Alice paused, eyes closed to remember, 'I believe his voice was strong and confident. Yes, I believe that is so.'

Thus alone on the waves Alice passed another interminable day.

When Alice next awoke it was deep night. She had a moment of confusion waking as she had from a dream. The pull of the bundle tied to her wrist had made her fancy that a large animal had been lashed to her arm and the considerable bulk of it was drawing her along. Alice had a vision of the far north woods as her location—huge trees leaping across her path as the beast charged along ahead of her.

'Stop, stop!' she cried but the creature did not seem to hear her protestations. Instead it only lunged on, dragging the unwilling young woman behind it. I shall never ask mother for a pet again, Alice woefully scolded herself. It was quite enough to have a pony, let alone this horrid beast that seemed bent on tumbling her into the next shire.

'Alice, you must keep hold of it!' Lizzie's calm voice seemed to cut through the murkiness of the forest, and Alice looked around in vain to find her sweet cousin and beg her assistance. 'Alice, the cheese!'

Alice wracked her brains to call to mind the purpose of the cheese. Everything seemed suddenly so confusing. She did seem to recall that the cheese was very important, but for what she was uncertain. Perhaps the animal that pulled her along so forcefully was in fact the cheese! Somehow it seemed right, but Alice found herself doubting the idea almost at once. Could a cheese be a beast? Could a beast be a cheese? The two questions paced back and forth across her head until Alice thought she might rather succumb to the dark shadows of the woods than consider the answers further.

Just as she was ready to give up all hope, a strange beast appeared before her. Was it the brute who had flung her along in its wake? Or was it some other fiend ready to torment her? The whooshing sound of the wind in the trees seemed very much like waves, she realised and as Alice stood looking at the strange creature she could feel them both sway back and forth as if on the seas.

The monster spoke. Monster, Alice thought, was perhaps uncharitable, but she was rather pressed to think of another word for something that appeared so curious in its form. Its head was like a gryphon's yet it had long black locks that seemed somehow familiar. The tiny wings at its back seemed unlikely to bear its weight yet the thing hovered just above the ground with the miniscule flaps. Its large shiny claws, gleaming from its furry paws and scaly feet, suggested a rather fiery temper, but its voice was soothing and kindly, if a bit rough and deep.

> *By the bone-white skull and the sad catbird*
> *You seek to find purchase on the sandy shores;*
> *The strangest stories that you ever heard*
> *Will pale next to tales of Alexander's wars.*

In the next instant, the peculiar beast flapped its wings

with finality and lifted up above the black treetops.

'Come back, come back! I don't understand!' Alice cried and awaked herself to fresh tears on the ink-dark ocean.

Alice awoke to the light of dawn—or so she hoped, for otherwise it was the last light of the day and she did not think she could bear the thought of darkness descending. It's not that it is so disagreeable to be in the dark, Alice thought to herself, fearing to be thought childishly timid, but that creatures might lurk unseen in the water when the sun went down and as we all know, unknown creatures do grow in the murky depths when the sun goes down.

'I should not fear a small tortoise,' Alice mumbled barely audible upon the gentle waves, 'but I should not like to meet a giant turtle. Not in the dark anyway.'

The light grew around her and Alice was comforted by the thought of being able to see dangers that might lurk nearby, although she quailed at the necessity of there being possible intruders near to her in the water.

She had forgotten, too, that the brilliant sun soon made her uncomfortably hot and thirsty. Alice had finally given in and rooted around in her bag to find the cheese secreted away, but she had had a great deal of trouble opening the swollen knots of chord and many tears had been shed (making her even thirstier, alas). As Alice had suspected, the cheese did refresh her somewhat but left her with a burning thirst afterward. It is a considerable tribute to the trust her cousin Lizzie inspired that Alice continued to avoid drinking the tempting liquid in which she was immersed.

By midday, however, Alice had become so delirious from thirst and heat that she was beginning to lose hope and the last shreds of discipline. Surely what was wet could slake her overpowering thirst. 'You must not drink the water, it will make you sick,' Alice repeated through lips so cracked that any one seeing them would feel a stab of empathetic pain. 'You must not drink the slaughter,' Alice continued speaking to a particularly attentive young fish, 'the peas will make it thick.' The fish seemed to wink at her and bow politely. Alice thought she should curtsey in turn, but she was unable to lift her head from the barrel to which she clung still.

'Peas,' Alice repeated, 'Peas are lovely and green.' The fish seemed to nod and encourage further thought, but Alice felt she had perhaps run out of wise words. What was it her father had always said? He had a Latin phrase for every occasion, which he would sternly intone from above the breakfast table, cowering all in the room with his erudite learning.

'Sic semper Saint Dennis,' Alice recommended to the fish.

'Seed o' Nelly,' the fish replied.

'I am far too tired for Latin now,' Alice said politely but firmly. 'I shall lie down now on this soft golden pillow.' Indeed she could feel the warm feather bed beneath her, softly responding to her fingers. 'Wake me for tea,' Alice told the fish, who nodded quickly and silently withdrew. It would not do to miss tea. I am so very thirsty, Alice reminded herself.

'*Quelle surprise, maman*! There's a young lady in the water,' Constance Forward called to her mother.

'Constance, you're supposed to be practicing your French. *En français, s'il vous plaît.*' Mrs. Forward did not look up from the gothic novel in which she was immersed. It was her considered opinion that Mrs. Radcliffe was far more exciting than life could ever be.

'Mama!' young Constance Forward continued with an unbecoming obstinacy, 'I do believe this young woman is in distress. In fact, I might hazard a guess that she is very near to drowning.' She heaved an exasperated sigh and tread her way into the shallow waters near the shore. 'I say, young person,' she said with some bursting curiosity and no little regard for tact, 'are you in distress?'

Alice looked up at the stork who seemed to be addressing her. 'We do not require cauliflower today,' she whispered, her voice a harsh wheeze. 'Come back again next Tuesday.'

'Mama,' Constance repeated with some excitement. 'Do come look. I believe this young woman is delirious. How very exciting!' Constance wondered briefly whether she ought not look for a stick with which she ought to poke the young woman, in the event that what appeared to be a damsel in distress might in fact be some sort of dangerous fish that only masqueraded in that guise. The natural world, Constance knew, was full of creatures with wiles beyond her ken. Or so her father always said, on those rare occasions when it came upon him to say anything at all. 'Mama!'

With a not inconsiderable sigh of disappointment, Mrs. Forward wrenched herself from the account of Montoni's machinations. 'Honestly, Constance, you are worse than an urchin. I do not wish to look at yet another dead fish. I have seen quite enough for a lifetime now and shall turn down the next salmon offered me.'

Mrs. Forward stopped short when she saw her daughter poking at a young woman tied to a barrel with a cautious finger. 'Constance, come away from that at once.' Oh my, the tender-hearted mother thought, shall I have to introduce the always-painful subject of death while on holiday in the south of France? It would quite take the *joie de vivre* out of the afternoon.

'Mama, look!' Constance said eagerly. 'Hasn't she got lovely hair?'

'Dear heart,' her mother said with some severity. 'It is not proper to compliment one when one is not conscious to appreciate it,' she reprimanded her headstrong issue, while nonetheless feeling relief that the steady rise and fall of the young person's form reassured her that death was not, in fact, before them.

'What's your name, dear?' Mrs. Forward asked, bending over the limp figure of Alice. 'Are you on holiday nearby?'

Alice blinked at the sound of a commanding voice, so like her own mother's in timbre, but saw only a giant penguin before her. We must of course blame her delirious state and the choice of a the very dark grey suit and white crinoline petticoats on the part of Mrs. Forward who thought one really ought not go to pieces just because one had gone to the strand.

'No fish, today, please,' Alice therefore beseeched her interlocutor. 'A drink of water is all I ask.' The effort proved too much and Alice sank back down upon her barrel as the gentle waves rolled it back and forth. It was almost as if she were on the *Bonny Read* once more.

'Yet I am not seasick!' Alice thought proudly as her vision greyed into unconsciousness.

'Call some gentlemen down here,' Mrs. Forward said decisively. 'We must rescue the girl!'

'How exciting!' Constance said before running up the sandy shore toward the cluster of gentlemen resting in the shade of a gaily-striped gazebo tent.

Alice was stirred awake by the arrival of a flock of penguins, some of whom seemed to be in nigh-on tropical colours. 'How very curious,' Alice muttered to herself as their nimble hands lifted her from the waves and into the blinding sun. I shall sleep extra late, Alice thought with a firm resolution, and no one shall make me stir until teatime. I simply won't move.

'Bring her into the shade,' the chief penguin ordered with admirable sternness. Alice could tell that this was not a bird with whom one would trifle. The thought was a comforting one and she had vague thoughts of Mrs. Perkins' tough but soothing ways, and her extraordinary blueberry scones.

It seemed odd that Lizzie was not here to remark upon something so odd as penguins. There was a reason she was absent, Alice thought, as gentle hands carried her drenched form to the welcoming shade of a gazebo. Why, Alice realised suddenly, there was that man. The man who wrote letters to her. Who was he? There had been something nearly revealed... but it was so tiring to think. 'Thank you,' she murmured to the stork at her left who leaned toward her with a tall beaker of water.

A small voice in her head said no, the water should not be drunk, though her lips and tongue cried out with fervour for a taste of the forbidden nectar. 'Is it safe?' Alice inquired of the stork, who nodded and urged the glass upon her. Alice hesitated a moment longer, but why should the semi-aquatic bird lie to her? Gratefully she drank the tepid water with relish, tipping the glass upward to drain every drop.

Holding the beaker away from her, Alice was startled to find that there was no stork before her but a very pleasant-looking young gentleman smiling at her. Behind him peeped a handful of others including the matronly woman whom she had mistaken for a penguin. Alice could see the woman did not much resemble the avian species (indeed she

was much larger) but was definitely looking with interest—
the edges of which had been politely concealed—at Alice
where she lay. She looked wonderingly about to find herself
in a beach gazebo surrounded by what could only be English
tourists on holiday.

'How very odd,' Alice said, then recalling her duties as
guest, continued. 'Thank you so much for rescuing me.'

'Our pleasure!' called one young man, who was immediately suppressed by a second, who undoubtedly thought him
a bit too keen. Alice smiled to herself. Surely she was looking anything but her best, yet it was quite agreeable to make
young gentlemen forget their manners.

'Please, where are we?' Alice asked, determined to find a
polite topic with which to begin acquaintance.

'You are not far from La Teste-du-Buch,' the penguin-lady
explained, then asked with what Alice felt sure was unnecessary severity, 'Where is your governess?'

Alice quailed before the sudden interrogation and felt a
whimper coming on. Yet under the clearly admiring gazes
of the young gentlemen, she felt a tad bit more courageous
and—holding the fine example of the pirate queen before
her—Alice worked up the courage to declare, 'I have no governess! I have been kidnapped!'

There was a pleasing gasp from all in attendance and Alice
could sense a crowd growing about the small gazebo. Why
did we not pack any hairbrushes in our little satchels? Alice
thought wistfully. Practical Lizzie would never have made it
a priority, but she should have thought about it herself. With
all the eager eyes upon her, Alice considered how she might
make herself somewhat more presentable in her wet clothes,
which suddenly struck her as shockingly indecent.

The penguin lady seemed to be coming to the same conclusion, perhaps helped along by this sudden declaration,
which appeared to suggest her to be a rather more salacious
young woman than her genteel demeanour might imply.
Alice was quite cheered by the thought.

'Kidnapped? How very odd,' the penguin woman said
with some apparent distaste. 'Constance, do move away from
this alarming child.' She took out a very ornate lorgnette

and peered at Alice through its focusing lens. 'Kidnapped, child? By whom? One cannot afford to be purloined by any common folk!'

Alice drew herself up fully as one helpful young gentleman set a mantle about her shoulders, which was extremely kind if a bit stifling. 'I was aboard the *Bonny Read* with the dread pirate Black Ethel.'

More gasps met that statement and Alice could feel herself expand with a great deal of satisfaction. The mantle, while well intentioned, made her rather warm with the damp heat of the strand.

'May I have a fan with which to cool myself?' Alice asked with admirable meekness, or so it seemed to her. The penguin woman, however, seemed as hard to please as Lizzie with her hard-headed practicality.

'Child, what is your name?'

Alice drew herself up to her full height—well, full as she could manage in the lounging chair in which she sat. 'I am Caroline Alice Mangrove, daughter of Lady Millicent and Lord Grenville Mangrove—the late Lord Grenville,' Alice added with a sombre note of remembrance. 'My friends call me Alice.'

The young gentlemen surrounding her added their immediate hope that they might call her Alice without any unwarranted sense of familiarity. The young woman in question was beginning to feel quite comfortable despite the unaccustomed heat, although a thought was beginning to nag at the back of her mind.

'That sounds reasonably sufficient,' the penguin woman admitted, 'However, it does not reconcile your singular state upon this deserted strand.' She looked rather disapprovingly through the lorgnette and Alice contemplated the fact that it was only possible to look quite that disapproving by means of a lorgnette.

'My dear cousin,' Alice recalled at last, 'she too is missing from the storm that threw us from the pirate's ship. Oh, my Lizzie! I am quite lost without her.' Alice got herself quite suddenly into a swoon and fainted dead away without another thought. It was a wise move.

143

When Alice awoke once more, she found herself far from the glare of the sunny strand and in a rather close, dark room. For a moment she experienced once more that sense of vertigo that often accompanies those enclosed after long exposure to open air, but it quickly passed. After all, Alice had spent most of her life—save for supervised excursions to well-cultivated gardens—within the civilizing presence of carefully tailored walls. The strangeness of the adventurous days that had passed of late slipped away from Alice's well-trained mind—well-trained as far as the habit of her family to ignore as much as possible anything unusual.

Her mother would certainly have approved. Her father, recent events tell us, might well have disapproved, but one feels he would have been disadvantaged by his position beyond this mortal coil.

Alice yawned and stretched, enjoying the peaceful moment of waking. She took the opportunity to look around the room in which she found herself. It was simply but well appointed, from which even she might draw the conclusion that it was a kind of inn that catered to gentle folk of a pleasingly similar rank. There were signs of a maid's careful attention in the toiletries lined up carefully across the bureau. Alice looked down at herself and was pleased to see that she had been dressed in a fresh linen shift.

There was no immediate sign of her own clothes, nor of the satchel, which had been tied to her wrist during the perilous journey. Alice had a momentary pang thinking of her dear Lizzie, but she quelled her discomfort with the thought that somewhere very nearby her cousin was likewise being rescued and they would soon be reunited. It was impossible to imagine otherwise, Alice told herself.

Hopping from the bed, she threw on the pink wrapper she found lying across the chair and pondered what to do next. She could see no way to ring for a servant, which seemed rather odd, but she was saved from further cogitation by the sound of a gentle knock on the door.

'Who is it?' Alice asked with a hopeful tone in her voice.

'Heavens, you're up at last!' Came the lively voice of young Constance Forward, soon followed by her animated face peering around the door. Seeing that Alice had dressed herself suitably, Constance sprang into the room. Alice was soon to discover that this was her normal mode of locomotion.

'Such a long time I have been waiting!' Constance continued, hurriedly taking a seat in the chair and motioning Alice into the window seat. 'I could hardly contain myself. I simply must hear your adventures! Mama said that I should let you rest and I have been hovering about waiting for any sign of life in here, so I could have a good excuse to come see you. How are you?' she concluded with a frank look up and down at Alice, who seemed to meet her expectations of reasonable story-telling health.

Alice, realising that a break had been left in the torrent of words, finally spoke. 'I am feeling much better. I am quite refreshed by the sleep and the care. Where are we, if you don't mind my asking?' Alice added with a shy smile.

'Our hotel, the Belle-something or other. I could never get the hang of French too much, you must teach me,' Constance charged on, oblivious to Alice's tentative cough indicating that she might not be as advanced in her French studies as the young lady assumed. 'Mama thinks my language skills ought to be improving much faster than they are, but there's simply so much to distract one from learning a skill when one is in foreign parts like this. Don't you find it so?'

While a question had been given, Alice found that there was not sufficient pause to make her way into the conversation at this point, and bided her time for the next pause.

'Mama says that I am incorrigible, by which I take her to mean that I am quite extraordinary in a way that seems to often exasperate her—I used to confuse exaggerate with exasperate, but not anymore. My tutor, well, the tutor I had before we came here, the one that was supposed to teach me French, which he didn't at all—he quit after one week and then we only had another two weeks or so before we left, so Mama said we didn't have time to hire another tutor and I would have to learn by immersion, which sounds rather like a teapot of some kind, don't you think? Anyway, my tutor explained the difference between the two. So, do tell me all about the pirates!'

Alice lurched forward, feeling as if a carriage had come to an unexpected halt. But Constance looked at her with such glowing admiration that surely she must be expected to speak. She had just opened her mouth to do so when Constance blurted out, 'It must be so exciting!'

'Indeed,' Alice said with some caution, but seeing her interlocutor poised very much like a spaniel intent on the throwing of a stick, she plunged into the start of her tale. 'We were spirited away from my father's funeral by persons unknown,' Alice began, taking on a breathless tone of her own.

It was simply too much for Constance, who immediately broke in with contrasting expressions of sympathy and excitement. 'Oh, you poor, sweet thing! Bereft of a father's love. I can't imagine how awful that must be, but then how thrilling to have been snatched away! Was it highwaymen? I have been in raptures since reading Rookwood; it must be so frightening and wonderful when they looked in with their masks and revolvers!'

Alice coughed and the torrent of words passed into a remembrance of respectful silence. 'It was not highwaymen,' Alice said, then reflected, 'that we could see. In fact we could see nothing at all of our captors for a long time.'

'How—' Constance began, then hastily covered her mouth, sitting back from the edge of her chair with a barely suppressed thrill, but compliant once more to be listener.

'We saw only rough servants who spoke cruelly to us and threatened us with knives, sabres and pistols,' Alice added, hoping that she was not distorting the memory too much, although one ought to be able to lend a story details of a pleasing nature. Already the conventions of novels seemed to have a greater influence over memory than Alice expected.

'Captive in our carriage, we were whisked along in a generally southern direction,' Alice said, immediately sensing the poor quality of her narrative. How do novelists keep their stories so compelling? she thought crossly. Constance was sure to interrupt her if she did not captivate her wandering attention quickly. Think! Alice turned her suddenly swift thoughts to Mrs. Radcliffe. What would she do?

'Our terror was supreme,' Alice continued with sudden

enthusiasm. 'We quaked considerably and started at each cruel word. How horrid to be addressed without civility, without gentility.' Alice choked on her own emotions and saw that Constance's eyes shone with similarly distilled and suppressed horror.

'If it had not been for my brave cousin,' Alice continued, pursuing a sudden inspiration, 'I should have simply fainted away at once.'

'How fortunate to have such a strong companion,' Constance burst forward, wringing her new friend's hand vigorously, but containing herself to that comment alone for the moment.

'Lizzie, dear Lizzie!' Alice said with genuine feelings, stirred at last by the inspiring account of her own adventures and her sympathetic audience. 'When shall I see her again? What has become of her? How cruel the wild sea is to a little girl like I,' Alice wept, overcome by her own suffering and a momentary lapse in grammar.

'Oh, poor child! If only we had rescued you both,' Constance joined her weeping, arm in arm like sisters.

It was thus in a sodden heap that Mrs. Forward discovered the girls, much to her dismay. Although this Alice seemed to be a genteel young girl of substantial birth, clearly she was not going to be a calming influence on her daughter. More's the pity, she muttered under her breath, but with her usual vigour, she roused the girls at once to more productive activities. 'It is time for luncheon. Do dress at once, Miss Mangrove!'

Chastened by the glowering presence of Mrs. Forward, Alice and Constance meekly complied with her orders. Alice dressed and Constance more or less silently accompanied her, which is to say the occasional interjection escaped along the lines of 'my goodness!' or 'oh mumbles!' while Alice felt a festering sense of resentment stir in her breast.

In vain, she tried to quash the feelings that, she was certain, both Lizzie and her mother would have disapproved of most vehemently. Alice thought of the debt owed to the kindly Mrs. Forward, who had not only rescued her from the sea waves and certain chill (well, eventually even the lovely strand might have given her a chill from those wet clothes), but also from the possibility (admittedly slim at that point) of a watery death.

Then she remembered how quickly the stern woman had shooed away the very nice circle of admiring young men who had done the requisite work of lifting her sodden form from the water while Mrs. Forward looked disapprovingly through her lorgnette.

Alice could sense her own lips taking on a rather stern expression of displeasure at the thought.

'Constance, my dear,' Alice said, holding out her sleeve to be buttoned by the fawning girl. 'Is your mother always so disagreeable?'

Constance nodded, the tip of her tongue sticking out at the corner of her mouth as evidence of her intense concentration upon the task before her. While Constance might never be known as one of the great minds of the century (or of any other century for that matter), she did have a wonderful sense of dedication to any simple task that she found herself capable of completing, generally greeting the accomplishment with a flourishing squeal of delight—as she did just then, having succeeded in buttoning Alice's cuff after several fruitless attempts. 'Mama is quite determined than I shall not be brought up with any vulgar traits or with any undue excitement of any kind.'

Alice's stern expression deepened. While her own mother might agree with such sentiments, Alice could not help feeling that there was something very middle class about such worries. Unconsciously, she had picked up that term from her dear cousin, but had never had a likely object upon who to pronounce such shortcomings.

Alice's rather livelier than expected life in recent days also contributed to her rather flashy assessment of the failures of the Forward household. She was now inclined toward a dangerous amount of pleasure and confidence. 'Lawks!' she therefore pronounced, revelling in the delighted gasp of her new friend. 'I live for excitement, my devoted Constance. I shall not let anyone stand in my way!'

Constance could hardly contain her amazement. In fact, she stared open-mouthed at Alice's cool confidence. 'Alice!

My…heavens,' she managed to squeak, nearly fainting away with her own daring. 'Whatever will you do?'

'What will we do?' Alice corrected her, taking her gloves in hand with a bold gesture. 'I do not plan to meekly obey.'

'Do you not?'

'Well,' Alice said with some uncharacteristic thoughtfulness, 'Not once I have had my luncheon.'

It was, Constance thought, the most brilliant thing she had ever heard.

'Mama thinks we should always take some air after eating,' Constance said with an air of uncertainty, for she half-feared, half-hoped that Alice would renew the rebellious proclamations she had made prior to their very fine luncheon of braised scallops and yummy red peppers. Constance was still in a dither of excitement about red peppers, if that was any indication of her state of mind. Heretofore having only seen green peppers, she was already in raptures about the wonders of the French experience. Her mother, naturally enough, considered this a bad sign of a potentially libertine nature and decided that henceforth luncheons would need to prove more instructively bland.

None of this had registered with Alice, however, for her thoughts throughout the luncheon had been a slightly petulant study of the same great lady's profile. Who is Mrs. Forward, Alice mused with a resentment tinged slightly by the red peppers' sweetness, to command me? I have sailed the seven seas with pirates, Alice told herself with a shake, who am I to fear this woman? Faithful readers, of course, will recognise that here Alice is fibbing slightly, or at the very least exaggerating, as she had sailed but one sea and that not for long. Perhaps Alice imagined the seas to be rather smaller than they are, believing that she had travelled more than her share. However, it would be difficult—even for a rather poor student of geography, which certainly Alice was—to imagine there were very many seas between England and France. One can only assume that truth had fallen by the wayside for this headstrong young woman, along with gratitude, geography and propriety.

I do not need to do as I am told, Alice continued, her

149

words sounding a little prickly even in her own head, as if in response to some perceived criticism, although all was silent as far as she could tell. By silent one must understand that there was a constant chatter on the behalf of the young Miss Forward throughout the meal, punctuated by the occasional reproving murmur from her mother. It was a noisy sort of silence, but one for which no audience was required nor attention from the participants.

I shall do as I please. She is not my mother, Alice said with decision. Not aloud of course, but she felt all the better for voicing the thought firmly in her head. It was as good as saying it out loud without the inconvenience of having to answer for one's words. When Mrs. Forward announced the required after-luncheon airing, Alice knew she must seize upon the opportunity. Her smile would have seemed crafty and mysterious to a careful reader of a thrilling novel, Alice was certain, then drew her mouth down suddenly in fear of discovery. Must not give away the plan.

Although there was not yet a plan to give away, Alice felt a decided thrill of excitement that she might be hatching a scheme. Now that they were out of sight of the inn, Alice ventured a glance at her companion, whose open face registered only the simple pleasure of walking with her new companion in the cheery seaside sunshine.

'Constance,' Alice said with sudden decision, 'would you like to have an adventure?'

Constance beamed. 'Yes, please!'

'Then we shall,' Alice said with all the confidence of a well-travelled young explorer.

'Where shall we go?' Constance asked, clapping her hands in delight.

'Er,' Alice said somewhat deflating her own burgeoning self-importance, 'I—I don't know.'

It was the crushed hopefulness of young Miss Forward that spurred Alice on to some kind of inspiration. She thought very hard about the options before them. It was a characteristically unfamiliar activity for Alice, but applying herself assiduously to the task, she soon found that indeed an idea appeared. 'We shall go to the strand and talk to young men unchaperoned,' she announced with decision.

Constance gasped. Alice revelled in her delicious sense of alarm. It was indeed a daring thought. Although the two of them traveling together stood little likelihood of arousing much of any talk amongst the easy-going French or even the scattered English tourists, Mrs. Forward would certainly be scandalised beyond all composure.

That was a thought worthy of savouring, Alice told herself with some satisfaction.

Constance reacted with a glee she found hard to contain. It manifested in her jumping up and down, clapping her hands together and pressing her lips together to suppress a squeal of delight. 'Oh, my, do you think we should—oh, we must! Won't mother—do you think the gentlemen will speak to us? I couldn't bear it if they did not speak to us!' Constance had gone from delight to terror in no time at all. All the bright colour evoked by the delighted hijinks had drained away to a pale wanness.

Alice, however, was confident. 'We shall even dare to speak first. Being gentlemen, they shall have to speak to us.'

Constance seemed convinced by this logic and flew at Alice to give her a rough embrace. 'You are simply the most amazing young woman, dear Miss Mangrove.'

Unaccustomed to this level of hero worship, Alice experienced an untoward dizziness of inflated self-esteem. It was bound to propel them into a properly indecorous adventure. That realisation caused Alice to briefly consider swooning with excitement. However, she gathered that firstly, Constance would not be of much use in the case of an emergency, but secondly, that finding herself in the newfound position of a leader, Alice sensed that it was necessary to maintain a sense of decorum.

Instead, Alice threw back her bonnet and let her luxuriant curls bounce in the sunlight. Constance gasped once more, then grinning a little too much like a lunatic Lizzie would have surely noted, threw back her bonnet as well. Unlike Alice, she was not able to keep from looking guiltily about the street for any observers. No one seemed to notice this bold move, however, so the girls giggled delightedly, linked arms and strode together down the high street in the direction of the strand.

Chapter Ten

'Lawks!' Mr. Tilney exclaimed for the umpteenth time. 'Such adventures you had with the pirates. I should never have guessed a slight lad such as you to have had the stomach for such goings on.'

'Indeed,' Lizzie said with some umbrage on behalf of her seized alter ego George Bennett, though she tried to contain her nettled tone. 'The size of the man is seldom any indication of character. I have known great men who quailed at the sight of a tiny mouse.'

'Now, now, don't kick up a fuss, Bennett. It's no reflection on a fine lad as yourself to say that one finds amazement in all you have accomplished at such a tender age. Duly impressed, that I am.'

Lizzie felt herself flush with pride, which her lively bay gelding seemed to sense and picked up his gait a little. They were riding along the eastward road and it was a gorgeous day, perfect for riding in that it was not too hot and the cool breeze from the sea was at their backs. It seemed ages since Lizzie had been on horseback—how strange an effect kidnapping had on one's life!

This was the best thing to happen to her in quite some time. While it did not make up for being orphaned from parents she genuinely loved, it was an improvement even on her secret romance, which, while quite thrilling to contemplate, remained a secret unshared, and thus, less than fully exhilarating (and in the genuine presence of a lively soul like Tilney, doubly so). There was the inconvenience and horror of the kidnapping itself, of course, but at this moment, Lizzie would not have traded the sequence of events for the world. Their life on board Black Ethel's ship was certainly extraordinary enough, but here she found herself on the road to Italy, and while her bay was not quite the fine stepper that Tilney's chestnut Darcey was, he was certainly a strong mount and a joy to bridle.

Tilney himself was a bit of a puzzle. He maintained such

an air of casual decadence with his perpetual cant and his lazy drawl, but those bewitching hazel eyes had a curious habit of probing deftly while his mouth produced an indolent smile. Lizzie knew she had to be on her guard with such a clever clogs. She even suspected once or twice that he had seen through her disguise, but as his behaviour betrayed nothing of the sort, she decided that it must be a mistaken worry on her part. It was not so difficult after all, masquerading as a man. She chuckled to herself to think that things would be entirely different in the opposite direction—what man could master the intricacies of the life of the fairer sex, where myriad strictures demanded an even greater plethora of subterfuges to circumnavigate their bindings. Lizzie chuckled to herself to think with admiration of the innumerable creativities of women.

'What are you thinking about, Bennett, that gives you such a saucy grin?' Tinley asked, reining in his chestnut momentarily.

'Women,' Lizzie said, the ambiguity of her thoughts and Tilney's appreciation merging in an unexpected frisson.

'Ah, Bennett, will you never learn?' The normally sunny disposition of her partner clouded briefly, Lizzie noticed. 'Women are treacherous, untruthful and deceiving. You should learn better and be forewarned.'

Lizzie gazed with frank curiosity at her companion. 'Mr. Tilney —' she began, but with an audible grumble from that target, remembered that she was not to address her pal so formally. 'Sorry, Tilney, just used to the demands of pirates. But as Black Ethel herself would no doubt argue, women are no more inclined naturally to vice than men.'

'You seem to have unusually strong feelings on the subject, Bennett,' Tilney said at last with a hearteningly sober tone.

'When you have voyaged with a pirate queen,' Lizzie said thoughtfully, 'you learn a lot about the worst of the lives of women.'

Tilney regarded Lizzie's comment for some time in silence, before admitting, 'Undoubtedly, it must take a great deal to drive a woman into piracy, Bennett.' He let his chestnut trot on for a few steps before continuing, 'But I think most gels might come by it naturally.'

Lizzie tried to cover her growing sense of irritation. 'If you had heard her story, Tilney, you would no doubt be moved to tears—even with your hard heart.'

'Oh I don't doubt it, old boy. Just the same, you take the average skirt flirter and you'll find the hardened heart of a criminal.'

Although he affected the same careless even tone, Lizzie could see in Tilney's bearing a growing sense of glowering ill humour. While she remained rankled by his comments on her sex in general, Lizzie was determined to find the root of this unfair prejudice. Surely he must not be too fixed in his opinion at such a young age. 'I think you should spill, Tilney. What unconscionable petticoat princess has tweaked your nose?'

'Oh, it's a boring old story,' Tilney muttered. 'The same you'd hear from a hundred others.' Nonetheless, his mood seemed to darken further and Lizzie found herself wanting to help her benefactor relieve the burden in his breast.

'Go on then, Tilney. It's a long ride and I'm sure it would help you to share this burden with one uniquely qualified to understand.'

Tilney laughed and sounded a little more like himself. 'Damn, Bennett! What makes a jackanapes like you at all qualified to understand the problems women cause?'

Lizzie grinned. 'Black Ethel took me under her wing in a way. Gave me some insight into the way their minds work. She may be an extraordinary example of one, but she's a woman for all of that.'

They rode along in silence for a few steps while Tilney seemed to turn the matter over in his mind. The fields beside them perked up in the golden light of the morning and the calls of doves came from the nearby copse. It was a lovely day.

'There was a girl,' Tilney said quietly at last. 'She was lovely as a summer's day, long golden hair, delicate hands and the finest of family graces.' Lizzie could not help thinking of her cousin Alice and bridling at the thought that golden locks were any indication of the qualities of a young woman, but kept her tongue in check. 'She promised to make me the happiest of men, Bennett, and then she threw me over for a long-limbed cad with a bigger fortune and better connections.'

'A not uncommon story,' Lizzie began, 'but —'

'A very common story if you ask me,' Tilney said with surprising fury.

'But one that can be told from either side,' Lizzie continued evenly. 'Why did you choose her in the first place but for her decorative beauty and family connections?'

Tilney did not respond at first, his clouded face staring fixedly at the ground. 'I was dizzy about her, Bennett. Wrote her poetry and all that malarkey. I was smitten.'

'But what did you know of her beyond polite agreeableness, good connections and long golden locks?' Lizzie persisted. 'You probably gave more thought to the cut of your waistcoat than you did to her suitability as your life's companion.'

Tilney looked at Lizzie with some annoyance. 'She was lovely, well-bred and perfect.'

'Did she wake early or late? Did she want to hear news from abroad or only from the local village? Did she read? Did she enjoy architecture? What did you really know of her character and spirit?'

Tilney pulled up short causing Darcey to snort with surprise. 'She was my intended, not a candidate for Oxford,' he said somewhat brusquely.

'Then I am not surprised she threw you over,' Lizzie said with a harsh laugh. 'You know your horse better than you knew her. Why do men treat women as if they were children?'

'I suppose they haven't had the benefit of piratical experience,' Tilney said, his tone returning to his relaxed drawl once more, but his eyes continued to look rather more fiery than usual.

Lizzie was grateful when the need for a luncheon became apparent and the two reined in a small country inn. The ride all morning had been noted for Tilney's unusual silence and lack of good humour. He appeared to be deep in thought and answered Lizzie's few conversational gambits with little more than a grunt.

They handed over their reins to the groomsmen and stepped into the cool comfort of the inn. It was a pleasant place of thick oak posts and lace-curtained windows. The landlord led the two of them to a small table in the corner from which they might glimpse the other folk filling the dining room that day.

There were two young ladies sitting quietly with an older woman, perhaps their mother. To the right, an elderly pair of men sat munching cheese and bread without a word to one another. A table of four held a lively pair of couples, chatting with animation and laughing frequently at one another's comments. It gave the room a fond cheery feel, Lizzie thought.

Tilney's thoughts clearly headed in another direction as he reflected misanthropically on the folks gathered there. 'Honestly, Bennett, look around us. What a sad reflection of the horrors of modern life.'

'Lud, Tilney. What are you talking about? I see nothing but a pleasant gathering of friendly folk. What could be cheerier?'

'Bennett, you are far too kind and trusting,' Tilney snorted. 'You look, but you do not see.'

'For instance?'

Tilney nodded his head toward the table with the two young women and their guardian. 'What does that table suggest to you?'

'Two young ladies, friends or sisters, under the careful watch of their mother or some such relative,' Lizzie said feeling a little puzzled by the hint of venom in his tone.

'Not at all,' Tilney said, a coldness creeping into his voice. 'Two young jackdaws in training with a senior member for advice on the craft.'

Lizzie laughed, a little too soprano at first, coughing to deepen it to a contralto. 'Tilney, you can't be serious. They look like nice country girls and their mother, or chaperone, looks kindly if dull.'

'Bennett,' Tilney chided with a shadow of his usual spirit, 'you ignore the details. Every aspect of their simple frocks has been designed to tempt the masculine gaze, to leave us besot-

157

ted with their beauty. They are, in short, snares. Hook our eyes and our purses are not far behind.'

'Ah, disappointed love has ruined your perspective, my friend. Do you not think girls dress to please themselves? They do tend to delight in the little touches of silk and lace that we often ignore. Who gives a hang about types of muslin but women? Is none of it for their own pleasure?'

Tilney waved away the suggestion. 'Snares for us, Bennett, and nothing more. We shall end up like those two bro-ken-hearted old men over there,' indicating the two elder gentlemen.

'Now, now,' Lizzie said, stranded somewhere between exasperation and amusement, 'Who's to say they're bro-ken-hearted? Perhaps they are merely enjoying the comfort of an understanding silence. They have known each other for decades and are perfectly content to share the fellowship of happy memories.'

'You are far too optimistic,' Tilney grumbled, reaching for a piece of bread, which he buttered with far too much force.

After a time, Tilney's light-hearted manner revived. 'Well, Bennett, perhaps you're right. Perhaps I do not give women enough credit. They're not all barques of frailty, I suppose.'

'Quite right,' Lizzie responded as she tucked into the fine country stew the landlord set before them. 'While women tend to be raised without a thought for their brains, there are many who work to develop innate abilities to the best of their circumstances.'

Tilney laughed and brandished his spoon at his friend. 'You seem to have an inordinate interest in some clever lass. Fess up, Bennett! Your colouring up gives you away.'

Lizzie had indeed blushed at the remark, fearing that Tilney might get too close to the truth of her disguise. 'Not at all, Tilney. I was merely thinking of a, erm, distant cousin of mine, I knew well in childhood. She corresponded in three languages, kept a collection of unusual insects catalogued and labelled carefully, and was seldom to be found without a book of some kind near to hand.'

'Ha!' Tilney said as if he were about to declare checkmate. 'And tell me, is she not in fact an old maid, ignored by all men, as dry and dreary as a gnarled wych-elm.'

'Not at all! She has long been considered a rather handsome woman.'

'But not married, surely,' Tilney said with finality, taking a healthy bite of bread as if to seal the fate of this unknown woman.

'Not yet, although,' Lizzie swallowed, afraid to reveal the secret so long contained, 'Although she is engaged to—a rather prestigious person in another country.' The secret confessed but still obscured left Lizzie with a pleasant feeling of both revelation and smug secrecy.

However, Tilney greeted this disclosure with a crow of laughter. 'Of course! Some foreigner who's never laid eyes on her—it's the only possibility. No Englishman will settle for such a homely bookworm.'

Lizzie tried not to show how nettled she had become, although Tilney's dismissive words struck very close to her heart. It was true the King of Naples had never laid eyes upon her, although she believed the pencil sketch she had sent to him—although from her most flattering angle—was a reasonably accurate depiction of her modest appearance. Lizzie knew she was not a beauty like Alice or her mother, but there was certain nothing hideous about her looks, either.

But Tilney could not know that George was really Lizzie, and a young man like George should not be quite so eager to support the vanity of a mere cousin. Be a man, Lizzie scolded herself—bluster, brag and lie as we imagine them to do when they are out of our sight.

"Pon rep, Tilney, I suppose you're right. You're the experienced one after all with the civilised side of womankind. I do well enough with the rougher sort. Tell me, how would you inveigle your way into the eyes of some young lass being such a notoriously picksome sort—say, those two country girls over there?'

'Oh, a conversation like that will require fortification,' Tilney drawled. Gesturing to the landlord, he called for wine, which made Lizzie worry a bit. Lord Mangrove did not approve of wine being wasted on young people without an educated palate, as he always said, so her experiences with the stuff were limited.

Nonetheless, she determined to press on. 'Go on then, Tilney. I'm curious to know how you work your way around a tempting armful.'

Tilney grinned. 'Well, the two before us hardly qualify, but I'll tell you the secret to getting on with the petticoats without trotting too hard.' He thrust a tumbler of wine at Lizzie with a laugh.

Oh dear, Lizzie thought and gulped a mouthful down.

Compared to the wine they had drunk with Black Ethel, this *vin ordinaire* seemed far rougher stuff, Lizzie thought to herself, not venturing to voice her opinion which Tilney would no doubt disparage with good natured jesting. So she was surprised to hear him comment upon that very quality.

'Palatable, but not much more. Eh, Bennett?' Tilney said, his head held at a speculative angle. 'In town this would be beneath my touch, but as we're in the country proper, I guess it will do.' He poured a little more into each of their tumblers and grinned at Lizzie. 'We'll get a little bosky and share the secrets of our amours.'

'Oh, that wouldn't really be sporting, now would it? I only asked for your advice in the broadest general terms, Tilney. No need to ramble through your conquests.'

Tilney laughed. 'No stories of your calf-loves, then? All right, I will share my secrets for success with the descendants of Aphrodite. Listen and learn, Bennett, and you will be a success with the pinkest of the pink when you return to our native land.'

'Lawks, man, on with your advice then,' Lizzie said, feeling emboldened by the wine's warm glow.

'The key,' Tilney said with a knowing look, 'is to flatter them of course.'

'Well, yes, that works with everyone, men included,' Lizzie interrupted.

'Ah, but you have to flatter women differently,' Tilney insisted. 'Men like to have their good qualities noticed. Girls on the other hand, need to have their imaginations awakened. Now listen first,' Tilney said, noticing Lizzie's impatient gesture. 'I know whereof I speak.'

160

'A woman needs to have a picture painted of the vision she forms in your mind. She can't bear to be simply what she is—lovely as that might be. Most of 'em have read far too many novels so they get these notions of dramatic scenes and romantic ideals. They want to be heroines, not just women, so you have to convince them that they are—at least to you.'

'I'm sure there are many sensible women whose imaginations have not been corrupted by the reading of novels,' Lizzie retorted a shade too vehemently, swigging a little more wine from her tumbler.

Tilney chuckled. 'Sensible women are no fun to flirt with.'

Lizzie flushed, feeling again as if this sharpish young man had somehow seen through her charade. 'I suppose that's true enough. Well, how would you spin such a web of deceit before a docile young maiden of the realm?'

'Oh, it needn't be all lies. After all, the truth is much easier to remember.' Tilney laughed a bit too heartily for such a slim joke, but poured more wine into his glass. 'You must praise every limb of her frame with excessive enthusiasm —'

'My mistress's eyes are nothing like the sun,' Lizzie intoned bitterly as she stared into her glass.

'Oh, yes, poetry is always good—provided it flatters,' Tilney said with a strange look at his drinking partner. 'Poetry sufficiently obscure might be passed off as one's own.'

'Then I suppose it helps to woo an ignorant girl.'

Tilney smiled but the expression stopped short of convincing. 'As the sweet sweat of roses in a still,' he intoned with a sonorous tone, 'As that which from chafed musk cat's pores doth trill, / As the almighty balm of th' early east, / Such are the sweat drops of my mistress' breast.'

'A girl might well be bewitched by your recitation,' Lizzie admitted, washing down a little more red, 'provided she is not scandalized by your choice of poets. Is Donne really fit for a gentle woman's ears?'

'What? A churchman of the first order, a loving husband —'

'And once a libertine who thought a true woman as rare as a falling star.' Lizzie looked frankly at her companion, wondering again what really lay beneath his too smooth exterior.

'He was onto something there,' Tilney said, staring off into the distance. 'Although he seemed to repent once he found such a gem.'

'Is it the nature of all libertines to repent at last?' Lizzie was hardly aware of speaking her thoughts aloud, but it did not matter, as Tilney appeared not to have heard.

Tilney seemed to awake from his momentary reverie, hastening to fill Lizzie's glass, which alarmed her. She could tell the effects of the wine were already creeping into her thoughts and it would take some effort to control them.

To distract him, she pressed for further information. 'What else, pray tell, do you do to win the hearts of the delicate ones?'

Tilney sighed. 'I have not been much of mood to do so lately, Bennett.'

'Now, now,' Lizzie said, trying to keep the arch tone out of her voice, although the roguish effect of the wine inclined her toward that outlook. 'You can't let one bad experience colour your actions, Tilney. Show a little spark.'

Tilney chuckled and gargled a little more wine. 'You're right, I suppose. But mind my words, young George, stay away from women with dimples. Dimples are a sure sign of a sensuous nature and a fickle heart.'

'What about men with dimples?' Lizzie said, taking care not to smile herself. 'For I noticed just now when you laughed that you have dimples yourself.'

Tilney looked rather sharply at her, one brow arched high. For a moment, Lizzie feared that she had gone too far, but then the young man at last burst into laughter that was not without an edge of bitterness. 'I suppose what is true of the goose must be likewise true of the gander. Damn, Bennett, but you're too clever by half. I shall have to watch myself around you.'

Lizzie felt a giggle coming on and was at great pains to stifle it. Oh dear, she thought, this must be a consequence of the wine. I must get Tilney talking and distracted. She reached across to fill his glass with the last of the bottle. Better him than me, Lizzie thought. 'Never mind that, Tilney, you were on to the next sure-fire trick in your bag. Tell on, I need educating in the habits of fine women.'

'Oh, let us not speak of women any more,' Tilney said, the animation draining away from his face. 'Let us speak of horses, trousers, banking schemes—anything but women. I am through with women for the nonce.' Tilney threw back the last of the wine and gestured for the landlord. Lizzie quailed at the thought that he might order more wine, but Tilney merely settled the bill and stood quickly to go.

Lizzie stood, too, and immediately felt how the wine had nudged her equilibrium off course. Swaying a little, she gripped the edge of the table and tried not to trip over her chair. Fortunately Tilney had not noticed her inebriation as he was already striding toward the door with his deliberate steps. Lizzie grabbed the last slice of bread to nibble as she followed tipsily in his wake. This will be an interesting ride, Lizzie thought.

As she passed by the table with the two young women, one surreptitiously caught her eye and smiled winningly. Lizzie smiled before she apprehended they were flirting at her, and hurried even more quickly for the door.

Lizzie felt her feet stumble with unaccustomed awkwardness, as if they were very remote from her instead of attached to the ends of her legs. 'Oh, mumbles,' thought Lizzie, 'I must be foxed!' It was a thought equally frightening and exhilarating. While she had seen Lord Mangrove stagger on occasion from an exquisite over-indulgence in West Indian rum, she had never imagined experiencing the effects herself. I must remember it all precisely and write it in a letter, Lizzie thought. To the King of Naples, she added quickly, then immediately knew that she could do no such thing.

This experience, although fascinating, could not have come at a more precarious time, for she needed to maintain the easy masquerade as George that she had taken up as well as concentrate on guiding her horse, for Mr. Tilney was already aboard Darcey and looking to be quite high in dudgeon, impatient to be on his way. Darcey had picked up his mood and stamped his feet with an excess of vital energy.

Lizzie's horse showed signs of the same restiveness and she had to hop helplessly on one foot as the pony danced around her, trying in vain to spring aboard the saddle. It was to her shamefaced embarrassment that the groom finally had to take a hand and help her up. She had no more than lighted in the saddle when Tilney took off at a sharp clip and Lizzie was forced to follow.

Although she wanted very much to go more slowly — and thought the sudden speed a less than prudent idea immediately after a meal and particularly when the horses were cold — Lizzie held her tongue and bounced along in Tilney's wake as well as she might, although the sloshing of the plonkplunk in her stomach soon proved discomforting.

I shall never drink again, Lizzie promised herself foolishly, particularly if I know that vigorous exercise on horseback will follow fast upon such indulgence. Her head had begun to ache unaccountably badly and she could feel a glow of perspiration exude from her forehead. The swiftly tilting scenery went past with a nacreous green glow.

All at once a sound rang out which Lizzie recognised from recent events to be the sound of pistol shot. Tilney's head whipped around in the direction from which the shot seemed to come, reining Darcey in slightly, but the lively chestnut was unwilling to stop altogether, shying coltishly away to the left while Tilney craned his neck left, a hand raised to shade his eyes.

Coming upon the pair so quickly and with the lag of liquor in her blood, Lizzie failed to rein in sufficiently, her horse bumping into Darcey, who reared and snorted loudly. Her more timid mount shied, cowering from Tilney's stepper. At that moment another shot rang out, rather close to the two riders and Lizzie's horse took this as sure sign of danger and bolted wildly, ignoring Lizzie's heartfelt cry of 'Stop! Stop!'

The rapid staccato tattoo of her mount's hooves echoed in Lizzie's ears as she pulled in vain at the reins. The shots had spooked him, though, and there seemed to be little hope of stopping him until his panic subsided. She could hear Tilney's hoof beats behind her, starting belated pursuit, but Lizzie could not help but fear that his arrival would come too late.

She cursed herself for the over-consumption of wine at luncheon. Had she been wiser, she would not have given in to Tilney's imprecations and would have been more alert — and likely far less woozy than she was beginning to feel just then. The rapid pace, normally a bracing one for that adventuresome rider, was taking a toll on her less-than-wholly settled stomach and knocking her slightly tipsy brain even further off kilter.

'Oh, mumbles,' Lizzie muttered, still pulling impotently at the reins, 'I shall fall off surely.' It was not a fate to be anticipated with any glee.

The track along which the runaway horse carried her was growing wilder. Somehow they had left the wide path that led from the public house and headed off into a more thickly forested area. Lizzie was alarmed to find the sound of shots repeated and at closer range. That some kind of danger lurked in the woods was certain, but it was a little difficult to think about it too much while she was desperately attempting to maintain her seat upon the horse. She cursed her poor training, cursed the copious wine and cursed her relative unfamiliarity with trousers.

Trousers were a revelation, indeed, she had discovered, but they did not immediately replace the expectations of a lifetime spent in skirts. Every thing, every motion seemed to take on a new shape. Who knew inexpressibles could have so profound an impact?

Her head filled with a soft susurration that promised to cloud out all logical process. Lizzie fought desperately against its force, but saw that her efforts were failing. I shall never be able to live with myself, Lizzie thought, if I faint away like some trifling girl. While a more dispassionate reader might find such a thing eminently forgivable given the particular circumstances, Lizzie was known for her unflaggingly harsh opinions when it came to her own conduct (for that matter, she was known to be a tad harsh when it came to the conduct of others as well, but we shall leave that by the side at present).

Just as she felt the agonizing slip into the murky state of unconsciousness, Lizzie sensed the light improving as the horse bolted into a clearing where a small number of men stood, pistols drawn and appearing to be just as surprised by her presence as she was by theirs. Even the runaway seemed to evince a puzzled air, for his steps surely slowed, allowing in that instant a breathless Mr. Tilney to dash up and make a grab for Lizzie's reins just as she slipped sideways in her saddle.

'So very sorry,' Lizzie muttered as she fell across Tilney's lap.

Lizzie could not have been unconscious for more than a moment or two before she awoke. She was somewhat flustered to find herself sprawled across Mr. Tilney's lap and struggled to rise from the indecorous position.

'Easy now,' came Tilney's steady reply. Did she only imagine it, or was there a hint of humour in his words? Lizzie did not hesitate, however, regaining her unsteady feet beside Darcey, who seemed unruffled by the sudden appearance of a second rider, although he was sweating from the exertion of their race.

Her own mount circled skittishly, still unnerved by the sudden surprise and the wild ride. Lizzie shook her head to clear it and took a step away from Tilney. Looking up she saw that he was now looking off in the distance, a view blocked from her by Darcey. His face looked suddenly grave. Lizzie bent down and peered under the horse's neck in the same direction.

Across the clearing was a group of men. Lizzie was quick to grasp what Tilney no doubt did — the men were engaged in a duel. The duellists stood some yards apart, surrounded by what were surely their seconds (or so Lizzie reckoned from her reading). There was a singular delight in seeing before her something she had read about so many times. Just as the first glimpse of the *Bonny Read* in full sail had filled her heart with a singing joy, the romantic sight of the battling rivals gave Lizzie a certain satisfaction and brought a smile to her lips. The smile faded when she beheld Tilney's expression. 'A duel,' she ventured to whisper toward him.

Tilney glanced down but his grimness remained. 'Duels are illegal,' he said simply.

Lizzie looked again at the knot of men and saw a similar grimness on their faces. It came to her, somewhat belatedly she understood, that they were in some danger. Once more she cursed the wine muzzing her head. It was slowing her reactions.

One of the men shouted at them in French, brandishing his weapon heavenward. Tilney looked down at Lizzie. 'What's he saying?' He could tell it was not good. 'Can you persuade him we will not interfere?'

Lizzie tried to clear her throat and felt a sudden strangle of fear around it. 'Pardon, *messieurs*!' She began, her voice stretching to a higher register than she had intended. What to say? Lizzie shouted that they were sorry and had come there by accident, but the men levelled their pistols at the two of them, announcing they were to come forward. She hastily explained to Tilney, who dismounted and stood by her side. It felt better to have him there and Lizzie had to resist the impulse to take his hand, something he would not at all expect from George Bennett.

'*Anglais?*' one of the duellists asked Lizzie as they approached. She nodded. His second squinted at Lizzie and looked back at his friend.

'*C'est une femme, no?*'

Lizzie felt a thrill of fear and stopped in her tracks. Tilney looked at her with surprise and then looked at the men with something like alarm. Lizzie had a moment to realise that every trace of the lazy drawler was gone from his frame. He looked ready to act.

She gulped. What to do now?

Chapter Eleven

'Is this the way to adventure?' Constance asked Alice rather meekly as they lingered outside a shop that appeared to be a green grocers. Alice had led the two of them around town with a wayward step, unwilling to admit that she wasn't exactly certain how to go about finding adventure.

In the most recent past, adventure had done the finding of Alice. She had very little idea of how to importune fortune's help and her every natural inclination laboured against seeking out the likeliest locations of adventure. But they had to start somewhere.

'In here,' she told her companion with a falsely hearty reassurance. 'We must have supplies for our adventure.' Alice pushed fearlessly into the shop but was immediately intimidated by the rather grumpy-looking middle-aged woman behind the counter tying up bunches of garlic. Alice turned adroitly as if intending all along to reconnoitre the loaves of bread lined up like soldiers along the shelf above the onions.

Alice made a great show of examining the loaves as if she were well versed in the qualities of fine baked goods. It was a wonder that Alice had never really examined a loaf of bread in its natural state. Toast with tea was already sliced and grilled. Alice selected a loaf and brought it to her nose. As she inhaled, the warm fragrance filled her nose with an image of the kitchen back home in Mangrove Hall. She felt a sudden surge of loss for the kindness of Mrs. Perkins and the peculiar habits of her mother.

'This is very good bread,' she told Constance, endeavouring to cover her uncomfortable feelings. Constance took this comment as gospel and welcomed the loaf into her arms as if it were a foundling, grinning broadly.

'Shall we have cheese as well?' Constance inquired, mindful of her mother's undoubted disapproval of such extravagance.

Alice nodded, for since her voyage upon the waters with a cheese she had become very fond of the substance indeed.

'Yes, certainly we must. And wine!' It seemed a good idea after all that an adventure might start with the right kind of meal.

'How shall we carry all this?' Constance asked suddenly, which made Alice realise that they were not at all prepared for their adventure. If they had had more time to plan — ah, but then would it be an adventure, she asked herself.

Alice eyed the woman behind the counter. She seemed an unlikely confederate, but there was little else in the way of possibility. People are not always what they seem, Alice reminded herself with a shake.

'*Pardon, madame, er, mademoiselle,*' Alice hastily corrected herself. '*Je n'ai pas un panier…*' The words seemed to crawl only unwillingly from her throat and once more Alice regretted her poor attention to lessons.

The shopkeeper looked irritated at first but taking in the open face of Constance and the ingratiating tone of Alice's speech, she mumbled something noncommittal, then pulled out a linen bag from under the counter and handed it to Alice, saying simply, '*et voila!*'

Alice grinned broadly and Constance clapped her hands with joy. The woman gave them a crooked grin, charmed by their simple cheerfulness. Alice selected a small bottle of wine and a couple of cheeses in close consultation with the shopkeeper. By the time they left, the three were firm friends. Alice waved a farewell as they turned the corner outside.

'Where now?' Constance asked brightly.

'I have a wonderful idea,' Alice said with a smile.

Clutching their impromptu picnicking feast, Alice turned decisively toward the strand. There it was that the young men were to be found walking this time of day. Yet surely there was nothing more seemingly innocent than two well-bred young girls enjoying the fresh air of the ocean.

Without chaperones!

The deliciousness of the thought thrilled Alice's admittedly sheltered heart and made her companion gasp with pleasurable alarm when she shared it.

'Mother will be so cross!' Constance gloated, excitement quickening her forward motion so that Alice had to step lively to keep up with her colleague. 'Think of it—cheese and young beaus of questionable family connections.'

'They may be complete strangers to us,' Alice added, not without the passing glimpse of her parted cousin's face before her. Surely Lizzie would not simply pass judgment on this recklessness, not after all they had been through together. It's not as if we were courting pirates, Alice, reminded herself. I have lived a wild life indeed, she asserted boldly as if her cousin were tsking at her just then. This little adventure is nothing compared to kidnapping.

Constance had no inkling of these tortured thoughts, instead aiming her mild face toward the sands that awaited their dainty steps. Surely adventure and dashing young heroes would be found in abundance there.

'This is so like a novel!' Constance crowed happily.

'Some novels,' Alice cautioned, the memory of Miss Fielding's instructive tome still weighing heavily upon her memory. That the novel in question had survived the sea-soaking seemed to Alice the height of inconvenience, particularly because Mrs. Forward had looked with a certain rapacious eagerness at its educational pages, wrinkled as they were by the voyage. While the book had yet to dry to a readable state, Alice was certain that the tiresome lessons of Mrs. Teachum's charges were sure to fill her evenings as soon as the pages dried.

'Oh, here's a nice spot,' Constance cooed, pointing to a large sandy opening close to the water's lap.

'Perhaps not,' Alice said after a moment's consideration. 'Do you notice how the sea encroaches upon each successive wave? We would be under water soon, my dear friend.' Constance looked rather crestfallen, so Alice cheered her by pointing to another spot nearby. 'See there? A couple of flat rocks will allow us to sit comfortably without sand marring our skirts.'

'Excellent, Alice. Oh, you are so very clever!'

Alice blushed at this unexpected acclaim. She had never met anyone quite as easy to impress as Constance. While Alice naturally enjoyed this unrestrainedly complimentary approval, she found herself missing the more measured assessment of her cousin Lizzie. Dear cousin, wherever she might be—no doubt Lizzie would not be embarking on such a wild adventure as this. Alice could not decide whether that realisation filled her with more fear or excitement.

The two young women seated themselves daintily upon the rocks, assuring one another that they were far more comfortable than any of the chairs in their pension (true enough, more's the pity), then spread the bounty before them, eager to sample the delights purchased.

'Alice,' Constance asked with sudden perturbation, 'how shall we open the wine?'

Alice's cheery smile evaporated. Here was a perplexing problem! Constance looked eagerly to Alice for answers, but the latter could only shake her head in confusion. A fine start to our adventure, Alice thought.

Just then the two young women heard a voice come tentatively across the sands. 'I beg your pardon…'

They looked up and saw a very nice-looking young man. Perfectly respectable, Alice thought, despite his ungentlemanly willingness to be helpful. Although he appeared to be French (his clothes were far too stylish for him to be an English tourist), his manner seemed admirably proper.

'I could not help but to notice that you were in search of a corkscrew. I can call my manservant at once and give you use of mine.' He nodded slightly as if to acknowledge their predicament.

Constance looked to Alice, who considered the proposition. Surely Mrs. Forward would be scandalized by accepting help from a stranger at such a juncture. That decided it. 'Yes, please, *s'il vous plait*,' Alice said with a slightly haughty curtsey. 'We would be delighted with the use of your implement.'

Constance giggled and looked slightly dazed. Such wild adventures! Nothing like this would ever have happened at home. Alice was certain of that as well, but relieved that their adventure had not quite reached the kidnapped/pirate ship levels of surprise. This was an adventure she could manage without assistance.

The gentleman turned slightly and called out imperiously, 'Tricheor! Fetch my wine case, *tout de suite*.' In no time, a

171

slightly hunched man appeared with a red leather case in his arms. Handing it over to his master, the man bent low. At first, Alice assumed this was a mere show of deference, but then the young man placed the case upon the man's back and popped it open.

'Forgive me for not doing so sooner, but allow me to introduce myself. I am Count Philippe de Graves.' He snapped a small nod in their general direction as he rummaged in the case, at last extracting a strange looking tool. '*Et voilà!*'

'Thank you—er, *merci*,' Alice said with a curtsey expressing both her growing discomfort with this individual and the oddness of seeing another man used as a table. France was indeed a peculiar land.

The count strode toward their picnicking area and held out his hand for the wine bottle. Alice handed it to him, smiling as if she were quite grateful for the intervention, although she was already regretting their off-hand acquaintance.

In no time, the count had the cork removed with a pleasing pop. He handed the bottle back to Alice, allowing his eyes to make an inventory of the young women's wardrobes that Alice found most indecent, but managed to conceal her consternation. 'How kind you are.'

'Have you anything in which to imbibe the wine?' The count was looking at their picnic with some amusement, Alice thought, which he ought not to do surely.

'I'm afraid not,' she answered. While she was loath to admit this failing, Alice was even more reluctant to show her uncertainty in front of Constance who even now looked with poorly concealed nervousness at the unfolding tableau. 'Do you also have glasses in that charming little case?'

'Indeed I do,' the count responded with a smile that looked rather like that a tiger might wear when facing a lame deer. 'Tricheor!' The hunched man walked somewhat awkwardly down the slight hill toward the three of them.

What else might this peculiar man have in that little case? Alice wondered suddenly.

Tricheor tumbled toward the little group with an odd, crab-like walk. 'Make haste,' the count nevertheless impressed upon his servant with a touch of ferociousness. Alice found herself developing a dislike for this man that trumped his carefully proper manners.

Well, apart from the carnivorous looks he turned upon the two young women. Perhaps I am imagining it, Alice thought. Mother would no doubt speak approvingly of the count's demeanour if not their manner of meeting.

Yet Alice found herself recoiling as the count reached for Constance's hand to settle her on the rock with a swiftly procured wine glass. The gesture was perfectly acceptable; however, the feral look in his eyes was something that Black Ethel would note with dismay—or perhaps, considering the pirate queen, with a drawn sword and a swift challenge.

Alice was no pirate, but she thought at that moment it would be a very useful occupation to have.

When it came to her turn to be helped to her seat, Alice smiled with what she hoped was confidence at her companion before taking the offered seat. Constance looked entirely meek and compliant, but filled with the heady excitement of their adventure.

Close up, the count's expression was even more predatory and Alice felt an unaccustomed sense of protectiveness toward her young friend. Perhaps adventuring was far too tedious to undertake without the proper precautions and the appropriate level of chaperonage. How Lizzie would scorn her! Not only had Alice failed to live up to expectations of excitement, but she was nearly ready to pack it in and return home in defeat.

What would a pirate do? Alice looked at the count, now pouring himself a glass of wine without invitation, and felt her jaw tighten. If there were no one to extricate the two of them from this unfortunate association, Alice would have to do it herself.

First, though, they must have their picnic.

'Shall we have some bread and cheese?' Alice said with all the confident pleasantness she could muster while keeping her misgivings buried. She could not know it but at that very moment, she looked quite the picture of her own mother.

'Delightful!' the count announced, turning to badger his servant once more with an abrupt pronunciation of his name

173

and an imperious gesture. Tricheor waddled forward until the count could reach a variety of implements that would help cut the cheese and bread. Alice blushed again to consider how ill-prepared they were for their meal, but quickly put away her doubts under a mask of pleasantness.

Could her father have seen it, he might have been grudgingly approving. It is perhaps an aspect of the spirit world that all places are one, and Lord Mangrove might well have turned up to take in the perilous adventures of his daughter. It may be telling that he chose not to do so.

'How kind you are,' Alice repeated with acid charm as the count handed her the platter he had produced and upon which she arranged the bread for slicing. 'Do let me have your knife. I shall have the bread ready to eat in a moment.'

She tried not to imagine that the count showed some reluctance in handing over the knife, nor what that might mean. Instead Alice smiled even more winningly and thus came to understand much more of the world.

Alice cut some generous slices of the sweet soft bread. Even as she sliced through the creamy interior, she inhaled the fresh scent of its grains. Had food always been this good? Or had she only begun to notice such things since her dunking in the ocean? Alice shivered to think of the horrible voyage once she had been washed from the deck of the *Bonny Read*.

In that time, she had feared that she would die upon the cresting waves. It was a wonder to sit here on the genteel strand and see the waves at a distance. For the moment, Alice found strength in the idea that she was safe and secure, despite her present company.

She sat up a little more straight in her impromptu seat. 'Count, please have a slice of bread. Constance?' Alice smiled comfortably, masking her discomfort. Constance was her responsibility and she felt compelled to protect her. The count might be a completely benign character (although she had begun to suspect he was not), nonetheless, Alice felt a strong desire to keep Constance from the harm with which she was so clearly ill-prepared.

'What a lovely spot,' Constance gushed, raising an eyebrow in the count's countenance. His lip curled as well with an expression that suggested a measure of contempt to Alice's scrutiny.

'More wine, my dear?' The count held the bottle at the ready for her friend. Alice noticed that Constance had indeed already imbibed her glass of wine. This would not do. Perhaps the young girl had not chanced to drink wine previously. Wine in large quantities, Alice had long ago discovered, led to drunkenness and loud speech. Both were objectionable in a man, but completely unforgivable in a young woman of breeding.

Something must be done.

'Constance, perhaps you should have a little more cheese and bread,' Alice said sweetly, handing over another generous helping to her friend. The count seemed to take this gambit into consideration as he poured Constance's glass.

'Tricheor,' he said with a smile that reminded Alice of something like a crocodile, 'Do fish around in my trunk for another bottle of wine. We seem to be getting near the end of this one.' The crouching servant shambled over so the count could rummage in the case balanced on the man's back.

Up close, Alice could see that Tricheor was sweating profusely and emitting a smell something like one of the less savoury cheeses they had passed up in the shop. Nonetheless, Alice felt a pang of pity for the man. Whatever had led him into the employ of the count, surely he was suffering as much as one might in such a position.

'It's awfully warm today,' Alice commented, filling the empty space of conversation with a perfectly suitable pleasantry. 'I rather wish we had brought parasols along with us. I fear we may not spend long in this sun. It would be quite calamitous for our complexions.'

'Never fear,' the count parried effortlessly. 'I can always send Tricheor for some suitable coverings.'

Alice heard the servant wheeze with effort as he adjusted his back from the count's searching hands. Things were going to be more challenging than she had expected.

Alice cleared her throat, wondering what would be best to do. Sudden recognition struck her: she sounded just like her mother making the same noise. Was her mother doing the same thing — playing for time — when she produced that sound? Alice discovered a growing sense of surprise that there was much more to her mother than the scolding disciplinarian she had always known. Perhaps her mother had more to teach her than she had ever suspected.

A minute stab of homesickness struck Alice's heart.

Here on the overly warm beach of southern France, she very much missed the damp dreariness of home with its darkened rooms, stuffy conservatory and fussy garden. While on board the *Demeter* and then the *Bonny Read*, when home seemed irredeemably lost, Alice had not longed half as much for her distant home.

Yet safely in the hands of civilized folk and surely, soon to be on her way home — after all, Mrs. Forward had seen to it that a proper message had been sent to Alice's mother inquiring as to the preferred method of returning this wandering daughter safely — somehow Alice felt more at sea than she had even in the dark swirling waters of the raging ocean.

The heart was a rather unpredictable cauldron of emotions, Alice thought.

Perhaps it was just the effect of their present company. The count's wolfish grin filled Alice with such loathing that she found it impossible to chew her food and set the bread down on the rock beside her. She was alarmed to see Constance looking decidedly goggle-eyed and knew she must do something decisive.

'This heat is simply unbearable!' Alice said with a languor that belied her growing panic. 'Count, would it be possible for you to arrange some sort of covering for us, perhaps a couple of those very large parasols?'

The look on his face genuinely frightened her, but within an instant it had been replaced by a bland expression allaying any sense of alarm. But Alice was not fooled. She knew she was working against time. '*Oui*, of course, *mademoiselle*. I shall send Tricheor to fetch the parasols. Tricheor!'

The servant so named wobbled slightly, uncertain whether to move under his burden or wait to be freed of it. After muttering somewhat darkly under his breath, the count rose to remove the case from his menial's back and set it on the sand.

With a peremptory gesture, he sent Tricheor off on his errand and turned back to the two young women.

Constance was looking a trifle pale. Alice did not like her shade. 'Constance, are you feeling ill?' Her friend could only nod, suddenly looking a distinct shade of green. Alice moved to put her arm around her shoulders. With a sudden return of hope, she looked up to the count with an expression her father would have recognised immediately.

'*Monsieur*, would you be so kind as to find some fresh water for my friend?'

Irritation spread across his countenance. Alice could see his struggle to master the occasion, but inevitably gave in to his failure at this moment. 'As you desire,' he said with a curt bow, but before he could actually depart, Alice heard with alarm voices nearby.

They were about to be discovered!

The voices turned out to presage a gaggle of young English tourists. Alice careered between delight and embarrassment at the thought of their peremptory arrival. Had she known young men better—at least the holidaying kind—she would have saved herself the blush of embarrassment, for such young men seldom notice or abide by rules of propriety and so would be little inclined to censure Alice and Constance for their untoward circumstances, finding themselves alone with peculiar and slightly unscrupulous Frenchman.

'What ho!' cried the floppy-fringed roisterer at the front of the pack as he caught sight of the tableau. His companions bayed in like fashion, a sound apparently expressing surprise and delight as far as Alice could discern.

So relieved was she to see fellow countrymen that Alice did not hesitate to greet them, much to the count's displeasure. 'Hello, how are you?' she asked somewhat breathlessly.

'Lawks,' cried another one of the lot, squinting in the sun in a most unattractive way. 'An English gel!' There was much hubbub as the scrum headed en masse down the dunes toward the sheltered cove.

There was much fussy shaking of hands with the count who icily responded to the hearty inquiries as to his health, though his frosty responses were ignored by the young men who only had eyes for the two young girls and favoured them with a tidal wave of compliments meant, no doubt, to break the ice and see if it held any water with them.

The noisy gaggle threatened to drown all the thoughts in Alice's head, but fortunately one among them seemed to be a young man of some sense. 'Lud, miss,' he said, gazing intently at Constance's green form, 'your friend seems to be a little worse for wear. Must be this cursed French sun, far too warm, if you ask me. We should get her to some shelter, tout de suite. Bertie, Stephen, Hugh, come now. We've got a lady in distress here.'

'Right-o, Reggie,' the floppy-haired one said cheerfully and the four crowded around Constance who was looking quite overwhelmed by the attention as well as the wine.

'Mind if we use this case?' Reggie said, taking up the count's little carry all. 'We can use it as a kind of seat to transport the young lady to a more congenial location.' The count was clearly displeased, but said nothing and the men took his silence as assent.

In a trice, Constance was whisked onto the case, which the energetic gents raised as if to carry Cleopatra herself. Alice could not keep from clapping her hands in delight. To have her poor friend rescued so delightfully and unexpectedly from their predicament was a wonder to savour.

Constance herself was a bit unnerved by the swiftness of the movement and the rocking motion of the well-meaning young centurions. Her pale green shade was approaching the colour of spring clover now and she convulsed suddenly, clutching her stomach.

'I feel...unwell,' she murmured with as much dignity as it was possible to maintain, before suddenly and violently vomiting to the west.

'Bingo!' cried Bertie.

'Heavens,' said Reggie. 'Awfully sorry.'

The latter words were addressed to the count, who bore the brunt of the explosive ejection, itself a rather rancid ruby tint with small chunks of comestibles.

'*Merde!*' was all he said.

The young louts, once they had adjusted to Constance's

outburst, carried the young heroine forward toward restorative shade and fresh water. This entailed some difficulty, as they could not entirely agree on which direction to head.

Alice, trailing at the back, torn between politeness required to their initial benefactor and loathing for the same, attempted to make polite conversation even as the count lagged further and further behind the eager if somewhat erratic steps of the young Englishmen.

'Hang on, Hugh! You're letting down the side!' Reggie called as the inattentive young hat rack became momentarily distracted by something shiny. Hugh recovered his footing and away they jounced poor Constance, who looked ready to release another volley of inclemency, but held herself in check with an admirable aplomb of which her mother would be quite proud.

Well, thought Alice, she would be if the whole display athletic conviviality did not scandalize her and if the thought of her daughter half-sprung on French plonk did not render her paralyzed with alarm. Best she not know, of course.

'Tilt her round, there's a good fellow,' Stephen reminded Bertie, who seemed to be inclined to follow Hugh's meandering path and so produce a split in the ranks. Poor Constance swooped with their movements and gasped for breath.

Alice found her brows to be furrowing in a manner entirely too reminiscent of her mother's habitual look and made an effort to relax her face. Nonetheless, she could not quite halt the words that wished to leap from her lips. 'Do be careful, gentlemen,' she said as casually as possible. 'You don't want to eject poor Miss Constance before you've had a chance to make her charming acquaintance and find out what a lovely dancer she can be.'

Alice had no idea whether Constance could actually dance at all— in fact she was rather inclined to guess that her impulsive friend was quite probably a reckless sort on the assembly room floor —but she thought it best to give her the benefit of the doubt as a matter of politeness and as a spur to more watchful care from the eager attendants.

It seemed to do the trick. Though Constance remained sick as a cushion, there was a very keen if friendly competition for the very next dance that might possibly come their way, along with a variety of spicy exclamations, from 'Tare 'n hounds!' to numerous ''Pon reps!'

Alice glanced over her shoulder at the count who, bereft of the assistance of Tricheor and without the captive audience, was stumbling along as best he could, stopping frequently to flick another spot of ejected foodstuff from his sleeve with an air of unutterable vexation. In the heat of the afternoon sun, Alice could almost believe that the count might just possibly burst into flames.

And it would not be the worst thing to happen, Alice said to herself with a toss of her head, which made her feel much more like her old self. The movement kept the hair out of her eyes normally, but this time it was solely to reassure Alice that there were some absolutes in the world that strange Frenchmen and kidnapping sailors could not extinguish.

'What ho, Reggie!' the lad called Hugh hallooed to his friend. 'Which way?'

'Right, then ahead,' he answered with admirable firmness, although Alice could not have ascertained where this would lead them. Nonetheless she acquiesced as it was sure to take them further and further from the site of her disturbing meeting with the count and his peculiar servant, whom she saw even now, was slowly approaching them from a distance.

Nonplussed by the image of his commander in a crowd of rowdy young gents, Tricheor's steps became even more irregular, Alice noticed. She turned her head and saw that the count still lagged somewhat behind the gaggle of Englishmen, his displeasure appearing to grow with every step. Tricheor's hesitation led to a sort of bobbing and weaving motion that threatened to empty the pitcher of water he carried and to make him lose hold of the parasol he had obtained somewhere.

While the young gentlemen recovered from another near accident with Miss Forward, Alice considered what would be best to do. She hated to re-engage in any obligation to the count, but she saw that poor Constance was fading fast under the bright sun of the strand. They might soon find shelter, but the last stretch of a journey was often the longest, she recalled well from the unpleasantness of her own travels.

Hang the count and hang propriety, Alice thought with determined brows. She picked up her pace and strode toward the struggling Tricheor. 'How kind you are to have arrived so punctually,' Alice said with as much pleasantness as she could muster. Close to she found the strange servant a most repellent object, oozing sweat from every pore and exuding a most curious odour. His skin indeed seemed uncannily coarse and hideous, causing Alice to avert her eyes as much as possible.

'Thank you for the parasol. My friend will be most delighted for its shade.' She held her hand out expecting the item to be passed along, but when it was not, she chanced to notice that the misshapen manservant was looking to his employer for confirmation, which irritated Alice to no end. Surely politeness needed no command. But the weary count affirmed the act with a curt nod and Tricheor handed over the prize.

Alice immediately handed it to Reggie, the seemingly competent one among the enthusiastic rabble, who popped the device open and placed it gently into Constance's limp hand. She sighed gently, which indicated a somewhat improved state, or so Alice hoped. His primary purpose concluded, Tricheor limped to the side of his master and continued with the same desultory limping pace beside him.

Up ahead, Alice could see a rather impressive tent, decorated with many colourful ribbons and flags. It appeared that the shambolic crew was making their way in that direction. While she blanched at the thought of being exposed to further public display of their misadventures, Alice found herself feeling more than sufficient relief at the thought that she need no longer be the person in charge. It had been an exhausting day of much thinking, evaluating and regretting.

Alice hoped for a return to childish innocence without realising that such thoughts were an inevitable sign that such innocence had already beat its wings and flown off.

'Perhaps they will have cake,' Alice mused, childhood nonetheless raising its head for a brief visit.

As they approached the gaily-colourful tent, Alice could divine that there was already a considerable crowd within from the vigorous conversation that bubbled across the strand to her ears. Again she blanched at the thought of exposing poor Constance to such a throng (and to so much potential irregularities of politeness) but there was little hope for avoiding it.

Besides, anything was preferable to their close encounter with the count. Alice sneaked a glance in his direction and was pleased to see that he was perspiring freely and looking rather worse for the travel. Suits him, she thought with a measured toss of her head. She was more certain than ever that he had been about nefarious intentions.

'Hey ho!' One of the celebrants within had noticed the approach of their inelegant train. 'Reggie, what's this?'

'Rescue mission, lads, with some of our finest flowers here,' Reggie nodded to indicate Alice, at which she coloured up prettily. It was very pleasant to be receiving compliments again.

'And this one?' another asked appearing to indicate the faltering Constance. 'A bit tap-hackled, eh?'

'Sick as a cushion,' Reggie affirmed as they looked around for a place to set their burden. 'Too much sun, poor little gel.'

Alice was very grateful to the steady young man who even at that moment was helping his boisterous colleagues to lower Constance next to a reasonably comfortable looking chair. She smiled at him to show her approval, but he was too busy settling her friend into the chair to see her approval. Alice could not help but think that it was rather irritating to try to do something nice for someone and not have them notice, but she decided that she would not hold it against their rescuer, and thus made another stride into the frightening world of adulthood.

Had she known, Alice would have backed away at once, but it is in the nature of these things that we seldom notice the steps until they have long passed into memory.

Because her friend was still sagging with exhaustion and illness, curious eyes turned upon Alice for answers to burning questions. While they were far too mindful of propriety to ask the direct question, 'Who are you?' they had no problem asking embarrassing questions like 'Are collars worn looser this year in Bath?' and 'Have you a lace edged handkerchief with Belgian lace?'

Alice found herself beset on all sides by eager young men, which in other circumstances (a genteel drawing room or an overly warm solarium) might have proved quite enjoyable, but at that moment was quite suffocating.

'Enough, enough,' Reggie at last intervened. Having sorted out Constance with a bevy of enthusiastic admirers fanning her—indeed they were well in the way of putting her in some danger of being blown off course—he turned his attentions to Alice and her circle of well-intended interlocutors. 'You must proceed one at a time and wait a sufficient time for an answer before advancing to the next question.

Alice smiled gratefully up at him and was gratified to see him notice.

It is hard work being a heroine, she sighed to herself before turning her attention to the young man inquiring as to the state of morning glories back in their native land.

After fielding the inquiry regarding British flora, Alice was pelted with further questions on collars, horse racing, quince jelly recipes and fireworks, which she answered with as much knowledge and good will as she could muster, however little that might be (particularly in the case of fireworks of which she could claim no knowledge whatsoever). She at last made an escape from the knot of well-meaning if entirely too bois-terous young men by claiming the role of friend to young Constance who suffered yet.

The young men graciously gave way while visibly admiring Alice's gentle and caring spirit. Alice herself was relieved to no longer face the firing line of rapid-fire questions about trivial matters that once enraptured her shallow heart.

Once again she felt a pang of longing for her parted cousin. Where, oh where could dear Lizzie be at this moment? Was she already home and safe back in Mangrove Hall? When would she at last join her there?

Mrs. Forward had written to her mother, so in all likeli-hood the time would come with appreciable suddenness, but at present Alice felt an entirely understandable longing for safety, comfort and cocoa that all heroines must sooner or later encounter.

Alice was pleased to note that Constance was looking more like her usual self. Under the overly energetic fanning of her companions she had recovered her lively colour and some animation. It was a relief to see her friend looking like herself again.

'Alice,' she called out, catching sight of her friend. 'There you are.'

Alice smiled seraphically as she had once seen Lady Hibbert do when the chrysanthemums had reached their peak of perfection on a warm summer day, although her heart was yearning to be immersed in just such a day instead of here on this harsh foreign strand. She could take comfort in the thought that her unexpected travels were near an end.

'Whatever will Mother say?' Constance whispered fearfully when at last Alice was within close confines with the fluttering younger girl. 'Should she know?'

Alice hesitated before answering, which allowed the seemingly always-attentive Reggie to offer an opinion.

'If you do not mind my saying so, Miss,' he said with an air of confidentiality that in no way presupposed any untoward familiarity, 'it may be helpful to point out some persons of interest in this somewhat unruly crowd.'

'Indeed,' Alice responded, hoping she included precisely the right balance of polite disregard and fervid interest in her tone.

'Yes, over there,' Reggie nodded indicating a pallid youth of ungainly proportions, 'You will see young Viscount Brackley, and over there,' he turned to indicate a rather toothy individual hard at work at the buffet table, 'you will find Sir Eliot Walter, a baronet, as is our friend Bertie, known in polite circumstances as Sir Bertram Thomas.'

'How enlightening, you are, Reggie,' Alice said with genuine warmth. 'We are much obliged. Thank you.'

'A delight, I assure you,' Reggie said with ease as he glided away into the throng.

A most useful man, Alice reflected. She decided it would be most advantageous to know the whole of his name and write him gracious words of thanks when she returned home. Such a man would be a compliment to her; even Lady Mangrove would approve.

Before she could rise to pursue the question further, Alice felt an unpleasant tug at her hem and turned to see the objectionable Tricheor scraping away at a grovel. She tried unsuccessfully to disguise her revulsion at the sight of his abjectness, but at last inquired somewhat sharply, 'Yes, what is it?'

Tricheor scraped even lower and said, 'My master bids you attend him for a swift moment outside.'

'Why does he not come in?' Alice said shortly.

'He wishes to return an item belonging to your friend that ah, how do you say, would be best returned without scrutiny.'

Alice was both puzzled and alarmed. What on earth could Constance have dropped on the beach? Better not to contemplate, she thought with a sudden blanch. 'All right.'

Tricheor led her to an opening in the side of the tent. Out in the bright midday sun, Alice blinked uncertainly and lifted up a hand to shade her eyes.

All at once, everything went black as a gunnysack was slipped over her head and hasty hands propelled her forward. Alice heard the sound of horses as she was thrust into a carriage roughly, the door slammed shut behind her.

'Kidnapped again,' she thought with surprising sanguinity. 'Will this ordeal never end?'

Chapter Twelve

'*Non, non,*' Lizzie said blushingly, but trying to drop her vocal tone to a lower register. '*Je suis un homme.*' Oh god, I do hope they believe me. It seemed easy enough to fool Tilney so far (although at various moments, she had had her doubts even about that), but could she fool the eyes and ears (and noses) of a bunch of Frenchmen?

Particularly a group of Frenchmen who were more than a trifle irritated by having their duel interrupted. '*Nous sommes ici par erreur,*' Lizzie hastened to add, because they had not dropped the aim of their pistols, which were still fixed upon the two of them.

'Can't you tell them we mean no harm?' Tilney said with a hint of irritation.

'I'm trying,' Lizzie growled with appropriate frustration for her George persona. '*Nous ne voulons pas nous mêler,*' she offered with what she hoped was a placatory tone.

At least now the men were exchanging glances with one another. It was a better sign than their previous grim humourlessness. For the hundredth time, Lizzie wondered why the French had such a peculiar lack of humour.

Undoubtedly, they thought the same of the English, she reflected.

'*Pardon, nous vous quitterons, ah, à vos affaires,*' Lizzie groped her way toward something diplomatic, revealing their knowledge of the illicit nature of their business and a determination not to interfere with it.

Not to mention her hope that she had persuaded them to imagine her a man.

One of the men, a tall one with a bare head, waved them over with his pistol. He seemed to be judging both Tilney and Lizzie with care. '*Venir ici, à la fois de vous.*'

Lizzie checked her tongue, which wanted to launch into a hurried explanation of their presence there, to tell the story of the runaway horse and the matter of too much wine, but her time spent with Tilney had already alerted to the fact that men preferred in general to say as little as possible. It would be best to remain silent.

The tall man, whose eyes were so dark they seemed almost solid black in the pupils, stared intently at the two of them as they walked closer, Lizzie trying her best to copy the exaggeratedly relaxed saunter that Tilney affected. His normal look of harmless laziness had likewise returned. Lizzie marvelled once more at how much lay below that superficial mask of gentle lassitude.

'You look 'armless enough,' the Frenchman said at last, startling them both with his abrupt change to English. 'It is unfortunate, however, that you happened upon our little altercation.'

'No business of ours, old boy,' Tilney practically yawned. 'What you French lot get up to is of very little interest to us. We were just blowing off a little steam after a heavy lunch. You know how it is.'

'*Tout à fait*,' the Frenchman replied. 'Nonetheless, we cannot let you leave.'

Oh dear, Lizzie thought, trying to hold in a wave of breathless fear. The pistols were once more levelled at them both and at this distance, they were bound to be lethal!

Lizzie tried to keep her wandering thoughts under control. The tension of the moment seemed to squeeze her middle so tightly that she found it hard to breathe. Tilney appeared to be completely relaxed, but Lizzie could tell from her close observation of him during the last few days that he was anything but.

'Marcel! Louis!' Their interrogator gestured peremptorily to his cohorts, indicating that they ought to train their weapons on the interloping English. Lizzie thought back to her time on board the *Bonny Read* and wondered what the fearless Black Ethel would do.

Not that it would help much, Lizzie thought to herself. I am no pirate. I wish I were fearless, but here I am consumed by fear.

'To even things,' the Frenchman continued, addressing them both with a haughty edge of contempt, 'one of you must serve on either side. *D'accord?*'

187

'We shall be happy to oblige,' Tilney said somewhat icily, irritated by the insistence that the two of them take part in this quarrel to which they had not been party. Lizzie was just relieved that they weren't going to have to be shot, so the full impact of the situation did not immediately hit her.

Tilney gave her a searching look, as if to signal concern for his young friend. Lizzie gulped, but tried to toss him a confident nod. He had to expect manly fortitude from young George Bennett and she was going to do her level best to deliver it.

If I die, he'll find out I'm a woman, Lizzie considered, but he ought not know before that.

Seeing the two compliant, the Frenchman once more wrangled his cohorts into place and the duel reassembled. Lizzie was somewhat surprised to see that their interrogator was one of the correspondents. His opponent was a pale and effete-looking Parisian who maintained an unconvincing air of hauteur. Lizzie did not make much of his chance and thus was somewhat nonplussed to find herself wrangled to his side of the altercation.

There seemed to be an inordinate number of seconds for a duel, based on her memory of novels and historical events. She had a vague recall of the playwright Ben Jonson felling an actor (thus ever the enmity between writers and their instruments, she pondered) and of course, Pitt the Younger, but the details of the events remained somewhat hazy.

Besides, French rules—like everything else about this country—might prove to be rather different than those of her homeland. Fair play might not even enter into the proceedings.

'Êtes-vous prêt?' their commander demanded of his opponent. Lizzie looked over at Tilney and felt a stab of fear that his handsome face might be marred by the violence of the moment. Somehow she could not bear the thought and felt herself grow faint once more.

This will not do, she told herself with a little shake. *You are a man, behave as a man must!*

'*Laissez-nous commencer!*' the Frenchman spoke firmly and at once the duel began.

The two men stood back to back and the seconds remained at rapt attention. A man all in black with a tall hat began to count in French. The duellists began to pace apart, pistols held high, faces grim. The cool afternoon breeze ruffled their shirts and hair, but Lizzie could not hear a sound.

It was as if she had been suddenly plunged into the pages of a novel. All the elements were here: Two men in a life or death struggle, tense guardians gathered round, a secret rendezvous in a sheltered location.

It must be love, Lizzie thought with an unaccustomed leap of her heart. These were emotions poorly suited to George Bennett, but she could not help the thought once it rose. Surely they were fighting for the love of a woman. How would it go? Surely the young man who had taken charge of the situation, who had forced them into service as seconds was hot-blooded enough to be the correspondent.

Lizzie looked over at the opponent, on whose side she had been drafted. While equally well dressed, Lizzie thought that she detected a certain petulant air that suggested the wronged party, the one who had lost something.

Again she felt a stab of worry over Tilney's fate. In the heat of the moment, when the bullets were flying, who could say what might happen? Lizzie was alarmed to comprehend how strong her feelings were. I am beholden to the King of Naples, she reminded herself. It was only proximity that had caused her to idly knit her thoughts toward Tilney and his cursedly devilish humour.

He looked anything but amused at present, however. As the duellists reached the end of the counting and turned, she could not stop herself from drawing a gasp of breath. The two men aimed their pistols and fired. The sudden cacophony rang in the ears of all those present.

Lizzie looked with alarm at Tilney, who—she was relieved to find—suffered no injury. The same could not be said of the combatants. The seconds, friends no doubt of the two in question, rushed forward with cries of some alarm.

Neither remained standing, so Lizzie feared the worst. She saw Tilney head forward to examine his duellist, so she thought she ought to do the same. Fighting her way into the crowd around the erudite Frenchman, she at last caught a glimpse of the man.

It was all she could do not to faint straight away.

Surely I have seen blood before, Lizzie thought even as she gasped for air. But the violence of the wound before her seemed vividly garish against the young man's bright white shirt. The shot had taken him in the shoulder and left behind a gaping hole though which blood poured even as the seconds tried to stanch the flow with an array of handkerchiefs.

His fellow combatant shouldered through the crowd, bleeding from the arm, but seemingly negligent of the injury and the pain. He looked fiercely at his foe, apparently trying to determine the extent of his injuries.

Good heavens, Lizzie thought dizzily, was he intending another go round?

'*Bien?*' he asked roughly, wrapping the bandage offered him around his forearm as he regarded his opponent with a cocky smile.

'*Très bien,*' the other croaked, as another man pushed through the crowd. This must be the physician, Lizzie deduced. The man in black threw down his bag and waved the others away from the injured man. Taking away the bundle of handkerchiefs, he tutted at the wound and turned back to his bag.

Extracting a large pair of pincers, he called to no one in particular for brandy. Several flasks were proffered and the physician grabbed one at random and put it gently to the lips of his patient, before taking a swig himself.

Handing the flask back to its owner, he motioned for the others to take hold of the young man's limbs. Once he was securely anchored, the doctor plunged the pincers into the wound and hunted for the ball lodged in the man's shoulder. The patient bellowed with pain and was rewarded with further helpful infusions of brandy.

At long last, the doctor grunted with satisfaction and extracted the ball triumphantly. The crowd cheered heartily and everyone looked relieved. The doctor bandaged the wound with alacrity and they all helped him, swaying, to his feet.

His opponent regarded him with clear triumph and not a little scorn. '*Il est decide, mon cousin?*'

Lizzie felt her eyes widen with surprise. They were family, and fighting like this? How horrible, she thought.

The defeated man nodded and said only, '*Oui*,' in a voice that plainly conveyed his defeat. He could not quite bring himself to regard his victor in the eye, which showed a want of character, Lizzie could not resist concluding.

The champion drew himself up to full height, ignoring completely the wound in his arm as he shook a warning finger at his enemy. '*Vous ne souillerez pas le fromage de mon famille toujours encore!*'

Lizzie could not have been more astonished. So it was not love after all, but cheese? She grimaced. The scene no longer seemed like one plucked from a beloved novel, but instead appeared all too cheap and petty. Gladiators! Rather they were petulant prigs—and worse, little more than merchants. To shoot one another over an insult to their family cheese? What nonsense!

She felt certain that somewhere Lord Mangrove was smiling at her naiveté.

Lizzie had no time to reflect upon this shift in illusions, for Tilney grabbed her sleeve and said, 'Let's make a run for it, Bennett—now while their attention is elsewhere!'

Lizzie glanced nervously over her shoulder, but the men seemed altogether occupied with helping the wounded combatants from the field. The two dashed to the bush where their horses had been hastily tethered and leapt into the saddles, or perhaps more accurately, Tilney helped Lizzie aloft then scrambled somewhat awkwardly on himself.

With a last glance at the knot of men muttering away yet more softly as they departed, the two turned their steeds and beat a hasty retreat in the opposite direction. As the hooves thundered along the path, Lizzie resisted looking back although she could not help imagining that a parting shot might be fired at any minute and strike her in the middle of her back, which gave her a very unpleasant itching sensation just there.

At last they turned back into the lane from which her bolting horse had deviated an interminable time ago. Tilney led the way as they rounded the corner and headed them once more east. After some minutes, they let the horses slow, and seeing they were not pursued, breathed mutual sighs of relief and let the winded horses amble along, their sides puffing with the exertion.

Tilney patted Darcey's neck in acknowledgement of his quickness, then grinned at Lizzie. 'A bit of adventure there, eh Bennett?'

'A bit more than I had bargained for,' Lizzie agreed. 'I can't believe it was all about cheese.'

Tilney's head flew back as he roared with laughter. 'Was it? Just cheese?'

'Admittedly, in the market, scorning the methods by which one produces cheese can be quite serious, casting aspersions on a family tradition and livelihood, but I had really thought it might be over a woman.' Lizzie still rankled at the thought, as much at realising the mercantile nature of the tussle as at finding her own feelings so easily moved by such silly romantic notions. Novels, as Lord Mangrove had warned so many times, indeed had an insidious effect on the imagination.

Tilney laughed again, although somewhat less heartily. 'Ah, men who go to pistols over a woman would do themselves a favour to aim for the heart and end it all.' Lizzie noticed that dark cloud, which sometimes crossed his face, had once more darkened his visage.

'You're such a terror, Tilney. Someday the right woman will come along and change your mind to something more hopeful,' Lizzie said with unaccustomed confidence. Some of the rush of excitement of the duelling must still charge her limbs, for she was not wont to take such a lively and chaffing tone with Tilney.

Tilney laughed, but there was something harsh in the tone. 'For the time being, I shall be happy to remain with a simple chap like you, Bennett. Let women keep their distance.'

Lizzie reflected that Tilney would be unlikely to guess that he was in much closer proximity to a female that he would have guessed, but had no intention of divulging that information. 'Shall we ride on until sunset?' she finally asked.

'Perhaps we might seek out a tavern sooner, or some kind of public house,' Tilney said, his voice a tight with strain, which made Lizzie dart him a quick look of concern.

'Are you in need of a restorative mug?'

Tilney gave her a lopsided grin, then reached to open his coat, revealing a crimson streak. Lizzie gasped in horror. 'I think I was shot,' he said finally.

'Good heavens!' Lizzie exclaimed, forgetting all propriety in her moment of alarm. 'What, what..!' There was nowhere for this sentence to go, fuelled only by panic and a vague knowledge that something must be done.

'Yes, my thoughts precisely,' Tilney said dryly if a tad weakly.

'Are you in pain?' Lizzie inquired, then immediately blanched. Of course he must be in pain! 'I meant, are you in unbearable pain?'

'Manageable, Bennett,' Tilney said, although his voice betrayed an evident weakness. 'But perhaps we should ride along and in hopes of coming to an inn very soon.'

Lizzie didn't like the pale look of his visage, but there seemed to be no other option. They touched their heels to the horses and set off again. She decided that it would be best to keep his spirits up and his thoughts distracted by chatting about their recent adventures with a lively air she did not feel. 'I wonder what sort of cheese was at the heart of the altercation,' she began tentatively, casting a glance at the pallid Tilney.

'I've always been partial to Red Leicester,' he said in return. The strain was evident, but he laughed nonetheless. 'I don't suppose there's much call for that around these parts.'

'Probably not. I'll bet it was far more likely to be Camembert, or possibly a variation on Brie.'

'If it was goat cheese,' Tilney coughed, 'I think they would both deserve to be shot.' Suddenly he collapsed against Darcey's neck and Lizzie cried out, distressed.

'Perhaps we should go back to the clearing. They did have doctors after all,' Lizzie reined in her mare and rose as close as she dared to Tilney, Darcey helpfully allowing her to do so without shying.

'No,' Tilney said, smiling wanly up at her. 'Just a bit farther. We can't be far from some kind of civilization. After all, the duellists had to be going somewhere, I suppose.'

Lizzie tried not to be terrified by the bloodless look of Tilney's face. His eyes were looking dull and sightless. The loss of blood was weakening him. What would she do if he fell off? She couldn't lift him, surely.

'Ahead,' he murmured. Lizzie looked and was immediately relieved to see a small group of buildings. Surely there would be someone who could help them!

'Just a little further now,' she encouraged Tilney and tried to urge the horses forward a little faster, though she grabbed onto his arm to keep him astride the gelding. When at last they got to the door of the first building, Lizzie shouted quickly for assistance in French and was relieved to see a woman in an apron appear in the doorway looking surprised and then distressed as she saw poor Tilney's appearance.

The woman gestured to bring Tilney forth and Lizzie struggled to get him safely off the horse and through the doorway. He staggered in her arms and Lizzie was terrified to see how much blood was soaking his shirt. The woman gestured to a table from which she had cleared a good amount of needlework. Lizzie helped Tilney to clamber up on the tabletop while she begged the woman to find a physician.

Tilney lay supine and Lizzie hardly knew what she should do. Surely the blood must be stopped. She grabbed a cloth from the mending pile and, after hesitating a moment, opened Tilney's shirt to reveal the wound in his side. It was useless to blush at the naked flesh before her, for the horrifying hole where the bullet had struck him continued to pour forth the precious red fluid.

Lizzie folded the towel and pressed it to his warm flesh. 'Hold on, Tilney,' she said quietly. His eye flickered but did not open. Lizzie felt tears well up in her eyes. It must not be too late. She could not bear to have those beautiful eyes close forever.

It seemed an eternity had passed, was passing while Lizzie stood silently beside the still body of her friend. The rich red seeped through the cloth she held at his side, but it did not seem to be leaking out as fast as before.

'Hang on,' Lizzie whispered, unwilling to break the silence with much more than that, as if the silence itself somehow suspended Tilney's fate. His face was pallid and slack, mouth slightly open. The stress of the injury was evident in his expression, which looked far more fatigued than his usual animated self.

The eyes, normally sparkling with barely suppressed laughter, remained stubbornly closed and Lizzie had to learn down to ascertain that he was indeed still breathing albeit shallowly. The pleasant features—not so much handsome as lively and well-formed, good humoured and quick—looked as wonderful as ever and Lizzie felt fear stab her heart again at the thought of losing him.

To her surprise, Tilney raised a hand to touch her fingers where they held the cloth to his wound. He licked his lips and then spoke. Lizzie had to bend low to hear him, her ear very near the barely moving lips.

'Bennett,' he whispered in a ragged tone, 'if I should not make it—'

'You will!' Lizzie hastened to say, laying her free hand on his shoulder for emphasis.

'But if I should not,' he continued doggedly, coughing with the effort, 'there are certain items in my bag that should be delivered to my family. Swear you will do this, Bennett.'

'I swear,' Lizzie repeated, a promise she knew not to be made lightly, but sworn as an oath on her life that very moment.

'You're a good chap, Bennett,' Tilney said, smiling weakly, eyes still closed, 'if a bit odd. I have grown very fond of you.'

'I will do whatever is necessary,' Lizzie told him, trying to keep the tears from spilling down her cheeks. 'But the physician is on his way and will no doubt patch you up in no time at all. You'll be fine, I'm sure of it.'

Yet she looked at the frightening red-soaked cloth and wondered if it were true.

'Tell my mother I am sorry,' Tilney said finally. 'I did not mean to punish her by going away, but I could not remain there any longer with, with—' He paused. 'No matter. The past is the past. But tell her, Bennett. You will, will you not?'

'I swear,' Lizzie repeated, the tears welling too fast to be detained any longer.

'Good man,' Tilney said and then was overtaken by a fit of coughing that struck terror into her heart.

Tilney sank back down to the table. If he had been pale before, he was nearly white now. Lizzie gasped and her tears fell freely. There was no one to see them now and she feared that Tilney could not hang on much longer.

Just then the door flew open and a harried man with a bag stepped in, closely followed by the alarmed seamstress, who was still blathering away wildly even as the physician waved her down. Lizzie was beyond relieved to see that a saviour had come.

'He's been shot, here,' Lizzie said frantically, indicating the shocking wound needlessly and forgetting her French. '*Ici, ici!*' she added, still holding Tilney's hand in her own.

'*C'est tout droit,*' the doctor said calmly, which maddened Lizzie to no end, but he stepped up to feel Tilney's pulse at the neck, frowned and then moved down to his side to peer at the wound.

'*Permettez-moi de travailler,*' he said abruptly to Lizzie, indicating she ought to move to the other side of the table and out of his way. Loath as she was to leave Tilney's side, Lizzie knew it was best to let the physician work.

He looked up at her, squinting a little. '*Plus de lumière, s'il vous plait,*' he said, then adding, '*monsieur,*' with such a crooked eyebrow that Lizzie feared she had been discovered. There was no time to think about that, however, when Tilney's life hung in the balance.

Lizzie and the seamstress moved to open the curtains of the shop and let more light in. The seamstress opened the door wider too. Lizzie hoped the fresh air from outdoors would prove bracing to the poor young man who seemed barely alive.

Oh, please do not take him from me, Lizzie fervently asked. I cannot bear to be parted from my dear friend. How could I know, how could I have imagined—

Lizzie found she was unable to finish the thought, save for

redoubled wishes that he be safe, please let him be safe and whole.

The doctor called for water and the seamstress galloped off to fetch a basin. He rummaged through his bag and pulled out what looked like a very large set of pincers. He looked over at Lizzie. '*Aidez-moi à le tenir*,' he said and she walked over as one in a trance, terrified at what was about to happen.

She leaned over and pressed her hands down on Tilney's shoulder, which felt icy to her touch. A sob threatened to break out from her throat, but through sheer force of will, Lizzie held it in. *I must not fail him now, when he needs me most*, she thought and inclined as far as she dared, then nodded to the physician.

The seamstress returned with a basin and stood ready beside the physician. He plunged the pincers into the wound and Tilney groaned, trying to rise from his weakened position. Even if Lizzie had not been holding him down, she doubted that he could have risen. He had become far too weak.

As the physician probed deeper, she felt the body under her hands become weaker. All at once there was a terrible cry that pierced Lizzie's ears with horror.

'Ah ha!' cried the physician. Grinning with pleasure, he held aloft the shot that had pierced Tilney's side. Lizzie realised that the cry had come from him and not the pale body before her. She grasped Tilney's hand and felt for a pulse at his wrist. It was still there, albeit weak.

'*S'il vous plaît le tenir encore*,' the doctor cautioned. Lizzie returned her hands to his shoulders although it seemed unlikely that he could move at all. However, when the surgeon started sewing up the wound, Tilney did indeed moan and move. Lizzie leaned down more firmly upon his shoulders and tried to restrain his movements.

The poor seamstress looked quite faint, clearly unaccustomed to such a sight in her little shop. But she held the basin steadily while the physician continued to mutter various oaths and imprecations under his breath as he tried to close the wound. Lizzie cast a glance at the work and blanched to see the terrible gash bound up with dark thread.

The physician, however, seemed quite pleased with his work. He reached into his bag to get a small bottle, which he then poured over the wound. Whatever was in the bottle must have been caustic, for it brought Tilney around with a shout and then a groan as he sank back down to the table.

'It must stay clean,' the doctor said in painfully slow English. 'Clean.' He placed a square of linen over the horrible stitches and then sought her help to wrap bandages around Tilney's waist to hold the square in place. They slipped the roll under his back and Lizzie was too occupied to consider the intimacy of the moment, which was doubtless just as well.

Her thoughts were already as confused as a mending basket in a windstorm. She put all thoughts of propriety and correspondence away from her mind and concentrated on what would help her friend pull through this unfortunate experience. The seamstress smiled kindly and patted Tilney's head with a cloth dampened from the basin.

'Brandy,' the physician said. '*La fièvre*, she always comes after. If he is strong, all will be well.' He turned to the seamstress and bade her go get some men from the inn to take Tilney to a room there. Lizzie was grateful for his help.

'I will come back tomorrow,' the doctor said, shaking Lizzie's hand. 'To see how he goes and to receive my fee, one hopes.' He chuckled, grabbed his bag and was out the door.

Lizzie leaned down to kiss Tilney's forehead. Already the heat of fever seemed to embrace it.

'Bennett?' he said weakly. 'Is that you?'

Lizzie froze.

Lizzie did not immediately know what to do and remained immobile as statue. Then she thought better of it and stood up hastily. 'Yes, Tilney, it is I. How do you feel…old fellow?'

'Weak,' he chuckled, eyes still closed and his cheeks looking drawn and pale. 'But at least I suppose I am still in this world. I had begun to think I might lose the fight, Bennett.'

'They're going to be taking you to an inn to recover. The physician says you need a good deal of rest to recover.' Lizzie restrained herself from fussing over him and adjusting his collar.

'Well, I got all the adventure I desired, I fear,' Tilney said with a weak smile. 'I wanted a wild life and I got it. Perhaps I only wished to play at adventurer.'

'You should recover completely from this, the physician said. You are young and hearty, Tilney. All will be well,' Lizzie could not restrain herself from patting his shoulder, but she thought perhaps it was a manly enough gesture.

'Let us hope so,' Tilney sighed. 'I suppose I really ought to write to let my family know that I will be laid up for some time. Perhaps it would be best not to disclose the complete details. No need to worry them unnecessarily.'

Lizzie nodded. 'You can dictate and I will write. I should make myself useful.'

Tilney reached for her hand and tapped it with his own. 'You have been invaluable, Bennett. I hardly know how to thank you.'

Lizzie blushed, relieved that he could not see her face. 'Not necessary, Tilney. You have done much for me, more than you know.'

'Nonetheless, I must say I owe you. I shall repay you.'

'What do you plan to do once you recover?' Lizzie asked, trying to move the subject away from the awkward expressions of debts owed. Surely the men from the inn would be arriving any moment.

Tilney sighed. 'I haven't the remotest idea. Perhaps I should go home and let you get on with your adventures, Bennett.'

'Ah,' Lizzie said, in surprise, struck for words. 'I suppose I might have to consider heading back to the homeland as well.'

'That precious stone set in a silver sea,' Tilney chuckled. 'At our lowest moments, home shines all the more brightly in our memory. Yet—'

'There were reasons to leave?'

'Indeed.' Tilney lay silent so long that Lizzie feared he had once more lapsed into unconsciousness, but at last he continued somewhat enigmatically, 'Problems must be solved, disappointments accepted, one supposes.'

'I guess so,' Lizzie said, her brow furrowed with puzzlement at his words. She looked up, hearing steps across the square. The men from the inn were coming at last. 'Here they come, Tilney.'

'Ah, very good,' Tilney said, opening his eyes again to meet Lizzie's gaze. 'I need to rest.'

'You do, indeed, sir.'

'Perhaps afterward,' Tilney said, 'we can discuss why a girl might pretend to be a boy, eh Bennett?'

Lizzie gulped, but the men from the inn were coming through the door, so she remained agonisingly silent.

Chapter Thirteen

Alice wondered if the rumbling of the carriage would ever stop. She had even dozed off after a time, so utterly bored by the endless journey that she very nearly wished for the presence of Miss Fielding's instructive tome, *The Governess*.

Well, nearly.

As she jounced along on the too-hard seat, Alice dully considered where her captor might be taking her this time. It was strange to realise that she was not overwhelmed by the knowledge that she had once more been kidnapped. Alice marvelled how not that long ago she had been quite distraught by the very same experience.

How long ago had her father's funeral taken place? It was hard to tell. She had had ample time to reacquaint herself with the proper calendar dates whilst in the kind keeping of the Forward family, yet she had not bothered. Had she suspected that a short time later she would once more be whisked away?

Or had she simply begun to live for the moment like some summery butterfly?

Alice was unaccustomed to such abstract considerations and gloomily wished yet again for Lizzie's kindly guidance. No doubt her beloved cousin would be able to wisely counsel her on the appropriateness of her musings and warn her away if they should dip too far into melancholy.

She had to admit that she did not feel overwhelmed by melancholy, although perhaps it was one of the characteristics of that dread state that one did not seem overwhelmed by it even when one was in fact engulfed by it. It would take much pondering, Alice mused.

Tired of musing, Alice tried to apply her eye to a crack in the tight blinds that darkened the carriage. Perhaps she might see something that would give her a clue as to her whereabouts. Try as she might, however, there was nothing to be seen but a slight glimmer of light and colour that flashed by the carriage's path. There was little information to glean from it.

Alice sighed. If Lizzie were here, she would entertain me. Alice considered the point. What would Lizzie do? Draw her out in improving conversation? What might they converse about? Geography would probably be hopeless. Literature? Well, certainly it would be better to broach that subject with some evidence of the products of it in hand.

No, surely Lizzie would have generous reserves of memory to draw up and discuss at length. What stories might I dig up from memory? Alice asked herself. She tried to retrieve some details of the last tome by Mrs. Radcliffe that she had devoured. Certainly at the time, the adventures had seemed vivid and breath-taking.

In vain, Alice sought for the strands of narrative that had gripped her so completely at the time. There had been a ghost, was there not? And a heroine, of course, in grave danger. Her father—or was it some other man—forcing her to marry against her will? There was a nun, she was almost certain—or had it been a priest?

Alice sighed. Why couldn't writers give one more to go on?

As she lapsed into consideration of the half-remembered plot of Mrs. Radcliffe's tome, Alice noticed a curious sound. It was a kind of rushing noise that she gradually figured out was a waterfall. This intrigued her and she returned to trying to catch a glimpse through the shutters of the carriage.

The sound continued to grow louder and Alice became quite certain that it was indeed a waterfall. Was this a good thing, she wondered? Would she be hurled off the waterfall to her death? That would be terrible indeed, Alice decided. Perhaps the waterfall would only mean a halt in their journey. Some kindly people in a mill would take pity on her and free her from this latest kidnapping excursion.

The rushing sound of the water increased and eventually slowly receded. Alice sighed. Even a horrible death would be a nice change from the monotony of the journey. Once one has braved pirates on the ocean and a close shave with a watery death, it was hard to get too concerned about lesser perils, she decided.

I suppose I have become quite brave, Alice congratulated

herself. If I were to face armed brigands I imagine I should remain quite calm. After all, I have stood in the midst of cannon-fire and did not tremble.

Readers will, of course, recall that Alice did a good deal more than tremble at the time she found herself in the pitched sea battle, that there was in fact a good deal of screaming and crying out in alarm. Let us not therefore suggest that Alice was deliberately fibbing. It is one of the peculiarities of memory for many of us, that we edit the copybook of time ever so subtly over the succession of days as to find ourselves in a rather different location than fact or the memories of others, might situate us.

One need not assume that the memories of others are any less prone to adjustment, nor that facts exist in a vacuum. After all, Alice might find herself on the side of philosophers who have suggested that the mere recording of observations change the things observed. However, Alice would have had to consider this matter at a much more subterranean level of thought than she had given it up to this point.

In fact, Alice's thoughts had already returned to unknotting the tangled memories of Mrs. Radcliffe's novel and had come to the conclusion that she was doubtless mixing together the strands of at least two novels. Her charming brow wrinkled inadvisably as she considered the story of the murdered mother and had the distinct feeling that this was from entirely another novel altogether.

It was quite confusing, but it did pass the time.

Just when Alice had determined that she had hold of the main narrative strand of *The Italian*, the carriage suddenly slowed. She was sufficiently surprised to once more drop the thin skein of memory and sit forward with eager anticipation for the next step in her own adventure.

The carriage came to a stop, the horses snorting and wheezing as they accustomed themselves to a stationary situation. An unseen hand snatched the carriage door open and Alice gasped.

It was a man whom Alice had never seen, but the alarming manner of his appearance did nothing to stifle the sense of alarm she felt. He was dressed all in black with a kerchief covering the lower half of his face, a broad brimmed hat on his head and he carried some kind of pistol in his hand.

'Alight from the carriage, *mademoiselle*,' he ordered with a peremptory air. 'You will not be harmed.'

Alice doubted that a mite, as you would expect, having seen more than her share of harmful types on the perilous journey since her father's funeral. But the ruffian offered her his hand to step down from the carriage, so—unlike the horrible Tricheor—he seemed at least to be a cultured person.

The rapidly setting sun did not leave much light for Alice to take in her surroundings, but there was enough of the roseate light to see that she had come to a large villa, suitably decrepit for any novel by Mrs. Radcliffe. One tower had in fact crumbled and fallen to the courtyard. Many cracks fissured the surface of the walls and a wild profusion of vines clawed along the walls as if desperate to escape some horrible fate.

Alice shuddered. It was not the warm pension in which she had spent the last few days with, as was clear to her now, all manner of bonhomie and friendly warmth. Poor Constance! She would be quite put out to find her friend gone. Mrs. Forward, doubtless, would consider her well out of it.

It was genuinely annoying to think that the redoubtable matron would probably assume this was some whim on Alice's part. How unfair!

Thus preoccupied, Alice only belatedly heard the masked man's words. 'I beg your pardon?' she said at once. 'What did you say?'

'I said you are my prisoner, *mademoiselle*. You will not be allowed to leave this villa.' His eyes seemed to flash with fire as he repeated these ominous words.

'Until?' Alice prompted, knowing the way these tales always went.

'I beg your pardon?' the man said unexpectedly.

'Until when?' Alice asked. 'Are you asking for a ransom, or merely forcing me to marry against my will? I assure you it is against my will, as I do not intend to marry anyone in a mask.'

Her captor seemed to have been caught up short by this

declaration. 'You are my prisoner,' he repeated, sounding less commanding than he had initially.

'That I am,' Alice agreed, 'but why?'

The masked man stared at her a moment, then waved her along with his pistol. 'Come inside. I will show you to your room.'

Alice sighed. This did not bode at all well for the start of an adventure.

She went along with the masked man with the pistol. What was the alternative? Alice was far too sensible to give into histrionics and after all, she was discovering that kidnapping did not have to be the end of things.

It was rather shocking to consider how frightened she had been the first time, Alice reflected as they walked through the gloomy and decrepit hall that provided an entrance to the strange villa. A world-weary air of pride filled her. It was quite easy now to assume that she would be rescued.

At the very least, she found it possible to anticipate being kidnapped by a competing interest. It suddenly struck Alice that one might circumnavigate the globe simply through being kidnapped by a variety of ruffians. She looked at her latest captor and considered voicing her thoughts aloud. It was difficult to suddenly realise one knew the proper use of a word like 'circumnavigate' and not have the proper chance to demonstrate that ability.

However, her current kidnapper's demeanour seemed more than a little disparaging, so she wisely kept such thoughts to herself as they ascended the rather dusty stairs to the next floor.

Continuing down a long hallway, Alice found herself aghast at the state of things. Having spent most of her short life under the stringent order of Mrs. Perkins and much of the rest on board the spic-and-span decks of the *Bonny Read*, she found it easy to be censorious. Such filth and no doubt, she was going to be asked to dwell here for an indeterminate time.

One really ought to have more of a say about where one spends one's captivity, Alice sighed.

At the end of the hall, the mysterious man unbolted a

door and indicated that Alice should enter it. 'Here is where you will be staying. A meal will be brought to you very, er, soon. Do not attempt to escape.'

He bolted the door behind Alice and she stared at it while listening to his retreating footsteps. A candle would have been nice, she considered, but acquiescing to the facts as they were, she turned to regard her prison.

It was a fairly large room. In a nicely kept villa, it would have been pleasurable indeed. While some feeble attempts had been made to remove the worst of the dirt, cobwebs remained in the corners of the room. The bed had been freshly made with what appeared to be clean linens, but the pitcher next to the bowl was filled with water long gone chill.

Mrs. Radcliffe could make much of a room like this, Alice thought.

Alice walked to the window and looked out curiously. The grounds of the villa were in similar disrepair. Mr. Radley would doubtlessly weep at the carnage. There were brambles overgrown through the hedges and a wild profusion of vines everywhere. Alice perked up somewhat when she saw that it was possible to see a very dramatic-looking waterfall in the distance, which must have been the direction in which they had arrived.

It wasn't much, but some sense of direction was helpful, if only to give a false sense of security.

Turning once more to regard the gloom of the room, Alice was delighted to spot a shelf of books. At last, entertainment!

Eagerly Alice approached the bookshelf to take a thick volume in her hands. The well-worn cover was impossible to decipher in the poorly lit gloom of the room, so she flipped the cover open to the title page. Disappointingly, everything seemed to be in some nearly indecipherable script with far too many flourishes and, Alice was almost certain, in German.

It was bad enough to have her hopes dashed, but to have them dashed so in such a decisively Teutonic manner was unforgivable. It was probably something dreadful and educational. Whoever this Goethe chap was, Alice was certain he could not possibly be any fun, as the letters of the book looked entirely too fussy and particular.

Sighing, she returned the volume to its place and sought another. Imagine her horror upon recognising the dread name of Fielding and knowing that she held yet another copy of the interminably instructive book by that good woman, *The Governess*.

If I wanted to be educated, Alice thought perhaps a bit unfairly, I shouldn't have bothered to be kidnapped. However, uncertain what else might lurk among the materials, she held the book in reserve. After all, Miss Fielding was better than nothing at all. She would not have credited it while engaged in her seemingly endless lessons with Miss Travers, but Alice actually missed reading and being quizzed about the contents of a story (though not enough to long for writing essays, it must be admitted).

Or Lizzie's interminable questions: with a sigh, Alice wondered yet again what might have become of her fair cousin, who was far more practical and resourceful and could be home already at that very moment. She was probably chatting comfortably with Alice's mother at that very moment, enjoying the scent of some fine orchids from Mr. Radley's greenhouse.

It should be remarked that Alice let a single tear fall thinking longingly of such a comfortable scene, but one should probably note that this was a rather restrained reaction for the young woman who once burst into tears because she could not have orange marmalade on her toast at tea on a particular April day.

With no one to comfort her, Alice turned again to the shelf in hopes of locating a tale of sufficient entertainment value to divert her thoughts from the terrible tediousness of being kidnapped in a strange villa by an unknown assailant.

Once, Alice thought, I would have thought that a very romantic and diverting scenario. The truth was that it had become more than a little tiresome. There were moments of kidnapping that were quite exciting, but there were an awful lot of aspects of the project where time lagged considerably. Her spirits rose slightly upon discovering a pile of matches that she used at once to light a candle.

Her attention returned to the shelf. The next volume,

although slim, looked far more weighted with potential. There was no author listed (always a good sign, as it suggested contents too scandalous to be acknowledged) and the title, while foreign, seemed to be steeped with mystery. And mentioning a Greek god in the subtitle could only be a good thing.

The Greeks, while famous philosophers, had lodged in Alice's mind as a plethora of scandalous figures. Taking the book and the light to her bedside, she felt the choice made had been a good one as the preface spoke of an 'impossible occurrence' and a 'work of fancy' and 'weaving a series of supernatural terrors.'

Here is something without any educational value at all, Alice told herself with great satisfaction.

Time passed unnoticed. Alice had found herself shivering as she read of Mr. Walton's journey north. The frozen climate was too horrible to consider as the night grew colder and colder. She looked up from the candlelit pages. Was no one coming to make her fire?

She pulled the duvet up close around her. It seemed odd to be reading in bed like this with the covers pulled up tight, but Alice had thought she might simply read a few pages and then feel sleepy. However, Mr. Walton's careful descriptions of the frozen north chilled her exceedingly and his longing for a bosom companion awakened a similar hunger in her.

Poor Constance! Alice wondered what she might be doing without her careful guidance. They had parted at a most inopportune moment, when Constance might well have needed her assistance in negotiating the rough waters of propriety with some natural flair. Doubtless Mrs. Forward would see to it that Constance had no further adventures in that foreign land with such dubious possibilities.

Well, it did nearly come to disaster, Alice remembered, somewhat abashed. The unpleasantness with the count and Tricheor had almost come to something quite awkward. She shivered with an even more profound cold at the memory of that situation. On top of the arctic descriptions from her book, it was enough to make tears well in her eyes.

Where is my companion? Alice thought, turning back a

few pages to find those words that had so moved her. Ah, there: 'I have no one near me, gentle yet courageous, possessed of a cultivated as well as of a capacious mind, whose tastes are like my own, to approve or amend my plans.'

It would not be so bad to be thus misused, kidnapped, taken from family and friends, Alice assured herself, if I had such a friend. I did have once, she thought, and I used her ill. How I would hang about poor Lizzie, complaining and wailing! What a poor companion I must have been for her. Alice looked out into the moonlit night. Where was Lizzie now? Did she know how sorry Alice was? Perhaps she is glad I am not with her, Alice told herself, feeling more wretched by the moment. If she is home already, she may well be enjoying the quiet and the peace.

With that thought, little Alice burst into real tears, her sobs echoing in the big room. No one heard her cries, or if they did, nothing came of them, for she was not disturbed by any sound or movement outside the room.

If you keep crying like this, Alice finally convinced herself, you will fill the room with tears and simply float away. That will not do. 'Stop crying at once,' she said, trying to be severe with herself. 'You don't want to find yourself swimming in a pool of tears.'

Besides, she thought with a little shake, won't it be interesting to find out who this curious man is who's just come up to Walton's ship in the middle of the frozen ice. Who could be lurking in such a place? Would Walton and his men perish where they were, rooted to the spot by the treacherous ice surrounding them?

I must find out, Alice decided and turned back to her novel as the night grew darker.

Alice shook herself awake in the pallid dawn light. She did not remember falling asleep, though the single candle had grown small. For a moment she still found her thoughts with Victor and his sad story. She had cried when his mother died and bristled with anger at his father's dismissive attitude. It seemed impossible that he should part from his beloved Elizabeth to travel to Ingolstadt, but Alice understood all too well that such partings might well happen despite one's best intentions.

Perhaps he will find much to sustain him in his studies, Alice reflected. Victor is bound to discover some exciting new worlds in his university. It very nearly made her consider the idea of education as something quite romantic.

I could study something, Alice thought, looking out onto the cold dawn light, which lit the wild shrubberies along the crumbling wall. It would be quite charming to know a lot about something useful, she mused. What a refreshing change it would be, when someone asked a question about something terribly complicated for me to be able to say, 'I know the answer to that.'

Alice pictured herself doing just such a thing, coolly nodding with sage authority as she found the needed answer upon her lips. Of course she had no idea what sort of subject she might be inclined toward, but Alice was suddenly certain that a sense of authority arising from knowledge would be quite pleasing.

But such thoughts were as fruitless today as thoughts of sandy beaches in the West Indies. Neither was within her reach. Alice pressed her nose closer to the cold panes of the window and dully observed the tangled garden below.

How Mr. Radley would despair, she thought. Underneath the chaos one could glimpse the garden that had once been there: statues draped in careless vines, benches now crowded out by overgrown bushes that would allow no one to sit upon them had they been level even for the purpose.

Such a waste, Alice sighed.

Just then she was startled to see a dark shape move furtively through the overgrowth. She drew in a sharp breath, wondering if this were some new danger—and then just as suddenly felt her spirits rise with hope. Perhaps rescue! But the shape disappeared, if it had been there in the first place. Alice could not help wondering if she had only dreamed it.

But the thought evaporated when Alice heard a loud step in the hallway. Someone was coming!

Unconsciously Alice pulled up the covers a little higher and listened to the steps get closer. Would it be her masked kidnapper? Or was there some further disturbing character come to claim her? Suddenly Alice thought about how much worse things might be.

I haven't even had a chance to get used to this place, she thought with a wistful twinge. Yet somehow I feel I shall miss it.

The steps halted outside the door. Alice held her breath. Slowly the door opened and a figure stepped inside.

Alice gasped.

It was the same figure who had faced her previously, clad in dark clothes and wearing a broad-brimmed hat with a kerchief over most of his face. She drew back, unsettled considerably by his sinister appearance. This was her kidnapper.

'Miss Mangrove,' he began, his voice raspy and low, his accent perhaps French. 'You are my prisoner.'

Well, that was obvious enough. In her irritation, Alice forgot a little to be afraid. It was more than a little vexing to always be dependent upon the kindness of strangers. While Alice had once counted on others to direct her daily activities, recently she had begun to find herself increasingly annoyed by the determined attempts by other people to control her days. In fact she had begun to have an irrational desire to not do anything at all until she had had a chance to think about things first.

Perhaps she had developed the taste first when leading Constance around. That eager young friend, whose absence once again caused Alice a stab of longing, had been all too ready to follow Alice even unto the very gates of Perdition, she recalled with a blush of shame.

It may have been her consciousness of that painful memory or some nascent sense of self, but Alice found a reserve of anger forming deep inside her.

'What right have you to imprison me here, of all places! There is no fire, I have had no food and have nothing to change into. If you wish me to perish, congratulations! I am well on my way to illness and death.'

Despite her words, Alice found she felt marvellously warm all of the sudden, stirred by her indignation to a warmer state. And as for fading away into weakness—well, quite the opposite effect seemed to stimulate her very limbs.

For his part, the kidnapper seemed taken aback and sputtered a little behind his masquerade. 'I—I—I—I'm sorry. I should have thought—'

All at once his voice seemed higher and less certain, not quite so French and almost familiar, Alice thought. Where have I heard that tone before?

However, before she could explore the matter further, he harrumphed and his voice returned to the previous gruffness. 'I will remedy the situation. You will be provided with appropriate food and I will have someone lay a fire for you.'

'Thank you,' Alice simply stated, unable to think of anything more appropriate.

'You are my prisoner,' he repeated, as if uncertain how to proceed next.

'Until when?' Alice prompted. It would be helpful to have some kind of schedule in mind. A young woman needed to have a calendar of events upon which to order her days. That was perhaps the worst thing about all this kidnapping; schedules were so irregular.

Despite the kerchief, Alice could tell that he was somewhat horrified by her failure to properly cow before his manly authority. 'Why, until you marry me!' he announced with evident pleasure.

Oh dear, Alice thought. How dreadful!

'And who are you that I should marry you?' Alice demanded.

'I am…' and he paused as if to heighten some theatrical sense of drama, 'Gilet de Sauvinage!'

'Do I know you?' Alice asked, somewhat nonplussed.

'No, of course not,' her kidnapper answered in a slightly more normal voice. 'You don't know me at all.' He also ceased to sound entirely French as well.

'I think perhaps I do,' Alice said slowly, her thoughts circling around the tinge of recognisable tenor in that voice.

'*Non, mademoiselle, non*,' he said hastily and very Frenchily. 'Now, I must hasten away.' With that he stepped back and closed the door suddenly. Alice heard the key turn in the lock and tried the handle. But the door would not move.

'How vexing,' Alice muttered.

After staring at the door impotently for a moment or more, Alice at last sighed and turned back to regard the room. The morning light had grown slightly stronger, but it was as yet only weakly stimulating. The fire would be welcome when it came, but there was no telling how long she might have to wait.

No tea, no fire, no food — it was quite barbaric. Alice tapped her foot. She felt Lizzie's absence ever more keenly. Surely her wise cousin would not stand still for such behaviour. Lizzie was so much better at commanding other people. She recalled how much more effective her cousin was at managing the recalcitrant Mrs. Perkins, who could be quite beastly to poor Alice when she was out of temper.

Thoughts of home, even of the often-disagreeable housekeeper, caused a lump to well up in Alice's throat. While she had much improved her overall command of the vagaries of life as a kidnapee, she was still a young person far from home and the comfort of friends, without even a cup of tea for solace.

It was indeed quite unbearable. Alice gave in to a sudden fit of tears, throwing herself on the bed as they flowed copious and seemingly unstoppable. It was so unfair! Alice badly wished for someone to whom she could state those very words. It would be so delightful to say them aloud and receive some kindly expressions in exchange.

'It's not fair,' Alice whispered, her voice barely audible in the large room. The tears still fell in rivulets across her pale cheeks. Hearing the words echo made her feel even more alone, which renewed her crying fit.

After a time, however, her sobs died down and her shoulders stopped shaking. As she wiped her tears away with her sleeve, Alice once more longed for a pocket in which she might have concealed extra handkerchiefs.

I shall never again complain about carrying a handkerchief, Alice thought, recalling all the times her mother had called after her, inquiring whether she carried that indispensable item and showing some consternation at Alice's cavalier attitude toward that accessory. Handkerchiefs were rather useful items after all, Alice admitted. How useful it would be if people simply carried extra ones with them at all times, so those without might prevail upon those who had them.

When he returns, I shall ask—no! Demand a handkerchief, Alice promised herself. Picking up the novel which lay on her pillow, she got up and sat in what appeared to be an uncomfortable chair to find out what might happen to poor Victor next. At least it would keep her from dwelling on her own considerable discomforts.

Chapter Fourteen

Lizzie paused at the window and regarded the sprightly village scene with nothing but fatiguing numbness. For three days now, Tilney had raved in the midst of a fever, seldom knowing her face or any rest. The physician seemed to shrug it off, but Lizzie was terrified at the sunken look Tilney's once-bright face had taken on.

There were dark circles under his eyes as well. Worse, he alternately raved or lay so still that she was frightened most of the time. Lizzie really couldn't decide which state was worse.

When he raved, there were things that made her blush with embarrassment. Sometimes Tilney cried out for someone named Thomasina, ardently weeping for her 'soft, pale hand,' then at other times he cursed her roundly in salty language that Lizzie might have expected to issue from the mouths of pirates, but not the lips of a well-bred Englishman.

But when he was wan and silent, it was she who wept, fearing any moment that his skin would turn cold as the grave and he would slip away from her forever, the unspoken mystery between them dying along with him.

Nonetheless he rallied again and again, sometimes regaining speech and lucidity for a short while. Tilney would wring her hand and call her friend. 'Bennett,' he would say, seemingly having forgotten his awareness of her masquerade, 'you're a stout fellow! Stay by me in this time and I will not forget your kindness.'

Lizzie had no doubt that he might well forget altogether the truth of her situation, but she was more concerned with his shifting health and inability to stay out of the weird world of shadows that illness seemed determined to place upon his brow.

'Tell my mother I am sorry,' he said repeatedly when he was straying once more from his best mind. It seemed to weigh much on his conscience. 'I did not mean to hurt her!' he said with a voice that tore the strings of Lizzie's heart.

Sometimes the words Tilney spoke had no connection to

reality at all, and Lizzie could not follow the logic of his ramblings on ants, bees and umbrellas. He was clearly raving. But it disturbed Lizzie as she saw him grow weaker day by day.

She tried to make him eat, but even soup had no appeal. The physician suggested wine, *d'accord*! But Lizzie was reluctant until everything else failed to tempt him. At last she gave in and it seemed to provoke even more heat within his ravaged frame. She had mopped his brow repeatedly this whole day and only now, when the afternoon sun seemed at its highest, did she finally pause to breathe in a little fresh air.

As these grim thoughts marched through her brain, Lizzie heard Tilney stirring afresh. Afraid that he was once more held in the coils of lunatic frenzy, she turned to re-wet the flannel that had served to wet his brow and lips, but found his eyes open and clear.

'Bennett, what has become of us?' he asked, his vision direct and frank.

Lizzie's heart leapt with hope.

'You are awake,' Lizzie said unable to conceal the delight in her voice, though she tried to smother the grin that tried to leap across her face. 'How are you feeling?'

'Decidedly odd,' Tilney muttered. Lizzie was encouraged to see that his eyes retained their focus if not yet enough of their accustomed sparkle. She dipped the flannel into the bowl and reached to wet his brow once more. He lifted a weakened hand to stop her.

'How long have we been here? Where are we anyway? What has happened?'

Lizzie paused before responding, wondering just how far she should backtrack in their adventures. It was most distracting to see his clever eyes scrutinize her face as if he suspected there was something that had not been entirely resolved between them.

'You were shot,' she began haltingly, sitting on the chair next to the edge of the bed. 'And you have been suffering from a fever some days, which quite alarmed me, I can tell you.'

'Have I alarmed you? I apologise, my friend.' His look was contrite and he laid his hand on hers. 'And you have been tending me, Bennett? How very kind.'

'It was nothing.'

'Tut—I am certain I was a great deal of trouble and I regret it most heartily,' Tilney said with evident regret. 'And where are we?'

'In a small village that goes by the name of Old Fénelon, although it is not clear that we are anywhere near what is known as Fénelon, which was the home of the author of *Telemachus*,' Lizzie added with a frown.

'Geography, Bennett, not history and literature,' Tilney said with a little more of his dry humour. 'Where are we in relation to things I would recognise?'

Lizzie coughed to disguise her embarrassment and, she had to admit, slight annoyance. The thing about having been on her own the last few days, and treated like a man, was that she had not been questioned or corrected in that time. That was the power of breeches.

'We are not far from where you were shot. Indeed, we could not have travelled far from that place as you were too gravely injured.'

'Do you think that wise?' Tilney asked, trying desperately to rise. Lizzie leaned down to try to help him gently to a sitting position, though he fussed and tried to do it himself. 'Those men might pursue us. We ought to have removed ourselves more decisively from the area.' His protestations were cut off by a violent fit of coughing.

'You should lay back down,' Lizzie scolded.

''Pon rep, Bennett. It's not like I'm befogged,' Tilney responded with considerable irritation, although he allowed her to help him back down onto the pillows. 'Lud, I'm weak as a kitten. What does the leech say about my chances for recovery?'

'He says that you'll be feeling corky in no time,' Lizzie said with every effort to conceal her discomfort in tossing off the cant Tilney used with such panache. 'Not in such words of course,' she added, hoping she had not gone too far, 'But the sense is there.'

'Do you think a fellow might get a bite to eat around here?' Tilney asked with studied laziness.

Lizzie took this to mean he was starving. 'I will get some soup for you *tout de suite*.' She hopped up to do just that but Tilney called to her at the threshold and she froze.

'And then there's a little mystery about which we need to speak, Bennett!'

Lizzie tried not to feel her heart beating in her throat, where it seemed to have leaped at the moment she heard his words. A mystery to clear up? He could only mean the secret of her identity, which he seemed to have figured out, at least insofar as he had deduced that she was not the boy she pretended to be.

As she hurried down the stairs, the feeling of panic rose. Lizzie's mind fluttered helplessly over the problem. What to do, what to do? If Tilney knew, what would he do? Would he send her away? Expose her? Or—worse?

No, Lizzie thought with a determined chin jutted out at no one in particular, she could not think Tilney a man capable of getting her started in the petticoat line. He might not be above a scrape or two, Lizzie assured herself, but underneath all that casual devilry, he was a regular gentleman.

She ordered some soup from the landlord, who had become accustomed to her self-assured commands and scrupulous accounting. Lizzie had been loath to use any more of Tilney's money than was absolutely necessary, but lacking any of her own, it was required.

The landlord seemed a bit spooked by her sudden appearance. He was a bit taken aback to see her so flustered and bustled himself to get the soup with all due speed. 'The young *monsieur*, he is awake?' he croaked in his limited English as he handed the tray to Lizzie, a generous half loaf of bread with a wedge of fine ham tucked in beside the bowl.

Lizzie smiled. '*Oui, monsieur*. I think he has begun to recover at last.'

'*Dieu merci*! Then perhaps you can get some rest, too. *Vous êtes très fatigue!*'

Lizzie smiled and shrugged in a most Gallic manner as she took the tray and headed back up the stairs. It was true, she was completely done in, as much by the worry as by the lack of sleep. She stifled a yawn. This would not do. There was still much to be done.

Pushing open the door to Tilney's room, Lizzie smiled. He looked very tired and wan, but there was more than a spark of life in his face now. 'Come now, old man. I have some fine soup for you here.' She laid the tray across his lap as he struggled up to a sitting position.

'Ah, Bennett, that has to be the best soup I have ever smelled,' Tilney said with relish as he seized the spoon. Lizzie grinned. It was only a simple peasant stew, but it must indeed seem heavenly to his deprived senses.

Tilney dove in, scooping up a few quick spoonfuls before he spoke another word. Lizzie satisfied herself with a little handful of bread torn from the loaf. Tilney looked up at her with a familiar twinkle in his eye.

'I say, Bennett, there is one thing we need to speak about very soon,'

Lizzie stiffened, her hand frozen with the bread at her lips. 'Indeed,' she said with an affectedly lazy drawl. She avoided raising her eyes and concentrated on nibbling at the piece of bread very slowly. 'And what would that be, Tilney?'

He paused, the soupspoon still clutched in his hand. 'What was the name of the sawbones who attended me?'

Lizzie felt herself relax a little. Was this all he was wondering? 'M. Sangsue. He ought to be coming sometime today in order to examine you further. He has been quite confident of your recovery when I was quite concerned.'

Tilney's face looked slightly clouded, as if he were trying to recall something elusive. 'It was he who fished out the shot from my side?'

Lizzie nodded. 'It was quite an exacting procedure. It took him a good long while to extract the ball from your wound. Quite a bit of delicacy involved. I'm sure you'll find *monsieur le docteur* to be a most trustworthy and painstaking task master.'

Tilney sighed, setting the spoon back in the cooling bowl of soup. 'Painstaking is correct. I say, Bennett, did you help with this procedure?'

'Indeed I did,' Lizzie answered, trying hard to maintain her lazy drawl even as she rose in excitement. Oh, if Alice could only see her then! How she would marvel at her cousin and her ability to sustain such a painful and difficult procedure, to say nothing of the blood. No doubt at all: it was a fabulous encounter and no less. Lizzie took unaccustomed pride in her careful charade. She had portrayed the male not only in the casual wearing of the clothes, but in the midst of shocking adventures, had maintained the role with all aplomb. 'It was quite horrifying, but I wouldn't have missed it for the world.'

'You have been a good friend, Bennett, and brave.' Tilney nodded sagely, leaning back against the pillows.

'Why thank you, Tilney. You're most kind.'

'Why, it's no less than the truth,' Tilney re-joined. 'Quite a lot to withstand—horror, blanche and blood,' he added, shaking his head as if in disbelief of it all. 'Especially when one is a girl, yes?'

Lizzie froze once more. He knew!

'How long have you known?' Lizzie couldn't decide between anger and dismay at Tilney's discovery. Surely if he had known…but ah! There was no good thinking about that.

'How long?' Tilney repeated. 'It's hard to say.' He paused and looked up at Lizzie speculatively. 'There was always a hint, I think.'

'A hint!'

Tilney shrugged, the bedclothes shrugging along with him. 'I knew something was not quite right.'

'Nonetheless —'

'Yes,' Tilney responded as if anticipating her comment, 'I did nothing.'

Lizzie stared at him. 'You knew and did nothing. Sir, I must ask —'

'No, no, no,' Tilney cried, his fist hitting the bed without a sound. 'I beg you not to think of me as some kind of commonplace mind, fiend seize it! I was uncertain if I was right and what's more, I knew that if you were undertaking such a charade, there must be some kind of excuse for it.'

'You mean —?'

'Yes, damn. I knew you were in some kind of havey-cavey business if you were engaging in this masquerade. I didn't know if you were in the suds with some kind of family matter or trying to escape some sort of unfortunate attachment. Lawks, Bennett, it's not as if you were easy to read.'

'I suppose not,' Lizzie admitted, flinging herself into the chair by the bedside, relieved at least to no longer have to carry off the disguise, although she had found it quite comfortable over time. 'I was doing my best not to bring you any trouble or dis-ease.'

'You were a cracking companion,' Tilney admitted with a half-smile. 'Lud, but you were cool-headed in the midst of that infernal duelling nonsense. I may have made a cake of myself getting shot, but I'm glad there was someone as sensible as you there to assist me, Bennett.'

'You—you are most welcome, Tilney.' Lizzie felt her face flush hot. As comfortable as she had been with Tilney all this time, she suddenly felt awkward and peevish now that he knew her secret and was complimenting her on her disguise.

'Not at all, Bennett,' Tilney responded, his eyes searching her face carefully. 'I say, what should I call you anyway, Bennett? I can't keep calling you Bennett. Nor George, I suppose.'

'My name is Bennett,' Lizzie said softly. 'Elizabeth. Lizzie.'

'Quite suits you,' Tilney said decisively. 'Lizzie it is.'

'Thank you. I think,' Lizzie said, marvelling at the sound of her name from his lips.

'Well then, what are we going to do?'

'Do?'

'Well, we're in the devil's own scrape here, Bennett—er, Lizzie.'

'What do you mean?'

Tilney guffawed. 'Let's see: you're a lone female traveling as a man, with a single gentleman for companion with a reputation as a bit of a rake, who's also been shot in the midst of a French duel. Bad form, Bennett, very bad form.'

'When you put it that way...' Lizzie paused. What on earth could they do?

They were both silent for a space of time.

'I can see nothing for it,' Lizzie said slowly, turning the thoughts over in her mind as she dared to say the words aloud, 'but to continue as we have done. At least for the moment, anyway.'

'Do you mean—?' Tilney frowned. 'As we have done?'

'I mean,' Lizzie said with the decision evident in her tone, even as she continued to sprawl luxuriously in the chair, 'that we cannot change things here, certainly. And it may not be safe to alter our arrangements as we travel.'

'Travel,' Tilney echoed, seeming somewhat nonplussed.

'Think, Tilney,' Lizzie said urgently, sitting up in her chair to regard him quite seriously. 'We're in a bind now. We've gone with this masquerade for so long now that people have been taken in by it. We cannot change anything at present—it would cause too much confusion. So we need to continue to pretend. Otherwise we will be in for difficulties for sure.'

Tilney frowned, but nodded his head. He must have realised she was right. 'But for how long shall we do this? Surely after we leave this place we can return you to your rightful situation. Whatever that may be,' he finished lamely, looking at her now with frank curiosity. 'What is your rightful situation?'

Lizzie sighed. 'I hardly know where to begin.'

Tilney leaned back, crossing his arms behind his head. 'I have no immediate plans.'

Lizzie sighed again and thought about where to begin. 'We were on the way to my cousin Alice's father's funeral,' she began, but paused. 'Perhaps I need to mention the King of Naples?'

Tilney raised an eyebrow. 'Miss Austen would enjoy your tale, I suspect.'

Lizzie could not entirely squelch the pleased grin that rose to her lips. 'Let us begin with the funeral and add other elements as they come along.'

'Were you close to your uncle?' Tilney quizzed her as he settled into his pillow.

'If you are going to ask those sorts of questions at every juncture,' Lizzie said with a narrowed eye, 'this will take much longer than it need do.'

'I am quite contrite,' Tilney said with a yawn. 'I will ask no more!'

Lizzie smiled. At this rate he would soon fall asleep and

she need not expose all of her lively details of the story. Accordingly she made her voice as even and droning as possible as she told the story of the funeral.

'It was a quiet day, very little in the way of plant growth or insect life,' she started and was pleased to see Tilney's eyelids droop precipitously. 'Alice and I were in our very finest mourning clothes and made sure that we had very neat and starched handkerchiefs in our pockets or sleeves, as that is certainly the most important part of funeral preparation.'

Lizzie noticed that Tilney's eyes were closed now and so droned on in a similar tone. 'We were riding along trying to recall what people had been wearing at the Assembly Ball,' which wasn't entirely true, but seemed perfect for lulling Tilney into slumber. 'I was trying to recall who had linen, whereas Alice tried to recall who had worn silk and we compared notes on who had been the more raucous.'

Tilney was not only asleep, but beginning to snore. Thank goodness, Lizzie thought. Now I can do a little thinking!

As Tilney snored on, Lizzie's thoughts raced. What indeed were they to do? What was her rightful situation at this point? She glanced down at Tilney's calm face, a little careworn to be sure, but just as open and appealing as it had been at her first sight of him.

That was the problem, after all.

By all that was right, she owed her affections to the hinted promises of the King of Naples, who, if he had been less than forthright in his declarations (a factor she put down to Italianate modesty), had nonetheless implied a very positive outlook in return for her attentions.

Despite his prodigious knowledge of insects, their habits and habitats, Lizzie had found that the immediate and tangible charms of Tilney had somehow made it very easy to forget the primarily literary appeal of the King. He was royalty, too, she tried to remind herself. Italian royalty to be sure, which was not quite the same thing; nonetheless, for a woman in her somewhat marginal position in English society, royalty of any kind was nothing to be sniffed at by any means.

Yet she must admit that she had hardly spared a thought for the King in some considerable space of time. Lizzie could not simply blame the rigors of caring for Tilney in his com-promised position. Tending a sick bed had often left her with ample time to peruse the informative letters posted by her Neapolitan friend, re-reading with interest his knowledgeable dissertations on the dining habits of the common cockchafer.

You have not shown the slightest interest in cockchafer lore, Lizzie scolded herself.

It was true: since meeting up with Tilney on that fateful day, she had spared little more than the occasional thought for the king and his little creatures. She looked down at her friend's slumbering visage. It wasn't that he was remarkably handsome. His face, while pleasant enough, did not have the dazzling attraction of someone like the elusive Kit Barrington, who had so fascinated her poor cousin, Alice.

Yet there was so much good humour and lively wit in that face when it was awake. That was the chief distraction, Lizzie thought with a sigh, a mind that kept up with her own. Be fair, she reminded herself, a mind that sometimes pulled ahead, too. Trapped in the well-intentioned enclosure of Mangrove Hall, Lizzie frequently tired of slowing her thoughts to match the pace of those around her. Love them as she might, she could not claim much in the way of intel-lectual stimulation for the kindly relatives who took her in. It was a pleasant change to be kept on her toes by a friend who was every bit as clever as she, and more than willing to chafe her verbally.

But duty was a thing a young woman ought not abandon completely. Lizzie felt a flush of shame at her own indulgent ways. As much fun as her adventures had been (in retrospect anyway; it was difficult to recall now just how frightened she had been when Tilney was shot), it behoved her to remember that pleasure was not the aim of life and she owed it to her relations and to the memory of her parents to do what was right.

'We shall go to Naples,' Lizzie said aloud. Tilney stirred at her words, but did not waken, turning his sweet face away from the light from the window. Lizzie felt a painful tugging at what were surely her heartstrings. Why must he look so thoroughly agreeable just then?

Lizzie felt the need to do something useful while Tilney slumbered and, tired of the endless repairing of clothes, steeled herself to do her duty. Certain that Tilney would not at all mind, she retrieved his letter case from his baggage and sat down to compose a letter to the King of Naples.

It was funny how comforting the very act of writing was. Sitting at the small table in the corner where the light shone to its best in the late afternoon, Lizzie uncapped the ink and sharpened the quill. With luck she would have some time before the physician arrived to check on his patient and see the improvement the day had brought.

She selected one of the smaller size papers among Tilney's collection. Dipping the quill in the tiny bottle, Lizzie drew a breath and quickly wrote the date at the top, marvelling again how much time had passed since that fateful day of the funeral. Another dip and she wrote 'Your Majesty,' in her usual manner, which was far too florid for her liking, but she found herself incapable of writing with the neat penmanship Lady Mangrove had always maintained in her own writing. However much she might control the rest of her life, Lizzie found it impossible to restrain her pen.

It was provoking. Lizzie often suspected that her handwriting revealed things about her that she would prefer to keep locked in her most private thoughts.

She dipped the pen once more into the inkpot and paused. As her hand hovered over the ink, allowing a stray drop to fall back into the bottle rather than blot the paper, Lizzie felt her good intentions sink.

What had she to say?

Her immediate thoughts were to apologise for the delay in clarifying her developing kidnap situation since the Pig & Whistle, but how then to explain what had happened in the succeeding interval? 'My excuse is rogues, pirates, destitution and a considerable amount of time spent in disguise as a young man.' Hardly satisfying to her correspondent, Lizzie imagined.

Nor flattering when put so baldly, she had to admit. Mrs. Radcliffe would make much of such a narrative, but Lizzie was certain she had neither the skill nor the patience to make much of the events. Besides, it wasn't really the point, after all.

What was the point, though? Telling the king that she would be coming to Naples somewhat unexpectedly? That she had taken the hinted promises as definite indications? Where did she stand with the king after all?

Lizzie stared at the clean white page and sighed. Such a terrifying tyranny in that empty space.

There was a step on the stair. Lizzie's heart leapt. It must be the physician, she told herself, and hastily rolled up the letter she had begun, tucking it into her pocket, then moving swiftly to cap the ink and return all the items to their places in the letter case.

She would finish the letter later, surely. Lizzie did her best to thrust away all disruptive thoughts nagging at her mind, suggesting that it wasn't a matter of time that was needed to complete the letter, but a decision about what the contents might be. Never mind that, she scolded. Somehow it would all work out.

Lizzie instantly recognised the steady rap at the door. Crossing to open it, she found the frowning physician on the other side. He entered the room with a curt nod and went straight to the patient.

'His colour looks much better,' he said placing a palm on Tilney's forehead. 'And the fever, she is gone. Excellent.'

'He was awake earlier,' Lizzie mentioned, trying to look as appropriately nonchalant as she could manage. 'I daresay he will be awake again soon.'

The sawbones nodded as if this were all according to plan. 'You must get him to eat. As much as possible. Do not accept his arguments. We need to restore his strength. There is always a chance he may have to fight off further infection. It was a deep wound.'

Lizzie, who had assumed the worst was over, worried anew. 'How will we know when he's out of danger?'

The physician shrugged in that peculiarly Gallic way. 'One cannot say. We shall simply have to observe.' He looked at Lizzie with his usual penetrating stare. 'You need rest as much as he. It will do no good to fall ill yourself.'

'Well, I—' Lizzie stammered.

'No,' he continued, waving away Lizzie's protests. 'You have worn yourself out. And even with a,' he paused searching for the right word, 'tenacious constitution like your own, your reserves are not endless.'

Lizzie swallowed and found she had nothing to say.

'Sleep, eat, rest.' He gestured down at the slumbering Tilney. 'Push him over. There is plenty of room for two.'

Lizzie did her best to conceal her alarm. 'Certainly, certainly. As you suggest.' As the physician stood by, she gingerly got into the bed next to her sleeping friend. I shan't be able to sleep a wink, Lizzie told herself.

Chapter Fifteen

Alice turned toward the window. The morning light was yet insufficient to presage the arrival of breakfast and she fidgeted uncomfortably, wondering how it was she had become accustomed to this part of the day so gradually. Not that long ago, such an hour would have been unthinkable. It was considerably astounding that the mere lack of servants, regular hours and required occupations should so disturb her day.

Such simple things, Alice thought. How disagreeable to have to do without them.

Worse, finding herself waking at a reasonable hour and occupying her long days with little more than reading, was beginning to make her feel a trifle old for her modest number of years. Alice blinked out the window and took in the unchanging landscape. At one time she had thought it exotic and full of promise.

Now, however, it only seemed to promise a neglect, which she shared. Daily Gilet de Sauvinage repeated his demand that she marry him and just as frequently, she refused. Apart from that, she had no contact with anyone. She surmised that someone must have been preparing the meals of which she partook, for de Sauvinage, despite his supposed Frenchness, did not seem to be quite capable of accomplishing them.

He never knew what was in the sauces, for instance.

Alice had never quite reconciled herself to the Gallic predilection for sauces. She understood gravy well enough and expected to see it on a pie, but expecting a good roast for her midday meal, she was always a bit nonplussed by the variety of sauces that had been appearing surrounding the meat that ought to have been the centre of the entrée.

While travel had indeed broadened her palate (she often remembered with a start the things she had consumed upon the decks of the *Bonny Read*) Alice longed for a simple beef roast and potatoes with peas to add a little colour.

What she usually received was some kind of meat in a rich sauce that clearly contained a good deal more butter and cream than was strictly necessary. She had to admit that the concoctions generally tasted quite good, but she longed for the simple tastes of her home.

Who could have imagined being wistful about Yorkshire pudding? But wistful she was.

Alice turned away from the window and sighed. The landscape offering no respite from her gloomy thoughts—in fact adding to them with the persistent drizzle that now came down from the heavens in the weak dawn light—she turned once more to Victor's tale of woe.

She had just begun to formulate some sympathy for the sad creature's tale of abandonment and woe—not to mention an indignation for Victor's abandonment of the same—when a knock on the door came which heralded her inevitable breakfast.

At least it will only be bread and butter, Alice thought with some relief. Good heavens, she thought, amazed at her own violent language, what will happen the day cook decides to add sauces to breakfast?

Upon approaching the door, however, she drew a sharp intake of breath signalling surprise and alarm as a figure stepped through the wood.

'Who are you?' Alice demanded with far more confidence than she felt.

From the figure, there came no reply. Its raven-black garments seemed to fluctuate with the passage of breezes, though there could surely be few such winds in the room. Alice could see no face beyond the chin, which poked out with an eerie paleness from below the hood that covered the rest of the head.

'Why do you not speak?' Alice said with considerably less gusto. She could feel a strange sensation trying to crawl up her spine toward her head and she had a terrible feeling that when it got there something awful might happen.

The figure before the doorway made a strange gesture with its hands—or what appeared to be its hands. The long sleeves of its accoutrements concealed any digits that might be found therein and Alice realised that the sensation rising to her brain was in fact panic and any moment now it might well be unleashed which would doubtless result in some sort of undignified outburst such as a scream or yelp. Either of which would surely convey a sense of terror that really ought not be revealed to apparitions of this sort, surely, Alice thought with an ever-so palpitating heart.

What would Lizzie do? Alice turned her swiftly scattering thoughts to the reliably comforting image of her cousin. In such a situation, Lizzie would be resolute even though frightened. She would think of something to say or do that would restore a sense of order to the chaos of the unknown.

Amidst the rapidly rising strangulation of alarm, Alice thought she must make some attempt to take control of the situation even as the strange figure swayed disturbingly before her.

'Did you bring my breakfast?' she blurted at last, the words squeaking out of her throat at a slightly higher pitch than normal.

The thing at the doorway uttered a sigh that stretched into a kind of disturbing moan that made Alice want to curl her toes right up. It seemed to speak the wordless misery and hopelessness of a deeply buried hell that it had risen from only momentarily and would soon be dragged back down into without mercy or respite.

'Well then,' Alice said with a decisiveness she did not feel, 'I will say 'good day' to you.' She turned on her heel with panic on her shoulder, leaping onto her head as she spun around and galloped most ungracefully toward the bed. Leaping into its centre, she pulled the bedclothes up to her chin and stared at the closed door.

Minutes ticked by and all remained silent. Alice could hear her own breathing in the small room and tried in vain to silence its noise. There was no movement or sound at the door. Perhaps the figure had moved on, seeking another door or another visitor to haunt. With luck it would not be back and there were surely many such rooms to investigate.

But it knows I'm here now, Alice thought. The realisation made her sink under the bedclothes and grow very quiet.

After some time had passed, Alice peeked up over the bedclothes. All was silent. More light shone through the window now and it's slightly cheerier ambiance helped to strengthen her resolve. Perhaps it was a dream, Alice told herself.

But she knew it was no dream. It was comforting, though, to try to make the incident turn hazy in her mind—as unpleasant things should become as quickly as possible. However, the fear still made her heart beat a little bit faster just thinking about the strange vision that had appeared in the doorway.

It did no harm, Alice thought with some relief. Perhaps it did not mean to frighten her. As she recalled its spooky black garments she could not suppress a shudder which roamed through her limbs like a gypsy wagon. Picturing the way its weeds moved to a wind that was not there made her feel distinctly unwell.

But it had done no harm. It had not even spoken to her. Perhaps it was seeking help. Alice tried to dredge up from her memory stories of ghosts and whether they had caused injury to anyone. Surely Mrs. Radcliffe had presented more than a few ghosts, many of whom seemed to be more suffering than suffered from.

Alice looked out the window at the breaking morning and could feel hope and confidence return to her. A blackbird whistled merrily and the sound revived her spirits. Perhaps, like so many of Mrs. Radcliffe's ghosts, this one was offering a warning to her.

What sort of warning?

Alice's heart raced again, fear propelling her thoughts. What if she were in some kind of danger?

Foolish girl, told herself with a shake. You've been kidnapped: of course you're in some kind of danger. But how much? Alice fretted for a moment, but the combination of the bright sunlight pouring in through the window, the blackbird's cheerful song and the complete lack of breakfast conspired to distract her thoughts from their morbid course.

Where is my breakfast? Alice thought. It should have been here by now. Even though it was generally a simple and entirely unexciting repast, the habit of breakfasting was one she was keen to keep, even if it had not yet included kippers much as she might keep hoping.

It must surely be kippers one day, she sighed. Even kedgeree would be a welcome respite from the sad porridge and toast. If one were going to go to the trouble of kidnapping a person, Alice speculated, it would be a welcome gesture to also plan for the kidnappee's keeping with a reasonable kitchen and some kind of staff.

Alice glanced out the window at the rather sad and unkempt garden, and thought for the hundredth time that it would be very nice indeed to be able to walk out in that garden, even if it had few delights for the eye. Alice had come to regard her mother's constant reminders about the importance of daily exercise as surprisingly well chosen.

She had nearly forgotten her fright when the sound of footsteps in the hallway jolted her back to contemplation of the door. As the steps grew louder and their maker closer, Alice sunk behind the bedclothes again, fearful and trembling as her anticipation grew. A knock came at the door and she gasped.

For a moment, there was no further sound after the knock. Alice quivered behind her protective bedclothes. She blinked a few times and then wondered if perhaps her visitor might be corporeal. A second knock at the door and the growling in her midsection convinced her that it was well worth ascertaining whether the apparition had returned or whether her breakfast might be waiting outside the door even now.

With trembling hands, Alice folded back the bedclothes neatly and swung her feet back over the edge of the bed. Gingerly she crossed the floor to the door, listening for any discernible noise on the other side of the door. Hearing nothing, she at last drew a deep breath and pulled on the knob. Unlocked? With a swiftly winging hope flying from her heart, Alice threw the door open.

Outside stood a very surprised Gilet de Sauvinage, holding a key in one hand and a tray with her breakfast in the other. '*Mademoiselle?*'

Alice looked quickly down the corridor in either direction. There was no one else to be seen.

'What is it, *mademoiselle?*' Her kidnapper seemed to speak in tones of concern, though it was hard to tell behind the kerchief that masked his face.

'I thought—' Alice began, then paused. 'Perhaps it was nothing.' Her nervous tone did not match the nonchalance of her words. 'Is that my breakfast?' she asked with more of her usual brisk tone.

'*Oui, mademoiselle, le petit déjeuner*. Let me bring it in to your room,' de Sauvinage said as he attempted to make his way into the room.

Alice blocked his entrance with a subtle movement. 'Do you think that is strictly necessary?' Alice asked though her stance clearly indicated it was not. 'I can take the tray myself.'

The unusualness of this statement in the context of her past did not strike the young lady at that time, unaware as she was of the many changes wrought by her adventures since the funeral of her father. The changes had been of a subtle nature, one by one. It was difficult for our heroine to glimpse that now increasingly distant time when she had been wholly dependent upon a range of servants and considerable parental guidance.

The Alice of not so many weeks ago would not have imagined demanding of her kidnapper, 'Have you heard or seen anything in the corridor this morning?'

'I do not know what you mean, Al—er, *mademoiselle*,' de Sauvinage said somewhat haltingly.

'I think you do,' Alice said. She wished very much for a lorgnette just then, for her mother had wielded one with such aplomb that no one could countenance her perusal with equanimity. Alice had seen many a stalwart young man cave before her scrutiny.

'I assure you—' he stammered, but Alice was not convinced.

'Tell me the truth! I insist.'

He seemed to be somewhat abashed at her insistence, at least as far as one might surmise under the disguise. 'The truth?'

'Indeed! You must admit the truth. There is an apparition haunting these halls, is there not?' Alice accused.

De Sauvinage appeared to pause and then nodded hastily. 'Yes, indeed there is, Miss. It's quite a chilling story in fact.'

Alice gasped. 'Tell me more!'

'I shall,' said de Sauvinage.

'Shall we set the tray down, first?' Gilet de Sauvinage asked Alice. It was a bit awkward with the two of them holding on to either side which held them immobile in the doorway.

'Just as you say,' Alice agreed, more intrigued by the thought of the mysterious story of the apparition than even with the idea of breakfast, although her stomach rumbled an appreciative reminder of the importance of that meal.

After some awkward fits and starts, Alice at last relinquished the tray with a sigh and retreated into the room so de Sauvinage could place the tray on the small table. The repast, once uncovered, proved to contain no kippers or even kedgeree, so Alice sighed and ate some of the toast.

'Now tell me of that apparition that haunts the hallways of this villa,' Alice demanded, pouring herself a cup of tea with the beginnings of a cross look etching into the furrows of her brow. If she had seen this furrowing, doubtless Alice would have been worried that such furrowing would lead to later wrinkling, but she remained blissfully unaware of that physical development, instead turning a severe eye upon her capture as she chewed her breakfast. It was impossible to see if that were having the desired effect, cloaked as he was by his mysterious disguise.

However, his words seemed to suggest that her look had prompted him to mindfulness. 'Yes, of course, miss. It is a strange and wondrous tale that may frighten you.'

Alice shrugged. A most unladylike gesture, but she had so far fallen form gentility on this journey that she failed to even notice the common tone of her body's movement. Her mother would have been shocked indeed, so it is just as well that she was not present to see Alice's shrug.

'I don't wish to frighten you,' de Sauvinage continued, now seeming more than a little reluctant to begin, which only increased Alice's irritation.

'I have been kidnapped and sailed with pirates,' Alice said, more than a little crossness slipping out between her lips with not a few crumbs of toast. 'I hardly think I will faint away at the mere story of a haunting.'

'As you wish, then, miss,' de Sauvinage said, his words and manner somewhat stiff.

I believe I have offended him, Alice thought, and smiled secretly to herself. It was quite enjoyable to have the whip back in her hand, so to speak. 'I do,' Alice said, feeling rather smug and superior. 'Tell on, please.' She stuffed the last bit of toast into her mouth and chomped it with satisfaction.

'Many years ago, in this very place—' de Sauvinage began.

Alice returned to the habit that annoyed her governess so, and immediately broke in for an explanation. 'In this very place, meaning this very room?' she asked somewhat pedantically.

'Well, I don't know for certain,' de Sauvinage said, non-plussed by her interjection. 'I—I believe it was in this wing, though perhaps in a different room. I cannot be too certain.'

'I think it would be very distasteful if it was this very room, and I would have thought it odd of you to choose to sequester me here,' Alice said, enjoying the use of this very important word, which had welled up from her admittedly spotty memory. 'Go on.'

'It was, in a word,' said de Sauvinage with a dramatic pause, 'murder!'

'Murder!' Alice said with alarm. That was rather more than she had expected. 'Murder?' she repeated, her voice decidedly less audible. 'Here?'

De Sauvinage nodded. 'It was more than forty years ago, when this villa was still occupied by the duke.'

'Which duke?' Alice asked, forgetting her terror for a moment.

'The duke of this villa,' de Sauvinage said with a touch of irritability. 'I don't know his name.'

'It's a rather important fact,' Alice said, her tone conveying a distinct shade of disapproval.

'Well, it is not one that I possess,' de Sauvinage said with finality. 'About forty years ago—no, I cannot be more specific than that,' he added, anticipating another interruption from his audience. 'The duke was away on business, of some unknown type,' he rushed to say, regarding Alice with a severe look, or so it appeared from behind the disguise. 'His younger brother was in charge of the estate and had some very questionable companions allowed as guests in his brother's absence.

'One of these men was the notorious Comte Belette, a reviled man of irregular hours and unpardonable tastes.'

Alice shivered. It was quite too horrible to contemplate.

'The comte had, unbeknownst to his host, had his henchmen spirit away a noble young lass and he received her in secret in this very house.'

'No!' Alice interjected. The horror of it all! She thanked her lucky stars once again that having had to be kidnapped, she had at least been spirited away by men who knew their place. Her heart went out to the poor unfortunate even as her finely honed sense of morality shrank from the likely (and only vaguely understood) fate the poor young woman suffered.

'Indeed,' Alice's own kidnapper continued. 'Sequestered in a room of this villa—'

'On this floor,' Alice filled in, her voice breathless with terror and excitement.

'On this floor,' de Sauvinage agreed, though once again reminding her, 'but probably not this room, he had her secreted away to use her for his filthy Gallic purposes.'

'How terrible!'

'Indeed,' de Sauvinage repeated. 'When night fell, he crept away from the other revellers and made his way to the room where the frightened young woman awaited her unspeakable fate.'

'Unspeakable,' Alice repeated with dread fascination.

'The story was told that she did her best to resist him, shrieking in terror and fighting off his advances with all decent outcry.'

'And did he…?' Alice could barely bring herself to ask.

Gilet de Sauvinage leant toward her, his voice dropping to a whisper. 'At the very last minute—'

'Yes?'

'She evaded his advances—'

'Hurrah!'

'By falling out the window and plunging to a horrible

236

death!'

'That's too horrible!' Alice exclaimed, leaping up in alarm. 'Was it this very window?'

Gilet de Sauvinage shrugged in a not especially Gallic way. 'I don't know which room it was, just that it was in this wing.'

Alice blanched. 'It could have been this very room. Oh, the poor unfortunate! Did her family demand justice?'

He shook his head. 'They never knew what had happened to her. The terrible Comte Belette never even sent them a ransom note or any kind of threatening message.'

'How awful!' Alice said, feeling an unaccustomed sense of faintness come over her. It had been some time since she had felt so weak. Perhaps she should eat more of her breakfast.

But there was also something niggling at the back of her mind. What could it be?

'Ever since,' de Sauvinage continued, unaware of Alice's wandering thoughts, 'many people have reported that they have seen wandering the corridors, a pale ghostly figure of a woman, searching, always searching.'

'What is she searching for?' Alice asked, subsiding again as she ate some of the porridge.

'Perhaps her killer,' he replied. 'Or perhaps she just wants someone to blame!'

'Well, it's not my fault,' Alice said with what had become her usual decided air. 'She can't want to haunt me. I suppose this comte is also dead.'

De Sauvinage shrugged again. 'I don't know. It's possible that he's still alive, but he is not here.'

'Do you know where he is?' Alice set her spoon down as an idea occurred to her.

'I haven't the slightest idea,' de Sauvinage said, sounding more than a trifle irritated with the line of questioning. 'I suppose he returned to his estate, wherever that might be.'

'I shall certainly tell the spectre if she returns,' Alice said, returning once more to her porridge. 'It is only fair that she know he is not here. She can seek her vengeance elsewhere.' The latter was less than entirely distinct as Alice was still masticating a mouthful of porridge during the speech, a collision of activities that would have well and truly scandalized her mother and most of the household had they been there to experience it.

'Well, one never can tell with ghosts,' de Sauvinage said. One might have caught a hint of irritation in his voice. Whether he was simply fed up with Alice's failure to be impressed with his tale or with her poor manners in speaking with her mouth full, it was difficult to ascertain.

However, he was startled when Alice suddenly dropped her spoon in horror. The utensil made an unpleasant wet smacking sound as it fell back into the porridge. She stared at de Sauvinage, her eyes round and her cheeks flushed.

'What is it, *Mademoiselle* Alice?' he asked, his voice choking up to a higher register and his French accent deserting him completely.

'Have you done it?' she shouted in a most unbecoming way.

'Have I done what?' Gilet de Sauvinage asked with irritation.

'Why,' Alice said, her tone suggesting that he ought to have known exactly what she meant, 'I meant exactly that. Have you sent a ransom request to my family?'

De Sauvinage blanched at her inquiry. 'How can you ask such a question?' he asked, his voice losing all trace of Gallic sanguinity.

'I ask because I must know,' Alice responded with more than a little forceful disapproval. As unaccustomed as she was to finding herself in a position of some authority, Alice nonetheless deciphered that there had been a kind of shift in the balance of power between the two of them. Invigorated by the story of the poor young woman's travails, Alice found herself determined not to give in to the same fate.

'Have you sent a ransom note to my family?' Alice reiterated. 'Tell me now!'

Gilet de Sauvinage quailed. Visibly, this was apparent.

It was not, Alice was certain, in the nature of villains to quail before heroines. She was somewhat disappointed to find that this was the calibre of villain she had attracted. Somehow it seemed a poor reflection on her.

If I were a better heroine, I would have attracted a more

accomplished villain, Alice thought sadly.

'I have had some delay,' de Sauvinage began.

'Why?' Alice demanded.

'I do not have a normal household staff, for one thing,' de Sauvinage blustered. 'If you knew what kind of efforts were required to keep a situation like this running smoothly, you would be surprised to say the least, miss — er, miss.'

Alice shrugged with a nigh on Gallic casualness. 'As the kidnapped person, I have no responsibility for those details. However, as the kidnapped person, I am horrified to find that you have done nothing toward securing my eventual rescue and ransoming. It is too shocking, too shocking by half,' Alice said with more than a touch of her mother's oft-exercised sense of high dudgeon.

'Do you know how long it takes to make porridge?' de Sauvinage asked with more than a touch of bitterness.

Alice raised an eyebrow in a gesture that would have made her sensible cousin Lizzie nod with approval. 'It is not my concern to know what porridge requires. You must ransom me or let me go.'

De Sauvinage looked more than a tad perturbed at her suggestion. 'Let you go? When it took me so long to acquire you? I do not think so.' He shook his head, but Alice was not yet daunted.

'Then ransom me,' she reiterated. 'My family will be grateful to have me returned to them, I am certain. I wish to be free.'

'I'm not sure that can be arranged,' de Sauvinage said with ominous intent.

'What on earth do you mean?' Alice demanded. It was more than a little provoking to find that while she had been kidnapped for some time, the ransoming process had yet to begin. 'Very bad form,' Alice added with a sternly disapproving look. 'Very bad form.'

'I don't think you comprehend—' Gilet de Sauvinage began, but Alice cut him off with an admirably peremptory gesture.

'I am displeased,' was all she said, however. But she suddenly appreciated the commanding tone her rather diminutive mother often used. It was surprisingly effective with many members of the public.

'I appreciate that,' de Sauvinage began, but Alice interjected once again.

'You may appreciate that,' she said with what she hoped was a studiously severe look, 'but I do not appreciate it. Such a thing is not at all to be tolerated.'

'I did not of course mean 'appreciate' in quite that sense, you understand—'

'It is immaterial,' Alice continued, allowing herself a very brief time in which she revelled in the thought that the word had sprung so easily to her lips. 'Quite immaterial. I have a reputation to maintain and a family who misses me to distraction, I am certain.' Though it was likely to be something less than the case, and in fact Alice suspected that the one family member who might well miss her a great deal was also missing and in dubious company—oh, poor Lizzie!—she nonetheless thought it rhetorically important to maintain such a façade, even if she could not quite recall the word 'rhetorically,' the concept was certainly clear enough in her thoughts.

'If you do not manage to arrange for a proper ransoming, I shall not be responsible for the consequences,' Alice warned with an admirable air of high dudgeon, before which her kidnapper quailed with surprising effectiveness.

'I don't see what you could possibly do,' he retorted nonetheless, clearly unwilling to allow Alice to seize control of the situation.

Alice drew herself up to her entire height, which was less impressive than desired while she was seated for breakfast, but she did do her best. 'If you do not properly dispatch with the necessary ransom note, I shall…' She paused.

After all, what ammunition had she?

A moment later, an imperceptible time for the tense circumstances, Alice smiled coldly. 'If you do not properly dispatch with the necessary ransom note,' Alice repeated, 'I shall summon the ghost of that dead young woman and be absolutely certain that I set her to haunting you day and night so you receive no rest whatsoever. That is what I shall do.' Alice folded her arms feeling rather smugly superior.

For his part, Gilet de Sauvinage gave every sign of having been beaten. 'I will acquiesce,' he said with obvious irritation in his manner. 'But I assure you I will ask for a substantial recompense that will make all this folderol worthwhile.'

Alice smiled. She might be forgiven for looking a trifle smug at that moment, but she had never quite triumphed in any kind of verbal exchange, so there was a quite an excuse for her gloating.

De Sauvinage bowed stiffly and backed out of the room. Alice felt a flush of excitement rise up to her cheeks, doubtless colouring them pink with delight. She had little time to relish her success, however, because a wispy voice rasped in her ear, 'How shall we punish him, Miss Alice?'

There was no doubt about it: a ghost hovered at her side.

Chapter Sixteen

'I must say,' Tilney drawled from far too close to Lizzie's ear, 'that I find this unexpectedly comfortable.'

Lizzie's eyes popped open and she sat bolt upright. After a moment's confusion, she remembered that she was lying in the bed next to Tilney. Were it not for the fact that he lay under the duvet and she on top of it, Lizzie might well have fainted with alarm right there.

'I-I—' she began stammering as she slipped off the bed. 'It was the surgeon. He insisted I rest. I did not wish to make him suspect anything was amiss, so I followed his orders.' She feared that her face had probably turned scarlet.

Tilney stretched and yawned. 'Well, I feel unaccountably better. And hungry. Do tell me I will be able to eat something now. Don't want that infernal sawbones to be forbidding me to put on the feedbag.'

'No, not at all. In fact, he was telling me to be sure to make you eat. Let me run down to the landlord and ask him for your supper.' Lizzie stepped toward the door, whisking away the lock of hair that decided to cover her eyes.

'Wait, Bennett,' Tilney said, his voice softer than before. 'Don't run away just yet.'

Lizzie paused, attempting to compose herself before she turned her face toward his. 'What is it, Tilney?'

To her surprise, his face did not reveal the usual lazy grin, but a rather more serious expression. 'I knew I fell asleep like a child while you were telling me your life story, but I do hope you will enlighten me to the cause of your present ticklish situation. I do want to know.'

The warmth that flushed her cheeks made Lizzie even more eager to depart. 'I shall,' she managed to say, her voice higher than usual from the strain of suppressing her conflicting emotions. 'Do let me get you some sustenance, first.'

'Bennett,' Tilney repeated. 'I want to know everything.' His smile returned but it was almost shy and his eyes had a kind of warmth in their gaze that made Lizzie blush further.

242

She nodded her head, not trusting herself to answer with words and hurried out the door.

In the dark of the corridor, Lizzie exhaled with relief. Why oh why, did she have to be kidnapped from her uncle's funeral, exiled on a white slaver's ship, rescued by pirates and nearly drowned in a storm just so she could run into Tilney in a small coastal village of France? It was as if some guiding influence wilfully threw her into one adventure after another for its own amusement.

If only she had not been thrown into Tilney's path! If only he had been a dullard and a fool! She would not be in the situation she was. Resolutely, she turned to head down the staircase. It would be best to get away from Tilney as quickly as possible. Lizzie could not bear to wrong him or herself. The less he knew, the better.

She would have to give him the slip, as they said, leave his side and go to the King of Naples. It was the only way. Yet her steps were heavy as she descended to the main floor.

As she stepped into the dining room of the inn, Lizzie found herself wistful. Contemplating her escape from this place suddenly made it seem so much homier. The dingy interior and well-worn accoutrements took on a nostalgic air as she tried to force herself into thoughts of escape.

Well enough to know she had to go away—for Tilney's good as well as her own, truly—but more difficult to actually act upon the knowledge. I can easily ride away, today or even tomorrow, Lizzie told herself.

But who would take care of Tilney?

Stop it, Lizzie thought with a shake. Tilney is well enough now, clearly on the way to recovery. He doesn't need you, she scolded. Lizzie did her best to ignore the stabbing pain in her chest. It didn't mean anything at all.

'*Monsieur*,' she asked the landlord, lowering her voice mid-word as it had crept up to a higher register than usual. 'If I could trouble your for some sustenance for my friend—'

The kindly landlord turned from his attentions to the glasses with mild surprise. 'Ah, *oui, oui*. I have some lamb stew that is *magnifique*, even if it is I saying so.' His smile was superseded almost at once by a more serious look, however.

'I have some news to share that you may not find so palatable, *monsieur*.'

Lizzie started. 'What is it?' The last thing she wanted was more surprises.

'The magistrate has arrived.'

'The magistrate?' That didn't sound good, Lizzie thought.

'*Oui*, he arrives periodically to review local disputes and such like. He has come a bit earlier than usual, however. I do not know for certain, but I fear that perhaps someone may have told him about the duel. One suspects that he may be more interested in the principal duellists themselves, of course,' and he gave a little Gallic shrug at this, 'but one can never predict the actions of *petit* bureaucrats.'

'Indeed,' Lizzie answered, her voice ringing hollow in the empty room. She watched the landlord bustle around scooping some of the stew into a tureen while her thoughts ran like spring colts around the corridors of her mind. Magistrate! Law, bother, difficulties—exposure! For both of them, no doubt. This could not be borne.

'*Merci, merci*,' Lizzie muttered as she took the tray from his hands. She made her way up the stairs as swiftly as it was safe to do, testing a wide variety of scenarios in her head as she struggled up the steps trying to keep the tureen level.

She burst through the door, startling Tilney who had a book open in his lap.

'We must depart today!'

'The fiend seize you, Bennett,' Tilney said with genuine surprise and irritation. 'What the devil do you mean, we have to leave?'

Lizzie smothered the smile that wished to bloom upon her lips. It was no good pretending that Tilney was not delightful, but she had to do her best not to make the thought plain. This will be so much more difficult now, Lizzie thought despairingly. 'The magistrate,' she offered. 'The magistrate has arrived earlier than usual, the landlord tells me. He may well be here to investigate the duel…'

'Ah, and its aftermath,' Tilney finished. His brow furrowed as he sat upright with decision. 'Then leave we shall. Help me up, Bennett.' He struggled to the edge of the bed.

'Nonsense!' Lizzie remonstrated. 'You cannot possibly be thinking of getting up.' In vain she tried to tuck him back into the bed.

'We have no choice, Bennett,' Tilney said with admirable firmness. 'Either we get on our way or we risk exposure. Be sensible, damn you. We'll be brought to Point Non Plus if the magistrate arrives and begins to ask uncomfortable questions.'

'I suppose,' Lizzie answered, hesitating as she tried to assail his logic, but finding no real recourse.

Tilney looked at her with cool appraisal. 'You may have grown accustomed to your telling of *Canterbury Tales*, but I think it best if we have to avoid spreading too many dubious legends in our wake. Much easier to keep track of the truth as much as possible, eh Bennett?' He crooked one eyebrow in her direction and Lizzie did her best to maintain a steadfast light-heartedness and not give in to the swooning feeling of giddiness that filled her heart at that moment.

'I suppose,' she merely repeated, frowning down at Tilney. 'How shall we proceed?'

'Help me up, Bennett,' Tilney croaked, making an effort to swing his pale legs out from under the bedclothes.

His face looked horribly pale, so Lizzie darted forward to steady his rise from the bed. 'Easy now, Tilney. We can't have you doing it much too brown, now.'

Tilney gave her a crooked smile. 'Curse you, Bennett, but you do have a flair for cant.'

Lizzie could feel her cheeks grow pink. 'Never mind that now, Tilney. We have important duties ahead of us.'

'Indeed we do,' he agreed, but Lizzie did not notice the gentle beam in his eyes as they took in her glowing face.

With her help, he was able to stand, but little more.

'Well, damn, Bennett,' said Tilney, his voice a little more gruff than usual. 'I feel unaccountably weak. Must be the surgery.'

'Agreed,' Lizzie agreed. 'But can you possibly travel? We shall have to hire a coach or phaeton, surely.'

Tilney regarded the issue with a passing solemnity. 'Do you suppose there is one to be had in this tiny village?'

'I can ask the landlord,' Lizzie said, 'But first let's get you into some kind of, er, state fit to be seen.' Lizzie could feel her face turn crimson with the thought. How could she be valet to this young man? It was not only improper, but also the thought was more than a little daunting to her sensibilities. She had a strange Alice-like sensation that she might just swoon with consideration of the situation.

That would not do.

How to negotiate then between Tilney's helplessness and her own sense of propriety? In vain Lizzie contemplated the options. There seemed to be little chance of escape from one scrape or another of a most perplexing kind.

'Ticklish situation, eh Bennett?' Tilney said. 'My suggestion is that you lay out my wardrobe on the bed and help me to this chair here,' he indicated the desired seat with and outstretched hand, 'Then, er, leave me to the task while you go inquire of the landlord whether there might be some suitable conveyance available. We can pursue things from there,' he said, smiling as Lizzie aided him to sit on the dressing chair.

'As you wish,' she sighed, looking askance at the effort this move had caused him while admiring the fine pink flush in his cheek. How she had ever considered Tilney's face to be anything less than the first chalk was a mystery. While it was not conventionally handsome, she nonetheless saw in its every line his character — at times exasperating, but always bright and observant.

In a flash, Lizzie had laid out the necessities of his wardrobe, sighing that she had had no chance to properly starch his cravat, but Tilney had taken to carelessly leaving it askew for so long, it was doubtless of little concern to him. She busied herself gathering up the details of his clothing. 'There you are,' she said at last, running her gaze once more over the accoutrements that littered the mattress. 'Do be careful.'

'I have been dressing myself for a good many years,' Tilney drawled, trying to hide his amusement not at all, though his cheeks were a good deal pink. It must be the strain of rising from the sickbed, Lizzie told herself.

After a moment, she finally stepped out of the room and into the hall, and so missed Tilney's odd look of both relief and perplexity.

'I'm afraid we must be asking for our bill,' Lizzie told the landlord. 'It is imperative that we leave quite soon, as we are expected in, ah, Italy soon, and Mr. Tilney tells me it is much further than we originally ascertained and the date necessary for our arrival quickly approaches.'

'*Oui, monsieur,*' the landlord agreed. He did not bat an eyelash at the patently outlandish story, by which Lizzie was made certain that he was indeed the soul of discretion.

This was indeed fortunate for them both.

While surely he did not believe the tissue of lies she had just woven, he was not in the least bit concerned. That was something positive that Lizzie could say about the French; they were far worldlier and far less inclined to judge than her fellow countrymen. Of course he had been taken in by her masquerade, but Lizzie did not count that against him, for she prided herself on her flawless performance as a boy.

'We shall also require a carriage or a phaeton—I'm not certain what you call them here, a smallish conveyance due to Mr. Tilney's injuries. I fear it will be too much effort for him to have to ride and I think it wiser to use this mode of transport.'

'*Oui, monsieur.* Will you wish to drive the carriage yourself, *Monsieur* George?'

Lizzie considered the question carefully. She hadn't really ever tried to drive a cart or carriage, but given her comfort with riding horses, surely it would be possible to manage them just as well in such a conveyance. Further, it would sidestep the need to involve an outsider in their little *ménage*, which would certainly decrease the chance of uncomfortable questions.

'Yes,' she told the landlord, 'That is precisely what we need.'

'Very good, *monsieur*. I will call my cousin, Armand. I think we can arrange for such a conveyance at least as far as the Italian border.'

'We can hire someone to bring it back here,' Lizzie said. 'That will be the simplest thing to do.'

The landlord went to fetch the boy from the kitchen to run this errand, while Lizzie considered if enough time had passed to allow Tilney to complete his toilette. She blushed at the thought of the intimate way they had somehow arrived at living. It was certainly not her intent to do anything untoward or unfitting for a young woman in her situation, but somehow since she had washed ashore in that coastal village Lizzie had been unable to reconcile her situation with propriety and so it had to be unless they unmasked altogether.

And where would they be then?

Lizzie sighed. What were they to do? She could not admit to herself that her feelings for Tilney were anything but grateful consideration for a corky individual like him, one to whom she could confide all the difficulties of her situation— well, almost all of her difficulties. Surely it was no more than that. And just as surely, he was no more interested in her than as a passing curiosity of course, she thought as she climbed the steps.

Lizzie knocked at the door. 'Are you ready, Tilney?'

'Ah, not quite, but you'd better come in,' came his strangled reply.

Alarmed, Lizzie threw the door open. 'Good heavens, what are you doing on the floor, Tilney!'

'Stupid thing, really,' Tilney said from his crumpled state on the floor. 'I just came over a bit weak.'

Lizzie charged forward to slip her arms under his. 'If you've torn out those stitches—'

'Steady on, Bennett,' Tilney said with as much verve as usual though his face had become several shades paler than when she left the room. 'I took care to collapse neatly enough. Even you should be impressed.'

Lizzie continued to mutter words of considerable derision under her breath as she helped Tilney regain seating on the bed. 'You might have caused additional injuries, you know,' she said trying very hard to look cross and not at all relieved that he seemed to have added no further harm. As she let go of him, Lizzie found it impossible not to blush at having had need to touch him so intimately again.

To cover her embarrassment and confusion, she told Tilney that the landlord had recommended his cousin as a procurer of transportation.

'Wonderful idea, Bennett,' Tilney said, looking a bit faint. His cheeks were flushed pink. Lizzie worried a bit that the strain had been too much for him, but he gamely finished knotting his cravat while she looked on. Her fingers itched to help him smooth out the fabric, but Lizzie willed them into compliance.

'I think a phaeton will be the best thing. We can doubtless hire a good sturdy carriage horse and let our mounts trot along behind us. We ought to make good time.'

Tilney gave her a penetrating look. 'And whither shall we wend, eh, Bennett?'

Lizzie froze. 'Whither?'

'You seem to have a destination in mind already,' Tilney continued, picking some imaginary lint off his spotless sleeve. 'Care to impart the location to your traveling companion?'

'Ah, well,' Lizzie began, but then halted abruptly. After a moment's consideration, she added with as casual an air as possible, 'I thought south would be safest, of course.'

'Of course,' Tilney re-joined. 'Why 'of course'?'

'Lud,' Lizzie drawled, 'they know we're English, after all.'

'Tare 'n hounds, Bennett,' Tilney said with evident irritation. 'What's that got to do with the price of cheese?'

'Sharpen up, Tilney,' Lizzie said with a small laugh. 'They're going to expect us to head north to get closer to home. We'll fool them all.'

'You are a bright chum to have in a scrape and no mistake,' Tilney said with a grin that warmed Lizzie exceedingly. 'Let's get all our gear together then, shall we? We'll be off once the landlord's relation gets here.'

Lizzie turned to the desk to begin packing Tilney's belongings up and so missed his puzzled look of perplexity.

A short time later they heard the landlord's step on the stair. The two had managed to pack up most of Tilney's belongings and were securing the items in their proper places. Lizzie had a moment of anxiety when it came time to put away the writing case, but she decided her letter would simply have to wait. There would be time yet to write to her Italian friend.

If that were indeed what she ought to do.

Lizzie stifled a sigh. She kept an eye on Tilney, but he seemed to be moving with care now. It was unlikely that he would tax himself beyond his capability and risk his pride. One fall was enough to encourage more attention to the weak state of his frame.

The landlord's polite knock came and Tilney called him in. '*Messieurs*,' he began, clapping his hands together with satisfaction. 'Your carriage has arrived. My cousin Armand is prepared to drive you where you wish to go, so you can depart at your leisure.'

'Ah,' Lizzie said, stealing a look at Tilney. 'We were under the impression that we were simply hiring a carriage, not a cousin.'

The landlord shrugged in his incomparable Gallic way. Lizzie found herself irked by the gesture's implacability and failure to communicate anything meaningful. Doubtless that was the intent of the movement all along.

'Armand is not eager to hand his carriage over to étrangers, you comprehend?'

Tilney harrumphed in a most officious manner. 'We are Englishmen after all.'

Another shrug, this one less careless. 'You have been good customers, *monsieur*. But when one leaves…' He paused, but did not seem determined to go on.

Lizzie looked uncertainly at Tilney, but the latter merely shrugged in his own inimitable style. 'As you say, one cannot predict the actions of strangers.'

They agreed on a price and the landlord descended the stairs once more, while Tilney and Lizzie conferred. 'This is far from ideal,' Lizzie hissed with some hint of venom. 'How are we to make a smooth exit if this bumpkin cousin attends to us?'

'Now who's prickly?' Tilney laughed. 'We shall manage, Bennett. Perhaps not at once, but we shall have more of an opportunity for concealment if we depart sooner rather than later. Recall we do have a pressing need to make ourselves scarce in this vicinity.'

Lizzie sighed again. 'I suppose you're right…'

'Of course I'm right!' Tilney crowed. 'Now let's get our

belongings together and quit this gloomy little corner. I am so very tired of being an invalid.'

'But you must be careful,' Lizzie scolded, gathering up the last of the handkerchiefs to tuck inside Tilney's traveling case.

'Come now, Bennett,' Tilney said with a roguish grin, 'Mustn't give the game away. Lawks! Someone will be thinking you're a female if you continue on in that vein.'

Lizzie coloured up considerably at his taunt, but said nothing immediately, instead busying herself with the clasps of the case. Finishing her exertions, she stood erect once more with the hope that the pink of her cheeks had diminished.

Tilney's grin seemed to suggest it had not. 'You're trotting too hard, Bennett.'

'And you're too ripe and ready by half,' Lizzie retorted. 'Let's see if we can get you downstairs without your making a mull of it.' She turned to open the door and thereby missed Tilney's satisfied grin.

'Careful now, old fellow,' Lizzie said with effort. It had taken her two trips to get Tilney's belongings down the stairs even with the landlord's help and Tilney took it upon himself to try to make his way down without her assistance. A very foolish move, for which she would have cursed him had she known anything stronger than 'damn!' or 'the devil take you!' both of which seemed far too flippant to match the level of irritation she had at present.

'I don't need much help,' Tilney said, his stubborn look much at odds with the frailty of his pale frame. Lizzie ignored his words and took his arm in hers as they wended their way down the steps. When they reached the ground floor, Tilney drew in a sharp breath.

'Bit sharp in the ribs, Bennett,' he croaked, seeking to conceal the effort those words cost him. Lizzie steered him to the nearest chair while the landlord looked on and tutted. The handful of people idling in the inn took in the scene with good-natured curiosity over their cups of cheer.

She noticed that no one stepped forward to lend a hand.

Tilney looked pale but maintained a chipper expression for the room. Only one who knew him as well as Lizzie did could ascertain the effort it took him to maintain that carefree look.

She felt a pang in her heart to know how he suffered, but restrained herself from making any comment on that fact.

The landlord stepped out from behind her and looked at Tilney with some concern. 'Ah, *monsieur*. Are you certain you should leave today? Perhaps another day of rest, no?'

Tilney should his head and gave a rakish grin. 'Things to do, old man, places to be.' He made as if to fumble with his cravat, but Lizzie could see the fingers tremble slightly as he fussed with the knot.

'*Monsieur*, could we purchase a bottle or two of your finest Bordeaux for our journey?' Lizzie inquired hastily, distracting the landlord from his frowning appraisal of Tilney's visage. He shrugged and went to fetch the bottles.

Lizzie knelt down before Tilney and mopped the light sheen of sweat from his brow with his handkerchief she had still kept in her sleeve. 'You'll be able to rest in the carriage,' she whispered. 'It will be fine.'

'Not feeling so corky,' Tilney muttered, closing his eyes for a moment. 'Damn surgeon should have stitched me tighter, I reckon.'

Lizzie couldn't entirely resist a smile. 'You're just fagged to death and will doubtless fall asleep at once, leaving me to entertain myself.'

'Oh, lud, you're just going to get jug-bitten and sing away the afternoon anyway,' Tilney said, a little colour filling his cheeks at the thought. 'I'll be lucky to get even a wink with your blasted drunken caterwauling.'

'It's a scandal,' Lizzie agreed, relieved to see him looking a bit less pale. 'I am the son of my father, truer words have never been spoken.'

'Well, I must look queer as Dick's hatband,' Tilney said, coughing into his sleeve. 'But I'm feeling a little less peaky now, so let us make the rest of the way out to the carriage. I have a bad feeling about this magistrate.'

'As you wish,' Lizzie said, the words echoing strangely in her ears. She had just got Tilney to the threshold of the inn when the landlord's voice rang out in alarm.

'*Monsieur*! The wine!' The landlord's voice carried across the yard. While the shout had initially startled Lizzie as she helped Tilney into the carriage, relief flooded her thoughts at once. Although the haste to get away might have made them a tad bit nervous, they had proceeded with sufficient care so as to not leave anything behind. There would be no returning to this place.

'*Merci, merci,*' Lizzie muttered as the landlord thrust the bottle and a parcel of bread and cheese into her hands. Tilney sighed a reedy thank you as well, but it could barely reach her own ears, let alone those of the landlord. 'This will speed our journey and make us much more comfortable.' She smiled and clasped his hand. 'Now if only we could take some of your lamb stew as well…'

The landlord beamed broadly at her praise. 'My cousin Armand shall take good care of you. I am sure he will bring good news upon his return of your safe travels and monsieur your friend's vast improvement. *Eh bien, Monsieur* Tilney? You will be well soon.'

'*Merci,*' Tilney uttered with some effort and Lizzie swung herself up into the carriage beside him. His paleness alarmed her, as did the renewed gleam of sweat across his brow.

'You shall rest now,' Lizzie said quietly but firmly, lifting her arm around Tilney's shoulders to brace him as the carriage took off. He tried not to react to the sudden shift, but she could tell how much it pained him.

'*Doucement s'il vous plaît, Monsieur* Armand,' Lizzie called out hopefully. 'My friend is still very much in pain.'

'*Oui, oui, je ferai ce que je peux,*' came the brusque response as the carriage rumbled on.

'I shall be fine,' Tilney said, eyes closed but with a weak smile.

'You should rest,' Lizzie cautioned, her voice softer now. She considered taking her arm from around Tilney's neck, given that its cushion was no longer as necessary, but he seemed comfortable at present, so she thought it might be best to wait until he drifted off into slumber before she took it away.

Surely it was his comfort and not her own she thought of as she admitted to the tingling warmth of his closeness.

'I can't sleep, Bennett,' Tilney said with some irritation. 'I

253

have been dozing for days.'

'But you need to rest and heal,' Lizzie said, her cheek much too close to his. 'Now you know it's best and I am right.'

Tilney chuckled. 'Never that, Bennett, never that. Oh, do tell me something amusing!' He closed his eyes but rather than fatigue she saw pain in his countenance.

'What shall I tell you?' Lizzie echoed, her words sounding hollow in her own ears as she became conscious of her heart beating more quickly.

Tilney leaned his head back but did not seem to find comfort. 'What about those mad tales of our adventures with the pirates? Not a word of truth there, I hazard a guess.' At last he leaned his head to the side until it touched hers. He sighed as if at last he were comfortable.

'On the contrary,' Lizzie continued softly, conscious of his ear being so close to her own. 'Nearly all of what I told you was true. We did indeed sail with the pirate queen herself, Black Ethel.'

'Did you indeed? Tell me more of your adventures, Bennett. I should like to be entertained.'

Lizzie inhaled the scent of his hair, then closed her eyes and began once more to narrate their wild adventures aboard the *Bonny Read*.

Chapter Seventeen

Alice could not recall breathing until she did it once again. The shimmering white figure by her side seemed to float in the air. She chanced to look down and saw that not only did the woman's feet not touch the ground, but that she did not indeed seem to have feet at all.

'I do beg your pardon,' Alice chanced at last to ask, 'are you in fact a ghost?' She hoped it was not an impertinent question to ask. As it did not touch upon money, rank or religion, it seemed safe enough to Alice, though she feared the query might fall under the rather considerable umbrella sheltering personal information, but sure the ghost's reaction would be indication enough as to whether she had crossed that line.

'Why, indeed I am!' the ghost answered emphatically, a slight elevation to her fashionably small chin accentuating her apparent pleasure in having this singular quality remarked upon.

What a relief, Alice thought. However, immediately upon the heels this rather agreeable realisation came the troubling thought of address. What did one call a ghost? Was 'Miss' sufficiently polite to recognise the bereaved nature of the circumstances? Was some further honorific required? Alice was perplexed. Her own brief acquaintance with funereal behaviour and requirements had been curtailed all too sharply by her kidnapping.

'O Miss Ghost,' she began, hesitating slightly to gauge her companion's reaction, 'I hardly know how I ought to address you.' Just to be on the safe side, Alice added a quick curtsey.

The ghost smiled. 'I am Judith Wychwood,' she said, making a curtsey of her own. 'The late Judith Wychwood, I suppose I should say, but I don't think that we are required to make use of that particular title.'

'If you think it is proper enough without...' Alice voiced tentatively.

'I think it is more informational than polite,' Miss

Wychwood said with a great show of seriousness. Alice was immeasurably impressed to have such a steady friend in evidence, which quite made her twinge with guilt over not missing her cousin Lizzie sufficiently.

At least I know Lizzie will be quite sensible and proper, Alice thought with sigh of longing.

'Please, do tell me your name, miss, so that we may be friends at once,' Miss Wychwood said, looking at Alice with a most agreeable expression of anticipation.

Alice was still young enough to marvel at the idea of someone desiring to be her friend, though it was a sign of her unfortunately growing sophistication that she also felt a glow of satisfaction for the novelty of having a friend who was also an apparition. Surely few of her friends could boast of the same.

'I am Alice, the only daughter of Lord and Lady Mangrove of Mangrove Hall. The late Lord Mangrove,' Alice hastened to add. 'My father haunted our house briefly after his untimely death,' she added, blushing shyly at her ability to claim some similarity to Miss Wychwood's situation.

Miss Wychwood nodded sagely, looking far wiser than her countenance might have suggested. 'Indeed, we spectres must frequent the location in which we met our respective demises.'

Alice gasped. 'You mean—!'

Miss Wychwood smiled sadly. 'Indeed, I died in this very room!'

'Would it be...awkward, Miss Wychwood,' Alice began, 'to, ah, ask about the manner of your demise?'

Miss Wychwood's diaphanous head shook emphatically. 'I have been eager to relate the circumstances of my tragic departure to some congenial person for a very long time.'

Alice halted just in time from asking how very long a time, feeling somehow that it might not be quite a polite question, all things considered. Yet again Alice wished Lizzie were there to appreciate the wise decision Alice had made on her own.

Where can my cousin be? Alice thought. Is she already home?

But Miss Wychwood was waiting eagerly, her gossamer

brow filled with the tale untold. 'Please, do share your story with me,' Alice said with genuine warmth. 'I should be most grateful.'

Miss Wychwood smiled. 'You are so kind. Other young women have been in this room before and they were invariably alarmed at my appearance. You must be made of much sterner stuff.'

Alice blushed at the unaccustomed praise. In many ways, she had become a much more remarkable young woman in the course or her adventures. However, she was unable to resist a chance to trot out the excitement of her own adventures. 'If one has survived kidnapping not once but twice and has survived pirates and being lost at sea,' Alice said in a rather breathless manner her former governess would have recognised from the schoolroom, 'One can be rather sanguine about unusual occurrences.'

'How admirable!' Miss Wychwood said with graceful generosity.

The changes in Alice were most evident at that moment, for instead of plunging into a lively account of her own perilous journey, she pulled herself up short and said quite without any trace of peevishness, 'But do share your history, Miss Wychwood. I am most keen to hear the details of your tribulations.'

The use of the latter word in addition to the selfless denial of centre stage would have made both Mrs. Martin (neé Travers) and Lizzie exchange a pleased expression of happy pride in the young woman. For the moment, we shall all have to settle for the knowledge that Alice has become a much more agreeable and self-sufficient woman.

She had improved so much so that she did not even congratulate herself on being so self-sacrificing, but simply listened attentively for Miss Wychwood's tale.

'I was once as you are now,' Miss Wychwood began, her voice fervent though her figure remained somewhat insubstantial. 'By that I do not simply mean alive, though I recall still how wonderful it was to be alive.'

'How terrible,' Alice offered, feeling helpless to locate more appropriate words of comfort. 'I know I should not wish to be…no longer alive.'

'There is a great deal one misses,' Miss Wychwood sighed. 'Warmth and food primarily. How I miss tea! And biscuits!'

Alice reached to take Miss Wychwood's hands in hers, but they passed through the mist of her form without contact.

Miss Wychwood smiled sadly. 'I miss, too, the comfort of human contact. Worse than having people cry out in alarm at one, it is wretched not to be able to feel anyone's embrace.'

'My poor dear Miss Wychwood,' Alice said with considerable feeling, a tear escaping from her eye. 'How did this horror begin?'

Miss Wychwood drew herself up to her full if incomplete height. 'I was kidnapped!'

The revelation that the present ghostly Miss Wychwood began her tragedy with being kidnapped, perhaps unsurprisingly, had an immediate and negative effect on Alice. 'How awful! And how, er, very like me!' Far too much like Alice's situation, in fact, for her to feel entirely sanguine about it.

'I know,' Miss Wychwood responded, vigorously nodding her head for emphasis. 'That is why I felt I must warn you despite the often alarming reaction people have to me in my present state,' she added with an admirable delicacy.

'Heavens!' Alice exclaimed, quite clearly alarmed. 'Do you mean you were also kidnapped by Gilet de Sauvinage?' Alice found it hard to believe that this petulant little man could possibly be a bloodthirsty villain suitable for one of Mrs. Radcliffe's gothic narratives. In the future, she might find herself doubting the veracity of writers if this sort of revelation were discovered to be more common than expected.

'No, quite another man altogether.'

'But English,' Alice added hopefully.

'No, I am afraid he was French.' The two shared their mutual sorrow in companionable silence.

'How did it happen? Your kidnapping, I mean,' Alice asked, seating herself on the bed. There was little use in remaining standing now that they had become friends. 'Do sit here and tell me all about it.'

This was an interesting situation, not least because she was rather curious to see whether the ghost could actually sit down, but also remarkable for the fact that Alice was not asking about poor Miss Wychwood's adventures merely to have an entrée into telling her own.

The apparition sat gingerly on the bed, almost hovering as if she were not certain where to locate the actual surface of the duvet. It was a near enough approximation that Alice was able to quickly stop watching Miss Wychwood with rather too much attention than was polite.

'I was traveling with my tutor,' Miss Wychwood began after a slight pause in which she seemed to focus on something very far away. Alice supposed that her home must seem to be very far away indeed having been forcibly ejected from the living. A shudder went through her. How very terrible the thought was.

'We were on our way to Paris on the coach. My parents thought a little sketching in the City of Light would be an ideal addition to my education,' Miss Wychwood said, her wispy voice sounding even more wistful at the memory.

Alice therefore checked herself from remarking on her delight at finding her new friend skilled in such an endeavour, recalling hastily that she would also be unable to carry on with that employment in her present state, and simply offered a sympathetic, 'Oh!'

'We were still in Normandy when we heard the alarming sound of hoof beats as dusk approached. The carriage held but just ourselves and a man with the unlikely name of M. Morte D'Allitee and we looked at one another with alarm for we knew what that dread sound meant.'

Alice gasped. 'Highwaymen!'

Miss Wychwood nodded sadly and ghostly tears fell from her orbs. 'Alas, yes.'

'And did they—?' Alice found herself unable to speak the terrible words.

'If only!' Miss Wychwood cried.

'You mean the highwaymen did not rob you?' Alice asked, the breath very nearly squeezed from her body in excitement

'Oh, they were more than just highwaymen,' the late Miss Wychwood said, the breath entirely gone from her body long ago, yet sighing with regret nonetheless. 'This was my kidnapper and his gang. Unrepentant brigands!'

'How awful!'

'Indeed, for they not only robbed the other people in the carriage, taking their money and any goods they had with them.'

'But not you?' Alice asked, aghast.

'Well, yes, they took my pocket money and my cameo necklace with a portrait of my older brother in it,' Miss Wychwood said, her bitterness evident even then. 'But worse, the leader of this reprehensible mob grabbed me and threw me across his saddle.'

'Did you scream?' Alice was overcome with delicious horror.

Miss Wychwood's spectre nodded with solemn assurance. 'I screamed most horribly!'

'Did he not feel pity?' Alice cried.

Miss Wychwood drew herself up to her full height, which while incomplete due to her insubstantial feet, nonetheless conveyed the depths of her despair. 'Not a jot.'

'How wretched!' Alice shook her head with wonder. How could there be such people in the world?

'I certainly thought so, once I was at liberty to gather my thoughts,' Miss Wychwood agreed. 'I must admit for quite some time I was unable to think anything, being nearly insensible with fear.'

'Perhaps it was a blessing,' Alice said, trying very hard to be sensible. 'I should think being insensible would be best when reality is far too horrid to contemplate.'

'I think you are right,' Miss Wychwood said as she sat back down, the dramatic peak of her narrative having been passed. 'There were stops along the way, but the first thing I remember clearly was coming to this villa.'

Alice was relieved to have the conversation turn to something with which she had had some experience. It seemed rather awkward to having very little to add to a conversation but the occasional interjection. 'Was it much the same when you arrived?' Alice asked eagerly.

Miss Wychwood sighed. 'You would not have known it,' she assured Alice. 'I will not pretend that I was here voluntarily, you understand—'

'Of course not!' Alice was quick to respond.

'But I was quite overwhelmed by my first sight of the villa,' Miss Wychwood said with a strange air. 'I had never seen anything quite like it.'

'I can believe that,' Alice said eagerly. 'I had something of the same impression, although,' she coughed, recalling that she had in fact arrived in the dark and had seen very little of the villa from the outside. 'I had a rather, ah, limited view of the villa as a whole.'

'It was quite a magnificent sight, I must admit. Quite unlike the neat lodge where I grew up,' Miss Wychwood said with a slightly regretful air.

'You were not then, ah—' Alice blushed. She dreaded that she had made a horrible faux pas. How Lizzie would reprimand her for such a thoughtless remark!

Miss Wychwood, however, had either not noticed her indelicacy or had decided to overlook it. 'I grew up in rather unremarkable circumstances, Miss Mangrove. It was my parents' ambition that I improve myself and perhaps achieve a higher position in society than they had. They were quite wonderful people,' she finished sadly.

'Oh, Miss Wychwood! Do they know your…present state?' Alice could not restrain herself from asking.

'Alas, no,' Miss Wychwood said and the two friends sighed together.

Alice looked very solemnly at her apparitional friend. 'I promise you, Miss Wychwood. If—no! When I escape from this place, I will carry your story to your parents, so they will no longer be troubled by the mystery of your fate.'

Miss Wychwood tried in vain to place a gentle hand on Alice's arm. 'You are too, too kind,' she said at last, her ghostly voice ragged with suppressed emotion. 'I am certain that is why I cannot rest. And I do feel ever so tired.'

'Poor dear,' Alice said, trying to pat her ethereal hand gently. 'Tell me more about your first sight of the villa,' she added, thinking it best to not allow her friend to linger on such a painful recognition. 'I have not seen nearly enough. Was the garden nice?'

'It was exquisite,' Miss Wychwood said, sounding a little distracted yet, but soon warming to the topic. 'It was in fact quite extraordinary to my eyes, accustomed to the simplicity of our own back garden.' She smiled wanly at Alice, as if to apologise for her simple pleasure.

Alice felt herself blushing a little to think of the extravagant garden at home and the beauties of the solarium. What a lucky girl I have been, she thought with wonder. And I didn't even know it. 'Oh, do tell me more, Miss Wychwood,' she begged her friend.

'In my first few days, I was allowed to walk in the garden, it being summer and the weather always fine. Of course they had a guard over me, but there was nowhere for me escape to from the walled garden. The hedges go quite all the way around.'

'Were there many flowering bushes?' Alice asked, amazed to find she was quite capable of drawing out a conversation when she had some interest in the person.

'So many!' Miss Wychwood cried. 'I have no idea what their names are or whether they are only native to this part of the world, but had it not been for the manner of my coming here, I should have quite liked to have stayed in the garden for some time. As it was, the strolls there were the only peace I had.'

'Oh, how awful for you to be in such danger!' Alice sympathized.

'My kidnapper was a hardened man with no pity,' Miss Wychwood agreed, phantom tears once more starting to fall. 'While he had hopes of remuneration, he treated me civilly enough. But once it became clear that no ransom would be forthcoming, he lost all patience and became quite brutal.'

Alice gasped. 'What a horror! You don't mean to say—'

Miss Wychwood nodded. 'They decided to make horrible use of me before discarding me.'

'No!' Alice could hardly breathe with terrified amazement.

'It was to be so, all that and more.'

'Oh, Miss Wychwood! How very terrible!'

'But I, too, had a desperate plan!' Her ghostly eyes flashed with unaccustomed fire. 'There was just one problem—'

'What was that?' Alice asked, her bright eyes betraying the eagerness she felt, caught up in Miss Wychwood's tale. 'What daring plan had you concocted to avoid that horrifying fate?'

Miss Wychwood looked out the window behind them. Below, the garden was a tangle of overgrown bushes that only hinted at the order which once made it beautiful. 'I made a desperate vow,' she said at last after a long sigh. 'When the nefarious men came for me, I would throw myself out this window to my death!'

Alice gasped. She was sure that Miss Wychwood was just about the most courageous young woman she had ever met. To even vow to do such a thing was quite remarkable. 'I do so admire you, Miss Wychwood,' Alice found the voice to say eventually. 'What a terrible choice!'

Miss Wychwood smiled, but it was devoid of humour. 'Considering the alternative, the soft embrace of the greenery seemed an almost pleasant way to die. But there was yet a difficulty in my plan.'

'What was that?'

'In addition to my being guarded day and night, there was also the problem that the window was bolted against just such a possibility.'

'Oh no!' Alice worried that Miss Wychwood's demise might be even more horrible a tale than she had surmised. The suspense was awful and she very nearly hoped it would last a good bit longer as it was rather delicious.

'Indeed. See here?' She pointed toward the top of the window where a sort of peculiar latch, rusted and askew, hung from the top. Alice got up to look at it, peering at the unfamiliar shape.

'That was the lock?'

'It was a work of my captor's own devising,' Miss Wychwood affirmed. 'It was certain to thwart the efforts of anyone seeking the escape of last refuge.'

'Good heavens!' Alice said, letting the words slip in her surprise. 'Then you mean —?' It was too horrible to be believed.

'Indeed,' Miss Wychwood agreed, her eyes brimming once more with tears, though her chin kept to a defiant height.

'There had been other young women held captive here. This is a singularly nefarious place.'

Alice's eyes seemed to be as wide as her mother's Wedgewood saucers. 'Have you... have you met other, ah, young women formerly in residence here?' It was a tricky sentence to construct, both to refer to Miss Wychwood's state indirectly yet with sufficient clarity to get the point across. Alice felt as if she needed a cup of tea to recover from the effort.

'I have not,' Miss Wychwood said, somewhat distracted at the thought, 'but this is a rather large residence. Perhaps there may be other women wandering in other parts of the villa.'

'It is quite possible,' Alice said, nodding. 'But please, do tell me more about your attempt to escape the clutches of the horrible kidnappers.'

Miss Wychwood seemed pleased to return the narrative to her own exploits. 'I used my fork to attempt to pry the lock open whenever I was not under immediate observation. I did not wish to arouse suspicion, so I did not seek to secret the fork away. But one day I had a most fortunate addition to my cutlery.'

'What was that?' Alice asked eagerly.

'A lobster fork!' Miss Wychwood said with triumph.

'A lobster fork?' Alice repeated with some measure of dubiousness in her tone. 'But they're so tiny!'

Miss Wychwood nodded, her insubstantial form curiously assured in the daylight. 'It was the smallness of the fork which allowed me to finally work my way under the latch.'

'Indeed,' Alice said, overcome with the cleverness of her ghostly friend.

'The servants were very careful with the usual cutlery, but completely overlooked the absence of the lobster fork.'

'How very clever of you,' Alice told her, feeling genuine warmth at the proximity of her to this very astute young woman, someone of whom Lizzie would surely approve. Alice was so excited by the thought of Lizzie's approval that she did not even feel the normal stab of sorrow at recalling Lizzie's absence from her life. 'And were you able to open the latch?'

'Not immediately,' Miss Wychwood continued. 'However,

the lobster fork gave me the foothold I needed. I would hide it at the end of every day when the horrible men came to check on me.'

'Where did you hide it?' Alice asked, wondering why she had never considered where she might conceal objects about the room. She quickly glanced around her to see if any spot jumped out. 'The bookshelf?' It seemed to her an intelligent response.

Miss Wychwood, however, shook her head. 'There was too great a risk that they might have wanted to take a volume from the shelf. There were a good many more books at that time.'

'I have been enjoying one,' Alice began, but then suppressed her own tangential thought. 'Do tell on, Miss Wychwood. Wherever did you manage to hide the purloined fork?'

Miss Wychwood smiled shyly but with a kind of satisfaction. 'Have you looked closely at the fireplace?'

'Only to see that it has seldom been lit,' Alice said with a peevish disregard for the import of the question. 'I have spoken most severely to M. de Sauvinage. It is simply barbaric,' she added with righteous indignation. 'Barbaric.' Alice found herself quite proud of the word.

'Indeed, in my time the same neglect applied. Because of that neglect, therefore, it was quite possible to conceal my useful tool where it was unlikely to be seen. I found a little ledge between the bricks where it was possible to rest my fork between uses.'

'And did you manage to loosen the latch with just a lobster fork,' Alice said, leaping up excitedly.

'It took a great deal of patience and time, but eventually I was able.'

'Oh, it is just like the Count of Monte Carlo!' Alice cried.

Miss Wychwood, the soul of kindness, did not correct her friend's misappellation. 'I often found solace in Edmond's tale, though I had no wish to seek revenge once I recaptured freedom.'

'Of course not,' Alice said with lively indignation for her new friend. 'You are far too good a person!'

Miss Wychwood's ghostly face blushed prettily. 'If you like, Miss Mangrove, I could show you my particular hiding place for the fork.'

'Oh, yes please!'

Alice thought she might nearly burst with excitement as the spectral Miss Wychwood led her toward the fireplace and the hiding place of her unusual instrument of freedom. Naturally, she was loathe to get any of the ash on her gown, so she crept forward carefully, but it was difficult to restrain the urge to clap her hands together.

One could only imagine the mess that would ensue, so it is fortunate that she did not actually do so.

Miss Wychwood's insubstantial arm pointed to a spot inside the chimney. Alice had to bend over and crane her neck to see the spot where she indicated. Sure enough, there was a little chink in the stones.

Gingerly, Alice reached up and sought with her finger-tips to find some kind of hidden shelf between the stones. Something moved under her touch and she fought the urge to recoil and instead pulled out the tiny silver lobster fork.

The tines were scratched and their tips uneven. Alice stared in wonder.

'Do you see!'? Miss Wychwood said, her eager tone con-veying the joy of sharing her small success at long last. 'It fit so snugly into that spot.'

'A perfect place of concealment,' Alice agreed, her tone gentle as she tried to hold back the tears that wished to burst forth. The story writ upon the grooved surface of the imple-ment was a horrific one.

How worn the little tines had become! Alice looked up to see Miss Wychwood now by the window.

'See here, where I pried up the latch bit by bit,' Miss Wychwood said, pointing to the spot as Alice drew near. 'It took so very long, you can imagine.'

'Yes,' Alice said absently, staring at the latch patinaed by age and neglect. 'How very patient you must have been,' she said finally, feeling as if she ought to comment somehow upon Miss Wychwood's ingenuity, even if she were loath to follow this discussion to its logical end.

'If only I had been able to discover the plan sooner,' Miss Wychwood sighed.

'Sooner?' Alice said, feeling a sudden ripple of even greater unease.

'Yes,' Miss Wychwood said drifting a little higher in the air than was necessarily required. 'A pity, that?'

'Whatever do you mean?' Alice could not help interrogating her friend, though her insides seized up in a kind of awful anticipation. 'Were you unable to put your plan into action?'

'Indeed I was not,' Miss Wychwood said, her face turned toward the gloomy haze outside the window.

'But you were able to free the lock?'

'I was,' she said, turning back to Alice. 'Though they have since repaired it—look! Here.' She leaned closely over the latch. 'I am quite certain they did no more than the minimum to repair it. You could use the same method, I think, to free yourself.'

'But if the plan did not, er, work…' Alice let her voice trail off, hoping Miss Wychwood would be able to construct the conclusion without her saying it.

'It was not the plan that was faulty,' Miss Wychwood said, her voice as cold as the grave. 'It was my captors.'

'Do you mean—' Alice gasped. It was too horrible to consider.

'They murdered me!'

'They murdered you!' Alice said wonderingly. It was awful to hear the words out loud. Alice could barely accept the notion. Miss Wychwood, such a charming young woman! How could anyone be so dreadful to her?

But all it took was the sight of her sad face to assure Alice that this terrible fact was true.

'Alas, it is true! And no one could mourn me, dear Miss Mangrove, because no one knew that I had died.' Sorrow suffused her handsome face and Alice suddenly realised how difficult her own situation was. Should she succumb too? Would they ever miss her at home? Tears fell easily and we must not feel too much approbation that many of Alice's tears were for herself—many were also for Miss Wychwood, for whom she felt a lively sympathy.

'Oh, Miss Wychwood! I mourn your death! And I swear, I swear, that I will acquaint those who love you with your sad fate. I shall cross oceans if necessary!' As indeed it would be necessary to do if she were to return to England.

'Thank you, Miss Mangrove,' came the sad reply, nonetheless suffused with all proper politeness.

'Please, do call me Alice,' the same said to her friend, trying again in vain but in earnest to take her hand. 'We must be as close as sisters, or at least as cousins. My dear cousin Lizzie is as close as a sister and I must include you among those dear to me!'

'Oh…Alice! You are too kind.' Miss Wychwood wept anew, this time for joy. 'Do please call me Judith. I ought to have asked you before, only I did not wish to be forward.' As best they could, one being entirely insubstantial, the friends embraced.

After a moment, the two smiled between their tears and continued their intimate conversation, no formal layer of politeness between them anymore. 'Alice, my dearest, you must try the method I had planned before I was so…'

'Untimely disrupted?' Alice was amazed at her own attempt to smooth over the sadness of her friend's demise. Oh Lizzie, you would be proud, she thought.

'Indeed! I was able to loosen the latch and would have sought egress, but for the arrival of the horrible miscreants. Surely you can loosen the latch, too.'

'I can but try!' Alice said and leapt up to do so. With Miss Wychwood's insightful coaching, Alice was quickly able to make good headway with the latch and soon, loosened it enough to be able to open the window.

The two young heads peeked out into the fresh air. The warmth was exquisite and Alice remembered it was not England that she found herself in.

'See, there?' Miss Wychwood asked, pointing her insubstantial arm out the sash. 'The ledge is fairly substantial, perhaps enough for one to make her way around to the balcony over there.'

Alice leaned out and swallowed nervously. It seemed a rather significant distance over which to traverse a rather small ledge. 'It certainly looks…possible,' she said at last.

'Do try! You do not wish to end up as I did,' Miss Wychwood reminded her.

Alice thought it over and knew she was right. 'Will you come with me?' she asked her friend.

'I will,' Miss Wychwood promised, her demeanour as solemn as death.

'All right, then,' Alice said and gingerly stepped out onto the ledge.

269

Chapter Eighteen

'Where the devil are we?'

Lizzie paused at the open door of the carriage. 'I take it you have awoken from your nap, Tilney.' He looked tired nonetheless and she worried again about the toll the trip was taking on him.

'And I asked a question, Bennett,' he continued irritably, rubbing his hair in such a manner that wisps of it stood up in a most amusing and undignified way.

'We are much further south than we were the last time we stopped, but still a rather long way from the border with Italy. We are angling to the east, if you would really like to know.'

'Indeed, for I cannot be certain that you would not lead us all the way to Zürich without my careful guidance,' Tilney said with a return to his familiar drawl. More than anything that tone cheered Lizzie for he sounded once more like himself. Now if only they could deal with the problem of the cousin driving the carriage and her own identity once they arrived in Italy.

'You should be grateful, you mountebank,' Lizzie scolded. 'I've secured a most appetizing lunch of fine smoked meat and the freshest goat cheese in the market square.'

Tilney raised one eye suspiciously. 'I do not think it right somehow that goats produce cheese. I'm not saying it's unnatural, mind you,' he said, peeking into Lizzie's parcel, 'but when a chap is accustomed to cows as the source of dairy, goats open up new vistas that boggle the mind.'

'Don't be an idiot,' Lizzie laughed.

'What's next?' Tilney continued with mock seriousness even as he spread the warm soft cheese across a baguette. 'Horses? Dogs? Hedgehogs? Beavers? It is against nature, I am certain.'

Lizzie could not eat her lunch for the hiccoughs of laughter that poured out her mouth. Since Tilney had recovered, life had become once more fun and entertaining. It was only in the last day or so that he had begun to question and argue with her, but Lizzie felt an immense weight lift from her shoulders as Tilney returned to his old self.

The wound of the bullet had been considerable, but she was grateful to think that his heart and mind were strong. 'I find this goat cheese to be quite mild and flavourful,' Lizzie said with mock umbrage. 'If you are not willing to eat what is put in front of you, then you, sir, will have to go do the foraging.'

'I certainly shall,' Tilney retorted, poking with suspicion at the sausages in the basket. 'Are there no peas here after all?'

'We are still in France, I must remind you, good sir,' Lizzie said with emphasis on the latter two words, 'where good food is required for every meal and people do not accept bland comforts in their place.'

'Bland comforts!' Tilney said, throwing his head back with haughty scorn. 'English food is the finest in the land.'

'Ah, but we are not in "the land" at present,' Lizzie corrected him. 'And when in Rome —'

'Eat anchovies, eh?' Tilney grinned and Lizzie felt that unpleasant leap in her heart.

'After that, goat cheese will not seem so bad.'

'So, Italy is still our destination?' Tilney asked with elaborate carelessness.

Lizzie, who had been caught up in the high spirits of their conversation, frowned. She had managed not to think too much about the road ahead, instead thinking only of the vaguely southward course as further away from trouble rather than toward a particular location. It was the direction they gave to the driver, but time was approaching when they must make a change.

'Italy, in one way or another,' Lizzie said with an equal attempt at a drawling casual air. 'I think we may need to make some changes once we get nearer to Nice.'

'Our fine charioteer will want to return home, doubtless,' Tilney said, tearing off another piece of fragrant bread and leaning back on the seat with a yawn.

'Do you think he will take us as far as that?' Lizzie asked, glancing toward the man in question who at present was letting the horses feed, too. It was a rather lovely day and she closed her eyes, imagining if this were only a day of relaxing fun instead of a brief respite on a troubling journey with an uncertain outcome.

'There is no telling what the man might do,' Tilney said with finality. 'He is French, therefore inscrutable and unpredictable.'

Lizzie laughed and looked at her companion. 'You are ridiculously close-minded about our sometime compatriots.'

'That is because they are our sometime combatants, too,' Tilney said, waving away the proffered goat cheese and taking up his glass of wine. 'While I cannot fault the French when they turn their hands to the vineyard, I am quite resolved that they only take up other endeavours with an eye toward disrupting the ease of all Englishmen.'

'And Englishwomen?' Lizzie asked a little tartly.

Tilney waved away the comment. 'It is terrible to think of Frenchmen appropriating English women. Or foreigners of any kind,' he added with a dark look.

Lizzie simply laughed. 'If Englishmen were more worthy of the love of Englishwomen, they would seldom have need to set out in search of more winning beaux.'

Tilney raised one eyebrow in a censorious arch. 'Beaux? This influx of *vocabulaire français* is most unnecessary. It is precisely the way things get quickly out of hand. French wines are one thing, but it beyond the pale to mix in so many superfluous words in a foreign tongue merely for effect or because you are thinking what to say in English.'

'What if there is no more exact word?'

'There is always a way to say something,' Tilney said, waving away her argument with his bread. 'And generally a better and more concise Anglo-Saxon way to say it.'

'*Sprezzatura*,' Lizzie said, allowing the syllables to roll off her tongue with delight.

'Oh, Italian now,' Tilney said, taking a bite of bread.

'Don't stall for time.' Lizzie grinned. 'What would you say is English for '*sprezzatura*'? Hmm?'

'Oh, I think it's far too warm to think of Italian. We will soon be forced to think on it, but I would rather not do so before we must. Or do you think otherwise?'

Lizzie had to admit to losing that particular manoeuvre, but wasn't willing to sacrifice the queen yet.

'If I were to make such a feeble escape from an argument,' Lizzie said as she sliced off a little more cheese, 'You would never let me hear the end of it, excoriating me for laziness and lack of aplomb.'

'Bennett, if it weren't so unseasonably hot, I would stridently argue for the natural superiority of English men over English women,' Tilney said pulling his hat low enough to cover his eyes from her gaze before yawning elaborately and sinking back. 'Lawks, but I'm fagged to death all of the sudden.'

'How very convenient for you. You're just in a miff because you can't defend your point. Concede, Tilney.'

'Nothing of the sort,' he muttered, sinking even lower and thrusting his legs out in front of him, the picture of perfect ease. 'Swallow your spleen, old man. My point's been made for me by better men than I. You just need to open a book.'

'You're too smoky by half,' Lizzie said with malicious glee. While his hat concealed his eyes from her merry gaze, it did not stop her from admiring his fine profile. There was determination in that chin, but good humour and kindness in his mouth, however much he might scowl. Lizzie felt herself blush at the thought of her stare being noticed and turned her attention to what was left of their lunch.

She wrapped up the bread and cheese and corked the wine, trying to keep the thoughts from racing through her mind again. It was far too difficult to concentrate on anything other than the agreeable young man now snoring softly nearby.

With determination, Lizzie attempted to take command of her thoughts and turn them toward their proper destination: the King of Naples. Think of it, Bennett, she said with mock severity, a king awaits you—one with a surprising interest in the habits and peculiarities of insects and arachnids, which certainly counted for much.

Tilney evinced no interest in such creatures. Indeed, Lizzie doubted whether he could tell a mosquito from a mosque.

Yet the fact remained all too vividly before her, that she had grown accustomed to his voice, to his slangy speech and moreover, the visage that slumbered before her now.

Lizzie frowned. She had never had a commonplace mind, but now she continually coloured up at the sight of Tilney, at his laughter, at his smile, at that warm voice she once feared she would never hear again after the duellist's bullet winged him. It was fortunate that she had been there to nurse him back to health from the terrible blow, but the idea kept fighting its way into her mind that he might never have been in the position of being shot were it not for her.

Stifling a tiny sob, Lizzie turned her head away from Tilney again. He was nearly recovered, certainly well enough for travel. Though he continued to tire easily, he was well out of danger. There was only one answer.

She would have to abandon him.

'*Monsieur*,' a familiar voice called.

Lizzie turned to see the kind landlord's cousin Armand, who approached quietly, seeing that Tilney had fallen once more into a slumber. 'What is it, Armand?'

'*Monsieur*, I know that I am to take you…what do you say, a ways, no?'

'*Oui*, that is so, Armand.'

'I need to get home soon, *monsieur*. My children, my wife—there is much to do at our farm.'

Lizzie looked at the man and saw a simple farmer far from home. Her heart felt a stab of sympathy quite remote from her own troubles. 'I know, Armand. I think we are near enough to the main thoroughfare to catch a mail coach to . . . ah, our destination.' Best to remain cagey about that, Lizzie reminded herself.

'*Oui, monsieur*,' Armand agreed. 'Do you think your *ami* will be ready to travel such an arduous way?'

Lizzie had her doubts, but she covered them with bonhomie. 'He is quite strong and will recover quickly. Why, he is already much more himself. We will be just fine, Armand. You need not worry.'

Perhaps it would make things easier, anyway. If Lizzie needed to make her own escape and head toward Naples, then she could leave Tilney to make his way homeward once more and be safe. She would have to do it and silence her

274

traitorous thoughts that whispered that she could not leave him not tomorrow, not ever.

What is the world, Lizzie thought, that allows us hearts and no way to express them? Allows us minds that must hold in their ruminations that might make this life less painful for many, that must leave to bland tradition the burning passions that wished to break free of such moorings and speak to authentic emotions and lives? What a world this is that gives us hearts to crack with longing and desire and yet no mind to comprehend the ways these hearts operate.

Armand took his seat once more, a hefty hunk of bread and some of the cheese beside him. The carriage rattled off and while the movement shook Tilney, he did not awaken, but slumbered on, leaning comfortably against Lizzie's shoulder as she stared off into the space beyond the window.

The French countryside that passed her view remained unseen. Her thoughts were filled with obligations made, tragedies already unfolded and the warm shape of Tilney's head pressed against her shoulder. Lizzie could smell the scent of his hair, a fragrance she had come to know well as she cared for his injured body. Such a foolish thing, she told herself, a mere animal sensation.

But it did not stop her from inhaling deeply the musky smell of his head, nor caressing with her free hand the dark curls of his head as he lay slumbering beside her. Surely, she remonstrated with herself, surely the King of Naples had charms in excess of this modest English gentleman. Surely the King would make her laugh as much as Tilney did, surely. And his knowledge of insects was vast. Tilney could not with certainty identify more than a dozen species.

'I hate insects!' he had announced quite decidedly when she brought the subject up in conversation. Lizzie leaned her head upon his and felt a tear fall from her eye.

The coach bounced along the country lane. Lizzie sat deeply in thought, Tilney's head still resting against her shoulder. She would have to decide soon what to do. Perhaps this journey will last forever and I need never think again, Lizzie told herself as the fields rolled by.

The darkening of the day seemed to match the unbidden

thoughts that returned to whisper that it could not be so. I shall have to leave him, Lizzie reminded herself. She looked outside and saw the gloomy light was not simply cloud cover, but the edge of a forest that drew them into its depths like a giant swallowing.

Just the place for hide and seek, Lizzie thought, then shivered for no reason. The sensation of having a goose step across her grave unsettled the young woman and she shifted a little under Tilney's weight.

What a thick forest this must be to shut out so much light! She had not thought that such woods grew in this part of France. As they approached the higher elevations, surely the trees would thin out. But it was impossible to deny that the forest grew thick hereabouts.

In another moment, Lizzie's sense of unrest grew. She turned her head. Surely that was a sound of hoof beats behind them! No need to be alarmed, Lizzie told herself, but she could not help the fluttering of her heart. Another set of travellers, doubtless. That was all. It was a road after all and what were roads for but to travel.

Set your mind at ease, Bennett, she scolded. Nonetheless, she wished Tilney were awake. It was not the time to feel on her own. But you're not on your own, Lizzie reminded herself. You have Tilney here beside you and stout Armand on the box. There was no reason to feel nervous.

Yet she could hear the hoof beats distinctly now.

They seemed to be making a speedy clatter on the hard earth. A carriage? She could distinguish no sound of wheels in the echo of the hooves, so that meant riders.

Why jump to the conclusion of brigands? After all, it might just be a group of young farm hands, traveling to the market or to a distant homestead. Perhaps it was a cadre of solicitors, traveling from one court to a higher one. Or soldiers, Lizzie told herself with some rising hope, keeping the roads of France safe from brigands just as the British navy kept the sea safe from pirates.

Well, Lizzie thought hastily, somewhat safe from pirates, that is.

She had nearly convinced herself that she would see the

bright colours of the gendarmes as they passed by the carriage, nodding politely as they rode past. But with a jerk, the carriage began to travel more quickly and Lizzie felt her heart leap to keep pace with Armand's team.

'What?' said Tilney, waking with an irritable exhalation. 'What are you gibbering about, Bennett?'

'Nothing, it's nothing,' Lizzie soothed. 'Go back to sleep.'

That was when the first bullet rang out. 'Lawks,' Tilney said with admirable calmness, 'Are we under fire again?'

Lizzie turned round on the seat with alarm, frightened that the next shot might harm Tilney or herself. 'I am not certain,' she said, attempting not to sound as breathless as she felt, 'but it appears that we may in fact be under fire.'

'I supposed it might be so,' Tilney drawled as another shot rang out. 'Remind me not to travel again with a losel loser like you, Bennett.'

Lizzie looked at him, aghast that he could be so nonchalant about another perilous situation. His crooked grin, however, charged her wits with much needed stimulation. 'I have a terrible feeling that we have much more to fear this time. These must be brigands, judging from Armand's pace.'

'We shall see,' Tilney said, eyes closed once more. 'There is little to be done until either we escape the peril or the brigands halt poor Armand's desperate measures.'

'How can you be so cool?' Lizzie asked, though her castigation was more habitual than actual. She craned her neck in vain to see if the furious hoof beats were in fact coming closer as she feared. Out the curtained window she could glimpse the legs of an approaching horse.

'They're beside us!'

Tilney sat up then. 'Damn! Why did I not carry a pistol?'

'No matter now,' Lizzie said, trying to gather her thoughts into something productive.

'I must protect you!' Tilney's eyes looked fierce. Lizzie had not seen such an expression on his face and while she worried that it would fatigue the poor man, she could not help feeling a sense of comfort that she had such a noble friend beside her in an hour of need. Gone was the extra burden of worry for her young cousin—poor Alice! Where could she be now? Surely safe, Lizzie told herself with some guilt, fearing it had been far too long since she had given her cousin even the most perfunctory passing thought.

Yet oh, what a relief in such a dramatic moment to know that she did not face the terror alone, but with a stalwart companion by her side who thought as much to protect her as she did him. 'What do we have to use as a weapon?'

'Fiend seize it, Bennett! Take cover, won't you?' Tilney said, his irritation plain on his face and in his voice.

'And where do you propose I take cover, Tilney?' Lizzie shot back as the drumming of hooves around them grew. 'We are in the devil's own scrape this time and there's little chance of getting out of it. We shall have to play by our wits assuming they give us the opportunity.'

Tilney looked at her, eyes wide. It was impossible to tell whether he was more astonished or angry. For a moment the decision seemed to hang in the balance and then he gave a sharp bark of laughter. 'Damn, Bennett, but you are a larksome lass.'

He looked ready to say more, at least it seemed to Lizzie there was a peculiar shine to his eyes, but just then they heard a loud thump as someone or something landed on the driver's box and the sound of fisticuffs emerged. The two of them exchanged glances.

The marauders were on the carriage!

The sounds of the struggle on the driver's box continued. Tilney and Lizzie trained their attention upon the unseen tussle, awaiting the outcome. They did not have long to wait. A cry of pain and then a loud thud came as a body fell from the carriage.

'But who has fallen?' Lizzie could not resist asking, though of course they could not know. The hoof beats surrounding them seemed ever louder, a sinister sound.

'We must have something with which to defend ourselves!' Tilney hissed.

'You are not even strong enough to do so and you must not endanger your health,' Lizzie said with equal spirit. 'Be sensible, Tilney.'

'Sensible!' Tilney looked daggers at her, then turned back

to rifling through the picnic basket in a vain attempt to find some kind of weapon. He hefted the wine bottle. It would have to do.

'We're slowing,' Lizzie said.

Tilney's face darkened. 'Stay behind me.'

'If they open the door on this side—' Lizzie began.

'Lizzie, do as I say,' Tilney said.

It was not so much the anger in his voice as the fear in his eyes that stifled her words of protest. They could hear the voices of men as the riders gathered around the carriage. The team pulling the carriage was slowing their steps with an abundance of snorts and seeming surprise as the driver shouted, 'Ho!'

'Lizzie,' Tilney said, his gaze on the door beside him, 'I do not know what will happen next.'

Lizzie touched his hand lightly. 'It will be all right, Tilney. We've been in a tight spot before.'

'I—I don't know,' Tilney said quietly. 'Things are different now.'

'How so?' Lizzie asked, her voice soft in the suddenly quiet interior.

'Oh, hang it, Bennett, don't make me say it.'

'Say what, Tilney?'

Just then they heard a pistol shot. Lizzie clutched Tilney's hand. Tilney grabbed her hand and brought it to his lips. 'Damn, Bennett. If I must die, I will not die without saying how much I love you.'

The door of the carriage flew open and the two lovers gasped, their eyes dazzled by the sunlight.

Lizzie could not tell what astonished her more: Tilney's peremptory announcement as he kissed her hand or the gang of miscreants who had appeared outside the carriage. It was impossible to see their faces as the sunlight behind them beamed brightly into the dark interior. The brigands' voices were a cacophony assaulting Lizzie's ears and she felt oddly bereft of breath.

Despite her confident words to Tilney, Lizzie feared that this was indeed the end of their extraordinary journey. They had been so fortunate—dodging bullets and French magistrates, not to mention her daily charade. All good things must come to an end, Lizzie thought as she blinked into the bright light, waiting for her eyes to adjust.

Tilney's grip on her hand had not loosened and Lizzie felt a flush of happiness as she heard his words echo again in her memory. If we die at the hands of these brigands, she thought, at least I will have had one moment of truly exquisite joy. She looked back at Tilney's face and admired once more the familiar lines of it. Though still touched by his injury and loss of blood, there was not a more handsome face in all the world, Lizzie thought with sudden certainty. Every line of it captured her heart, every imperfection only added to her delight that this man should say he loved her. If this were the end, then it was all worth it. She had found the man who had won her heart.

To her surprise, however, Tilney stared at the brigands crowded outside the door—and he was laughing!

Lizzie turned to regard the fearsome creatures and saw that they were smiling, too. Her jaw fell open. What could this mean?

'Tilney! 'Pon rep, but we had a devil of a time finding you,' shouted one young lad, who seemed not at all sinister now that Lizzie could see him clearly.

'Lawks, but you're the very last person I expected to see kicking up a lark among the froggers. Damn, Stephenson! We thought you were the worst sort of highwaymen.' Tilney laughed heartily. 'Bennett and I thought we were done for.'

'I landed a facer on that devilish driver of yours,' Stephenson said, his face glowing with pride. 'A regular highwayman couldn't have done any better, I warrant. You should have seen us go at it wild.'

'Oh, poor Armand,' Lizzie said, her sympathy going out to the innocent driver.

'Well, I fear we have had a bit of a scrape and got the wrong handle on the basket, I think,' Stephenson said rather confusingly. 'Aren't you being kidnapped, old man?'

'Kidnapped?' Tilney said, exchanging a look with Lizzie, evidently as befuddled as she. 'You're too ripe and ready by half, lads. We've had a few scrapes of late, but never kidnapped.'

'Come out here into the light so we can see you, Tilney,' Stephenson insisted, grabbing hold of the young man's arm and making him grunt with pain.

'Leave him alone,' Lizzie shouted, 'He's been shot!'

'By one of us?' Stephenson said with alarm. 'Good heavens, old man. Sorry about that.'

Tilney laughed, but Lizzie saw the strain on his face. 'No, this was another fiasco.' But he leaned forward and with Lizzie's help, was able to step out into the sunlight.

'Now, who's this friend?' Stephenson said with evident curiosity as he scrutinized Lizzie's face. 'Say, don't I know you?'

Lizzie quailed.

It was bad enough to suddenly be blinking in bright daylight after the darkness of the coach, but Lizzie found it impossible to bear Stephenson's scrutiny with equanimity. Fortunately a distraction occurred while she helped brace up Tilney.

'Reggie, we've brought him around once more,' another young man cried from the front of the carriage where the horses stamped their hooves with what seemed to Lizzie's fanciful mind to be Gallic indignation.

Perhaps it was just her amplification of the bewildered scowl on poor Armand's face. As he hove into view supported on either side, she could hear him muttering a string of words that were unfamiliar to the young woman until he got to '*fils*' and '*chienne*' and then she turned away quickly to cough.

'Bertie! Brackley!' Tilney cried with delight. 'I say, what a wonder.'

'Tilney, old boy! 'Pon rep—did we shoot you? Heavens!' Bertie looked ready to drop the staggering Armand in his eagerness to see his friend, while Brackley gaped open-mouthed.

'Poor Armand!' Lizzie said. 'How could you frighten him so?'

Stephenson looked at her rather more sharply. 'I say, Bennett—'

'What the devil are you all doing here?' Tilney cut in,

much to Lizzie's relief. 'Aren't you all supposed to be on the sunny strands? Hugh!' he added, as another young man appeared leading their horses.

'Tare 'n hounds! Tilney, you've survived!' Hugh dropped the reins of the horses and made ready to clap his friend on the shoulder, until he noticed how Tilney winced. 'Good god, man—did we wing you?'

Tilney laughed. 'Anyone else along for the ride? I don't want to have to retell the tale each time.'

'Eliot meant to come,' Stephenson said with a familiar sort of lazy drawl, 'but he caught a cold.'

'He caught a Constance, you mean,' Bertie said, crowing with laughter.

'As you have guessed, Bennett,' Tilney said to Lizzie, the usual lopsided grin on his face, 'all my friends are quite mad. You will have expected no less.'

Stephenson laughed heartily at this. 'That rotter Eliot has betrayed the brotherhood and fallen in love with a most unlikely lass.'

'French, you mean?' Tilney said, eyebrow arched.

'Luckily no,' Hugh said. 'Sir Eliot managed to come all the way to the land of the frogs and fall in love with an English woman.'

'Reggie lost his heart, too!' Bertie said. 'But fortunately he lost the girl as well.'

Stephenson's looks glowered darkly and, for a moment, Lizzie thought he might truly explode in anger, but the look passed and he laughed genuinely enough, though the sound rang a little hollow in her ears. 'Yes, the illness and the cure in one fell swoop.'

'Right,' Hugh sniffed. 'That's why we had to set off in pursuit of her so quickly.'

'I thought you were running to my aid,' Tilney laughed.

'Well, we heard about you on the way,' Stephenson admitted. 'But we had set off in search of poor Alice.'

'Alice!' Lizzie cried. Could it be—?

Stephenson looked at Lizzie with a rather uncomfortably penetrating gaze. 'Yes. A young English woman named Alice whom we met under the most remarkable circumstances and then almost as quickly, ah—' he paused, searching for the right word.

'Then we lost her,' the one called Bertie said with a jolly laugh that did not suit Stephenson's sudden look of consternation. 'We had barely gotten to know the two delightful young ladies when poor Alice was whisked away most precipitously.'

'And we had every reason to suspect foul play,' Stephenson added darkly, his eyes flashing anger. 'One minute she was there, the next—poof!'

'Well, we gave that suspicious little man Tricheor a good natter,' Hugh said with a decided nod. 'A bit of the havey-cavey about him, but he was trembling so, it was not possible he could have been behind such a daring caper.'

'And this Alice,' Lizzie said as calmly as she could manage. 'She was English?'

'Indeed,' Hugh said, but Stephenson broke in.

'Yes, a very nice young English woman, a bit over her head, but quite plucky for all that.'

'Did you learn her last name?' Lizzie asked, her tone as carefree as she could manage.

'You did, did you not?' Hugh said, turning to Stephenson, who looked somewhat careless himself.

'Yes, I think so,' Reggie continued to look as unconcerned as possible, infuriating Lizzie, who nonetheless sought to not betray that feeling.

'And?' She managed to keep her question succinct. She could not help noticing Tilney's close attention to her, however.

'I believe,' Reggie Stephenson drawled, 'that her family name was—Mangrove.'

Lizzie could not contain her gasp. 'My long lost cousin!' she exclaimed.

Tilney gaped at her in surprise. 'Your cousin?'

Stephenson's eyes seemed to want to burn through her words into her very brain. 'You know the young lady,' he said with a coldness that seemed quite at odds with his previous excitement.

Bless him, Lizzie thought, he is quite smitten. Oh heavens,

he imagines me a rival! 'Indeed, I believe that sounds like my dear cousin Alice, daughter of the late Lord Mangrove. She and—er, she had been kidnapped from her father's funeral and spirited away.'

'She has been spirited away again,' Stephenson said with considerable passion. 'We were hoping to find her when we ran across word of Tilney's plight.'

'Damn, man. We must rescue Bennett's cuz,' Tilney broke in. 'It's the only thing to do.'

Lizzie shot him a grateful look. 'Tell us what you know,' she begged Stephenson as the others gathered around. 'We must find Alice!' Her heart warmed with excitement at the thought they she might be reunited with her dear cousin soon.

Chapter Nineteen

'Miss Wychwood, er, Judith,' Alice whispered, although it was unlikely that anyone would over hear them. 'Is the balcony getting closer perhaps?'

The disconcertingly ethereal voice of Miss Wychwood hovered somewhere off to Alice's right, not quite on the same ledge, but then again, ghosts did not require even the insubstantial support of its narrow width. 'Only a few steps further,' came the encouraging reply. 'Just don't look down.'

Now Alice had certainly had no intention of looking down. When she had begun her perilous journey out of the window, one promise she made herself was that she would certainly not look down. Alice knew what lay below, as she had glanced out of the extremely untidy windows many times, but she had no real desire to remind herself of that geography without the safety of a dirty windowpane between her and it.

But a funny thing happens to the most obedient child when told not to do something.

Alice looked down and immediately dizziness overwhelmed her. The ground, which had seemed so nearby from the safety behind the glass, now seemed perilously distant. After all the falls I have taken, after all the adventures I have survived, Alice thought somewhat nervously, perhaps I should think nothing at all of falling into the garden below.

'Miss Alice!' cried Miss Wychwood. 'Take my hand!'

Alice craned her neck around to the side where Miss Wychwood hovered anxiously. Without a thought she stretched her hand out to her friend and clasped hers. The two inched along the ledge without drawing another breath it seemed, but Alice could feel the dizziness that had attacked her subsiding.

The balcony loomed ahead like a shimmering oasis in the desert. Alice found herself as thirsty for it as a camel that had been on a very long holiday indeed and had only had a very dry bread for tea with no butter at all.

'Just a few more steps,' Miss Wychwood encouraged.

Alice tried to think nothing at all and concentrated only on the sound of her friend's voice and the touch of her hand. Step, step, step. Minute movements, but progress, surely, Alice told herself.

'We're there!' Miss Wychwood cried. 'Alice, you're safe!'

Alice looked down and they were indeed at the balustrade for the balcony. She let go of Judith's hand to grab the railing and ever so carefully boosted herself over it. Trembling, Alice nonetheless found herself filled with triumph. 'We did it!' she cried with a voice that very nearly sounded like a sob.

Miss Wychwood clapped her hands with joy. 'Indeed!'

'Judith!' Alice said, her eyes wide and mouth open. 'I could feel your hand!'

They both gasped with surprise and delight and embraced at once.

Miss Wychwood's touch was wispy and uncertain, but it was indeed palpable. Alice could not believe her delight in having her friend even this slight bit tangible. It was so wonderful to feel the affection of a friend, one whose words and advice had already proved a comfort.

'Judith, my dearest friend,' Alice said, tears filling her eyes. 'How delightful to feel your hands in mine.' She took her friend's hands between her own as if to demonstrate the delight.

'Oh Alice, it has been so long!' Judith cried ghostly tears of joy and relief. 'I do not feel quite so bereft now.'

'It must have been awful for you,' Alice said with feeling. 'I do not know how you had the courage to manage.'

Judith blinked her tears away and smiled. 'You are so very kind, Alice dear. I'm sure you would have figured out the secret much sooner.'

'It was the crisis,' Alice said, nodding her head sagely. It was the first time she had been able to carry off such a gesture. She was certain it improved her appearance markedly. 'Under extraordinary circumstances, one is able to accomplish remarkable feats.' Alice worried that her tone sounded entirely too brash and softened the statement by adding, 'I believe my cousin Lizzie once told me that.'

'Alice, I am quite certain you are correct,' Miss Wychwood cried, doubtless impressed whatever the source of the knowledge. 'What shall we do now?'

Alice looked around them with a sense of mild alarm. The balcony had been their goal, but now that they had achieved it, what were they to do? Alice looked carefully at the French doors that led to the balcony. It was entirely possible that they would be locked. 'We need to get inside again,' Alice said, her voice losing a bit of cheeriness as the difficulty of doing so squashed her confidence a bit.

'Do you suppose it is locked?' Miss Wychwood inquired, anticipating Alice's own thoughts.

'We can but try,' Alice said with a confidence she did not feel. She stepped forward and tried the handle. It proved immobile. Oh dear, Alice thought. This did not bode well. Alice leaned down to peer in the keyhole, but it was too dark to see anything.

'Perhaps I can pop inside and see if there is a key in the lock,' Judith suggested.

'Excellent,' Alice said, but there was not much hope in her voice. If there were a key, it would nonetheless be on the wrong side of the door.

'The key is here,' Miss Wychwood's muffled voice announced.

Alice perked up. 'Can you turn it?'

Judith's face lit up with excitement. 'Let me see!' She bent at once to her task, concentrating on grasping the key with her ethereal fingers. Her brow furrowed with concentration, but she did not seem to be able to get a firm grip in the key. Doubtless it had sat idle in its place for some time.

Alice felt her hope sinking. There was a sudden clatter and the key fell to the floor.

'Oh dear!' Miss Wychwood said, her dismay apparent in both her voice and her face.

Alice had a flash of inspiration. 'Judith, dear, can you push the key under the door?'

Judith clapped her hands together. 'I believe so.' With stately grace, she leaned down and pushed away at the rusty key. Gradually it inched its way under the door until the teeth poked through where Alice's eager fingers could grip it. With a flourish, she brandished the key and set it to the lock. After a moment's hesitation, the key turned with a click and Alice was able to pull the door open.

'Oh, Alice!' Miss Wychwood cried and the two confederates embraced happily once more.

Alice looked up from her embrace with Judith Wychwood. The corridor appeared to be empty, its dark silent and untroubled by any presence, spirit or flesh. The way to escape was clear.

'Quick, Judith,' Alice whispered, suddenly feeling the need to restore the cloak of secrecy to their actions. 'Let us make our way toward the entrance. Surely we will be able to slip out that way.'

The two joined hands and walked as quickly and as quietly as they could manage, most of the worry on the side of Alice, who was after all the only one who made any sound. At any moment, Alice feared someone might pop out and rudely demand where she thought she was going. She very nearly worried that her heart might give them away, pounding away as it did in her bosom very like a little hammer.

It put her in mind of the blacksmith in the village, which set up a kind of metallic clanging echo in her head that in turn fuelled the sense of panic even more, like coals on a fire.

They paused at the top of the stairs. 'Do you hear anyone, Judith?'

Miss Wychwood bent her insubstantial frame toward the foyer below. 'I do not hear a peep,' she whispered to Alice, though the sound would not have been much should she have chosen to speak aloud

Cautiously Alice trod down the stairs, hoping there would not be much in the way of creaking. The whole process suddenly reminded her of the stairs that led down from the nursery and how the third one, no matter how carefully she might step, would always give a lamentable groan that alerted her tutor Miss Travers (as she then was, Alice reminded herself, finding she had kind thoughts in absentia even of the disappointing Mr. Martin who had married that tutor), who would then recall a new lesson that Alice ought to be learning while she tried to nap a little longer or whatever it was that her tutor did when not occupied in tuition.

Sometimes Alice suspected her of writing a three-volume novel, but it was only in mischievous fits of mild unkindness.

The two escapees could be forgiven for their growing confidence that their flight would remain undetected. After all they had made it nearly to the bottom of the considerable staircase without mishap when at last the penultimate step groaned heavily beneath Alice's dainty foot.

Pausing mid-step in an attempt to curtail the unfortunate sound, Alice was alarmed to hear the groan turn into a horrendous crack and leapt to the parquet as the rotten wood gave way. Miss Wychwood and she embraced once more, their faces masks of horror.

'Oh, dear!' Miss Wychwood said helplessly.

Alice gasped, for in the same moment she heard footsteps coming from a not inconsiderable distance. 'I fear we have been discovered!' The two young women clasped hands and turned to face the danger together. Whatever might happen, Alice thought with a surge of grateful warmth, they were not alone.

The steps grew louder. Alice cast her glance around vainly hoping for some avenue of escape, but the capacious hall revealed little in the way of concealment. The large size of the entry door suggested a need for more force than the two young women could provide. There was not a single piece of furniture behind which they might crouch. Unladylike as that may appear, the idea held some certain appeal for Alice at that moment.

Judith Wychwood's ethereal arms wrapped tightly around her, which gave Alice some reassurance. She straightened her back. As her father would no doubt bark, she was a Mangrove and there was a legacy to that name of proud and haughty daring. Had not her grandfather faced down the savages of Orkney? Had not her uncle single-handedly triumphed over a gaggle of recalcitrant chimney sweeps in the midst of Mayfair? Had not her own father once stunned a trumpeter swan with a blow of his badminton racket? She had much to live up to and live up to that legacy she would.

'Be not afraid,' Alice whispered to her friend. 'I shall face him down with the courage of all the Mangroves dead and gone.' Judith squeezed her hand as tightly as she could, but Alice felt a whisper of fear at the thought that she too might become a Mangrove dead and gone.

However, she straightened once more with the succeeding thought: 'What would Lizzie do?'

Alice lifted her chin and tried to make her eyes blaze as heroines' eyes in novels seemingly did.

She had composed herself just in time. The repugnant shape of Gilet de Sauvinage appeared from the gloom and started suddenly. 'What are you doing out of your room?' he snapped.

Alice drew in a breath, the better to calm herself. 'We have decided to escape!'

'We?' the dark figure said, pausing in his forward motion.

Alice and Judith exchanged a look. 'He cannot see me!' Judith crowed.

'What's wrong with you?' her captor said in a remarkably not-French accent.

'He can't hear you either,' Alice said, the triumph in her voice evident.

'Can't hear whom?' the kidnapper said, beginning to strut forward once more, his step impatient now.

'I have an idea,' Judith said, then shot away with ethereal speed until she crouched most indecorously in the very path of Gilet de Sauvinage. Alice gasped. That her dear friend would go to such lengths to assist her. She pressed her hand to her heart, impossibly moved, tears springing from her eyes as if from a fountain.

Her captor stared incredulously until the very moment that he fell over Miss Wychwood and went sprawling!

Alice could not stifle the laughter that bubbled forth from her lips. In fact, the exquisite tension of the perilous journey from her room to this spot gave power to the merriment and her chortles took wing and grew very swiftly into guffaws, which made her clutch her middle because of their force. It had been many a year since the carefree young woman had laughed quite that hard and it made Alice quite giddy.

From the floor below, Judith extricated herself from the sputtering kidnapper with as much decorum and dignity as she could manage. She seemed puzzled to see his arm pass through her skirts without effect, but drew herself up to her full height once more, the better to express her disapprobation.

'You, sir,' Miss Wychwood said with a strong tremor of emotion, 'are no gentleman.'

The fellow in question, however, seemed to take no notice of her severity, continuing to mutter nearly inaudibly and pat the parquet around him in search of something. 'The fiend seize it! If I have lost my sliver of Edmund's tree—'

A strange sensation seized Alice. Her body went rigid. A flush painted her cheeks. *I know that voice!* She hurried down the steps toward the figure on the floor and the bewildered Miss Wychwood and snatched the kerchief from the man without the slightest blink of fear.

'I knew I recognised that voice!' Alice announced with triumph.

Arthur Boylett cowered back in surprise. 'Miss Mangrove, I—I—' but there he stopped for Miss Mangrove had never looked so very much like her mother, though towering at least a good half a foot higher, which made her a rather imposing figure indeed.

Alice had never imagined herself to be capable of so much indignation. It flared through her veins like a fire, as if she had swallowed a large spoonful of laudanum, the sort Miss Travers used to give her on particularly warm summer afternoons when they had both gravitated toward an internecine peevishness that had no outlet in propriety. 'Arthur Boylett, I demand you tell me what on earth you have been doing! Deceiving me! Holding me captive—and with what possible purpose?'

Miss Wychwood's face shone with admiration for her friend and she, too, rounded on the would-be kidnapper. 'You mountebank! How dare you treat the lovely Miss Mangrove with such roughness and ill will! I am shocked and appalled by your inconsiderate behaviour.' The latter phrase gave the young insubstantial woman a real sensation of quickness and she appeared to grow a trifle more tangible.

For his part, Arthur had continued in vain to locate the lost saintly king's relic—a sliver of wood upon a wood floor after all being much in the same position as a jade earring in a clover field, he was not having much in the way of success—while gaping with growing irritation at his would-be fiancée. 'It is really most provoking, Alice—'

'Miss Mangrove,' Alice corrected, her voice reaching a register of frigidity unheard of below the Polar Regions.

'I mean to say, Miss Mangrove,' he said with due emphasis on the latter two words, 'that given your mother's recalcitrant nature and downright hostility to me, I feared that she would not allow our engagement.'

'Hostility!' Alice said, straightening her back even further as her indignation soared. 'How very rude you are, Arthur.'

He halted his fruitless search and looked up at her with patent affront. 'You did not hear the unkind words she decided to fling at me that day.'

Alice closed her eyes and did not deign to regard him. 'My mother would not be anything but the soul of propriety. If she used unkind words, as you say, they were doubtless required by the situation.' She looked down at Arthur then, folding her arms across her chest. 'It makes me wonder what unseemly language you used.' Alice hoped that her look was as severe as her mother's could be behind her best lorgnette. The surge of pride she experienced for her remaining parent suddenly filled her with an exquisite mixture of anger and loss. 'How dare you insult my mother!'

Arthur grimaced as he strove to rise to his feet. 'She did shoot me, you will recall, Miss Mangrove.'

'That's no excuse!' Miss Wychwood squeaked with acute indignation, for she felt the pangs of Alice's distress most heartily.

'Who's there?' Arthur asked with some consternation and not a little fear.

'That's Miss Wychwood,' Alice said with a sigh. 'She tripped you.'

Miss Wychwood gave a stiff curtsey, acceding to politeness but making her disapproval evident.

Arthur stared. 'Where?'

Alice indicated with her hand where her friend stood. 'Miss Wychwood, I apologise for Mr. Boylett's opacity.' She endeavoured not to smile with pleasure at that particular word, but carried on with her introduction. 'He is—that is, he was once thought to be my fiancé. That is to say, he was my late father's preferred choice. However,' she said, turning her disapproving look back to Arthur, 'I am certain, had he lived, papa would have reconsidered such an alliance.'

Miss Wychwood's face grew dark with displeasure at the thought of her friend joined to such a nefarious man. 'I will greet you politely,' she said with the same haughty regard Alice had been trying on, 'but my civility stops there!'

'Did I hear something?' Arthur asked, his brow furrowed with concentration. 'I almost thought I heard something.'

'I demand that Miss Wychwood and I be allowed to leave at once!' Alice said, her mind now firmly made up. 'Bring round your coach and let us depart. I am certain my mother would very much like to see me.'

Arthur narrowed his eyes, which made him look rather surprisingly like a tortoise. 'Coach?'

'Yes, coach—the coach in which you brought me here.' Alice raised an eyebrow. Her mother's ability to wield that instrument was equalled by none in all of England, so Alice could not hope to reach her level of mastery at once, but she was pleased to see Arthur quail before her, if only slightly.

Arthur wrung his hands with evident discomfort. 'I'm afraid—I'm afraid it was in fact,' he paused and swallowed, 'a hired coach.'

Alice found herself too furious for words. Miss Wychwood gasped and put her hand to her mouth. A blush grew upon her cheek. Its glow made her even more tangible and Arthur stared toward her with growing alarm. He fidgeted away from her.

All at once a preternatural sense of calm infused Alice. 'So, it was you who abducted Lizzie and me from the very train of my father's funeral procession?'

'Yes,' Arthur mumbled, reaching for his handkerchief to dab at his moist brow.

'Allowing us to be man-handled by the horrid man? And taken to a public house?' Alice's eyes could properly be said to blaze just then. It would also be fair to note that her outraged dismay was giving way to a kind of pleasure, the source of which she could hardly have grasped, having never been in the grip of a righteous anger.

Arthur cringed. 'I had to conceal my connection to the—er, adventure.'

'Crime!'

'But I had to be sure no one would suspect me! I was with your mother the whole time, not that it helped much. She seemed to get so irritated with me.'

'I wonder why,' Miss Wychwood said, voice both dry and ethereal, though the sound startled Arthur even more.

Alice spoke the next words very slowly. Perhaps she was remembering imperfectly an actress she had seen once in a tragic role and it was this that gave her the inspiration to unfurl a litany of wrongs with a measured cadence of the stage. 'You sold my cousin and me to a nefarious sea captain who had…unspeakable designs upon our persons!'

Arthur gasped. 'I did no such thing! My orders were very specific. In fact I paid that man far more than he would have received…had…I wanted…which I did not!' The young man's face turned very red and his eyes looked ready to pop out of his skull.

Alice was pleased. Admittedly, she would have been far more pleased had Arthur flung himself at her feet and demanded her forgiveness tearfully, but Alice had learned much from her experiences and recognised when her expectations might be a bit fanciful. 'Miss Wychwood and I will not spend another moment in your presence, Mr. Boylett. If you are incapable of providing us with proper accommodation, we will depart on the feet with which God provided us!'

So saying, Alice linked arms with Judith, who looked like she might very nearly pop with pride and admiration, and strode toward the door. One could be forgiven for noticing that Alice positively glowed and that it was not simply from righteous anger, but also from a bit of uncharitable pride in her performance.

She was not, however, quite finished. At the door, the two women halted and Alice glanced back at the now abject Boylett. 'I was never moved to like you much, Mr. Boylett, and knowing the dark depths of your character now, I must say that even if you were the last man in the world, I could never be prevailed upon to marry you.'

The door that had seemed far too imposing for her to open before, moved with a creak at her touch. There was a glorious delight in slamming the door behind them, Alice thought, although the noise was not everything she would wish. The two strode arm in arm down the rubble-strewn steps with broad smiles of satisfaction across their faces.

Chapter Twenty

However, upon reaching the bottom of the steps, the two of them paused. 'Where shall we go?' Miss Wychwood asked quietly, her voice barely a susurration in the gentle winds.

Alice hardly wished to disclose that she had no idea, but there was little choice. 'Let us stroll down the lane and see what we can see,' she said with as much hopeful buoyancy as possible, but the reality was already sinking in. Two young women without chaperones—one admittedly rather physically insubstantial, though her sense of propriety remained solid as ever—were an invitation to disorder and the likely prey of all manner of nefarious figures.

The world was a large place and full of danger for two such as them.

Alice could feel her haughty confidence shrink as the lane passed under their feet, making the villa smaller and the wide-open countryside even vaster. On another day, passing through it in a pretty carriage, Alice would have thought it a most agreeable region. But now it oppressed her with cautionary thoughts that she recognised, rightly, as that of common sense and not simply repeated lectures.

'Perhaps,' she said, hesitating to gather her courage and the better to expose her quailing heart. 'Perhaps we should—'

'Listen,' Judith broke in, her amorphous face rigid as she hearkened to the distance. 'Do you hear that?'

Alice was about to answer negatively when she caught the sound at last: hoof beats! Her heart leapt up, but then sank down again. Yes, it might be their salvation, but it could also mean danger. Clearly Miss Wychwood's thoughts did not incline in that direction, which might be forgivable considering her situation far beyond the veil, but the fluttering in Alice's breast grew as they stared in anticipation.

The most provoking thing was the bluff behind which, which the lane disappeared. They could hear the hoof beats of coming horses—how many? At least a half dozen, surely—but could see nothing at all. When the riders came around the curve, they would be in sight, though still a distance away. Perhaps we can still run back to the villa for shelter, Alice thought. She distracted her worried musings by glancing around for other possible sources of shelter. The rocks within sight were far too small. Trees there were none. Such vegetation as there was, while green and leafy, also tended to be low to the ground.

Alice took a tighter grip on Judith's arm. Her friend looked at her with some confusion and a dawning understanding. 'Oh Alice, do you think we might be in danger?'

'Let us hope for the best,' Alice said with a lightness she did not feel. She drew in a deep breath as the noise grew louder and just when it seemed impossible to bear the suspense any longer, the riders came into view. There were a half dozen riders as well as a carriage heading toward them at a startlingly expeditious clip. Were they confederates of Mr. Boylett's? Or were they rescuers? There was no way of knowing as the gap between them shortened.

'I'm not afraid,' Miss Wychwood whispered, though Alice could feel her tremble.

'Neither am I,' she whispered back nonetheless, laying her hand on Judith's arm for reassurance. I am afraid, Alice thought, but I will stand here beside my friend and hope for the best.

As the riders approached, they called out and hope surged in her heart again. Would evil brigands call out in advance of murder? Alice wondered. Surely not.

'Are they calling 'Miss Mangrove'?' Judith asked in astonishment.

Alice grinned. 'I believe they are!' There was no doubt about it: the riders were Englishmen and they were calling her name. If only I had my mother's lorgnette! Instead she squinted into the distance hoping to divine the identities of the gentlemen, for gentlemen they surely proved to be. Indeed, the one at the front looked distinctly familiar. Alice's jaw dropped as she recognised the man.

'Alice, is it all right?' Judith asked, her anxious eyes darting from her friend's face to the oncoming entourage.

'Yes, we are safe!' Alice grabbed Judith and hopped up

and down with her. For Alice had divined the person of one Reggie Stephenson, the fine young gentleman who had rescued both poor Constance and herself from that revolting Count de Graves and his unctuous servant Tricheor. It did not seem possible to be so glad to see a person of such short acquaintance, but Alice remembered with joy the ease with which Mr. Stephenson had taken command of their fortunes and set everything right.

And here he was again, most unexpectedly!

He was waving energetically at Alice who waved back just as heartily, which moved Miss Wychwood to do the same. Alice remembered that his friends who travelled with him were an assortment of viscounts, baronets and even an earl, so there could be no objection in introducing them to her friend.

And in the carriage? Perhaps it was her dear Constance! I do hope she is well now, Alice told herself, already having made up her mind that she would have the delight of seeing her impressionable friend once more. She could not stop smiling as she watched the dashing Mr. Stephenson approach.

For his part, the eagerness seemed well matched, for he rode ahead of the others and far in advance of the carriage. In fact he seemed to be coming so quickly that Alice felt a touch of alarm. She need not have worried, for as his large chestnut mount approached, he threw up his head as Stephenson pulled him to a stop and leapt from the saddle.

It was altogether quite satisfying, Alice thought.

'Dashing,' Judith whispered with awe in her voice, 'simply dashing!'

Mr. Stephenson dropped to one knee and reached his hands before him. 'Miss Mangrove, do forgive my hasty arrival and precipitous dismount. My concern for your good health and safety must serve as my excuse.'

Alice admired both the words and the tone, and could not fail to notice the touching way his thick crop of hair flopped over his brow as he stared up at her with a sincere look of concern. Kit Barrington? Why did I ever think him handsome? 'Mr. Stephenson, I cannot say with what delight I greet your arrival. I am quite well now, though I have been through a rather harrowing experience with my friend here.'

Mr. Stephenson looked at the space where Alice appeared to be patting someone's hand, and then looked back at Alice. He was silent a moment, wracked with indecision, but he quickly recovered. 'What can I do to make you more comfortable? Command me, Miss Mangrove, and it shall be done!'

The other gentlemen had arrived as well, remaining on their restive mounts as they called cheery helloes to Alice, those who knew her, for she perceived unfamiliar faces among the known. 'My only wish now is to go home to England.'

The gentlemen cheered this and clamoured to carry out that very task.

Alice smiled and waited for them to quiet. 'Once there, I hope you all will aid me in locating my dear cousin Lizzie, the bravest, most noble—' Alice found she could not finish the thought. Safe once more, her heart broke to think of her beloved cousin adrift in the ocean or lost on an island somewhere, friendless and alone. A sob tried to force its way from her throat.

Mr. Stephenson and Miss Wychwood both stepped forward to comfort Alice, meeting awkwardly at her elbow, much to the former's surprise and the latter's annoyance.

'Oh, Alice,' Judith sighed.

'Oh, Miss Mangrove,' Mr. Stephenson said in a much brighter tone. 'Please step over to the carriage, I have a most wonderful surprise for you!' The carriage pulled near even as he spoke and the door flew open.

'Constance?' Alice asked with a grateful yet suddenly fatigued air. It seemed improbably that she should suddenly feel so tired, but she could not wait to collapse on the doubtless uncomfortably hard seat of the carriage. It shall feel as comfortable as a featherbed.

But her heart leapt once more as a figure hopped from the carriage and stared at her. The breeches and waistcoat were not familiar, but the face was and it proved to be the greatest restorative to Alice's spirits that she could imagine. 'Lizzie!'

The two cousins flew at each other and embraced with a flurry of enquiries that neither could hear nor respond to while they both continued to speak. The gentlemen around them around them grinned happily at the pair and at one another. The happy reunion was only silenced when at last a second figured struggled from the carriage, blinking in the late day light.

'Alice,' Lizzie announced, grinning broadly, 'This is Mr. Sydney Tilney. Careful, he's been shot.'

'Shot!' Alice said, her eyebrows shooting skyward once more. 'Good heavens!'

'Alice,' Lizzie scolded gently, though she continued to smile. 'Whatever has happened to your manners?'

'How do you do, Mr. Tilney?' Alice said, ignoring Lizzie's remark and looking at the gentleman who seemed quite unperturbed by his injury or at least highly amused at something.

'So this is the famous cousin Alice,' Mr. Tilney said as he took her hand gently. 'I see you don't need rescuing after all. How fortunate.' He leaned back against the carriage and laughed. Alice noticed the way Lizzie immediately fussed at him, seeking to persuade him to sit inside the carriage once more.

'Oh! And let me not forget my manners,' Alice said, turning to her friend with a smile, 'This is Miss Judith Wychwood, who helped me to escape the horrible kidnapper, who turned out to be none other than Arthur Boylett,' she finished bitterly.

Lizzie looked intently at the seemingly empty space beside Alice. 'Is Miss Wychwood a ghost?' she asked at last. Mr. Stephenson jumped a little at that and looked somewhat perplexed.

'Yes, I'm afraid so,' Alice said, squeezing her friend's hand. Miss Wychwood faded for a moment, but then became more substantial entirely through force of will.

Lizzie smiled and held out her hand. 'I am so grateful to you, Miss Wychwood, for aiding my dearest cousin in her time of need.' Whether she could feel Judith's mild grip was uncertain, but she wished to imagine it was so.

Mr. Stephenson gamely held out his hand, too, murmuring, 'So pleased to make your acquaintance, Miss

Wychwood.'

'There is so much to tell!' Lizzie crowed, unable to contain herself.

'I have so much to tell as well,' Alice said, matching her enthusiasm. 'It's been so long since we parted in the storm. I have undergone so many strange things—and I,' she paused, fearing it would be boasting to claim what she was about to claim, 'I have become so much better than I was, at least I hope I have.'

She blushed, but her cousin took it not amiss. 'Alice, so much has changed. I have every confidence that you have become a credit to your family name in every way.' Lizzie lowered her voice. 'And I have written to the King of Naples, for I am no longer free.' It was her turn to blush, which she did as she turned her shining eyes up Mr. Tilney, who looked every bit as enchanted as Alice's cousin.

Alice exchanged a happy look with Judith. To think of Lizzie in love! Tears sprang to her eyes and once more she found herself without a handkerchief.

Lizzie noticed her distress and extracted just the thing from the pocket of her waistcoat. 'Here, Alice.'

Alice took it gratefully and hugged her cousin impulsively and they both cried and laughed at once.

'Come, let us get in the carriage and on our way home,' Lizzie said, wiping the tears from her cheek with the back of her hand. 'I have so much to tell you!' She turned and helped Tilney back up into the vehicle.

'May I offer my assistance to you and Miss Wychwood?' Mr. Stephenson said gently at Alice's elbow.

Alice could only nod, for she saw a look in his eye that answered all the questions she might have had about why such a gentleman had sought her rescue on such short acquaintance. 'Yes, Mr. Stephenson, I would be very grateful to you for your hand.'

Epilogue

'I do understand that, Mr. Radley,' Alice said with a touch of severity. 'Nonetheless, I do wish that you would deal more directly with the rhododendrons.'

'I would, Miss Alice, I would,' Radley muttered, not quite meeting her eye, 'but they can be a bit—'

'Stroppy?' Alice anticipated his response. 'We are English,' she reminded him, 'We did not bow to Napoleon. Surely you are not suggesting we bow to a mere shrub!'

Radley was nonplussed by this and moved off muttering to himself about having seen something move out of the corner of his eye. Alice felt a glow of triumph and headed toward the morning room, where her mother tended to spend her afternoons. She had not quite left the solarium when the shimmering form of Miss Wychwood joined her. Alice hugged her friend gaily. 'Judith! How are your parents?'

'They are much better,' the young ghost sighed. 'Not quite used to me, but pleased to be able to scold me for my failings.'

'Nonsense,' Alice said with a decided tone. 'They should be terribly impressed with your courage and resourcefulness. Think where I would be without you.'

Judith smiled happily, but her response was interrupted by the petulant tones of Lady Mangrove.

'Alice, do have a word with your father. He is irritating me to no end,' she said as Alice and Judith entered the morning room to find Lady Mangrove and the late Lord Mangrove both poring over the local newspaper and its account of important events.

'Your mother ignores the encroachment of foreign novelists,' Lord Mangrove's insubstantial form barked. 'We cannot allow this aggression to subsist.'

'You will have to continue this argument without me,' Alice said, hearkening to a familiar step in the hall. Her face shone with a wide grin as the beloved face appeared at the door.

'Am I interrupting anything?'

'No, not at all, my dear,' Alice said, throwing herself into a large chair. 'You look like you have news.'

'Indeed!' Reggie crowed, holding forth a letter with exquisite seals. 'From Italy!'

'Lizzie!' Alice cried, jumping from her seat. 'What does she say?'

Reggie chuckled. 'My dearest wife, as if I would deny you the first view of your dear cousin's letter. Do open it at once, I am bursting with curiosity.' He leaned down to kiss Alice's cheek. She did not so much as blush at this display, but took it entirely in stride. Her parents however dropped their bickering for a moment and raised eyebrows at one another, a silent commentary on the decadence of this new generation.

'The baby is born!' Alice said excitedly as her eyes hungrily devoured the page. 'A boy! I knew it would be.'

'And how is the King of Naples?' Reggie said, his tone becoming serious.

'Very well, very well,' Alice said absently, scanning the next page of the letter. 'Apparently things in the Mediterranean have calmed considerably since last summer.'

'And Tilney?' Reggie said, trying to look over his darling wife's shoulder.

'He is quite the proud papa, Lizzie writes,' Alice said laughing and pulling the letter out of reach of Mr. Stephenson's hands. 'And he and the king have become the best of friends, except for the insect collection, about which they have agreed to disagree.'

'And when do they come home?' Reggie said, folding his arms around Alice's shoulders and kissing her on her ear with scandalous abandon.

'They will be home in a month,' Alice said with a sigh.

'Assuming there are no further adventures,' Reggie laughed.

'Adventure?' Alice said, folding the letter to re-read later. 'What ever could you mean?'

THE END

ACKNOWLEDGEMENTS

Like its heroines, this book has travelled down many interesting paths. In 2010 it came out in an edition from Tease Books: 'Big thanks to Gail, Stella and everyone at Tease for their hard work on my book.' In 2013, Tirgearr Publishing in Ireland put out a new edition. Thanks to Kem and all for taking a chance on it.

Before that, it was a serial written online: 'Thanks to the constant readers who began this journey with the blog I started in my Texas exile, when I feared (groundlessly) that I would not have time to keep up my fiction writing. Thanks as well to those who caught up later on TextNovel and offered their support and encouragement. Thanks to Cheryl Le Beau, who won the contest to name the story and thus got to be immortalized in its pages (along with her nattily dressed bosun, Joey). Big thanks to my new friends in the Romance realm, especially Dana Fredsti, David Fitzgerald, Saranna deWylde, Isabel Roman, Susan Hanniford Crowley, Stella Price, Debi Chowdhury, Jackie Kessler, [the late] Jack C. Young and of course, our delightful hostess at UnBound, Adele Wearing.'

You may not know that the latter thanks is to the woman we know better as Auntie Fox. We have both been through a number of changes since then. I remain grateful for all our fun and collaborations and I hope the third time proves the charm for this book and it brings something useful (cough: lucrative) to Fox Spirit Books. Skulk for life! Ever may we floof!

Thanks endlessly to Jane Austen, Charlotte Brontë, Elizabeth Gaskell, Barbara Pym, and Georgette Heyer for inspiration. Last and far from least, big hugs to the friends I couldn't do without: Stephanie, Wendy, Paul, Byron, Chloë and the rest of the Skulk, Jane and the SpeakEasy Dames, my Wyrd Sisters—and my own Lochee.

**Thank you for buying this Fox Spirit Book.
We hope you enjoyed it.**

Fox Spirit believes that day to day life lacks a few things.
We need the fantastic, the magical, the mischievous and
even a touch of the horrific to stave off the banal and
humdrum. Let the skulk bring you stories full of wonder
and mischief delivered with a sharp bite.

Join the Skulk at foxspirit.co.uk